PENGUIN BOOKS
Crescent Dawn

Clive Cussler is the author or co-author of a great number of international bestsellers, including the famous Dirk Pitt® adventures, such as *Arctic Drift*; the NUMA® Files adventures, most recently *Medusa*; the Oregon Files, such as *The Jungle*; the Isaac Bell adventures, which began with *The Chase*; and the highly successful new series: the Fargo adventures. His non-fiction works include *The Sea Hunters* and *The Sea Hunters II*: these describe the true adventures of the real NUMA, which, led by Cussler, searches for lost ships of historic significance. With his crew of volunteers, Cussler has discovered more than sixty ships, including the long-lost Confederate submarine *Hunley*. He lives in Arizona.

Dirk Cussler, an MBA from Berkeley, worked for many years in the financial arena, and now devotes himself full-time to writing. He is the co-author with Clive Cussler of *Black Wind*, *Treasure of Khan* and *Arctic Drift*. For the past several years, he has been an active participant and partner in his father's NUMA expeditions and has served as president of the NUMA advisory board of trustees. He lives in Arizona.

D1513634

Crescent Dawn

CLIVE CUSSLER
and DIRK CUSSLER

PENGUIN BOOKS

PENGUIN BOOKS

Published by the Penguin Group

Penguin Books Ltd, 80 Strand, London WC2R ORL, England

Penguin Group (USA) Inc., 375 Hudson Street, New York, New York 10014, USA

Penguin Group (Canada), 90 Eglinton Avenue East, Suite 700, Toronto, Ontario, Canada M4P 2Y3
(a division of Pearson Penguin Canada Inc.)

Penguin Ireland, 25 St Stephen's Green, Dublin 2, Ireland (a division of Penguin Books Ltd)

Penguin Group (Australia), 250 Camberwell Road, Camberwell, Victoria 3124, Australia
(a division of Pearson Australia Group Pty Ltd)

Penguin Books India Pvt Ltd, 11 Community Centre, Panchsheel Park, New Delhi – 110 017, India

Penguin Group (NZ), 67 Apollo Drive, Rosedale, Auckland 0632, New Zealand
(a division of Pearson New Zealand Ltd)

Penguin Books (South Africa) (Pty) Ltd, 24 Sturdee Avenue, Rosebank,
Johannesburg 2196, South Africa

Penguin Books Ltd, Registered Offices: 80 Strand, London WC2R ORL, England

www.penguin.com

First published in the USA by G. P. Putnam's Sons 2010
First published in Great Britain by Michael Joseph 2010
Published in Penguin Books 2011

001

Typeset by Palimpsest Book Production Limited, Falkirk, Stirlingshire
Printed in England by Clays Ltd, Elcograf S.p.A.

978-0-241-50780-3

www.greenpenguin.co.uk

MIX
Paper from
responsible sources
FSC® C018179

Penguin Books is committed to a sustainable
future for our business, our readers and our planet.
This book is made from Forest Stewardship
Council™ certified paper.

To Teri and Dayna,
who make it all fun.

PROLOGUE
Hostile Horizons

Galley Chase

A.D. 327

The Mediterranean Sea

The drumbeat echoed off the wooden bulkheads, reverberating in a rhythmic staccato of flawless precision. The *celeusta* rapped methodically at his goatskin drum in a smooth yet mechanical fashion. He could bang for hours without missing a beat—his musical training based more on endurance than harmony. Though there was a recognized value to his steady cadence, his audience of galley rowers simply hoped that the monotonous performance would soon reach an end.

Lucius Arcelian rubbed a sweaty palm across his leggings, then tightened his grip on a heavy oak oar. Pulling the blade through the water in a smooth motion, he quickly matched strokes with the men around him. A young native of Crete, he had joined the Roman Navy six years earlier, attracted by lucrative wages and an opportunity to acquire Roman citizenship at retirement. Physically tested in the years since, he now aspired only to advance to a less laborious position aboard the imperial galley before his arms completely gave out.

Contrary to Hollywood myth, slaves were not used aboard ancient Roman galleys. Paid enlistees propelled the ships, typically recruited from seafaring lands under the empire's rule. Like their legionary counterparts in the Roman Army, the enlistees endured weeks of grueling training before being put to sea. The oarsmen were lean and strong, capable of rowing twelve hours a day, if need be. But aboard the Liburnian-type *bireme* galley, a small and light warship that featured just two banks of oars on either side, the oarsmen acted as supplemental propulsion to a large sail rigged above deck.

Arcelian gazed at the *celeusta*, a minuscule bald man who drummed with a pet monkey tied beside him. He could not help but notice a striking resemblance between the man and the monkey. Both had big ears and round jolly faces. The drummer wore his mug in a constant look of mirth, grinning at the crew with bright wily eyes and chipped yellow teeth. His image somehow made the rowing easier, and Arcelian realized that the galley's captain had made a wise choice in selecting the man.

"*Celeusta*," called out one of the rowers, a dark-skinned man from Syria. "The wind blows fierce and the waters seethe. Why hath we been given the command to row?"

The drummer's eyes lit up. "It is not for me to question the wisdom of my officers or else I, too, would be pulling an oar," he replied, laughing heartily.

"I would wager that the monkey could row faster," the Syrian replied.

The *celeusta* eyed the monkey curled up beside him. "He is a rather strong little fellow," he replied, playing along. "But in answer to your question, I know not the answer. Perhaps the captain wishes to exercise his talkative crew. Or perhaps he simply desires to run faster than the wind."

Standing on the upper deck a few feet above their heads, the galley's captain gazed fitfully astern at the horizon. A pair of distant blue-gray dots danced on the turbulent waters, gradually increasing in size with each passing minute. He turned and looked at the breeze filling his sail, wishing that he could run much, much faster than the wind.

A deep baritone voice suddenly disrupted his focus.

"Is it the wrath of the sea that weakens your knees, Vitellus?"

The captain turned to find a robust man in an armored tunic staring at him with a derisive gaze. A Roman centurion named Plautius, he commanded a garrison of thirty legionaries stationed aboard the ship.

"Two vessels approach from the south," Vitellus replied. "Pirates both, I am most certain."

The centurion casually gazed at the distant ships, then shrugged.

"Mere insects," he said without concern.

Vitellus knew better. Pirates had been a nemesis to Roman shipping for centuries. Though organized piracy in the Mediterranean had been wiped out by Pompey the Great hundreds of years ago, small groups of independent thieves still preyed on the open waters. Solitary merchant ships were the usual targets, but the pirates knew that the *bireme* galleys often carried valuable cargo as well. Contemplating his own vessel's lading, Vitellus wondered whether the seaborne barbarians had been tipped off after his ship had left port.

"Plautius, I need not remind you of the importance of our cargo," he stated.

"Yes, of course," the centurion replied. "Why do you think I am on this wretched vessel? It is I who has been tasked with ensuring its safety until delivery is made to the Emperor in Byzantium."

5

"Failure to do so would mean fateful consequences for us and our families," Vitellus said, thinking of his wife and son in Naples. He scanned the seas off the galley's bow, noting only rolling waves of slate-colored water.

"There is still no sign of our escort."

Three days earlier, the galley had departed Judaea with a large *trireme* warship as escort. But the ships had become separated during a violent squall the night before, and the escort had not been seen since.

"Have no fear of the barbarians," Plautius spat. "We will turn the sea red with their blood."

The centurion's brashness was part of the reason that Vitellus had taken an instant disliking toward him. But there were no doubts about his ability to fight, and for that the captain was thankful to have him near.

Plautius and his contingent of legionaries were members of the *Scholae Palatinae*, an elite military force normally assigned to protection of the Emperor. Most were battle-hardened veterans who had fought with Constantine the Great on the frontier and in his campaign against Maxentius, a rival Caesar whose defeat led to the unification of the splintered empire. Plautius himself bore a wicked scar along his left bicep, a reminder of a fierce encounter with a Visigoth swordsman that nearly cost him his arm. He proudly wore the scar as a badge of toughness, an attribute that nobody who knew him dared to question.

As the twin pirate ships drew near, Plautius readied his men along the open deck, supplemented by spare galley crewmen. Each was armed with the Roman battle accoutrements of the day—a short fighting sword called a *gladius*, a round laminated shield, and a throwing lance, or *pilum*. The centurion quickly divided his soldiers into small fighting groups in order to defend both sides of the ship.

Vitellus kept a fixed eye on their pursuers, who now stood within clear sight. They were smaller sail- and oar-driven vessels of sixty feet in length, roughly half the size of the Roman galley. One displayed pale blue square sails and the other gray, while both hulls were painted a flat pewter to match the sea, an old disguise trick favored by Cilician pirates. Each vessel carried twin sails, which accounted for their superior speed under brisk winds. And the winds were blowing strong, offering the Romans little chance of escape.

A glimmer of hope beckoned when the forward look-out shouted a sighting of land ahead. Squinting toward the bow, Vitellus eyed the faint outline of a rocky shoreline to the north. The captain could only speculate as to what land it was. Sailing primarily by dead reckoning, the galley had been blown well off its original course during the earlier storm. Vitellus silently hoped they were near the coast of Anatolia, where other ships of the Roman fleet might be encountered.

The captain turned to a bulldog-shaped man who wielded the galley's heavy tiller.

"*Gubernator*, steer us to land and toward any leeward waters that may avail itself. If we can take the wind out of their sails, then we can outrun the devils with our oars."

Belowdecks, the *celeusta* was ordered to beat a rapid-fire rhythm. There was no talking now between Arcelian and the other oarsmen, just a low bellow of heavy breathing. Word had filtered down of the pursuing pirate ships, and each man concentrated on pulling his oar as quickly and efficiently as possible, knowing his own life was potentially at stake.

For nearly half an hour, the galley held its distance from the pursuing vessels. Under both sail and oar, the Roman vessel pushed through the waves at nearly seven knots. But the smaller and better-rigged pirates ultimately gained ground again. Pushed to the brink of exhaustion, the galley's oarsmen were finally allowed to slow their strokes to conserve energy. As the brown, dusty landmass arose before them, almost beckoning, the pirates closed in and made their attack.

With its companion ship holding astern of the galley, the blue-sailed vessel worked its way abeam and then, oddly, moved ahead of the Roman ship. As it passed, a motley horde of armed barbarians stood on deck and loudly taunted the Romans. Vitellus ignored the shouts, staring at the coastline ahead. The three vessels were within a few miles of shore, and he could see the winds diminish slightly in his square-rigged sail. He feared it was too little and too late for his exhausted oarsmen.

Vitellus scanned the nearby landscape, hoping he could put in ashore and let his legionaries fight on soil, where they were strongest. But the coastline was a high-faced wall of rocky bluffs that showed no safe haven to run the galley aground.

Speeding almost a quarter mile ahead, the lead pirate ship suddenly pivoted. In an expert tack, the vessel swung completely around and quickly veered head-on toward the galley. At first glance, it appeared to be a suicidal move. Roman sea strategy had long relied upon ramming as a primary battle tactic, and even the small *bireme* was outfitted with a heavy bronze prow. Perhaps the barbarians were more brawn than brains, Vitellus considered. He'd like nothing more than to ram and sink the first ship, knowing the second vessel would likely retreat.

"When she turns again, if she turns, follow and impale her with our ram at any cost," he instructed the steersman. A junior officer was stationed in the ladder well to await directional orders for the oarsmen. On deck, the legionaries held their shields in one hand and their throwing spears in the other, awaiting first blood. Silence befell the ship as everyone waited.

The barbarians held their bow to the galley until they were within a hundred feet. Then as Vitellus predicted, the adversary tacked sharply to port.

"Strike her!" the Roman shouted, as the helmsman pushed the tiller all the way over. Belowdecks, the starboard rowers reversed their oars for several strokes, twisting the galley hard to starboard. Just as quickly, they reverted to forward propulsion, joining their port-side oarsmen at maximum effort.

The smaller pirate ship tried to slip abeam of the galley, but the Roman ship turned with her. The barbarians lost momentum when their sails fell slack as they tacked, while the galley surged ahead. In an instant, the hunter became the prey. As the wind refilled its sails, the smaller ship jumped forward, but not quick enough. The galley's bronze ram kissed the stern flank of the pirate ship, ripping a gash clear to the transom. The vessel nearly keeled over at impact before righting itself, the stern settling low in the water.

A cheer rang out among the Roman legionaries, while

Vitellus allowed himself a grin in belief that victory had suddenly swung in their favor. But then he turned to face the second ship and instantly realized that they'd been had.

During the engagement, the second vessel had quietly drawn closer. As the galley's ram hit home, the gray-sailed ship immediately drew along the galley's port beam. The crunch of shattered oars filled the air as a fusillade of arrows and grappling hooks rained down on the deck. Within seconds, the two ships were drawn and lashed together as a mass of sword-wielding barbarians flooded over the side.

The first wave of attackers barely touched the deck when they were impaled by a barrage of razor-sharp spears. The Roman slingers were lethally accurate, and a dozen invaders fell dead in their tracks. But the invasion barely slowed, as a dozen more barbarians took their place. Plautius held his men back until the horde swarmed the deck, then rose and charged. The clang of sword on sword rang over the dying shouts of agony as the slaughter ensued. The Roman legionaries, better trained and disciplined, easily repelled the initial attacks. The barbarians were used to attacking lightly armed merchants, not well-armed soldiers, and they faltered at the stiff resistance. Beating back the boarding party, Plautius rallied half his men to press the attack and personally led the way as the Romans pursued the barbarians onto their own ship.

The barbarians quickly broke ranks, but then regrouped at the realization that they vastly outnumbered the legionaries. Attacking in groups of three and four, they would target a single Roman and overrun his position. Plautius lost six men before quickly organizing his troops into a fighting square.

On the stern deck of the galley, Vitellus watched as the Roman centurion cut a man in two with his sword, mowing through the barbarians like a scythe. The captain had gamely turned the galley inshore during the fight, with its pursuer lashed alongside. But the pirate ship dropped a stone anchor, which eventually found bottom and ground both ships to a halt.

Meanwhile, the blue-sailed vessel had curled around and attempted to rejoin the fight. With flooding from its damaged hull slowing its pace, it aimed clumsily for the galley's exposed starboard flank. Duplicating the move of its sister ship, the vessel slipped alongside, and its crew quickly flung grapples.

"Oarsmen to arms! Report to the deck!" Vitellus shouted.

Belowdecks, the exhausted oarsmen rallied to the cry. Trained as soldiers first, the oarsmen and every other sailor aboard were expected to defend the ship. Arcelian followed his brethren in line as they gulped down a splash of cold water from a clay pot, then rushed to the deck with a sword in hand.

"Keep your head down," he said to the *celeusta*, who had passed out the arms and now followed at the end of the line.

"I prefer to look the barbarian in the eye when I kill him," the drummer replied with his trademark grin.

The oarsmen joined the fight none too soon as the second wave of pirates began storming the starboard rail. The galley's crew quickly engaged the attackers in a mass of steel and flesh.

As Arcelian stepped onto the main deck, he was aghast

at the carnage. Dead bodies and severed limbs were scattered everywhere amid growing pools of blood. Untested in battle, he unwittingly froze for a moment, until an officer ran by and yelled at him, "Sever the grappling lines!"

Spotting a taut rope stretching off the galley's bow, he sprang forward and sliced the line free with his sword. He watched as the cut line whipped back toward the blue-sailed ship, whose deck stood several feet below his own. He then peered down the galley's rail and noticed a half dozen more grapple lines affixed to the pirate ship.

"Cut the lines!" he shouted. "Shove the barbarian clear."

The words fell on deaf ears, as he realized that nearly every crewman aboard was engaged with the barbarians in a fight for life. Only at the stern of the galley did he observe with encouragement that the *celeusta* had joined the effort, attacking a grapple line with a small hatchet. But time was short. Aboard the slowly sinking pirate vessel, the barbarians began making a determined effort to board en masse, realizing their ship had little time left afloat.

Arcelian stepped over a dying shipmate to reach the next grapple and quickly raised his sword. Before the blade came down, he heard a whistling through the air, and then a razor-tipped arrow bit into the deck an inch from his foot. Ignoring it, he swung the blade through the rope, then dove beneath the rail as another arrow darted overhead. Peering over the edge, he spotted his assailant, a Cilician archer wedged at the top of the pirate ship's mast. The archer had already turned his attention away from the oarsman and was aiming his next arrow astern. Arcelian looked on in horror as he realized that the archer was aiming at the *celeusta*, who was about to cut a third grapple line.

"*Celeusta!*" the oarsman screamed.

The warning came too late. An arrow ripped into the little man's chest, burying itself nearly to the quiver. The drummer gasped, then dropped to his knees, as a flow of blood turned his chest red. In a final act of allegiance, he slammed the hatchet through the grapple line, then fell over dead.

The barbarian ship began settling lower in the water, inciting a final rush to the galley. Just two grapple lines remained binding the ships together, a point lost on all of the pirates save the archer. Still perched in the mast, he took aim and fired again at Arcelian, sending an arrow whizzing over his head.

Arcelian saw that the remaining grapple lines were amidships, although the two vessels were touching at the stern and the fighting had drifted aft. The oarsman dropped to all fours and scurried beneath the rail to the first line. A dying barbarian lay nearby, his midsection a jagged mass of exposed flesh. The strong oarsman approached and nimbly hoisted the man over his shoulder, then turned and stepped to the grapple line. Immediately there came a thwack, and an arrow drove hard into the barbarian's back. With his free hand, Arcelian swung the sword and sliced the line in two as a second arrow burrowed into his human shield. The oarsman collapsed to the deck, rolling the now dead barbarian off his shoulder while catching his breath.

Nearly spent from his ordeal, Arcelian surveyed the final grapple, which had clawed into a yardarm a dozen feet above his head. Peeking over the rail, he spotted the enemy archer, who had finally abandoned his perch on the mast and was descending toward the deck. Seizing the opportunity, Arcelian jumped up and ran down his own deck, climbing onto the rail where the grapple line sloped down. Catching his balance, he started to swing the sword, but momentum beat him to the punch.

The force of the two divergent ships on the single line was too powerful to bear, and the iron grapple lost its grip on the masthead. The rope's high tension flung the grapple like a projectile, spinning it in a low arc toward the water. The sharpened barbs whizzed past Arcelian, barely sparing him a bloody demise. But the rope looped around his thigh and jerked him off the rail, throwing him into the water just ahead of the pirate vessel's bow.

Unable to swim, Arcelian splashed wildly, trying to keep his head above water. Flailing about, he felt something hard in the water and latched onto it with both hands. A chunk of wooden railing from the pirate ship knocked loose during the earlier collision, the flotsam was just large enough to keep him afloat. The blue-sailed pirate ship suddenly loomed over him, and he kicked frantically to escape its path. He was carried farther away from the galley in the process, catching a current that was just too much to overcome in his weakened state. Kicking weakly to hold his position, he watched wide-eyed as the pirate ship caught a gust of wind and accelerated toward the shore, its deck riding low above the water.

While Arcelian had freed the starboard grapples from

the Roman ship, Vitellus and a junior officer had cleared the port-side lines, save for a remaining grapple near the stern. Leaning against the tiller with an arrow protruding from his shoulder, the captain yelled over to the centurion on the adjacent ship.

"Plautius, return to the vessel," he said in a weakened voice. "We are cast free."

The centurion and his legionaries were still battling fiercely on the opposite vessel, though their fighting numbers had diminished. Plautius pulled his bloodied sword from the neck of a barbarian and gave a quick glance toward the galley.

"Proceed with the cargo. I shall detain the barbarians," he yelled, plunging his sword into another attacker. There were but three legionaries left standing with him, and Vitellus could see that their remaining breaths would be few.

"Your bravery shall be recorded," the captain yelled, cutting the last line. "Farewell, Centurion."

Free of the anchored attack ship, the galley leaped forward as its lone sail filled with the breeze. His *gubernator* long dead, Vitellus muscled the steering oar landward, feeling the grip turn slick with his own blood. An odd silence crept over the deck, prompting him to stagger to the forward rail and peer down. The sight below stunned him.

Littered across the deck was a mass of dead and dismembered bodies, Roman and barbarian intermixed, in a wash of red. A nearly equal number of attackers and crewmen had engaged one another, fighting to a mortal standstill. It was a scene of carnage like no other he had ever witnessed.

Shaken by the sight and faint from loss of blood, he stared at the heavens.

"Protect thee for thy Emperor," he gasped.

Swaying back to the stern, he wrapped his tired arms around the tiller and adjusted its angle. Cries for help echoed up from men afloat in the water, but the captain's ears fell deaf as the ship sailed by. With his eyes staring vacantly at the land ahead, he gripped the tiller with his last bit of energy and fought for the final moments of his life.

Drifting in the choppy waters, Arcelian looked up in surprise to see the Roman ship sailing clear, suddenly bearing down on his own position. Crying for help, he watched in anguish as the galley slipped past him, ignoring him in complete silence. A moment later, he caught a profile of the ship as it turned and he saw with horror that not a single soul stood upon her main deck. Only the lone figure of Captain Vitellus was visible, slumped over the tiller on the raised stern. Then the ship's sails rustled in the wind, and the wooden galley darted toward shore, soon disappearing completely from sight.

June 1916

Portsmouth, England

The naval dock was abuzz with activity, despite the dampening effects of a cold drizzle. Royal Navy stevedores busily worked beneath a steam-powered derrick, hoisting huge amounts of food, supplies, and munitions aboard the gray leviathan moored at the dock. On board, the crates were neatly stowed in the ship's forward hold, while a throng of sailors in heavy woolen peacoats readied the ship for sea.

The HMS *Hampshire* still maintained a spit-and-polish finish, despite more than a decade at sea and its recent action at the Battle of Jutland. A Devonshire class armored cruiser of ten thousand tons, she was one of the largest ships in the British Navy. Armed with a dozen large deck guns, she was also one of the deadliest.

In an empty storehouse a quarter mile down the quay, a blond-haired man stood by an open siding and studied the ship's loading through a pair of brass binoculars. He held the binoculars to his eyes for nearly twenty minutes until a green Rolls-Royce appeared, crossing the dock and pulling up in front of the main gangway. He watched intently as a band of Army officers in khaki uniforms quickly materialized, surrounding the car and then assisting the vehicle's occupants up the gangway. From their dress, he judged the two arrivals as a politician and a high-ranking military officer. He caught a quick glimpse of the officer's face, smiling to himself as he noted that the man wore a heavy mustache.

"Time to make our delivery, Dolly," he said aloud.

He stepped into the shadows, where a weather-beaten cart was hitched to a saddled horse. Stuffing the binoculars under the seat, he climbed aboard and slapped the reins. Dolly, an aged dappled gray mare, lifted her head in annoyance, then shuffled forward, pulling the cart out into the rain.

The dockhands paid scant attention to the man when he pulled his cart up alongside the ship a few minutes later. Dressed in a faded woolen coat and soiled trousers, a flat cap pulled low over his brow, he resembled dozens of other local paupers who survived by the odd job here and there. In this instance, it was an acted role, embellished by a failure to shave and a liberal dousing of cheap scotch on his clothes. When it was deemed time to perform, he made his presence known by advancing Dolly to the base of the gangway, effectively blocking its use.

"Get that nag out of the way," cursed a red-faced lieutenant overseeing the loading.

"Aye got a d'livry for the '*Ampshire*," the man growled in a Cockney accent.

"Let me see your papers," the lieutenant demanded.

The deliveryman reached inside his jacket and handed the officer a crumpled page of watermarked stationery. The lieutenant frowned as he read it, then slowly shook his head.

"This is not a proper bill of lading," he said, quietly eyeing the deliveryman.

"It's wot the general gave me. That and a fiver," the man replied with a wink.

The lieutenant walked around and surveyed the crate, which was roughly the size of a coffin. On the top was an address stenciled in black paint:

PROPERTY OF THE ROYAL NAVY
TO THE ATTENTION OF SIR LEIGH HUNT
SPECIAL ENVOY TO THE RUSSIAN EMPIRE
C/O CONSULATE OF GREAT BRITAIN
PETROGRAD, RUSSIA

"Humph," the officer muttered, eyeing the paperwork again. "Well, it is signed by the general. Very well," he said, passing the paper back. "You, there," he barked, turning to a nearby stevedore. "Help get that crate aboard. Then get this wagon out of here."

Rope was strung around the crate, and a shipboard derrick yanked it into the sky, swinging it over the rail and depositing it in the forward hold. The deliveryman gave a mock salute to the lieutenant, then slowly drove the horse off the dock and out of the navy yard. Turning down a nearby dirt road, he ambled past a small port warehouse district that ended at an expanse of open farmland. A mile farther down the road, he turned into an uneven drive and parked the cart beside a dilapidated cottage. An old man with a game leg limped out of a nearby barn.

"Make your delivery?" he asked the driver.

"I did. Thank you for the use of your cart and horse," the man replied, pulling a ten-pound note out of his wallet and handing it to the farmer.

"Begging your pardon, sir, but that's more than my horse is worth," the farmer stammered, holding the note in his hands as if it were a baby.

"And a fine horse it is," the man replied, giving Dolly a farewell pat on the neck. "Good day," he said to the farmer, tipping his hat without another word, then walking up the drive.

He turned down the road and hiked a few minutes until detecting the sound of an automobile headed his way. A blue Vauxhall touring sedan rounded a corner, then slowed to a stop beside him. The deliveryman stepped closer as the rear door of the sedan opened and he climbed in. A staid-looking man in the attire of an Anglican priest slid across the backseat to make room. He stared at the deliveryman with a shroud of apprehension masking his dull gray eyes, then reached for a decanter of brandy mounted to the seat back. Pouring a healthy shot into a crystal tumbler, he passed it to the deliveryman, then directed the driver to proceed down the road.

"The crate is aboard?" he asked bluntly.

"Yes, Father," the deliveryman replied in a sarcastic tone of reverence. "They bought the phony bill of lading and loaded the crate into the forward hold." There was no longer any trace of a Cockney accent as he spoke. "In seventy-two hours, you can bid farewell to your illustrious general."

The words seemed to trouble the vicar, though they were what he had anticipated. He silently reached into his overcoat and retrieved an envelope stuffed thick with banknotes.

"As we agreed. Half now, half after the . . . event," he said, passing over the envelope as his words fell away.

The deliveryman smiled as he eyed the thick stack of currency. "I wonder if the Germans would pay this much to sink a ship and murder a general," he said. "You wouldn't happen to be working for the Kaiser, now, would you?"

The minister firmly shook his head. "No, this is a theological matter. Had you been able to locate the document, this would not have been necessary."

"I searched the manor three times. If it was there, I would have found it."

"As you have told me."

"You are certain that it was carried aboard?"

"We've learned of a meeting on the general's schedule with the Father Superior of the Russian Orthodox Church in Petrograd. There can be little doubt as to the purpose. The document must be aboard. It will be destroyed along with him, and so the secret shall die."

The Vauxhall's tires touched wet cobblestone as they entered the outskirts of Portsmouth. The driver navigated toward the city center, passing block after block of tall brick row houses. Reaching a main crossroads, he turned into the rear driveway of a nineteenth-century stone church labeled St. Mary's as the rain began to fall with intensity.

"I'd like you to drop me at the railway station," the deliveryman said, observing the large motorcar bisect a churchyard cemetery and pull to a stop behind the rectory.

"I was asked to drop off a sermon," the minister replied.

"Won't take more than a moment. Why don't you join me?"

The deliveryman suppressed a yawn as he looked out the rain-streaked window. "No, I think I'll wait here and keep dry."

"Very well. We'll return shortly."

The minister and driver walked away, leaving the deliveryman to count his blood money. As he attempted to tally up the Bank of England notes, he had trouble reading the numbers and realized his vision was blurring. He felt a wave of fatigue sweep over him and quickly tucked the money away and lay down on the seat to rest. Though it seemed like hours, it was only a few minutes later when a mist of cold water struck his face and he pried open his heavy eyelids. The stern face of the minister looked down upon him amid a shower of rain. His brain told him that his body was moving, but there was no feeling in his legs. He focused his blurry eyes enough to see the driver was carrying his legs, while the minister dragged him by the arms. A mute sense of panic rang within his skull, and he willed himself to retrieve a Webley Bulldog pistol from his pocket. But his limbs refused to respond. The brandy, he thought with momentary clarity. It was the brandy.

A canopy of green leaves filled his vision as he was carried beneath a grove of towering oak trees. The minister's face still swayed above him, a sullen mask of indifference illuminated by two frigid eyes. Then the face fell away, or rather he did. He heard more than felt his body drop into a trench, splashing down hard into a muddy puddle. Flat on his back, he gazed up at the minister, who stood high over him with a faint aura of guilt.

"Forgive us our sins in the name of the Father, the Son, and the Holy Spirit," he heard the minister say solemnly. "These we take to the grave."

The back side of a shovel appeared, followed by a clump of soggy dirt that fell and bounced off his chest. Another shovelful of dirt tumbled down, and then another.

His body was paralyzed and his voice frozen, but his mind still operated with reason. With crushing horror, he fully grasped that he was being buried alive. He fought again to move his limbs, but there was no response. As the dirt piled high within his grave, his screams of terror blared only within his mind, until his last breath was painfully snuffed out.

The periscope cut a lazy arc through the boiling black water, its presence nearly invisible under the night sky. Thirty-five feet beneath the surface, a baby-faced German naval *Oberleutnant* named Voss slowly rotated the viewing piece three hundred and sixty degrees. He lingered over a few speckled lights that rose high in the distance. They were lantern lights from a scattering of farmhouses that dotted Cape Marwick, a frigid, windswept stretch of the Orkney Islands. Voss had nearly completed his circular survey when his eye caught a faint glimmer on the eastern horizon. Dialing the viewing lens to a crisper focus, he patiently tracked a steady movement of the light.

"Possible target at zero-four-eight degrees," he announced, fighting to contain the excitement in his voice.

Several other sailors stationed in the submarine's cramped control room perked to attention at his words.

Voss tracked the object for several more minutes, during which time a quarter moon broke briefly through a bank of thick storm clouds. For a fleeting moment, the moonlight cast a sheen on the object, exposing its dimensions against the island hills behind it. Voss felt his heart flutter and noticed his palms suddenly grow sweaty on the periscope handgrips. Blinking hard, he confirmed the visual image, then stood away from the eyepiece. Without saying a word, he sprinted from the control room, scrambling down the tiny aft passageway that ran the length of the sub. Reaching the captain's cabin, he knocked loudly, then slid open a thin curtain.

Captain Kurt Beitzen was asleep in his bunk but woke instantly and flicked on an overhead lamp.

"*Kapitän*, I've spotted a large vessel approaching from the southeast approximately ten kilometers off. I caught a brief glimpse of her profile. A British warship, possibly a battleship," Voss reported excitedly.

Beitzen nodded as he sat upright, flinging off a blanket. He had slept in his clothes and quickly pulled on a pair of boots, then followed his second officer to the control room. An experienced submariner, Beitzen took a long look through the attack periscope, then barked out range and heading coordinates.

"She's a warship," he confirmed nonchalantly. "Is this quadrant clear of mines?"

"Yes," Voss replied. "Our nearest release was thirty kilometers north of here."

"Stand by to attack," Beitzen ordered.

Beitzen and Voss moved to a wooden chart table, where they plotted a precise intercept course and relayed orders to the helm. Though submerged, the submarine rocked and pitched from the turbulent seas overhead, making the urgent task more stressful.

Built in the shipyards of Hamburg, the U-75 was a UE-1 class submarine, designed primarily for laying down mines on the seafloor. In addition to a large stock of mines, she carried four torpedoes and a powerful 105mm deck gun. Her mine-laying duty was nearly complete, and none of the crew was expecting an encounter with an enemy warship.

Under Beitzen's command, the U-75 was on only its second mission since being launched six months earlier. The current cruise had been deemed a minor success already, as the sub's mines had sunk a small merchant ship and two trawlers. But this was their first crack at a prize of major stature. Word quickly rippled through the crew that they were targeting a British warship, boosting the focus and tension to high levels. Beitzen himself knew that such a kill would guarantee him the Iron Cross.

The German commander gently guided the submarine to a position perpendicular to Marwick Cape. If the warship held her bearing, she would pass within a quarter mile of the lurking sub. The U-boat's torpedoes had an accurate range of less than half a mile, necessitating an uncomfortably close firing position. In World War I, most merchant ships were actually sunk by the U-boats' deck guns. The U-75 didn't have that option against the heavily armed cruiser, particularly in the present rough seas.

Positioned for the kill, the captain hung to the periscope,

waiting for his quarry. Another flash of moonlight revealed that the *Oberleutnant* was close to the mark. The vessel appeared to be an armored cruiser, somewhat smaller than the fearsome dreadnoughts.

"Tubes one and two, stand by for firing," Beitzen commanded.

The cruiser was now less than a mile away, its imposing size nearly masking the horizon. Beitzen quickly double-checked the torpedoes' firing profile, then eyed the target once more. The vessel was quickly approaching their strike range.

"Open bow caps," he ordered.

A few seconds later, a reply rang through the control room, "Bow caps open."

"Tubes one and two ready."

"Ready," came the reply.

Beitzen tracked the cruiser through the periscope, waiting patiently while the crew around him held their breaths. He watched until the big surface ship appeared directly in front of them. Beitzen parted his lips to give the fire command when a bright flash suddenly filled his eyepiece. A second later, a muffled explosion rocked through the sub's steel bulkheads.

Beitzen stared dumbfounded through the periscope as flames and smoke burst from the cruiser, lighting the night sky with a blaze of persimmon red. The big warship shuddered and shook, and then her bow burrowed under the waves. The stern quickly rose up, hung suspended in midair for a few moments, then chased the bow down toward the seafloor. In less than ten minutes, the mammoth cruiser disappeared completely from sight.

"Voss . . . you are certain there are no mines in this quadrant?" he asked hoarsely.

"Yes, sir," the officer replied, double-checking a chart of minefield locations.

"She's gone," he finally muttered to the anxious crew awaiting his orders. "Close bow caps and stand down."

As the disappointed crew resumed their duties, the captain clung to the periscope, staring blankly through the eyepiece. A handful of survivors had escaped in lifeboats, but there was nothing he could do to help them in the turbulent waters. Watching the empty black sea before him, he struggled to find an answer. Yet none of it made sense. Warships just didn't blow up by themselves.

It was a long while before Beitzen pried himself away from the periscope and staggered quietly to his cabin. Fated to die later in the war, he would never learn the truth of why the *Hampshire* had blown up. But in his remaining days, the young *Kapitän* never shook the image from his mind of the cruiser's last minutes, when the massive warship seemingly died without cause.

PART I
Ottoman Dream

Yerebatan Sarnici

I

July 2012

Cairo, Egypt

The noonday sun burned through the dense layer of dust and pollutants that hung over the ancient city like a soiled blanket. With the temperature well over the century mark, few people lingered about the hot stones that paved the central court of al-Azhar Mosque.

Situated in eastern Cairo some two miles from the Nile, al-Azhar stood as one of the city's most historic structures. Originally constructed in the year A.D. 970 by Fatimid conquerors, the mosque was rebuilt and expanded through the centuries, ultimately attaining status as Islam's fifth most important mosque. Elaborate stone carvings, towering minarets, and onion-domed spires vied for the eye's attention, reflecting a thousand years of artistry. Amid its fortress-like stone walls, the centerpiece of the complex was a wide rectangular court surrounded by rising arcades on every side.

In the shade of an arcade portico, a slight man in baggy trousers and a loose-fitting shirt wiped clean a pair of tinted glasses, then surveyed the courtyard. In the heat of the day, only a small number of youths were about, studying the architecture or walking in silent meditation. They were students from the adjacent al-Azhar University, a preeminent institution for Islamic learning in the Middle East. The man touched a thick beard that covered his own youthful face, then lifted a worn backpack to his shoulder. With a white cotton *keffyeh* wrapped about his head, he easily passed as just another theology student.

Stepping into the sunlight, he trekked across the court toward the southeast arcade. The façade above the keel-shaped arches featured a series of ornate roundels and niches cut into the stucco, which he noticed had become favored roosting spots for some local pigeons. He walked toward a protruding central arch topped by a high rectangular panel, which signified the entrance to the prayer hall.

The call to midday *salat*, or prayer, had occurred nearly an hour earlier, leaving the expansive prayer hall nearly empty. Outside the foyer, a small group of students sat cross-legged on the ground, listening to a university instructor lecture on the Qur'an. Skirting around the group, the man approached the hall entry. There he met a bearded man in a white robe, who eyed him sternly. The visitor removed his shoes and quietly offered a blessing to Muhammad, then proceeded in with a nod from the doorman.

The prayer hall was an open expanse of red carpet punctuated by dozens of alabaster pillars that rose to a beamed ceiling. As in most mosques, there were no pews or ornate altars to provide orientation. Cupola-shaped patterns in the carpet, outlining individual positions of prayer, pointed toward the head of the hall. Noting that the bearded doorman no longer paid him any attention, the man made his way quickly along the pillars.

Approaching several men kneeling in prayer, he spotted the *mihrab* across the hall. An often unassuming niche carved into a mosque's wall, it indicated the direction of Mecca. Al-Azhar's *mihrab* was cut of smooth stone and arched with a wavy black-and-ivory stone inlay that had a nearly modern design.

Moving to a pillar closest to the *mihrab*, the man slipped off his backpack, then lay prone on the carpet in prayer. After several minutes, he gently pushed his pack to the side until it wedged against the base of the pillar. Spotting a pair of students walking in the direction of the entrance, he rose and followed them to the foyer, where he retrieved his shoes. Passing the bearded elder, he muttered, *"Allahu Akbar,"* then quickly stepped into the courtyard.

He pretended to briefly admire a rosette in the façade, then quickly made his way to the Barber's Gate, which led out of the mosque compound. A few blocks away, he climbed into a small rental car parked on the street and drove in the direction of the Nile. Passing through a dingy industrial neighborhood, he turned onto the lot of a crumbling old brickyard and pulled behind its abandoned loading dock. There he pulled off his loose trousers and shirt, revealing a pair of jeans and silk blouse underneath. The eyeglasses were removed, along with a wig, and then the fake beard. The male Muslim student was no more, replaced by an attractive, olive-skinned woman with hard dark eyes and stylishly layered short black hair. Ditching her disguise in a rusty garbage bin, she hopped back into the car and rejoined Cairo's sluggish traffic, crawling away from the Nile to the Cairo International Airport on the northeast side of town.

She was standing in line at the check-in counter when the backpack exploded. A small white cloud rose over al-Azhar Mosque as the prayer hall roof was blown off and the *mihrab* shattered into a pile of rubble. Though the explosion had been timed to detonate between daily prayers, several students and mosque attendants were killed and dozens more injured.

After the initial shock subsided, the Cairo Muslim community was outraged. Israel was blamed first, then other Western nations were targeted when no one claimed responsibility for the blast. In a few weeks, the prayer hall would be repaired and a new *mihrab* quickly installed. But to Muslims across Egypt and around the world, the anger at the assault on such a sacred site lasted much longer. Few could have recognized, however, that the attack was only the first salvo in a strategic ploy that would attempt to transform the very dominance of the entire region.

2

"Take the knife and cut it free."

An angry scowl covered the Greek fisherman's face as he handed his son a rusty serrated knife. The teenage boy stripped down to his shorts, then leaped off the side of the boat, the knife held firmly in one hand.

It had been nearly two hours since the trawler's fishing nets had first snagged on the bottom, much to the surprise of the old Greek, who had safely dragged these waters many times before. He ran his boat in every direction, hoping to work the nets free, cursing loudly as his frustration mounted. Try as he might, the nets held firm. It would be a costly loss to cut away a portion of his nets, but the fisherman grudgingly accepted the occupational hazard and sent his boy over the side.

Though windswept on the surface, the waters of the eastern Aegean Sea were warm and clear, and at thirty feet down the boy could faintly see the bottom. But it was still well beyond his ability to free-dive, so he halted his descent and attacked the dangling nets with his knife. It took several dives before the last strand was cut free and the boy yanked to the surface with the damaged nets, exhausted and out of breath. Still cursing over his loss, the fisherman turned the boat west and putted off toward Chios, a Greek island close to the Turkish mainland, which rose from the azure waters a short distance away.

A quarter mile farther out to sea, a man studied the fisherman's plight with curiosity. His frame was tall and lean yet robust, his skin deeply tanned from years in the sun. He lowered an old-fashioned brass telescope from his brow, exposing a pair of sea-green eyes that flickered with intelligence. They were reflective eyes, hardened by adversity and numerous brushes with death, yet they softened easily with humor. He rubbed his hand through thick ebony hair flecked with gray, then he stepped onto the bridge of the research vessel *Aegean Explorer*.

"Rudi, we've surveyed a good chunk of the bottom between here and Chios, haven't we?" he asked.

A diminutive man with horn-rimmed glasses looked up from a computer station and nodded his head.

"Yes, our last grid ran within a mile of the eastern shore. With the Greek island situated less than five miles from Turkey, I don't even know whose waters we're in. We had about ninety percent of the grid complete when the AUV's rear sensor blew a seal and flooded with salt water. We'll be down at least two more hours while our technicians repair the damage."

The AUV, or autonomous underwater vehicle, was a torpedo-shaped robot packed with sensing equipment that was dropped over the side of the research ship. Self-propelled and preprogrammed with a designated survey path, the AUV would cruise above the seafloor collecting data that was periodically relayed back to the surface ship.

Rudi Gunn resumed tapping at the keyboard. Dressed as he was in a tattered T-shirt and plaid shorts, nobody would have guessed he was the Deputy Director for the National Underwater and Marine Agency, the prominent government organization responsible for the scientific study of the world's oceans. Gunn was normally confined to NUMA's Washington headquarters rather than stationed aboard one of the turquoise-colored research vessels that the agency used to gather information on marine life, ocean currents, and environmental pollution. An adept administrator, he relished escaping the hubris of the nation's capital and getting his hands dirty in the field, especially when his boss had escaped likewise.

"What sort of bottom contours have we seen in the shallows around here?"

"Typical of the local islands. A sloping shelf extends offshore a short distance before abruptly plunging to thousand-foot depths. We're in about a hundred and twenty feet of water here. As I recall, this area has a fairly sandy bottom, with few obstructions."

"That's what I thought," the man replied, a sparkle growing in his eye.

Gunn caught the look and said, "I detect a devious plot in the boss's head."

Dirk Pitt laughed. As the Director of NUMA, he had led dozens of underwater explorations, with remarkable results. From raising the *Titanic* to discovering the ships of the lost Franklin Expedition in the Arctic, Pitt had an uncanny knack for solving the mysteries of the deep. A quietly confident man with an insatiable curiosity, he'd been enamored of the sea from an early age. The lure never waned, and drew him out of NUMA's Washington headquarters on a regular basis.

"It's a known fact," he said cheerily, "that most inshore shipwrecks are found by the nets of local fishermen."

"Shipwrecks?" Gunn replied. "As I recall, our invitation from the Turkish government was to locate and study the impact of algae blooms reported along their coastal waters. There was no mention of any wreck searches."

"I only take them as they come," Pitt smiled.

"Well, we are out of commission for the moment. Do you want to drop the ROV over the side?"

"No, the nets of our neighborhood fisherman are snagged well within diving range."

Gunn looked at his watch. "I thought you were leaving in two hours to spend the weekend in Istanbul with your wife?"

"More than enough time," Pitt said with a grin, "for a quick dive on the way to the airport."

"Then I guess this means," Gunn replied with a resigned shake of the head, "that I gotta go wake up Al."

Twenty minutes later, Pitt tossed an overnight bag into a Zodiac that bobbed alongside the *Aegean Explorer*, then climbed a portable ladder down into the boat. As he took his seat, a short barrel-chested man at the stern twisted the throttle on a small outboard motor, and the rubber boat leaped away from the ship.

"Which way to the bottom?" Al Giordino shouted, the cobwebs from an afternoon siesta slowly clearing from his dark brown eyes.

Pitt had taken a visual bearing using several landmarks on the neighboring island. Guiding Giordino inshore on a decided angle, they motored just a short distance before Pitt ordered the engine cut. He then threw a small anchor over the bow, tying it off when the line went slack.

"Just over a hundred feet," he remarked, eyeing a red stripe on the line that was visible underwater.

"And just what do you expect to find down below?"

"Anything from a pile of rocks to the *Britannic*," Pitt replied, referring to a sister ship of the *Titanic* that was sunk by a mine in the Mediterranean during World War I.

"My money's on the rocks," Giordino replied, slipping into a blue wet suit whose seams were tested by his brawny shoulders and biceps.

Deep down, Giordino knew there would be something more interesting than an outcropping of rocks at the bottom. He had too much history with Pitt to question his friend's apparent sixth sense when it came to underwater mysteries. The two had been childhood friends, in Southern California, where they'd learned to dive together off Laguna Beach. While serving in the Air Force, they'd both taken a temporary assignment at a fledgling new federal department tasked with studying the oceans. Scores of projects and adventures later, Pitt now headed up the vastly expanded agency called NUMA, while Giordino worked alongside him as his Director of Underwater Technology.

"Let's try an elongated circle search off the anchor line," Pitt suggested, as they buckled on their air tanks. "My bearing puts the net snag slightly inshore of our present position."

Giordino nodded, then stuffed a regulator into his mouth and slipped backward off the Zodiac and into the water. Pitt splashed in a second later, and the two men followed the anchor line to the bottom.

The blue waters of the Aegean Sea were remarkably

clear, and Pitt had no trouble seeing fifty feet or more. As they approached the darkened bottom, he noted with some satisfaction that the seafloor was a combination of flat gravel and sand. Gunn's assessment was correct. The area appeared to be naturally free of obstructions.

The two men spread apart a dozen feet above the seafloor and swam a lazy arc seaward around the anchor line. A small school of sea bass cruised by, eyeing the divers suspiciously before darting away to deeper water. As they angled around toward Chios, Pitt noticed Giordino waving at him. Thrusting his legs in a strong scissors kick, Pitt swam closer, finding his partner pointing to a large shape ahead of them.

It was a towering brown shadow that seemed to waver in the thin light. It reminded Pitt of a windblown tree, its leafy branches sprouting skyward. Swimming closer, he saw that it was no tree but the remnants of the fisherman's nets drifting lazily in the current.

Leery of entanglement, the two divers moved cautiously, positioning themselves up current as they approached. The nets were caught on a single point, protruding just above the seafloor. Pitt could see a faint trench scratched across the gravel-and-sand bottom, ending in an upright spar tangled with the nets. Kicking closer to the obstruction, he could see that it was a corroded T-shaped iron anchor about five feet in length. The anchor was tilted on its side, with one fluke pointing toward the surface, the fisherman's nets hopelessly ensnarled around it, while the other fluke was embedded in the seafloor. Pitt reached down and fanned away around the base, revealing that the buried fluke was wedged between a thick beam of wood and a smaller cross frame. Pitt had explored enough shipwrecks to recognize the thick beam as a ship's keel.

He turned away from the nets and eyed the wide, shallow trench that had recently been scratched across the bottom. Giordino was already hovering over it, tracking it to its origin. Like Pitt, he had surmised what happened. The fishing nets had snagged the anchor at one end of the wreck and dragged it along the keel line until it had caught a cross frame and held firm. The action had unwittingly exposed a large portion of an aged shipwreck.

Pitt swam toward Giordino, who was fanning sand from a linear protrusion. Clearing the protective sediment revealed several pieces of cross frame beneath the keel. Giordino gazed into Pitt's dive mask with bright eyes and shook his head. Pitt's underwater sense had sniffed out a shipwreck, and an old one at that.

Uncovering bits and pieces as they swept the perimeter, they could tell that the ship was about fifty feet long, and its upper deck had long since eroded away. Most of the vessel had in fact disappeared, with just a few sections of the hull surviving intact. Yet at the stern, portions of several small compartments were evident beneath soft sand. Ceramic dishes, tile, and fragments of unglazed pottery were visible throughout, although the ship's actual cargo was not apparent.

With their bottom time beginning to run low, the two divers returned to the stern and scooped away sections of gravel and sand, searching for anything that might help identify the wreck. Poking through an area of loose timbers, Giordino's fingers brushed upon a flat object under the sand and he dug down to find a small metal box. Holding it up to his mask, he could see a pin-type locking mechanism was encrusted to the front, though the shackle was mostly corroded away. Carefully wrapping it in a dive bag, he checked his watch, then swam over to Pitt and signaled that he was surfacing.

Pitt had uncovered a small row of clay pots, which he left undisturbed as Giordino approached. He was turning to follow Giordino to the surface when a small glint in the sand caught his eye. It came from opposite the pots, where his fins had brushed up some bottom sediment. Pitt swam around and fanned away more sand, exposing a flat section of ceramic. Though it was caked with concretions, he could see that the design featured an elaborate floral motif. Digging his fingers into the sand, he grasped the edges of a rectangular box and pulled it free.

The ceramic container was about twice the size of a cigar box, its flat sides emblazoned with a blue-and-white design that matched the lid. The box felt heavy for its size, and Pitt carefully tucked it under one arm before kicking toward the surface.

A steady afternoon breeze was building from the northwest, pestering the water with whitecaps. Giordino was already aboard the Zodiac, yanking up the anchor, when Pitt appeared. He kicked over to the rubber boat and handed Giordino the box, then climbed aboard and stripped off his dive gear.

"Guess you owe that fisherman a bottle of ouzo," Giordino said, starting up the outboard motor.

"He certainly put us on an interesting wreck," Pitt replied, drying his face with a towel.

"Not an amphora-carrying Bronze Age wreck, but she still looked pretty old."

"Possibly medieval," Pitt guessed. "A mere child, by Mediterranean wreck standards. Let's get to shore and see what we've got."

Giordino gunned the motor, driving the Zodiac up on its keel, then turned toward the nearby island. Chios itself was two miles away, but it was another three miles up the coast before they entered the small bay of a sleepy fishing village called Vokaria. They tied up at a weather-beaten pier that looked like it had been built during the Age of Sail. Giordino then threw a towel down onto the dock, and Pitt laid out the two artifacts.

Both items were covered in a layer of sandy concretion, built up over centuries underwater. Pitt located a fresh-water hose nearby and carefully scrubbed away some of the layered muck on the ceramic box. Free of grime and held aloft under the sunlight, it dazzled the eye. An intricate floral pattern of dark blue, purple, and turquoise burst against a bright white background.

"Looks a bit Moroccan," Giordino said. "Can you pop the top off?"

Pitt carefully worked his fingers under the overhanging lid. Finding a light resistance, he gently forced it free. Inside, the box was filled with dirty water, along with an oblong object that glittered faintly through the murk. Pitt carefully tilted the box to one side, draining it.

He reached in and pulled out a semicircular object that was heavily encrusted. To his shock, he could see that it was a crown. Pitt held it up gingerly, feeling the heavy weight of its solid-gold construction, the metal gleaming from portions that were free of sediment.

"Will you look at that?" Giordino marveled. "Looks like something straight out of King Arthur."

"Or perhaps Ali Baba," Pitt replied, looking at the ceramic box.

"That shipwreck must be no ordinary merchant runner. You think it might be some sort of royal vessel?"

"Anything is possible," Pitt replied. "It would seem somebody important was traveling aboard."

Giordino took hold of the crown and placed it on his head at a rakish angle.

"King Al, at your service," he said, with a wave of his arm. "Bet I could attract a fine local lady wearing this."

"Along with some men in white jackets," Pitt scoffed. "Let's take a look at your lockbox."

Giordino set the crown back into the ceramic case, then picked up the small iron box. As he did, the corroded padlock slipped off, dropping to the towel.

"Security ain't what it used to be," he muttered, setting the box back down. Emulating Pitt, he worked the edges of the lid with his fingers, prying the top off with a pop. Only a small amount of seawater sloshed about inside, for the container was filled nearly to the rim with coins.

"Talk about hitting the jackpot," he grinned. "Looks like we may be in for an early retirement."

"Thank you, no. I'd rather not spend my retirement years in a Turkish prison," Pitt replied.

The coins were made of silver and badly corroded, several of them melded together. Pitt reached to the bottom of the pile and pulled out one that glimmered, a lone gold coin that hadn't suffered the effects of corrosion. He held it up to his eye, noting an irregular stamp, indicative of hammered coinage. Swirling Arabic lettering was partially visible on both sides, surrounded by a serrated ring. Pitt could only guess as to the age and origin of the coin. The two men curiously examined the other coins, which in their condition revealed few markings.

"Based on our limited evidence, I'd guess we have an Ottoman wreck of some sort on our hands," Pitt declared. "The coins don't look Byzantine, which means fifteenth century or later."

"Somebody should be able to date those accurately."

"The coins were a lucky find," Pitt agreed.

"I say fund the project another month and avoid going back to Washington."

A battered Toyota pickup truck approached along the dock, squealing to a halt in front of the men. A smiling youth with big ears climbed out of the truck.

"A ride to the airport?" he asked haltingly.

"Yes, that's me," Pitt said, retrieving his overnight bag from the Zodiac.

"What about our goodies?" Giordino asked, carefully wrapping the items in the towel before the driver could examine them.

"To Istanbul with me, I'm afraid. I know the Director of Maritime Studies at the Istanbul Archaeology Museum. He'll find a good home for the artifacts and hopefully tell us what we found."

"I guess that means no wild night out on Chios for King Al," Giordino said, passing the towel to Pitt.

Pitt glanced at the sleepy village ringing the harbor, then climbed into the idling truck.

"To be honest," he said as the driver began pulling away, "I'm not sure Chios is ready for King Al."

3

The commuter plane touched down at Atatürk International Airport in Istanbul just before dark. Scurrying around a mass of commercial jumbo jets like a mosquito in a beehive, the small plane pulled into an empty terminal slot and bumped to a halt.

Pitt was one of the last passengers off the plane and had barely stepped into the tiled terminal when he was mauled by a tall attractive woman with cinnamon-colored hair.

"You were supposed to beat me here," Loren Smith said, pulling away after a deep embrace. "I was afraid you weren't going to come at all." Her violet eyes beamed with relief as she gazed at her husband.

Pitt crooked an arm around her waist and gave her a long kiss. "A tire problem on the plane delayed our departure. Have you been waiting long?"

"Less than an hour." She crumpled her nose and licked her lips. "You taste salty."

"Al and I found a shipwreck on the way to the airport."

"I should have guessed," she said, then gave him a scolding look. "I thought you told me flying and diving didn't mix?"

"They don't. But that puddle jumper I flew in on barely cleared a thousand feet, so I'm plenty safe."

"You get the bends while we're in Istanbul, and I'll kill

47

you," she said, holding him tight. "Is the shipwreck anything interesting?"

"It appears to be."

He held up his overnight bag with the artifacts wrapped inside. "We retrieved a couple of artifacts that should be revealing. I invited Dr. Rey Ruppé of the Istanbul Archaeology Museum to join us for dinner tonight, in hopes that he can shed some further light."

Loren stood on her toes and looked into Pitt's green eyes, her brow wrinkled.

"It's a good thing I knew when I married you that you'd always keep the sea as a mistress," she said.

"Fortunately," he replied with a grin while holding her close, "I have a heart big enough for the both of you."

Grabbing her hand, they waded through the terminal crowd and collected his baggage, then caught a taxi to a hotel in Istanbul's central historic district of Sultanahmet. After a quick shower and change, they hopped another cab for a short ride to a quiet residential area a dozen blocks away.

"Balikçi Sabahattin," the cabdriver announced.

Pitt helped Loren out onto a quaint cobblestone lane. On the opposite side of the street was the restaurant, housed in a picturesque wood-frame house built in the 1920s. The couple waded past some tables outside to reach the front door and entered an elegant foyer. A thick-set man with thinning hair and a jovial smile stepped up and shoved out a hand in greeting.

"Dirk, glad you could find the place," he said, crushing Pitt's hand in a vise grip. "Welcome to Istanbul."

"Thanks, Rey, it's good to see you again. I'd like you to meet my wife, Loren."

"A pleasure," Ruppé replied graciously, shaking Loren's hand with less vigor. "I hope you can forgive an old shovel jockey's intrusion on dinner tonight. I'm off to Rome in the morning for an archaeology conference, so this was the only opportunity I had to discuss your husband's underwater discovery."

"It's no intrusion at all. I'm always fascinated by what Dirk pulls off the seafloor," she said with a laugh. "Plus, you have obviously led us to a lovely dining spot."

"One of my favorite seafood restaurants in Istanbul," Ruppé replied.

A hostess appeared and escorted them down a hallway to one of several dining rooms fitted into the former house. They took their seats at a linen-covered table aside a large window that overlooked the back garden.

"Perhaps you can recommend some regional favorites, Dr. Ruppé," Loren said. "It's my first visit to Turkey."

"Please, call me Rey. When in Turkey, you can never go wrong with fish. Both the turbot and sea bass are excellent here. Of course, I can never seem to eat my fill of kabobs, either," he grinned, rubbing his belly.

After placing their orders, Loren asked Ruppé how long he had lived in Turkey.

"Gosh, going on twenty-five years now. I came over one summer from Arizona State to teach a marine archaeology field school and never left. We located an old Byzantine merchant trader off the shores of Kos that we excavated, and I've been busy here ever since."

"Dr. Ruppé is the foremost authority on Byzantine and Ottoman marine antiquities in the eastern Mediterranean,"

Pitt said. "His expertise has been invaluable on many of our projects in the region."

"Like with your husband, shipwrecks are my true love," he said. "Since taking the maritime studies post at the Archaeology Museum, I regrettably spend less time in the field than I'd prefer."

"The burden of management," Pitt concurred.

The waiter set a large plate of mussels with rice on the table as an appetizer, which they all quickly sampled.

"You certainly work out of a fascinating city," Loren noted.

"Yes, Istanbul does live up to its nickname as the 'Queen of Cities.' Born to the Greeks, raised by the Romans, and matured under the Ottomans. Its legacy of ancient cathedrals, mosques, and palaces can grip even the most jaded historian. But as a home to twelve million people, it does have its challenges."

"I've heard that the political climate is one of them."

"Is changing it the purpose of your visit, Congresswoman?" Ruppé asked, with a grin.

Loren Smith smiled at the allusion. Though a long-serving House representative from the state of Colorado, she wasn't much of a political animal.

"Actually, I only came to Istanbul to visit my wayward husband. I've been traveling with a congressional delegation touring the south Caucasus and just stopped off on my way back to Washington. A State Department envoy on the plane mentioned that there were U.S. security concerns about the growing fundamentalist movement in Turkey."

"He's right. As you know, Turkey is a secular state that is ninety-eight percent Muslim, mostly of the Sunni faith.

But there has been a growing movement under Mufti Battal, who's centered here in Istanbul, for fundamentalist reforms. I'm no expert in these matters, so I can't tell you the actual extent of his appeal. But Turkey is suffering economic distress like other places, which breeds unhappiness and discontent with the status quo. The hard times seem to be playing right into his hands. He's visible everywhere these days, really attacking the sitting President."

"Aside from upsetting the Western alliances, I can't help but think that a Turkish shift toward fundamentalism would make the entire Middle East an even more dangerous place," Loren replied.

"With a Shia-controlled Iran flexing her military muscle, I fear your concerns are quite valid."

Their dinners were brought to the table, Loren receiving a baked sea bass dish and Pitt a grilled grouper plate, while Ruppé dined on Black Sea turbot.

"Sorry to ruin the meal with politics, it's a bit of an occupational hazard," Loren apologized. "The sea bass is outstanding, I'm happy to report."

"I don't mind, and I'm sure Dirk is used to it," Ruppé said with a wink. He turned to his old friend. "So, Dirk, tell me about your project in the Aegean."

"We're investigating a number of low-oxygen dead zones in the eastern Mediterranean," Pitt replied between bites. "The Turkish Environment Ministry has steered us to a number of regional spots in the Aegean where recurring algae blooms have snuffed out all marine life. It's a growing problem we've been seeing in many places around the globe."

"I know that it's been a major concern in the Chesapeake Bay, right in our own backyard," Loren remarked.

"Dead zones in the Chesapeake have become quite large in recent summer months," Pitt acknowledged.

"All due to pollutants?" Ruppé asked.

Pitt nodded. "In most instances, the dead zones are located near the delta areas of large rivers. Low oxygen levels are usually a direct result of nutrient pollution, primarily in the form of nitrogen from agricultural or industrial runoff. The nutrients in the water initially create a mass growth of phytoplankton, or algae blooms. When the algae ultimately die and sink to the bottom, the decomposition process removes oxygen from the water. If the process reaches critical mass, the water becomes anoxic, killing all marine life and creating a dead zone."

"What have you found so far in Turkish waters?"

"We've confirmed the presence of a moderately sized dead zone between the Greek island of Chios and the Turkish mainland. We are continuing to conduct survey work in the region and will ultimately map the perimeter and intensity of the zone."

"Have you traced its source?" Loren asked.

Pitt shook his head. "The Turkish Environment Ministry is helping identify potential industrial or agricultural polluters in the area, but we're not close to identifying the source, or sources, just yet."

The waiter appeared and cleared their dinner dishes, then brought a tray of fresh apricots and three coffees to the table. Loren was surprised to find that her coffee was already sweetened.

"Dirk, is your shipwreck located in the dead zone?" Ruppé asked.

"No, but not far off. We were actually laid up repairing our sensing equipment when we discovered the site. A fishing boat that is now short a few feet of net gave us some help."

"In your call, you mentioned retrieving some artifacts?"

"Yes, I actually brought them with me," Pitt replied, nodding toward a black bag that sat near his feet.

Ruppé's eyes lit up, then he looked at his watch. "It's after eleven, and I've probably kept you up too late as it is. But the museum is just a few minutes down the road. I'd love to take a look at the items, and then you can leave them in the safety of my lab, if you like."

"Don't be ridiculous," Loren piped up, averting potential disappointment for her husband. "We're both dying to have your assessment."

"Great," Ruppé smiled. "Let's enjoy our coffee, and then we can go to my office to take a proper look at what you found."

The coffee cups drained and the check paid, the trio wandered out of the restaurant and up the street. Ruppé stopped in front of a green Volkswagen Karmann Ghia convertible parked at the curb.

"My apologies for the lack of legroom, I know the backseat is pretty cramped," he said.

"I love these old VWs," Loren said. "I haven't seen one this nice in ages."

"She's getting on in years but still runs like a top," Ruppé said. "I've found it to be a great car for zipping around the cramped streets of Istanbul, though I miss having air-conditioning."

"Who needs that when the top goes down?" Pitt

mused, taking the passenger seat after Loren had wedged herself into the backseat.

Ruppé drove back into the heart of the city, then turned through a large arched gate.

"We're entering the grounds of Topkapi, the old Ottoman palace," he explained. "Our museum is located near the entrance to the inner courtyard. You should take a tour of the palace, if you have the chance. But go early, it's a tourist favorite."

Ruppé motored through a parklike setting studded with historic buildings. Driving up a slight rise, he pulled into an employee parking lot at the rear of the Istanbul Archaeology Museum. A half block away rose the high wall that surrounded the inner palace of Topkapi.

After uncoiling themselves from the cramped car, Loren and Pitt followed Ruppé toward a large neoclassical building.

"The museum actually encompasses three buildings," Ruppé explained. "There's the Museum of the Ancient Orient around the front, next to the Tiled Kiosk, which houses the Museum of Islamic Art. I kick around here in the main building, which houses the Archaeology Museum."

Ruppé led them up the back steps of the columned building, constructed in the nineteenth century. After he unlocked the back door, they were greeted by a night watchman stationed just inside.

"Good evening, Dr. Ruppé," the guard said. "Working late again?"

"Hi, Avni. Just a quick visit with some friends, and then we'll be gone."

"Take your time. It's just me and the crickets."

Ruppé led his guests through the main hallway, which was filled with ancient statues and carvings. Exhibit halls on either side showcased elaborate tombs from across the Middle East. The archaeologist stopped and pointed out a massive stone sarcophagus covered with bas-relief carvings.

"The Alexander Sarcophagus, our most famous artifact. The scenes along the sides depict Alexander the Great in battle. Nobody knows who's actually inside, though many believe it's a Persian Governor named Mazaeus."

"Beautiful artwork," Loren murmured. "How old is it?"

"Fourth century B.C."

Ruppé guided them down a side corridor and into a spacious office overflowing with books. A large lab table occupied one wall, its stainless steel surface covered with artifacts in varying stages of conservation. Ruppé flicked on a bank of overhead lights, which brightly illuminated the room.

"Let's take a look at your soggy goods," he said, pulling a couple of stools up to the table.

Pitt unzipped the bag and pulled out Giordino's iron box, unwrapping it carefully from the towel.

"Somebody's piggy bank, I believe," he said. "The lock came off by itself," he explained with a guilty grin.

Ruppé slipped on a pair of reading glasses and studied the box.

"Yes, it looks like the equivalent of a strongbox, quite old from the appearance."

"The contents might make dating it a little easier," Pitt remarked.

Ruppé's eyes widened as he opened the lid. Spreading a cloth on the table, he carefully laid out the silver and gold coins, seven in all.

"I should have let you pay for dinner," he said.

"My word, is that real gold?" Loren asked, picking up the gold coin and noting its heavy weight.

"Yes, looks to be from an Ottoman mint," Ruppé replied, studying the stamped inscription. "They operated several around the empire."

"Can you read any of the writing?" she asked, admiring the swirling Arabic script.

"It appears to be a rendition of *'Allahu Akbar,'* or 'God is great.'"

Ruppé crossed the room and scanned his bookshelf, finally retrieving a thick-bound volume from the shelves. Flipping its pages, he stopped at a photograph of several antique coins. Comparing the image with one of the coins, he nodded in satisfaction.

"A match?" Pitt asked.

"Spot-on. Identical to coins known to be minted in Syria, during the sixteenth century. Congratulations, Dirk, you've likely discovered an Ottoman wreck from the Age of Suleiman the Magnificent."

"Who's Suleiman?" Loren asked.

"One of the most successful and admired of the Ottoman sultans, perhaps only behind the reigning founder of the empire, Osman I. He expanded the Ottoman Empire across southeastern Europe, the Middle East, and North Africa during his reign in the mid fifteen hundreds."

"Perhaps this was a gift or offering to the Sultan," Pitt

said, removing the ceramic box from his bag and slowly unwrapping it. Loren's eyes brightened at the intricate design in blue, purple, and white that adorned the lid.

"What beautiful artistry," she remarked.

"The old Muslim craftsmen did wonders with tile and ceramic," Ruppé said. "I haven't seen anything quite like this, however."

He held the box up to the light and studied it carefully. There was a small uneven crack on one side, which he rubbed a finger over.

"The design is similar to items I've seen known as Damascus ware," he said. "It's a pattern from the well-known ancient kilns of Iznik, Turkey."

He carefully pried the lid off, then removed the encrusted crown from inside.

"Oh my," Loren said, inching closer.

Ruppé was equally impressed. "That's something you don't see every day," he said, holding it for study under a portable lamp. He picked up a small dental pick and lightly scraped off a particle of sediment.

"This should clean up quite nicely, given a careful scrubbing," he said. Examining it a bit closer, he squinted with a furrowed brow. "That's odd," he said.

"What is it?" Loren asked.

"There appears to be an inscription on the inside rim. I can just make out a few letters, but it appears to be Latin."

"That doesn't make much sense," Loren said.

"No," Ruppé agreed. "But I think after a bit of conservation, we'll be able to figure it out. Should allow us a good chance at identifying its origin."

"I knew we came to the right place," Pitt said.

"It would seem that your shipwreck may contain more than one mystery," Ruppé said.

Loren looked at the crown through tired eyes, then suppressed a yawn.

"I'm afraid I've kept you up far too late," Ruppé remarked, placing the crown in a wall safe, then putting the lockbox, coins, and ceramic box into a plastic bin filled with fresh water. "I'll be anxious to examine the items in more detail with the help of my associates as soon as I return from Rome."

"I'd like to know what a gold crown inscribed in Latin is doing on an Ottoman shipwreck," Pitt said.

"We may never know, but I'm curious to see what else is on that wreck," Ruppé replied. "Strange as it seems, there's actually been only a small number of Ottoman wrecks discovered in the Med."

"If you can notify the Turkish authorities of our find, we'll do what we can to help," Pitt said. He handed Ruppé a nautical chart with the wreck's location marked in red. "It's pretty close to Chios, so the Greeks might have something to say about it."

"I'll make a call first thing in the morning," Ruppé said. "Is there any chance you and your vessel could help initiate a full survey of the site?"

Pitt smiled. "I'd like nothing more than to figure out exactly what we found. I'll manage to divert our vessel for a day or two. We have an archaeologist already aboard who can help direct the work."

"Fine, fine. I'm on good terms with the Turkish Ministry of Culture. They'll be pleased to know that the wreck is in good hands."

He looked at Loren, who was fighting to keep her eyes open.

"My dear, forgive my historic ramblings. It's very late, and I need to get you back to your hotel."

"You better, before I lie down to sleep on one of the sarcophagi outside."

Ruppé locked up his office, then escorted them past the guard and out of the building. As they were descending the museum's steps, a pair of muted explosions erupted in the distance, and a series of nearby alarms sounded suddenly, echoing over the high walls of Topkapi. The trio stopped, astonished, and listened to the faint voices of men shouting and then the pop of gunfire rattling through the night sky. More shots were fired, the sounds drawing closer to them. Seconds later, the door to the museum opened behind them, and the security guard came running toward them with a horrified look on his face.

"The palace is under attack!" he yelled. "The Chamber of the Sacred Relics in Topkapi has been raided, and the guards at Bâb-üs Selâm are not responding. I must make sure the gate is barricaded."

Bâb-üs Selâm, or the Gate of Salutations, was the main entry point into the enclosed sanctuary of Topkapi Palace. It was a high-towered palisade resembling a Disneyland castle, where tourists lined up in the morning to explore the palace and grounds of the grand Ottoman sultans. A security station was located just inside the gate, which housed several Turkish Army guards assigned to night duty. Situated just up the road, the gate was clearly wide open, and no guards were visible.

The museum guard, Avni, sprinted past Ruppé and across the parking lot. About a hundred yards from the gate, he ran past a white utility van parked just off the road. The van's motor immediately turned over and coughed to life.

Its headlights were turned off, immediately triggering an uneasy feeling in Pitt. Sensing something amiss, he instinctively followed after Avni.

"Be right back," he grunted, then took off at a sprint.

"Dirk!" Loren shouted, confused at her husband's sudden reaction. But he didn't bother to answer when he noticed the white van begin to pull forward.

Pitt knew what was about to happen but was powerless to prevent it. When the van lurched forward with a whining squeal from its motor, he could only watch as if it were a movie scene in slow motion. The van aimed for the museum guard and quickly picked up speed. Running at full tilt, Pitt shouted a warning.

"Avni! Behind you!" he yelled.

But it was a futile gesture. With its headlights still turned off, the van lurched forward and struck the museum guard from behind. His body flew high off the vehicle's hood, then cartwheeled to the pavement with a thud. The van continued accelerating, then screeched to a stop in front of the open gate.

Pitt kept running, quickly approaching the prone guard. From the grotesque shape of the man's head, Pitt could tell that the guard's skull had been shattered, killing him instantly. Unable to do anything for him now, Pitt proceeded toward the van.

The van driver sat behind the wheel, anxiously staring

through the open Bâb-üs Selâm portal. With the engine running, he failed to detect Pitt's footsteps until he was alongside the van. He turned to look out the open side window and was met by a pair of hands that reached in and grabbed him by the collar. Before he could even resist, his head and torso were yanked halfway through the window.

Pitt heard additional footfalls approach, but only caught a shadow out of the corner of his eye as he wrestled with the driver. He had looped an elbow beneath the man's chin and was nearly ripping his head off. The driver regained his wits and struggled to release Pitt's grip, jamming his knees under the steering wheel and flailing with his arms. But Pitt was able to exert pressure on the driver's throat until he gasped for air, then started to fall limp in his arms.

"Let him go," a female voice suddenly barked.

Pitt turned toward the prone body of the dead museum guard while maintaining his grip on the choking van driver. Loren and Ruppé had followed him up the road to assist Avni and were now positioned alongside the dead man. Ruppé was leaning down on one knee, holding his hand to a bloody gash inflicted across his forehead, while Loren stood alongside looking at Pitt with fear in her eyes.

Standing beside them was a short woman wearing a black ski mask, sweater, and pants. She stood with her arm extended, pointing a pistol at Loren's head.

"Let him go," she said once more to Pitt, "or the woman dies."

4

Topkapi Palace was the grand residence of the Ottoman sultans for nearly four hundred years. A sprawling maze of garnished tiled buildings and chambers built on a hillside compound overlooking the Golden Horn, the palace contained a treasury of Turkey's rich history. The popular and crowded guided tours provided a glimpse into the personal lives of the ruling sultans, while showcasing an impressive collection of art, weapons, and jewelry. Yet amid the royal opulence, the palace contained a serious collection of holy Islamic relics revered throughout the world. And it was these objects that the thieves had targeted.

A catering van had easily smuggled a small cache of arms and plastic explosives into the palace grounds several days before. The thieves merely entered the complex as tourists late in the day and quietly slipped aside, hiding in a groundskeeper's shed. Under cover of darkness, long after the last tourists had left and the entrances secured, the thieves collected their weapons and moved on the Chamber of the Sacred Relics, where many of the holy objects were stored.

The actual assault took barely a minute, as they blasted their way through a side wall with the explosives, then shot and killed a nearby guard. They quickly gathered their desired relics, then escaped through the damaged wall.

The thieves had carefully orchestrated a series of small,

diversionary explosions at various points around the compound as they made their way south on foot. Once past the main gate, they would be whisked off the grounds in the waiting van. It would take only a few minutes from there to reach the maze of Sultanahmet's winding streets and become lost to the night.

Police sirens wailed in the distance as two men in black sprinted through Bâb-üs Selâm, each toting a canvas bag. The woman aiming the handgun at Loren immediately barked clipped orders to the men as they approached the van. The two thieves threw their bags in the back, then dragged the semiconscious driver there and laid him out. One of the men hurried around front and climbed into the driver's seat, while the second man produced his own pistol and leveled it at Loren. The woman barked again at Pitt.

"You. Away from the van," she ordered, training her gun on Pitt. "This woman is coming with us. If you wish to see her alive again, you will tell the police we escaped through the Gülhane Park Gate." She motioned her weapon toward the northeast side of the compound.

Pitt's hands clenched into fists, and his eyes nearly shot flames of anger, but there was nothing he could do. The woman sensed his wrath and leveled her gun at his head.

"Don't even think about it," she said.

The gunman grabbed Loren by the arm and roughly shoved her into the back of the van, then climbed in and closed the door behind them. The woman backpedaled to the front passenger door, holding her gun on Pitt until she jumped inside. The new driver immediately floored it, and the van squealed away with its tires smoking.

Pitt quickly ran to Ruppé, who had staggered to his feet

but wobbled from the blow to his head administered by the woman.

"Your car," Pitt said hurriedly.

Ruppé quickly fished out the keys.

"You go now. I'll just slow you down."

"Are you all right?"

"Just a scratch," he replied with a weak smile, eyeing his blood-smeared hand. "I'll be fine. You go ahead, and I will inform the police when they arrive."

Pitt nodded as he grabbed the keys and dashed off toward the Karmann Ghia. The old Volkswagen fired on the first turn of the key. Pitt immediately jammed it into gear and chirped the tires as he sped off after the van.

The exterior grounds of Topkapi were laid out in the rough shape of a tilted *A*, with an entry gate at the base of each leg. Anticipating a more likely police response through the northern Gülhane Park Gate, the thieves headed for the Imperial Gate to the south. Despite a daily influx of tourist buses to the palace, the tree-lined roads through the grounds were narrow, curving affairs that limited speed.

Pitt took to the main road on which the van had exited, but it was well out of sight by now. Passing several small side drives, Pitt felt his heart beat faster in the fear that he might not be able to locate the van. Professional thieves were usually not murderers, he tried telling himself. They would probably let Loren free at the first opportune moment. But then his mind flashed back to the image of the museum guard being intentionally run over. They had heard plenty of gunshots over the palace wall as well. An uncomfortable pang hit him at the realization that these thieves were in fact not afraid to kill.

He pushed the accelerator down harder, eliciting a painful wail from the Volkswagen's air-cooled motor. The Karmann Ghia was far from a fast car, but its size and weight made it a nimble cornering vehicle. Pitt pushed the little car to its limits, constantly shifting between second and third gears as he shot down the curving road. Once he pushed it a little too far, sending a hubcap bounding into an elm tree when the back wheel kissed a curb.

The roadway straightened for a short stretch, then ended at a crossroads. Pitt slammed on the brakes, skidding into the empty intersection, as he contemplated which way to turn. A quick glance to either side revealed no traffic and no sign of the van. Pitt thought back to the woman's remark about the Gülhane Gate. He had no clue where it was but recalled her wave of the pistol. Despite the twists and turns he had driven, he was certain that she had motioned to what was now his right. Jamming the gearshift into first, he stomped on the gas and popped the clutch, shooting off down the paved road to his left.

The wide canopies of aged oak trees whizzed by overhead as he accelerated hard, following the road as it faded to the right. Dropping down a low hill, he came to another crossroads. This time, he spotted a road sign in English, "Exit," with an arrow pointing to the right. Slowing only slightly, he screeched through the turn with a squeal of blistering rubber, the Volkswagen drifting into the oncoming lane that was thankfully devoid of traffic.

The road opened onto an extended straightaway that led through the Imperial Gate. Pitt could sense an increase in light radiating ahead, as the trees and shrubs of the palace grounds gave way to the crowded urbanization of

Istanbul's ancient city center. Staring down the road, Pitt caught a glimpse of taillights turning just outside the gate.

It was the van.

Pitt felt a surge of hope as he held the throttle down and raced to the gate. The thieves must have been right, he thought. If the Istanbul police were responding to the alarm, they hadn't yet made it to the Imperial Gate. As he approached the gate, he caught a glimpse of what appeared to be the bodies of two Turkish soldiers lying beside the road.

He ignored the sight, bursting past the gate and making a sharp right turn, slowing to avoid a loud squeal of tires. A glance ahead revealed that the van had cut south, down a perpendicular boulevard. Pitt quickly followed suit, flicking off his headlights as he made a sharp turn, then closed in on the van.

A congested mass of cars and people by day, the city's historic Sultanahmet center was oddly quiet late at night. Pitt sped around a beat-up taxicab, then slowed as he saw the van stopped at a traffic light.

They were traveling past Hagia Sophia, one of the grandest monuments surviving from the Byzantine era. Built as a basilica by the Roman Emperor Justinian and later converted to a mosque, it stood as the largest domed building in the world for almost a thousand years. Its ancient frescoes and mosaics, along with its towering architecture, made it one of Istanbul's most important cultural landmarks.

The van turned right again, crossing Sultanahmet Square and the forecourt of Hagia Sophia, where a handful of tourists milled about, taking photos of the illuminated exterior. Pitt tried to edge closer to the van but was cut off by a pair of taxis pulling away from the curb.

The van slowed its pace to avoid attention as a police wagon stormed by on a cross street with its lights and siren blazing, heading up the hill toward Topkapi. The small congregation of vehicles moved out of the square and down a block before stopping at a red light. A rusty garbage truck ambled down the cross street, then stopped near the corner to pick up a pile of trash. The truck momentarily blocked the van, which was wedged from behind by one of the taxis.

Sitting two cars behind that, Pitt watched a slow-moving garbageman attack the trash pile and decided the situation afforded him the chance to act. Without hesitation, he leaped out of the Karmann Ghia and rushed toward the back of the van, crouching low while hugging the sides of the taxis to avoid detection. The van's rear panel doors had tinted windows, but Pitt could make out a figure seated on the right side who either had very short hair or was wearing a ski cap.

The light turned green, and the van lurched forward, then stopped, forced to wait while the lackadaisical garbageman slowly disposed of the pile of bulging plastic trash bags. Pitt approached the van in a crouch and placed a foot on its bumper, then grabbed the door handle with his right hand. Flinging the door open, he lunged in, his balled left fist coiled to strike.

It was a risky move, one that could get both Loren and himself killed. But he had the element of surprise on his side and rightly figured the gunman in the rear had let his guard down and was relishing the success of the theft. Deep down, there was another motive for abandoning caution. Pitt knew he could never live with himself if he failed to act and something happened to Loren.

With the door flung open, Pitt peered into the rear compartment while already in motion. He had gambled correctly and found the uninjured gunman seated on a bench to the right. Seated opposite was the original van driver, who was slowly regaining his color. Loren was seated beside him, wedged against a partition that divided the rear from the driver's compartment. In the fraction of a second that they made eye contact, Pitt could see a look of fright in his wife's eyes.

Surprise was completely his, as the gunman didn't even have his pistol on Loren but was holding it down at his side. He gave Pitt a startled look through his ski mask before Pitt's balled fist struck him on the chin. With surging adrenaline and controlled rage, Pitt could have probably put his fist through the van's side panel had he aimed differently. The blow instantly knocked the man cold, sending him teetering to the floorboard without ever raising his weapon.

The other man reacted quickly, perhaps relishing the opportunity to retaliate against the earlier assault. He dove onto the back of Pitt's outstretched body, pinning Pitt's torso against the floor. The man had a gun in his pocket, which he struggled to retrieve while wrapping his other arm around Pitt. Pushed flat, Pitt immediately raised himself with his arms but couldn't quite shake the man's half bear hug. Seeking any measure of leverage he could, Pitt wedged a foot against the rear bumper, then tried shifting his weight to the rear. With his attacker glued to his back, Pitt heaved with both his arms and legs, flinging himself backward and out of the van.

The taxicab was idling just a foot or two behind the van. Hurtling through the air, the two intertwined bodies slammed backward onto the cab's hood, the van driver sandwiched beneath Pitt and bearing the brunt of the impact. The man gasped as the breath was knocked from his lungs, and Pitt felt the grip around his torso soften. Spinning to his feet, Pitt pulled the man's arm away, then shoved an elbow into the driver's head with repeated blows. It was enough to stun the man into submission and he sank to the pavement before he could find the grip on his gun.

Catching his breath, Pitt looked up to see Loren scampering out of the van. In her hand, she was clutching one of the black bags.

"Quick, let's go," he urged, grabbing her arm and pulling her down the street. They staggered a few steps to the sidewalk, Loren resisting any attempts at speed.

"I can't run in these shoes," she pleaded.

Pitt heard a yell from the direction of the van but wasted no time looking. Instead, he roughly grabbed his wife and shoved her toward the alcove of a small square building a few steps away. He dove after her as two quick cracks from a pistol rang out. A pair of concrete chips flew in the air as the bullets peppered the ground near their feet.

The doorway provided cover, but just temporarily. It would only be seconds before the woman with the pistol stepped down the street far enough to have a clear shot at the two of them.

"Where to now?" Loren gasped, her heart pounding in fear.

Pitt quickly surveyed an ancient weathered door that stood at the top of the steps.

"A simple choice, I'd say," he replied, nodding toward the door. "We go in."

5

Two firm kicks on the wooden door were sufficient to dislodge the well-worn dead bolt from its housing and force an opening. Loren and Pitt quickly slithered into a plain, empty room, sided by a counter and cash register. At the back of the room was a wide, dimly lit stairwell that led to a lower level.

From outside the door, they could hear the sound of running footsteps approach. Pitt turned and swung the door closed as he caught a glimpse of the woman in black sprinting around the back of the taxi. He missed seeing the muzzle flash from her pistol as she fired again, but he saw the slug bury itself into the door a few inches from his face.

"I guess we go down," he said, grabbing Loren's hand and rushing to the stairs. They had hopped down a few of the carved stone steps when Loren yanked on his arm.

"I can't make it that far in heels," she said, noticing that the stairwell descended a considerable distance below them. She quickly yanked off her pumps, then proceeded to scurry down the stairs.

"Why does practicality never enter into the design of women's shoes?" Pitt asked, catching up with her.

"Only a man would have to ask," she grumbled, breathing hard from their exertion.

They continued plunging down the stairs, which

descended over fifty steps. Their argument over footwear was lost to a sense of awe as their surroundings unfolded before them under sparse lighting.

They had descended into a huge man-made subterranean cavern. It was a totally unexpected and somewhat bizarre structure to find in the middle of bustling Istanbul. The steps ended at a wooden platform, which overlooked the deep cavern. Pitt admired a forest of thirty-foot-high marble columns that stretched into the darkness by the dozen, their capitals supporting a towering multi-arched ceiling. A bank of red overhead lights lightly illuminated the space, lending it a mysterious, almost hellish appearance.

"What is this place?" Loren asked, her voice echoing off the stone walls. "It's breathtaking, in more ways than one."

"It's an underground cistern. A huge one, by the looks of it. The Romans built hundreds of them under the streets of Istanbul in order to store water, which was transported in from the countryside via aqueducts."

They stood in what was actually the largest cistern in Istanbul, the Yerebatan Sarnici. Originally constructed by Emperor Constantine and later enlarged by Justinian, the structure stretched nearly five hundred feet in length. In its day, the cistern's mortar-lined floor and walls were capable of holding 2.8 million cubic feet of water. Abandoned during the Ottoman reign, it became a forgotten, mud-filled bog until restored by the Turkish government in the twentieth century. As testament to Roman construction prowess, the floor of the cavern still stored a few feet of water for effect.

The vast chamber was nearly silent but for the splattering of water that occasionally dripped from the ceiling. The silence was suddenly disrupted by the sound of footsteps overhead as the armed woman in black rushed through the office and started down the stone steps. Pitt and Loren immediately took off running, following a raised wooden ramp that led toward the far end of the chamber.

The ramp ultimately split into a circular walkway that allowed tourists to view the myriad of carved columns that supported the cistern's ceiling. Beneath it, the flat, shallow waters made a tranquil home to hundreds of colorful carp that never saw the light of day. Pitt and Loren had little time to admire the fish as they sprinted to the far end of the chamber.

The wooden ramps were wet from the dripping ceiling, and Loren slipped repeatedly in her stocking feet. Falling as they rounded a sharply angled corner, she lay for a second, catching her breath, until Pitt helped her to her feet. The sound of shoes rushing down the stone steps behind them echoed through the chamber.

"Why is she still bothering with us?" Pitt asked aloud as he dragged Loren around the corner.

"Might have something to do with this," she replied, holding up the black bag still clutched in one hand. "I took it from the van. I thought it might be important."

Pitt smiled at his wife's instincts. "Yes, it probably is," he said. "But it's not important enough to get killed over."

The pursuing footfalls had reached the bottom of the stairs, their tone changing to a muted thump on the wooden ramp. Pitt and Loren ran a few more yards, turning down a section of ramp that suddenly terminated in a dead end.

"Give me the bag, and you may walk away."

The woman's voice echoed through the cavern in angry repetition. After a silent pause, her steps resumed at a quickened pace. Though still out of view under the dim lights, she was audibly closing the gap.

"Into the water," Pitt whispered, grabbing the black bag from Loren while guiding her to the rail. In her long dress, she clumsily climbed over the rail, then let Pitt help lower her quietly into the waist-deep water. Her body gave off an involuntary shiver, from both the cool water and the threat at hand.

"Move to the back of the far column and stay out of sight until I call for you," he directed quietly.

"Where will you be?"

"Giving her the bag back."

He leaned through the rail and gave her a quick kiss, then watched as she waded past several rows of marble columns before disappearing from sight. Satisfied that she was safely hidden, he turned and moved back down the platform. A thundering boom caused him to pause as a chunk of wooden railing splattered into the water a few feet ahead of him. He spotted the figure of the shooter a hundred feet away and he quickly sprinted ahead until a row of columns blocked her from view.

His mind raced in the few seconds of cover he had. He quickly contemplated the black bag, which was lightly weighed down by two separate objects. There was no place for concealment on the empty wooden ramps, so his eyes drifted upward at the huge columns nearby. He noted that every third column or so had a small red light fixture mounted near the crown, which backlit the cistern. As the sound of the woman's footsteps drew closer, Pitt hoisted the bag and split the two objects through the exterior cloth. He then twisted the loose center cloth until the bag resembled a barbell, with the weighted objects at either end.

"Drop it!" he heard the woman's voice yell.

In the dim light, Pitt gambled that she was still too far away for an accurate shot, so he took two quick steps toward the railing. The pistol barked again, twin muzzle flashes clearly visible out of the corner of Pitt's eye as the shots thundered through the chamber. One bullet hit the rail while the other whistled past his ear. Already in motion, all he could do was keep moving.

With a third step, he swung the bag up from the floor and flung it upward with all his strength. Without breaking pace, he grabbed the top railing and pulled himself over the side. The bag spun like a pinwheel and was still drifting skyward when Pitt hit the water. He immediately spun under the surface toward the ramp, under its supports, kicking in the direction of the woman. With a controlled effort, he swam smoothly in the shallow water, trying not to break the surface. An old hand at free diving, he easily covered seventy-five feet before gently easing up for air.

He held perfectly still, quietly catching his breath beneath the ramp while checking where the woman was located. He correctly gauged that he had bypassed her beneath the ramp as she ran toward the point of his initial splash. Peering from the water's edge, he saw her pacing on the far side with her gun pointed at the water.

Slipping back under the ramp, he cautiously followed it in the other direction until it made an angled turn. There was more illumination in the area than he preferred, but the bend offered a point of concealment as a staging area for attack. He started to pull himself up a support beam when he detected a new set of footsteps pounding down the stone stairs. A car horn honking on the street blared in the background.

"Miss Maria, we must leave at once," shouted a male voice in Turkish. "The police are beginning to search outside of Topkapi."

Pitt crept back into the water as the woman broke into a run in his direction. Hearing her pass overhead, he held perfectly still, listening as she began climbing the stone steps. Nearing the top, she hesitated for a moment, then a shrill voice boomed through the cistern.

"I shall not forget you!" she shrieked.

The sound of her footsteps fell away, and the car horn ceased honking. Pitt sat still in the cold water, listening to the eerie echo of the falling water droplets. Satisfied that the assailants were in fact gone, he climbed onto the ramp and made his way to the end, calling out Loren's name along the way.

His freezing wife appeared from behind one of the columns and waded to the ramp, where Pitt hoisted her up. Though her hair was a mess, her dress soaked, and she shivered with cold, she still looked radiant to Pitt.

"You all right?"

"Yes," she said. "Are they gone?"

Pitt nodded, holding her hand as they walked down the ramp.

"Nasty people," she said. "I wonder how many they killed during the heist."

Pitt could only speculate. "Did they hurt you?" he asked.

"No, but they clearly weren't afraid to kill. They didn't seem to care at all when I told them I was a U.S. Congresswoman."

"They must have less regard for politicians here than in America."

"Did you give her the bag?"

"No, I'm afraid she had to leave empty-handed. As you heard, she doesn't intend to forget us."

"Where did you hide it?"

Pitt stopped and pointed toward the crown of a marble column that rose from the water just a few feet away. Wrapped around a high-mounted light fixture atop the column, the twisted black bag hung dangling over the water.

"It's not hidden," he said with a slight grin. "It's just a tad out of reach."

6

"Another cup of tea, Sheikh?"

The guest nodded slightly as his host proceeded to refill his cup with black tea. Barely thirty, he was the youngest of five sons born to one of the ruling royal families of the United Arab Emirates. A slight man, he wore a perfectly pressed, bone-white headdress wrapped with a gold-threaded *agal*, which barely hinted at the multibillions of petrodollars that his family controlled.

"The Mufti's movement appears to have a sound footing in Turkey," he said, setting the teacup down. "I am pleased at the progress you have reported."

"Mufti Battal has a devoted following," the host replied, gazing toward a portrait of a wise-looking man in black robe and turban hanging on the far wall. "The times and conditions have been conducive to expanding the movement, and the Mufti's personal popularity has enhanced its appeal. We have a real opportunity ahead to change Turkey and her role in the world. Achieving such change, however, requires considerable resources."

"I am committed to the cause here, as I am committed to the Muslim Brotherhood in Egypt," the Sheikh replied.

"Like our Egyptian brothers, we will unite in the way of Allah," the host replied with a bow.

The Sheikh rose and crossed the high-rise office, which looked and felt like the interior of a mosque. Small *kilim* prayer rugs were aligned in an open space, facing a tiled *mihrab* aimed at Mecca. On the opposite wall, a high bookshelf was filled with antique copies of the Qur'an. Only a huge illuminating picture window warmed the otherwise austere and reverent interior.

The Sheikh moved to the window and admired the panorama before him. The office building was situated on the Asian bank of the Bosphorus and offered a breathtaking view of old Istanbul on the European shore, just across the slim waterway. The Sheikh stared at the towering minarets of the Süleymaniye Mosque in the distance.

"Istanbul has an earnest respect for its past, as it should," he said. "One cannot attain greatness without building on the past."

He turned to his host. "My brothers are all Western educated. They wear British-made suits and crave sleek automobiles," he said with disdain.

"But you are not like them?"

"No," the Sheikh replied thoughtfully. "I attended the Islamic University at Madinah. Since an early age, I have devoted myself to Allah. There is no greater purpose in life than to expound the words of the Prophet." He turned slowly from the window with a distant look.

"The threats to our ways never cease," he said. "In Cairo, the Zionists bomb al-Azhar, yet there is no global outrage."

"Mufti Battal and I are outraged."

"As am I. Such affronts cannot be ignored," the Sheikh said.

"We must strengthen the foundation of our house to withstand all outside forces."

The Sheikh nodded in agreement. "As you know, I have been blessed with a sizable fortune. I will continue to support the way of the Sunnah here. I share in the wisdom of Istanbul in venerating our past."

"Upon it, we will build great blessings to Allah."

The Sheikh eased toward the door. "I will arrange the transfer of funds shortly. Please pass my blessings to Mufti Battal."

"He will be both grateful and delighted. Praise be to Allah."

The Sheikh responded in kind, then joined an entourage waiting for him outside the door. When the Arab contingent had left the foyer, the host closed the door and returned to his desk, where he removed a key from the top drawer. Stepping to an inconspicuous side door, he turned the lock and entered an adjacent office nearly three times the size of the former. The room was not only large but also grand in appearance, and nearly the opposite in ambience. Brightly lit, it featured a stylish mix of contemporary art and classical oil paintings, unique tribal floor coverings, and nineteenth-century European furniture. Accented by overhead spotlights, the room's prominent features were opposing banks of built-in shelves, which were loaded with expensive antiques and relics from the Ottoman era, including porcelain vases, detailed tapestries, and jeweled weaponry. In the center of one shelf was the collection's showpiece, a gold-threaded tunic on a mannequin in a glass-enclosed case. A placard inside indicated that the tunic had been worn by Mehmed I, an Ottoman Sultan who ruled in the fifteenth century.

A petite woman with short black hair was seated on a

divan, reading a newspaper. Her presence stirred a touch of annoyance in the man's face, and he walked past her without saying a word. Reaching a carved desk near the window, he peeled off a *keffiyeh* and black robe, revealing a sport shirt and slacks underneath.

"Your meeting with the Sheikh was productive?" she asked, lowering her paper.

Ozden Aktan Celik nodded in reply.

"Yes, the nitwit runt of the royal litter has agreed to another infusion of cash. Twenty million, to be exact."

"Twenty?" the woman replied, her eyes widening. "Your skills at persuasion are impressive indeed."

"Simply a matter of playing one spoiled rich Arab off another. When our Kuwaiti benefactor learns of the Sheikh's contribution, he will be forced to exceed it out of ego alone. Of course, your recent visit to Cairo helped up the ante."

"Amazing how the Zionist threat can be milked for such profits. Just think of the money that would be saved if the Arabs and Israelis ever kissed and made up."

"They'd each find another scapegoat to antagonize," Celik said, taking a seat behind the desk. He was a well-proportioned man, with thinning black hair combed back on the sides. His nose was wide, but he had a strong face, and would not have looked out of place on the cover of *Gentlemen's Quarterly* magazine. Only his dark eyes hinted at a personality quirk, dancing constantly in a pirouette of emotional intensity. They twitched with anger as they focused on the woman.

"Maria, I would have preferred that you not show yourself so quickly. Particularly given your chaotic performance last night." His eyes centered on her with a glowering intensity.

Whatever intimidation he intended had absolutely no effect on the woman.

"The operation went off entirely as planned. It was only the intrusion by some meddling bystanders that delayed our exit."

"And subverted the acquisition of the Muhammad artifacts," he hissed. "You should have killed them all on the spot."

"Perhaps. But as it turns out, two of them were U.S. government officials, including a Congresswoman. Their deaths would have overshadowed our objective. And our objective seems to have been attained." She folded the newspaper she was reading and tossed it over to Celik.

It was a copy of *Milliyet*, a Turkish daily newspaper, its blazing headlines proclaiming "Murdering Thieves Attack Topkapi, Steal Holy Relics."

Celik nodded. "Yes, I've read the accounts. The media is blaming domestic heathens for stealing and desecrating our nation's sacred Muslim relics. Exactly the headlines we intended. But you forget that we have paid influence with a number of local reporters. What is it that the police believe?"

Maria took a sip from a glass of water before responding. "We can't be certain. My informant within the department was only able to obtain an electronic copy of the incident report this morning. It appears they have no real suspects, though the American woman did give some physical descriptions and reported that our team appeared to be speaking in Arabic."

"I told you I didn't like the idea of using Iraqi operatives."

"They are well trained, my brother, and, if caught, still provide a safe scapegoat. A Shia thief, even if from Iraq, is nearly as productive as a Western infidel for our purposes. They are well paid to keep quiet. And besides, they falsely believe they are working for their Shia brethren. I couldn't have obtained this without them," she added, opening a small suitcase at her feet.

Reaching inside, she pulled out a flat object wrapped in loose brown paper. She stepped over and placed the package on the desk in front of Celik. His darting eyes zeroed in on the package, and he began unwrapping it with trembling fingers. Beneath the paper he uncovered a green taffeta bag. Opening the bag, he gently removed its contents, a faded black banner that was missing chunks along its border. He stared at the banner for nearly a minute before gently picking it up and holding it reverently in the air.

"Sancak-ı Şerif. The sacred standard of Muhammad," he whispered in awe.

It was one of the most treasured relics of Topkapi, and perhaps the most important historically. The black woolen banner, created from the turban of a defeated foe, had served as the battle standard for the prophet Muhammad. He had carried it with him into the key Battle of Badr, where his victory had allowed for the very rise of Islam itself.

"With this, Muhammad changed the world," Celik said, his eyes a sparkling mixture of reverence and delusion. "We shall do the same."

He carried it over and set it on the glass case housing Sultan Mehmed's tunic.

"And how were the other relics lost?" he asked, turning and facing the woman.

Maria stared at the floor, pondering a reply. "The American woman grabbed the second bag when she escaped the van. They hid in the Yerebatan Sarnici. I was forced to leave before I could retrieve it," she added with disdain.

Celik said nothing, but his eyes bored through the woman like a pair of lasers. Again his hands trembled, but this time in anger. Maria quietly attempted to stave off an explosion.

"The mission was still a success. Even if all of the targeted relics were not obtained, the impact is the same. The entry and removal of the battle standard will generate the desired public response. Remember our strategic plan. This is just one step in our quest."

Celik slowly cooled but still sought an explanation.

"What were these American tourists doing at Topkapi in the middle of the night?"

"According to the police report, they were at the Archaeological Museum, near the Bâb-üs Selâm Gate, meeting with one of the curators. The man—his name is Pitt—is some sort of underwater expert for the U.S. government. He apparently discovered an old shipwreck near Chios and was discussing the artifacts with the museum's nautical authority."

Celik perked up at the mention of the wreck. "Was it an Ottoman vessel?" he asked, eyeing the encased tunic before him.

"I don't have any other information."

Celik stared at the colorful threads of the aged tunic. "Our legacy must be preserved," he said quietly, as if in a trance that had taken him back in time. "The riches of the empire belong to us. See if you can find out more about this shipwreck."

Maria nodded. "It can be done. What of this man Pitt and his wife? We know where they are staying."

Celik continued staring at the tunic. "I do not care. Kill them if you want, but do it quietly. Then prepare for the next project."

Maria nodded, a thin smile crossing her lips.

7

Sophie Elkin dragged a brush through her straight black hair, then took a hurried look at herself in the mirror. Dressed in worn khaki pants and a matching cotton shirt, and, without any makeup, she would have been hard-pressed to make herself appear any plainer. Yet there was no hiding her natural beauty. She had a narrow face with high cheekbones, a petite nose, and soft aquamarine-colored eyes. Her skin was smooth and flawless, despite the many hours she spent outdoors. The features were mostly inherited from her mother, a French woman who had fallen in love with an Israeli geology student studying in Paris and had migrated with him to Tel Aviv.

Sophie had always minimized her looks and femininity. Even at an early age, she spurned the dresses her mother would buy, preferring pants so she could join the neighborhood boys in rough-and-tumble activities. An only child, she'd been close to her father, who had ascended to the head of the Geology Department at Tel Aviv University. The independent young girl had relished accompanying him on field expeditions to study the geological formations in the surrounding deserts, where she raptly absorbed his fireside tales of biblical events on the very grounds where they camped.

Her father's work led her to study archaeology in college. While attaining her advanced degrees, she was jolted by the arrest of a fellow student for stealing artifacts from the university archives. The incident introduced her to the dark world of underground antiquities trading, which she grew to detest for its impact in the destruction of historic cultural sites. Upon receiving her doctorate, she abandoned academics and joined the Israel Antiquities Authority. With passion and dedication, she worked up to head of the Antiquities Robbery Prevention Unit in a few short years. Her devotion left little time for a personal life, and she dated infrequently, preferring to spend most nights working late.

Grabbing a handbag, she left her small hillside apartment overlooking the Mount of Olives and drove toward the Old City of Jerusalem. The Antiquities Authority was housed in the Rockefeller Museum, a sprawling white limestone structure situated near the northeast corner of the Old City. Employing just twelve people, her department was tasked with the impossible duty of protecting the roughly thirty thousand ancient cultural resource sites located around Israel.

"Good morning, Soph," greeted the department's senior detective, a lanky, bug-eyed man named Sam Levine. "Can I get you a coffee?"

"Thanks, Sam, I'd like that," she said, covering a yawn as she squeezed into her cramped office. "There was some sort of all-night construction going on near my apartment last night. I slept terribly."

Sam returned with the coffee and plopped down on the other side of her desk.

"If you weren't going to sleep, then you should have joined us on recon last night," he said with a grin.

"Any apprehensions?"

"No, our Hebron grave robbers must have taken the night off. We gave up by midnight but did come away with a nice stack of picks and shovels."

Perhaps the world's second-oldest profession, grave robbing ranked near the top of the Robbery Prevention Unit's criminal hit list. Several times a week, Sophie or Sam would lead a late-night stakeout of ancient grave sites around the country where signs of recent excavation had been observed. Pots, jewelry, and even the bones themselves could usually find a ready buyer in the underground antiquities market that pervaded Israel.

"Now that they know we are onto them, they'll probably lay low for a couple of weeks," Sophie said.

"Or move elsewhere. Assuming they've got enough cash to buy some new shovels," he added, smiling again.

Sophie glanced through some reports and news clippings on her desk, then passed one of the articles to Sam.

"I'm concerned about this excavation at Caesarea," she said.

Sam quickly skimmed the article.

"Yes, I've heard about this. It's a university-sponsored excavation of the old port facilities. It says here that they have uncovered some fourth-century seaport artifacts and a possible grave. You really think the site is a theft target?"

Sophie drained her coffee, then set down the cup with an agitated stare.

"The reporter might as well have put up a banner and flashing lights. Any time the word 'grave' finds its way into print, it's like a magnet. I've begged the news reporters a thousand times to avoid publicizing grave sites, but they are more interested in selling papers than protecting our heritage."

"Why don't we go down and take a look? We're scheduled for a recon tonight, but I could reassign the boys down there. They'd probably enjoy a trip to the coast."

Sophie looked at her desk calendar, then nodded. "I'm free after one. I suppose we could go check it out, and stay the night if it looks worthwhile."

"Now you're talking. For that, I'll go steal you another cup of coffee," he said, jumping out of his chair.

"Okay, Sam, you got a deal." Then she looked at him sternly. "But just don't use the word 'steal' around me!"

Situated on the Mediterranean coast about thirty miles north of Tel Aviv, Caesarea was a lightly populated enclave easily overshadowed by its historic past as a seat of Roman power. Built by King Herod the Great as a fortified port city in the first century B.C., Caesarea featured the famous hallmarks of Roman architecture. A high-columned temple, a grand hippodrome, and an ornate palace along the sea all graced the city, which was fed cool inland water via massive brick aqueducts. Herod's most impressive engineering feat was not on land, however. He designed and built massive breakwaters out of concrete blocks, using them to create the largest protected harbor in the eastern Mediterranean. The success of the harbor propelled Caesarea to greater importance as the capital of Judaea under Roman rule, and the city remained a key commerce center for over three hundred years.

Sophie was well acquainted with the remains of the

ancient city, having spent a summer at the site while in college. Turning off the busy coastal highway, she eased the car through a luxury-home development, then entered the remains of the Roman site, which was now a protected state park. The centuries had not been kind to the original construction, its old Roman buildings having long since crumbled. Yet many remnants of the city's ancient features were still intact, including a large section of an arched aqueduct that stretched across the ocher sands, not far from a sizable amphitheater that faced the sea.

Sophie parked the car in a lot near the hilltop entrance, adjacent to some Crusader-era fortifications.

"The university team is excavating near the harbor," she said to Sam. "It's just a short walk from here."

"I wonder if there's anything to eat around here?" He eyed the barren park hills around them with trepidation.

Sophie tossed him a water bottle from the backseat. "I'm sure there are some restaurants back near the highway, but you'll have to settle for a liquid diet for now."

They walked down a trail that weaved toward the beach, broadening at several points along the bluff. They passed a long-forgotten road that had once been lined with residences and small businesses, their ghostly remnants little more than disorderly piles of stone. As they descended the trail, the small harbor opened up before them. There was little left to recognize its boundaries, as the original breakwaters had become submerged centuries ago.

The trail led to a wide clearing, where little piles of stone were scattered across the field in all directions. A cluster of beige tents was assembled farther down, and

Sophie could discern a few people working under a large awning in the center. The trail continued another hundred yards down the hill, to where the waters of the Mediterranean lapped at the beach. Two men were visible working on a small spit of land, bracketed by a pair of generators that hummed loudly in the distance.

Sophie headed toward the large awning, which she could see was erected over an area of active excavation. Two young women stood near a mound of dirt, filtering the soil through a screened box. As she stepped closer, Sophie could see an older man hunched over in a trench, picking at the soil with a small trowel and brush. With rumpled clothes, a close-cropped gray beard, and a pair of glasses perched at the end of his nose, Keith Haasis bore the marked appearance of a distinguished university professor.

"How much Roman treasure have you unearthed today, Dr. Haasis?"

The bearded man stood up in the trench with an annoyed look on his face, which immediately transformed into a wide grin when he recognized the inquisitor.

"Sophie!" he thundered. "How good to see you." He hopped out of the trench and rushed over, giving her a big bear hug.

"It's been too long," he said.

"I just saw you two months ago at the biblical archaeology conference in Jerusalem," she chided.

"Like I said, much too long," he laughed.

In her younger days, Sophie had attended numerous seminars held by the archaeology professor from the University of Haifa, which had led to a professional friendship.

Haasis was a highly valued contact, as both an archaeology expert and as a source of information on newly discovered sites and destructive activity.

"Dr. Haasis, this is my assistant, Sam Levine," she said, introducing her companion. Haasis introduced his nearby students, then led Sophie and Sam to a circle of camp chairs that surrounded a large cooler. The professor passed out chilled cans of soda, then wiped his brow and plopped into a chair.

"Somebody needs to turn up the ocean breeze today," he said with a tired smile. Then, gazing at Sophie, he asked, "I presume this is an official visit?"

Taking a drink, Sophie nodded in reply.

"Any particular concerns?"

"A bit of overstated publicity in yesterday's *Yedioth Ahronoth*," she said, retrieving the newspaper article from a shoulder bag. Passing the article to Haasis, she coldly eyed Sam drain his can of soda and snatch a second from the cooler.

"Yes, a local reporter stopped by for an interview a few days ago," Haasis said. "His story must have been picked up in Jerusalem."

He smiled at Sophie as he passed the article back.

"Nothing wrong with a little publicity for some proper archaeology," he said.

"Nothing, that is, except a brazen invitation to every thief with a shovel," she replied.

Haasis waved his arm through the air. "This site has been plundered for centuries. Any 'Roman treasure' that was buried around here is long gone, I'm afraid. Or didn't your agent think so?"

"What agent?" Sophie asked.

"I was up in Haifa for a meeting, but my students said an antiquities agent stopped by yesterday and surveyed the project site. Stephanie!" he called over his shoulder.

One of the girls at the screened box hurried over. A gangly coed of barely twenty, she stood before Haasis with a look of devotion.

"Stephanie, tell us about this fellow from the Antiquities Authority who came by yesterday," he said.

"He said he was with the Robbery Prevention Unit. He wanted to check the security of our artifacts, so I gave him a tour of the site. He seemed most interested in the harbor excavation and the papyrus document."

Sophie and Sam looked at each other with raised eyebrows.

"Do you recall his name?" she asked.

"Yosef something. He was kind of short, dark-skinned, with curly hair. Looked Palestinian, to be honest."

"Did he show you any identification?" Sam asked.

"No, I don't think so. Is anything the matter?"

"No, not at all," Haasis said. "Thanks, Stephanie. Why don't you take some drinks down to the others?"

Haasis waited until the girl left with an armful of cans, then turned to Sophie.

"Not one of your agents?" he asked.

Sophie shook her head. "Certainly not from the Robbery Prevention Unit."

"Maybe he was from the national parks authority, or one of your own regional offices. These darn kids don't seem to remember anything these days."

"It's possible," she replied in a doubtful tone. "Can you show us your excavation sites? I'm most interested in the tomb. As you know, the grave robbers around Jerusalem have created a cottage industry as of late."

Haasis smiled, then jerked his thumb over his shoulder. "It's right behind us."

The trio stood and walked around to a wide trench that ran behind the chairs. A sprinkling of red plastic markers was pinned into the ground surrounding a small section of exposed bones. Sophie recognized a femur among the remains embedded in the dirt.

"There's no formal tomb. We've just uncovered a single grave at the edge of the site. It's really unrelated to the diggings here," Haasis explained.

"What is this site?" Sam asked.

"We believe it was something of a shipping warehouse. We targeted the area after a set of bronze scales was uncovered here some years ago. Our hope is to collect samples of grains, rice, and other food staples that might have come through the port. If successful, it will provide us a better understanding of the type and volume of trade that passed through Caesarea when it was a thriving center of trade."

"How does the grave fit in?" Sophie asked.

"We haven't performed any dating, but my guess is this fellow was a casualty of the Muslim invasion of the city in A.D. 638. The grave lies just outside the foundation of the building, so I think we'll find that he was a lone body hastily buried against the wall."

"The newspaper article called it a tomb 'rich with artifacts,'" Sam noted.

Haasis laughed. "Journalistic license, I'm afraid. We found a few buttons made of animal bone and the heel from a sandal before we halted excavation. But that's the extent of any 'rich artifacts' from the grave site."

"Our friendly neighborhood grave robbers are liable to be sorely disappointed," Sam said.

"Indeed," the professor replied. "For our real riches have been uncovered along the seawall." He nodded toward the Mediterranean, where the hum from the generators still drifted up the hill. "We discovered an early papyrus document that has us very excited. Come, let's take a walk down to the water, then I'll show you the artifact."

Haasis led Sophie and Sam to the trail, then guided them down the hill. Small ridges of scattered stone broke the soil in odd patterns around them, faint reminders of the city's once congested multitude of buildings that had long ago been reduced to rubble.

"Using molds to pour and set his concrete blocks in place, King Herod constructed two large breakwaters that circled toward each other like a pair of arms," Haasis lectured as they walked. "Warehouses were built atop the breakwaters, and a towering lighthouse stood at the harbor entrance."

"I recall that an early research project mapped a large number of stones underwater believed to have fallen from the lighthouse," Sophie said.

"A shame Herod's work didn't survive the sea's ravages," Sam said, looking out at the water and finding little visible evidence of the original breakwaters.

"Yes, most all of the blocks are now completely

submerged. But this is where the heart of my interest lies," Haasis said, motioning toward the invisible bay. "The warehouse up the hill makes a nice field school for the students, but the port facility is what makes Caesarea unique."

They crossed the beach and hiked onto a small finger of land that poked into the wave-driven sea. Two male students were laboriously excavating a deep pit in the center of the rocky spit. Nearby, a diver could be seen working in the water, applying a compressor-driven water jet under the surface.

"This is where the main breakwater originated," Haasis explained, speaking loudly to overcome the drone of a nearby compressor. "On this site we believe was situated the equivalent of a customs house. One of the boys recovered the papyrus document in a shattered pot over there," he said, pointing to a nearby trench. "We expanded some test trenches in several directions but have found no other artifacts."

"Amazing that it would survive so close to the water," Sam said.

"We've found fragments of the foundation that are still above mean high-tide levels."

They peered into the active test pit, where one of the students pointed out a small flat section of marble tiling.

"Looks like you've reached the basement," Sophie remarked.

"Yes, I'm afraid there may not be much left to excavate."

"What's the diver up to?"

"He's a marine engineer helping reconstruct the layout

96

of the original port facilities. He seems to think there may be a subterranean chamber to our customs house and is poking around for an underwater access."

Sophie walked over to the edge of the embankment and stared down at the diver. He was working in ten feet of water almost directly beneath her, manhandling a water jet against the hard-packed bottom. Without noticing the audience above him, the diver broke off his probing and began to ascend. He held the nozzle of the water jet upright, which sprayed a fountain of water skyward when he broke the surface. Standing right in its path, Sophie was doused with a blasting spray of salt water before she could jump out of the way.

"You damn fool!" she cursed, wiping the salt water out of her eyes with her dripping sleeves.

Realizing what he had done, the diver quickly spun the nozzle seaward, then swam to the edge of the embankment and shut off the compressor. Turning to his victim, he gazed at the wet clothes clinging tightly to her body, then spat out his regulator.

"Behold, a goddess from the sea?" he said with a wide smile.

Sophie shook her head and turned her back on him, growing angrier at the sight of Sam laughing out loud. Haasis suppressed his own mirth and came to her rescue.

"Sophie, there's a towel in my tent. Come, let's get you dried off."

The diver popped his regulator back into his mouth and disappeared under the surface as Sophie followed Haasis up the trail. They reached the professor's tent, where she rubbed her hair and clothes dry as best she could. The warm breeze would dry her clothes quickly, but she shivered at the sudden evaporative cooling effect on her damp skin.

"May I see the artifacts you have excavated?" she asked.

"Certainly. They're right next door."

The professor led her to a large peaked tent that was open at one end. Inside were the artifacts recovered from the warehouse site, mostly potsherds and tile fragments, strewn about a long linen-covered table. The student Stephanie was busy with a camera and notebook, carefully numbering and recording each piece before storing them in thin plastic boxes. Haasis ignored the artifacts and led Sophie to a small table at the back of the tent. A single sealed box was on the table, which Haasis handled cautiously as he removed the lid.

"I wish we had found more," he said wistfully, standing aside to let Sophie peer into the box.

Inside was an elongated patch of brown material, pressed between two plates of glass. Sophie immediately recognized it as papyrus, a common writing surface in the Middle East up to the end of the first millennium. The sample was worn and frayed, yet clean rows of handwritten symbols were plainly visible down most of the document's length.

"It appears to be a port facility record of some sort. I can make out references to a large quantity of grain and a herd of livestock being off-loaded at the wharf," Haasis said. "We'll learn more after laboratory analysis, but I think it might be a customs bill for a merchant vessel delivering goods from Alexandria."

"It's a splendid find," Sophie complimented. "With

luck, it will enhance the information gathered from the warehouse site."

Haasis laughed. "My luck, it will prove entirely contradictory."

They both turned as a tall figure entered the tent carrying a large plastic bin. Sophie saw it was the diver, still clad in a wet suit, his loose dark hair streaked with water. Still angered over her dousing, she began to make a caustic remark but felt her voice wither when she was met by a bright smile and a pair of deep green eyes that bored right through her.

"Dirk, there you are," Haasis said. "May I introduce the lovely but damp Sophie Elkin of the Israel Antiquities Authority. Sophie, this is Dirk Pitt, Jr., on loan from the U.S. National Underwater and Marine Agency."

The son and namesake of the agency head, Dirk walked over and set down the bin. Still flashing a disarming smile, he warmly shook hands with Sophie. She didn't offer a protest when he was slow to release his grip.

"My apologies for the shower, I didn't realize you were standing there."

"No trouble, I'm nearly dry now." She was inwardly startled at how her anger had suddenly been displaced by an odd tingle. She absently patted her hair to prove her point.

"I hope you'll allow me the honor of buying you dinner tonight to make amends."

Dirk's forward proposal caught her off guard, and she stumbled to answer, muttering something unintelligible. Somewhere a voice inside screamed at her for losing her normally unflappable manner. Haasis thankfully intervened to save the awkward moment.

"Dirk, what's in the box?" he asked, eyeing it curiously.

"Just a few goodies from the subterranean chamber."

Haasis's mouth dropped. "It truly exists?"

Dirk nodded.

"What chamber?" Sophie asked.

"While I was surveying the remains of the inshore breakwater, I found a small underwater opening near Keith's test pits. I could only squeeze my arm in, but I could feel my hand break the water's surface. That's why I was using the water jet, to blast a larger hole through the mud and concretions."

"How large is the cavity?" Haasis asked excitedly.

"It's not much bigger than a crawl space, about six feet deep. But most of it is above water. I'll go out on a limb and speculate that it was part of a cellar used for storage or records archives."

"How did you come to that conclusion?" Sophie inquired.

Dirk dried off the plastic bin he had carried in and carefully pulled off the watertight lid. Inside were several ceramic boxes, rectangular in shape and colored a reddish orange. He pulled one out and handed it to Sophie.

"Hopefully you can decipher its contents," he said. "They didn't teach me ancient texts in marine engineering school."

Sophie set the box on a table and gently prised off the lid. Inside were a half dozen tightly wound rolls of material.

"They're papyrus rolls," she said in a shocked voice.

Haasis could no longer contain himself, slipping on a pair of white gloves and squeezing in alongside Sophie.

"Let me take a look," he said, pulling one of the rolls out and slowly unrolling it across the tabletop. An odd but orderly script filled the page, handwritten with a bold stroke.

"It appears to be Coptic Greek," Sophie said, looking over the professor's shoulder. An ancient text developed in Egypt using the Greek alphabet, Coptic script was a common written language in the eastern Mediterranean during the time of Roman rule.

"Indeed," he confirmed. "It appears to be an annual record from the harbormaster, for port fees and dockage. These are the names of vessels, with their lading," he said, running a gloved finger down a pair of columns.

"Isn't that a reference to the Emperor?" Sophie asked, pointing to a block at the top.

"Yes," Haasis replied, trying to interpret the heading. "It's titled a report of Caesarea port fees, or something to that effect. Written on behalf of Emperor Marcus Maxentius."

"If my memory serves, Maxentius was a contemporary of Constantine."

"Maxentius ruled in the west and Constantine in the east, before the latter consolidated power."

"So this must date to the early fourth century."

Haasis nodded with a glimmer in his eye, then looked at the other scrolls. "These may offer us an amazing glimpse into life in Judaea under Roman rule."

"Ought to provide fodder for a good thesis or two from your students," Dirk said, as he emptied the bin of three additional ceramic boxes. Tucking the empty bin under his arm, he turned and headed out of the tent.

"Dirk, you just uncovered a magnificent historical find," Haasis said with wonder. "Where on earth are you going?"

"I'm gonna go get wet like a damn fool," he replied with a twisted grin, "because there's plenty more where those came from."

8

Ozden Celik arrived at the Fatih Mosque, one of Istanbul's largest, an hour after morning *salat* and found the ornate interior halls of the complex mostly empty. Bypassing the main prayer hall, he followed a side corridor to the rear of the structure, then exited into a small courtyard. Marble paving stones led to a nondescript building located in an area cordoned off from tourists and worshippers. Celik made his way to the threshold and entered through a heavy wooden door.

Stepping inside, he found himself in a bright and bustling office. Cloisters of gray cubicles extended in all directions, fronted by a large wooden reception desk. The clamorous din of churning laser printers and ringing phones filled the air, lending the feel of a telemarketing call center. Only the odor of burning incense and photos of Turkish mosques on the walls indicated otherwise. That and the absence of any women.

Celik noted that all of the office workers were bearded men, many wearing long robes, tapping at their computers in apparent incongruity. A young man behind the counter stood as Celik approached.

"Good morning, Mr. Celik," he greeted. "The Mufti is expecting you."

The secretary led Celik past a line of cubicles to a large corner office. The room was sparsely decorated, containing only the requisite Turkish rugs on the floor for expression. More notable were the sagging rows of bookshelves that lined the walls, packed tightly with religious tomes reflecting the scholarly background of an Islamic Mufti.

Mufti Altan Battal sat at a barren executive desk, scribbling on a writing pad, with a pair of open books on either side of him. He looked up and smiled as the secretary ushered Celik into the office.

"Ozden, you have arrived. Please, take a seat," he offered. "Hasan, let us talk in peace," he added, shooing away the secretary. The assistant quickly backpedaled, closing the door on his way out.

"Just putting the finishing touches on Friday's sermon," the Mufti said, setting a pencil down on the desk beside a cell phone.

"You should have one of your Imams do that for you."

"Perhaps. But I feel that it is my calling. Deferring to one of the mosque Imams might create jealousies as well. I would rather ensure that all of the Imams of Istanbul speak with one voice."

As Mufti of Istanbul, Battal was the theological leader of all three thousand of the city's mosques. Only the President of the Diyanet İşleri, a nonelected post in Turkey's secular government, technically wielded greater spiritual authority over the country's Muslim population. Yet Battal had developed far greater influence over the hearts and minds of the mosque-going public.

Despite his seniority, Battal appeared nothing like the stereotypical stern gray cleric with a raging beard. He was a tall, powerfully built man with an imposing presence.

Not yet fifty years old, he had a long face that expressed the sunny disposition of a Labrador puppy. He often wore suits instead of robes and inflected a deprecating sense of humor that made his brand of fundamentalist Islam almost seem fun.

Yet despite his sunny persona, the message he sold was a bleak one. Raised on the extreme fundamentalist tenets of Islamic interpretation, he vocally supported Islamism, the expansion of Islam as both a religious and political movement. His worldview taught the subjugation of women's rights while strongly turning away from Western culture and mores. He had gradually built a power base by railing against the forces of foreign influence, then turned his sights on the secular government as economic conditions within Turkey soured. Although he hadn't publicly taken a militant stance, he believed in *jihad* for the defense of Islamic territory. Like Celik, he was driven by a powerful ego, and privately aspired to command the country as both its religious and political leader.

"I have some very good news to report, on several fronts," Celik said.

"My friend Ozden, you are always working behind the scenes on my behalf. What is it that you have done for our cause now?"

"I recently met with Sheikh Zayad of the Emirati Royal Family. He is pleased with the work you have done and wishes to make another substantial contribution."

Battal's eyes widened. "On top of his earlier generosity? This is wonderful news. I am still at a loss, however, as to his interest in our movement here in Turkey."

"He is a man of vision," Celik replied, "who supports

adherence to the Sharia path. He is troubled by the growing threats against us, as evident by the recent mosque attacks here and in Egypt."

"Yes, despicable acts of violence against our holy sites. And on top of that, there is the recent theft of the Prophet's relics from Topkapi. These are intolerable assaults on our faith by outside forces of evil."

"The Sheikh concurs with your sentiments. He sees his country's security, and that of the entire region, being safer under a fundamentalist Sunni rule."

"Which leads to your next bit of news?" Battal said with a knowing grin.

"So, the birds have been singing, eh? Well, as you may know, I met with the Felicity Party's leadership council, and they have agreed to accept you as their presidential candidate. They actually appeared ecstatic at your willingness to replace Imam Keya as their presidential candidate."

"A tragedy that he was killed in the Bursa Mosque blast," Battal said with sincerity.

Celik suppressed a knowing look and nodded his head. "The party leadership has expressed their willingness to adopt your platform demands," he continued.

"We are similar in philosophy," Battal replied agreeably. "You are aware that the Felicity Party only garnered about three percent of the vote in the last presidential election?"

"Yes," Celik replied, "but that was not with you atop the ballot."

It was an alluring appeal to Battal's ego, which had blossomed with his recent rise in popularity.

"The election is only a few weeks away," he noted.

"Which is perfect for us," Celik replied. "We will catch the ruling party by surprise, and they will barely have time to react to your candidacy."

"Do you think I really have a chance?"

"Polling figures indicate that if you entered the race, you'd be less than ten percentage points behind. It's a deficit that could easily be overcome by events."

Battal stared off at his bookshelf of Muslim writings. "It may be a singular opportunity to erase the wrong-doings of Atatürk and lead our country back to its rightful path. We must adhere to Sharia, the law of Islam, in every aspect of our governance."

"It is your duty to Allah," Celik replied.

"There will be strong opposition to my candidacy, particularly on constitutional grounds. Are you positive we can overcome the challenges?"

"You forget that the Prime Minister is a hidden ally to our cause. He has kept his true faith concealed from the public and will be with us in forming a new government."

"I enjoy your confidence, Ozden. I will of course have a key role for you in leading our new state, praise Allah."

"I am counting on it," Celik replied smugly. "As for your announced entry into the presidential race, I will assist your advisers in coordinating a large public rally. With some of the Sheikh's money, we will be able to create a media blitz that will flood the opposition. I am also working on some other programs to boost your popularity."

"So be it," Battal said, standing and shaking hands with Celik. "With you by my side, my friend, what can we not achieve?"

"Nothing, my master. Nothing at all."

Celik left the meeting with a skip in his step. The foolish naïf could be played like a violin, he thought. Once elected, Celik would be pulling all the strings. And should Battal have a change of heart, Celik had a slew of dirty tricks up his sleeve to keep the Mufti in line.

Exiting the mosque under an unusually clear and sunny sky, he felt the future was looking very bright indeed.

In a dimly lit cubicle within the secured walls of Fort Gordon, Georgia, Turkish language analyst George Withers listened to the conversation through a set of cushioned headphones. An employee of the NSA's Georgia Regional Security Operations Center, Withers was one of an army of linguists paid to eavesdrop on Middle East communications from the Army base tucked amid the forested hills surrounding Augusta.

Unlike most of his voice intercept work that involved real-time translation of phone calls captured from satellite transmissions, this conversation was hours old. The data had originated from a listening post at the U.S. Embassy in Istanbul, which had intercepted a cellular phone call to the Turkish National Intelligence Organization. The call had been digitally recorded and encrypted, then sent to Fort Gordon via an NSA relay station in Cyprus.

Withers had no way of knowing that the call had actually originated from Battal's own cell phone. Sitting idle on his desk, the phone had been remotely activated by the Turkish intelligence agency. Like most modern cell phones, Battal's had a built-in tracking device, which allowed it to be targeted with a secret software download.

Sitting unused or even turned off, the cell phone's microphone could be turned on remotely, gathering all nearby audio inputs. Once activated, the audio could be transmitted through a normal cell call without the user's knowledge. The Mufti had been placed on a watch list by Turkey's Intelligence Director, a hardened secularist who had grown nervous of Battal's growing popularity and power. Battal's conversation with Celik, and every other person who entered his office, was now on a direct feed to the Turkish intelligence agency. The American linguist listening in was therefore an eavesdropper on an eavesdropper.

Correctly gauging the nature of the call and guessing that it was transmitted by an unauthorized recording, Withers decided that it was worth forwarding to an intelligence analyst for further assessment. Glancing at a desk clock and seeing that it was time for his lunch break, he quickly typed in a computer command. Seconds later, a written transcript of the conversation appeared on his computer monitor, courtesy of the agency's voice recognition software. Withers reviewed the transcript, correcting a few errors and clarifying a comment or two that the software failed to decipher, then added his own comments to a summary page. E-mailing it to an agency specialist in Turkish affairs, he rose from his desk and headed to the cafeteria, thinking that the report would probably never again see the light of day.

9

The U.S. Director of National Intelligence sat quietly through his weekly staff briefing on Eurasian and Middle Eastern affairs. A taciturn retired Army general named Braxton, he was the President's chief intelligence funnel for the Defense Department, Homeland Security, the CIA, and a dozen other agencies responsible for protecting the nation's security.

The briefing was dominated by the usual field updates of events taking place in Afghanistan, Pakistan, Iraq, and Iran. A parade of intelligence officers and Pentagon officials marched in and out of the secure conference room at the Liberty Crossing Intelligence Campus, the recently constructed home of the DNI located in McLean, Virginia.

The briefing was on its third hour before the agenda turned to Israel. John O'Quinn, a deputy national intelligence officer for western Asia, slipped away from the mammoth conference table to refill his coffee cup as a CIA intelligence officer discussed the latest developments on the West Bank.

"All right, all right, there's nothing new there," Braxton interrupted impatiently. "Let's move on to the rest of the Med. What's the latest on the al-Azhar Mosque bombing in Cairo?"

O'Quinn hurried back to the table as the CIA officer fielded the question.

"The final death toll was only seven, as the blast occurred at a time of sparse attendance. We don't know if that was intentional or not. There was a single explosion, which severely damaged the mosque's main prayer hall. As you know, al-Azhar is considered the state mosque of Egypt, and is also one of the oldest and most revered sites in Islam. The public outrage has been intense, with several anti-Israel marches taking place throughout the streets of Cairo. We're quite sure that the protests are being organized by the Muslim Brotherhood."

"Does Cairo know who is responsible for the bombing?"

"They don't," the CIA man replied. "No one with any credibility has taken responsibility, which isn't surprising given the nature of the attack. Our fear is that the Muslim Brotherhood will gain renewed traction from the attack to make further inroads into the Egyptian parliament."

"That's all we need is for the Egyptians to go fundamentalist on us," Braxton muttered with a shake of his head. "What's our intelligence assessment as to who pulled it off?"

"We really don't know, sir. We're looking at potential al-Qaeda connections, but have nothing firm at the moment. There's a somewhat curious detail from the Egyptian National Police, and that is that they claim to have found residue samples of HMX from the blast site."

"The meaning being?"

"HMX is a tightly controlled plastic explosive. It's high-end stuff, mostly used for nuclear devices and rocket propellant. It's not something we'd normally associate with al-Qaeda, and we find it a bit odd that it surfaced in Egypt."

Sitting in an adjacent chair, O'Quinn felt the hair on the back of his neck rise. He quickly cleared his throat.

"You sure it was HMX?" he asked.

"We're awaiting our own test samples, but that's what the Egyptians reported."

"That mean something to you, O'Quinn?" General Braxton asked.

The intelligence officer nodded. "Sir, there was a planted bomb explosion at the Yeşil Mosque in Bursa, Turkey, three days before the al-Azhar blast. You may have seen a field brief on it. Three fatalities, including a prominent leader in the fringe Felicity political party. Like in Egypt, it was an old, venerated mosque." He took a quick sip of his coffee, then added, "The Turkish authorities have confirmed that the blast was caused by a planted parcel of HMX explosives."

"So we have two planted bombs in two countries three days apart," the general stated. "Both in historic mosques, both ostensibly with a low designated kill rate, and both ostensibly using the same explosive material. All right, then, somebody please tell me who and why."

An uneasy silence filled the room before O'Quinn finally braved to speak.

"Sir, I don't think anyone was aware of the similarities in explosives until just now."

The CIA man agreed. "We'll get some analysts to search for a possible link right away. Given the nature of the explosives, I might speculate that the Iranians have some involvement."

"What do the Turks think?" Braxton asked.

"Like Egypt, there have been no claims of responsibility. We have had no indication that the Turks have identified any suspects."

The general began fidgeting in his seat, his cobalt blue eyes boring into O'Quinn like a pair of drill bits. O'Quinn had worked for the general for less than a year but had slowly gained his professional respect. He could tell by his demeanor that the Director wanted more, and finally he asked for it.

"What is your assessment?" the general asked gruffly.

O'Quinn's mind churned to expel a coherent reply, but he had more questions than answers.

"Sir, I can't formulate the Egyptian blast, but, as far as the Bursa mosque bombing, some believe there may be a link to the recent artifact thefts at Topkapi Palace in Istanbul."

"Yes, I read about that," the general replied. "I understand a Congresswoman was somehow involved in the incident."

"Loren Smith, of Colorado. She recovered a portion of the stolen artifacts but was nearly killed in the process. She somehow managed to keep her name out of the papers."

"Sounds like someone I could use on my staff," Braxton muttered.

"I believe some sort of explosives were used during the Topkapi break-in," O'Quinn continued. "I will make an immediate inquiry to determine if there is a match to the Bursa and Cairo bombings."

"What would be the motive?"

"The typical incidences of mosque bombings, as we've seen in Iraq, are Shia attacks on Sunni mosques, or vice versa," offered the CIA officer. "Though in the case of Turkey, I believe the Shia Muslims in the country are a nonviolent minority."

"That's correct," O'Quinn stated. "A more likely culprit would be Kurdish separatists. Turkey is holding national elections in less than four weeks. It's possible that the Turkish attacks were instigated by the Kurds, or another fringe political party trying to stir up trouble, though I'm not sure that would explain a link to Cairo."

"I would think the Turkish authorities would have been quick to publicly blame the Kurds if they thought they were actually behind the attacks," Braxton said.

"You're probably right," O'Quinn replied, flipping through his briefing notes. His fingers stopped at a copy of the NSA intercept transcript recorded by George Withers.

"Sir, there's another development on the Turkish front that may be cause for alarm."

"Go ahead," the general said.

"Altan Battal, the Muslim Mufti of Istanbul and a leading fundamentalist cleric in Turkey, will be entering the upcoming presidential election, according to an NSA call intercept."

"President Yilmaz has had a stable leadership run for several years," Braxton noted. "And Turkey is strongly secular. I can't imagine that this Battal fellow represents more than a marginal candidacy."

"I'm afraid that's not the case," O'Quinn replied. "President Yilmaz's popularity has waned considerably due to the poor state of the economy, and he's been stung by recent corruption charges within his administration.

Mufti Battal, on the other hand, has become a rising public figure in the country, particularly with the poor and unemployed. There's no telling how he'll perform as a political candidate, but many fear he could represent a legitimate challenge to the incumbent."

"Tell me more about this Battal," the general asked.

"Well, sir, his claimed bio states that he was orphaned at an early age and forced to fight for survival in the ghetto slums of west Istanbul. He escaped a life of poverty when he came to the aid of an old man being robbed by a neighborhood thug. In gratitude, the man, a mosque elder, sent Battal to a private Muslim school, where he paid the boy's room and board well into his teens. The school was heavily fundamentalist, which apparently drives his views today. He has a heavy scholarly bent yet also a gift for oration, which helped accelerate his rise through Istanbul's Muslim hierarchy. He now stands as the chief theologian for all of Istanbul. Though personally charming, his writings and sermons espouse Taliban-like interpretations of Islam, with plenty of rallying about the evils of the West and the dangers of foreign influence. There's no telling what would happen if he was elected, but we'd have to face the real possibility of losing Turkey overnight."

"Does he have a chance to win the election?" Braxton asked with rising dread in his voice.

O'Quinn nodded. "Our assessment is that he could have a real shot at it. And if the Turkish military should sustain his election, then all bets are off."

An Air Force colonel seated at the table gasped. "A fundamentalist takeover of Turkey? That would be an unmitigated disaster. Turkey is a NATO country and one of our strongest allies in the region. We have a variety of military resources in the country, including tactical nuclear weapons. The Air Force base at Incirlik is critical for our operations in Afghanistan."

"Not to mention the listening posts on their soil we use to monitor the Russians and the Iranians," added the CIA man.

"Turkey is currently a key transfer point for supplies into Afghanistan, as they were for Iraq," grieved an Army major seated beside the colonel. "Loss of those supply lines would jeopardize our entire Afghan campaign."

"We foresee all kinds of potentially disastrous scenarios," O'Quinn added quietly, "from a closure of the Bosphorus, and its flow of Russian oil and gas, to an emboldened Iran. The entire Middle East would be affected, and the impact of such a change on the balance of power is nearly impossible to predict."

"Turkey has been a quiet friend and trading partner of Israel, exporting large quantities of food and fresh water, among other things," the CIA officer said. "If Turkey and Egypt were both to make a turn toward fundamentalism, it would heighten Israel's isolation. In addition to emboldening Iran, I would fear a greater aggression from Hamas, Hezbollah, and other frontline adversaries of Israel, which would only lead to greater violence in the region. Such a turnabout in ruling power could in fact become the trigger point that we have long feared, the one that sparks World War Three from the heart of the Middle East."

The room fell silent as Braxton and the others digested the words with quiet dread. The general finally shook off the uneasy tension and barked a stream of orders.

"O'Quinn, I want a full report on this Mufti Battal on my desk first thing in the morning. I'll also need an executive summary for the Presidential Daily Brief. We'll reconvene here Friday, where I expect a full assessment from both State and CIA. Assign whatever resources are necessary," he added with clenched teeth, "but don't let this get ahead of us." He slammed his briefing book shut, then glared at the CIA man.

"World War Three?" he hissed. "Not on my watch!"

10

The call to morning *salat* drifted through the open hotel window, waking Pitt earlier than he would have preferred. Leaving the warm comfort of Loren's side, he rose from bed and peered out the window. The black-tipped minarets of Istanbul's Sultanahmet Mosque scratched a hazy sky just a few blocks away. Pitt noted wryly that the Islamic call to prayer no longer came from a *muezzin* shouting from the heights of the minaret but rather from loudspeakers situated around the mosque.

"Can you turn that racket off?" Loren mumbled from beneath a blanket.

"You'll have to take it up with Allah," Pitt replied.

He closed the window, then gazed through the pane at the towering architecture of the nearby mosque and the blue waters of the Sea of Marmara just beyond. A large contingent of freighters was already assembling in line, waiting their turn to sail up the narrow Bosphorus Strait. Loren materialized out of the bed, slipping into a robe and joining her husband at the picture window.

"I didn't realize that blaring came from the mosque," she said a bit meekly. "It's quite beautiful. Built by the Ottomans, I presume?"

"Yes, in the early seventeenth century, I believe."

"Let's go have a look after breakfast. But after last

night's excitement, that may be all the sightseeing I'll be up for today," she said with a yawn.

"No shop-till-you-drop at the Grand Bazaar?"

"Maybe next time. I want our lone full day together in Istanbul to be relaxing."

Pitt watched a red freighter chug off the shoreline, then said, "I think I have just the ticket."

They quickly showered and dressed, then ordered breakfast brought to their room. They were readying to leave when the phone rang. Pitt answered and spoke for several minutes, then hung up the receiver.

"It was Dr. Ruppé, calling from the airport. He wanted to make sure you were okay," he explained.

"I'd feel better if you told me the police had captured those criminals."

Pitt shook his head. "Apparently not. Rey is a little irate, as the local media is blaming the break-in and murders on an anti-Muslim movement. Apparently, some valuable jewelry was ignored at Topkapi in favor of several Muhammad relics."

"You said murders in the plural," Loren remarked.

"Yes, there were a total of five security guards killed in the ordeal."

Loren grimaced. "The fact that several of the murderers were Persian-looking didn't clue the police in another direction?"

"The police have our account. I'm sure they are operating under a different scenario." Deep down, Pitt wasn't so sure but hid his anger at the thought of his wife's kidnappers escaping scot-free.

"The other news, according to Ruppé," he continued,

"is that they kept our names and involvement out of the paper. Apparently, there is widespread outrage at the theft, which is being viewed as a deep insult to the Muslim community."

"Even after our near-death experience, that's okay with me," Loren mused. "By the way, what exactly did they end up stealing?"

"They made off with a battle standard that belonged to Muhammad. Apparently, the outrage would have been even more magnified if you hadn't liberated the second black bag."

"What did it contain?"

"A cloak of Muhammad's, called the Holy Mantle, along with a letter written in his hand. Part of what is known as the Sacred Trusts."

"It's terrible that somebody would try to steal such relics," Loren said, shaking her head.

"Come on, we better go see the rest of this town before anything else disappears."

They exited the lobby of the hotel and entered the bustling streets of old Istanbul. Pitt noticed a man in mirrored sunglasses staring at Loren as he passed on his way into the hotel. Tall and sporting a near-ballerina figure, Loren seldom failed to attract the male eye. Dressed in light slacks and an amethyst blouse that nearly matched the color of her eyes, she looked vivacious despite the turmoil of the night before.

Walking down a block or two, they stopped and peered in the window of an upscale rug shop called Punto of Istanbul, admiring an elegant Serapi carpet that hung on the wall. Strolling to the end of the street, they crossed the

Hippodrome, a long, narrow park around which the chariots raced in the Byzantine era. Just beyond was the mosque of Sultan Ahmet I.

Completed in 1617, it was the last of Istanbul's great imperial mosques. The exterior featured a rising cascade of domes and semidomes that climbed in height and grandeur until culminating in a massive central dome. By the time Pitt and Loren had entered the mosque's arched courtyard, most of the morning worshippers had been replaced by camera-toting tourists.

They made their way into the prayer hall, its expansive interior dimly lit by high banks of stained-glass windows. Overhead, the curving domes were covered in a maze of intricately patterned tiles, many in shades of blue, which gave the building its nickname, the Blue Mosque. Pitt studied an archway filled with familiar-looking floral tiles, which were manufactured in the nearby city of Iznik.

"Look at that design," he said to Loren. "It's nearly identical to the pattern on the ceramic box we pulled from the wreck."

"You're right," Loren agreed, "though the coloring is a little different. Congratulations, it's more evidence that your wreck sank around sixteen hundred."

Pitt's satisfaction was short-lived. Eyeing a green-tiled wall on the opposite side of the prayer hall, he spotted a man in sunglasses looking in his direction. It was the same man who had gawked at Loren outside the hotel.

Without saying a word, Pitt slowly herded Loren toward the exit, consciously staying close to a group of German tourists on a guided tour. He casually surveyed the crowd scattered about the mosque, trying to discern whether Sunglasses had any partners. Pitt noticed a thin Persian man with a bushy mustache shuffling along nearby, a serious scowl on his face. He appeared incongruous among the other tourists standing with their necks craned toward the ceiling. It seemed unlikely that the Topkapi thieves would have tracked them down so quickly, though Pitt recalled the threatening words of the woman in the cistern. He decided to find out for sure.

Following the Germans out of the prayer hall, Pitt and Loren pulled on the shoes they had removed earlier and followed the tour group into the courtyard. Pitt watched from the corner of his eye as the Persian followed suit.

"Stay here," Pitt told Loren, then turned and quickly strode across the marble tile toward the man.

The Persian immediately turned, pretending to study a nearby column behind him. Pitt strode right up and gazed down at the man, who stood a head shorter.

"Excuse me," Pitt said. "Can you tell me who's buried in Atatürk's tomb?"

The man at first avoided Pitt's gaze, peering instead toward the prayer hall exit where Sunglasses now stood. Spotting a shake of the head, he turned and faced Pitt with a look of contempt.

"I wouldn't know where that dog lies," he spat, his eyes glistening with an arrogant intimidation born of a hardened life in the streets. An undercover police agent he was clearly not. When Pitt noticed the telltale bulge of a holstered handgun under the man's loose shirt, he decided not to press the issue. He gave the man a cold, knowing look, then turned and stepped away. Walking back to Loren, he half expected a bullet in the back and silently hoped the crowds and mosque security were sufficient deterrents to spare an immediate attack.

"What was that about?" Loren asked as he returned.

"Just checking the time. Come on, let's see if we can catch a cab."

The German tour group was slowly moving toward the courtyard exit, but Pitt grabbed Loren's hand and dragged her past them, slipping out before they converged on the doorway. Pitt didn't bother looking back, knowing full well that Sunglasses and the Persian would be in pursuit. Prodding Loren to the street, he got lucky and commandeered a cab that was off-loading an elderly pair of tourists out front.

"To the Eminönü ferry docks, as fast as you can," he directed the cabdriver.

"Why all the rush?" Loren asked, slightly agitated at being hustled into the car.

"I think we are being tailed."

"That man you spoke to inside the mosque?"

Pitt nodded. "And another fellow wearing sunglasses who I saw earlier outside our hotel."

As the cab pulled into traffic, Pitt looked out the back window. A small orange sedan screeched up to the curb with a lone driver inside. Pitt looked across the mosque grounds to see the German tourist group still congregated around the mosque exit. He smiled as he spotted the Persian clumsily fighting his way through the thick crowd.

"Why don't we go to the police?" Loren asked, a rising note of alarm in her voice.

Pitt flashed a reassuring grin. "What, and ruin our one and only relaxing day in Istanbul?"

11

The yellow taxi quickly melted into traffic, leaving the domed mosque and its minarets in the rearview mirror. Had the driver turned north and wound through the crowded maze of the historic old city, he would have easily lost the orange sedan to thick traffic. But the judicious cabdriver, thoughtful to make good time, instead turned south and headed toward a divided motorway called the Kennedy Caddesi.

The pursuers desperately attempted to catch up. The orange sedan sped away from the mosque after picking up its two passengers, nearly getting sideswiped by a tourist bus as it wove through traffic.

"I think they turned right," the driver said in a hesitant voice.

"Go," Sunglasses directed from the front passenger seat while nodding at the driver to follow his instincts.

The car turned south, bolting through a red light, before slowing behind a procession of crawling vehicles. Seated in the backseat, the Persian suddenly pointed down the road, spotting a yellow cab two blocks ahead turning onto the Caddesi.

"I think that is their cab," he shouted.

The driver nodded, his knuckles tightening around the steering wheel. There was little he could do to prod his way through the clogged traffic, and he anxiously cursed the surrounding vehicles while the seconds ticked by. Finally spotting a break in oncoming traffic, he burst down the left lane for a block, then nosed back into the right lane. The traffic moved forward, and he quickly entered the Caddesi, flooring the accelerator and weaving down the highway like a Formula 1 racer.

The highway looped around the eastern boundary of Topkapi, hugging the Bosphorus shoreline. Traffic moved briskly as the road turned north then west along the Golden Horn, a natural water inlet that divided the European sector of Istanbul. Pitt looked down at the waterway, admiring a large green dredge ship that was churning the waters off the shoreline. As the cab approached the Galata Bridge, which stretched north over the Golden Horn into the district of Beyoğlu, a throng of cars and buses suddenly materialized, impeding movement to a crawl. The cab exited the Caddesi at the first opportunity, snaking down to a ferry dock near the base of the bridge.

"Boğaz Hatti dock at Eminönü," the cabdriver announced. "The next ferry departure will be right over there," he added with a wave of his arm. "If you hurry, you can just catch it."

Pitt paid the driver, adding a healthy tip, then surveyed the road behind them as he exited the cab. Seeing no sign of the orange sedan, he casually escorted Loren to the ticket window.

"You just can't stay away from the water, can you?" Loren said, eyeing several large ferryboats on the waterfront.

"I thought a relaxing cruise on the Bosphorus was just what the doctor ordered."

"Actually, that does sound enticing," she admitted, relishing some fresh-air sightseeing. "Just so long as we're alone and there's lunch involved."

Pitt grinned. "Lunch is guaranteed. And I think we've lost our friends."

Purchasing their tickets, they walked down one of the busy docks and boarded a modern passenger ferry, grabbing some seats by a window. A triple blast of the ship's horn signaled its departure before the gangway was pulled aside.

On the road out front, the orange sedan screeched to a halt, its two passengers flying out of the side doors. Bypassing the ticket booth, they sprinted down to the dock, only to watch the ferryboat churn into the strait. Panting to catch his breath, Sunglasses stared at the ferry, then turned to the Persian.

"Find us a boat," he hissed. "Now!"

At twenty miles in length and seldom more than a mile wide, the Bosphorus Strait was at once one of the world's busiest and most scenic waterways. Dividing the heart of Istanbul, it had been a historic trading route, utilized by the ancient Greeks, Romans, and Byzantines. In modern times, it had become a major conduit for Russia, Georgia, and other countries bordering the Black Sea. Tankers, freighters, and containerships constantly clogged the narrow waterway that split the European and Asian continents.

The ferryboat steamed north at a comfortable clip, easing past the hilly skyline of Istanbul under a clear blue sky. The vessel soon passed under the Bosphorus Bridge and later the Fatih Sultan Mehmet Bridge, both towering suspension bridges that rose high above the waterway. Pitt and Loren sipped hot tea while surveying the neighboring boat traffic and the hillside architecture. The crowded shoreline slowly receded into a line of stately waterfront mansions, diplomatic missions, and former palaces that resided against a green forested backdrop.

The ferry made several leisurely port stops before approaching almost within sight of the Black Sea.

"Care to go up to the top deck for a better view?" Pitt asked.

Loren shook her head. "Looks too breezy for me. How about another tea instead?"

Pitt duly agreed and walked over to a small café and ordered two more black teas. Had they climbed to the top deck, Pitt might have observed the small speedboat carrying three men that raced up the strait toward the ferryboat.

The ferry soon turned toward the European shore and docked beside a pair of smaller car ferries at the Port of Sariyer. An old fishing village, Sariyer still exuded the historic Turkish charm of many upper Bosphorus havens that were slowly being overrun with affluent retirees.

"There are supposed to be some good seafood restaurants here," Loren said, reading from a tour book. "How about we get off for lunch?"

Pitt agreed, and they soon joined a throng of sightseers clogging the gangway to exit the ship. The dock was near the base of a large hill, with the town spread along shoreline flats to their right. The town's main road fed into a small waterfront park to their left, which caught Pitt's eye when an old Citroën Traction Avant motored onto the grassy field.

They walked through a small fish market, observing a

fresh catch of sea bass being unloaded from a small fishing boat. Ambling past a row of competing seafood restaurants, they selected a small waterfront café at the end of the block. A spry waitress with long black hair seated them at a patio table along the water's edge, then quickly covered their table with meze, small appetizer portions of various Turkish dishes.

"You have to try the calamari," Loren said, shoving a rubbery blob into Pitt's mouth.

Pitt playfully crunched one of her fingers with his teeth. "A nice match with the white cheese," he replied after swallowing the fried squid.

They enjoyed a leisurely meal, watching the sea traffic maneuvering down the strait, along with the tourists bustling through the adjoining restaurants. Finishing their seafood dishes, Pitt was reaching for a glass of water when Loren suddenly clutched his arm.

"Swallow a bone?" he asked, noting a tight-lipped grimace on her face.

Loren slowly shook her head as she released her grip. "There's a man standing outside the door. He was one of the men in the van last night."

Pitt took a drink from his water glass, casually turning his head toward the café's front door. Outside the entrance, he could see a brown-skinned man in a blue shirt milling about the door. He had turned toward the street, obscuring his face from Pitt.

"Are you certain?" Pitt asked.

Loren saw the man steal a quick glance through the window before turning away again. She looked at her husband with fear in her eyes and nodded.

"I recognize his eyes," she said.

Pitt thought the profile looked familiar, and Loren's reaction convinced him she was right. It had to be the man Pitt had slugged in the back of the van.

"How could they have tracked us here?" she asked, slightly hoarse.

"We were the last ones on the boat, but they must have been close enough to see us board," Pitt reasoned. "They probably followed in another boat. It wouldn't have taken long to scout the restaurants near the ferry dock."

Though he kept a calm demeanor, Pitt felt a deep uneasiness over the safety of his wife. The Topkapi thieves had proven last night that they weren't afraid to murder. If they had taken the trouble to track them down, it could be for only one reason—retaliation for disrupting the burglary. The threat by the woman in the cistern suddenly didn't sound so hollow.

The café's waitress appeared and, while clearing away their lunch dishes, asked if they wanted dessert. Loren started to shake her head, but Pitt spoke up.

"Yes, indeed. Two coffees and two orders of your baklava, please."

As the waitress scurried back to the kitchen, Loren admonished Pitt.

"I can't eat any more. Especially not now," she added, glaring toward the front door.

"Dessert is for him, not us," he replied quietly. "Make a show of heading for the restroom, then wait for me by the kitchen."

Loren responded immediately, pretending to whisper in Pitt's ear, then slowly rising and moving down a short hall that led to both the kitchen and restrooms. Pitt noted the man at the door stiffen slightly as he observed her movement, then relaxed when the waitress delivered the coffee and dessert to the table. Pitt surreptitiously slipped a stack of Turkish lira on the table, then poked a fork into the thick slab of baklava. Taking a peek toward the door, he saw the blue-shirted man turn again toward the street. Pitt dropped his fork and rose from the table in a flash.

Loren stood waiting at the end of the hallway as Pitt rushed by, grabbed her hand, and yanked her into the kitchen. A startled chef and dishwasher simply stopped and stared as Pitt smiled and said hello, then squeezed past some boiling pots with Loren in tow. A back door opened onto a small alley that curved to the main front street. They hustled up to the corner and turned to head away from the restaurant when Loren squeezed Pitt's hand.

"How about that trolley?" she asked.

An antiquated open-air trolley used to shuffle locals and tourists from one end of town to the other was moving slowly down the street toward them.

"Let's board on the other side," Pitt agreed.

They crossed the street just before the trolley approached and then quickly jumped aboard. The seats were all taken, so they were forced to stand as the trolley passed by the front of the café. The man in the blue shirt still stood out front and casually surveyed the trolley as it motored by. Pitt and Loren turned away and tried to screen themselves behind another passenger, but their cover was limited. The man's eyes froze at the sight of Loren's purple blouse, then he swung around and pressed his face to the restaurant window. Pitt could see the shock in the man's face as he turned back and watched the trolley recede down the street. Quickly stumbling after the trolley, he yanked a cell phone from his pocket and frantically dialed as he ran.

Loren looked at Pitt with apologetic eyes. "Sorry, I think he spotted me."

"No matter," Pitt replied, trying to stifle her fears with a sure grin. "It's a small town."

The trolley made a brief stop at the fish market, where most of the passengers climbed off. Observing their tail still in pursuit a block away, Pitt and Loren grabbed a seat and crouched low as the trolley resumed speed.

"I think I saw a policeman earlier near the dock," Loren said.

"If he's not around, we might be able to short-hop another ferry."

The trolley cruised another block, then approached its stop near the ferry dock. The old vehicle's wheels were still turning when Pitt and Loren jumped off and scurried toward the dock. But this time, it was Pitt's turn to grab Loren's arm and freeze.

Ahead of them, the dock was now empty, the next ferry not due for another half hour. Of greater concern to Pitt was the appearance of two men near the dock's entrance. One was the Persian from the Blue Mosque, pacing about the quay, alongside his friend in the sunglasses.

"I think we best find some alternate transportation," Pitt said, guiding Loren in the other direction. They quickly stepped toward the road, where a 1960s-era Peugeot convertible rambled by, followed by a small group of locals on foot trailing it to the waterfront park. Pitt and Loren approached the Turks and tried to melt into the small party for cover. Their attempt failed when the blue-shirted man from the restaurant appeared down the road. Shouting to his cohorts on the dock, he waved excitedly, then pointed in Pitt's direction.

"What do we do now?" Loren asked, seeing the men on the dock move in their direction.

"Just keep moving," Pitt replied.

His eyes were dancing in all directions, searching for an avenue of escape, but their only immediate option was to keep moving with the crowd. They followed the group into the park, finding the open grassy field now lined with two uneven rows of old cars. Pitt recognized many of the highly polished vehicles as Citroën and Renault models built in the fifties and sixties.

"Must be a French car club meet," he mused.

"Wish we could actually enjoy it," Loren replied, constantly gazing over her shoulder.

As the group of people around them began to disperse across the field, Pitt led Loren to a cluster of people in the first row. They were congregated around the star of the show, a gleaming early-fifties Talbot-Lago with a bulbous body designed by Italian coachmaker Ghia. Working their way to the back of the crowd, Pitt turned and surveyed their assailants.

The three men were just entering the park together at a brisk pace. Sunglasses was obviously the team leader, and he promptly directed the other two men to either edge of the field while he slowly moved toward the center row of cars.

"I don't think we'll be able to leave the way we came in," Pitt said. "Let's try to keep ahead of them. We might be able to cut up to the main road from the other end of the park and flag down a car or bus."

"I wouldn't be opposed to attempting a carjacking at this point," Loren replied grimly. She moved quickly, skirting around and between the cars, with Pitt a step or two behind. They tried as best they could to use other onlookers as cover, but the crowds thinned as they moved down the row. They soon reached the last car, a postwar two-door convertible painted metallic silver and green. Pitt noticed an older man seated inside taping a "For Sale" sign to the windshield.

"The last of our cover," Pitt remarked. "Let's move fast to the trees."

Pitt grabbed Loren's hand, and they started to run across the last section of grass field. A thick line of trees circled the park's perimeter, beyond which Pitt was certain the coastal road lay just to the west.

They'd run just twenty yards when the sight ahead ground them both to a dead stop. Beyond the trees, they could now see a high stone wall that enveloped the southern half of the park. As a deterrent to the private residence on the other side, the wall was topped with shards of broken glass. Pitt knew that even with his help there was no way Loren could quickly scale the wall and outrun their pursuers, let alone avoid a bloody scrape in the process.

Pitt wheeled around and quickly spotted the three men. They were still picking their way through the cars, slowly converging on them. Tugging Loren's hand, Pitt began walking back toward the line of cars.

"What do we do now?" Loren asked, fear evident in her voice.

Pitt looked at her with a devilish sparkle in his eye.

"In the words of Monty Hall, let's make a deal."

12

"Does she sport a Cotal transmission?" Pitt asked.

The older bearded man leaned over and opened the car's driver's-side door.

"She certainly does," he said in a clearly American accent. "You familiar with Delahayes?" His face perked up as he gazed at the tall, dark-haired man and his attractive wife.

"I've long admired the marque," Pitt replied, "especially the coachwork-bodied vehicles."

"This is a 1948 Model 135 convertible coupe, with a custom body from the Paris shop of Henri Chapron."

The large two-door convertible had clean but heavy lines that exemplified the simple designs of auto manufacturers immediately after World War II. Loren admired the striking green-and-silver paint scheme, which made the car look even longer.

"Did you restore it yourself?" she asked.

"Yes. I'm a miner by trade. I ran across the car at an old dacha in Georgia while working a project on the Black Sea coast. It was in rough shape but all there. Brought it back to Istanbul and had some local talent help me with the restoration. It's not concours quality, but I think she looks nice. They squeezed a lot of speed out of her six-cylinder engine, so she runs like a demon." He reached out a hand toward Pitt. "My name is Clive Cussler, by the way."

Pitt shook the man's hand, then quickly introduced himself and Loren.

"She's a beauty," Pitt added, though his eyes were focused on the nearby crowd. The man with the sunglasses was staring at him from five cars away, walking casually in his direction. Pitt spotted the other two men farther afield but closing from the flanks.

"Why are you selling the car?" he asked while quietly motioning Loren to approach the passenger door.

"I'm headed over to Malta for a bit and I won't have room for it there," the man said with a disappointed look. He smiled as Loren opened the left side suicide door. A black-and-tan dachshund sleeping on the seat gave her an annoyed look, then hopped out and ran to its owner. Loren slid into the leather-bound front passenger seat, then waved to Pitt.

"You look good in the car," Cussler said, turning on the sales charm.

Loren smiled back. "Would it be all right if we took it for a little test-drive around the park?" she asked.

"Why, of course. The keys are in it." He turned to Pitt. "You're familiar with the Cotal transmission? You only need to use the clutch to start and stop."

Pitt nodded as he quickly slipped behind the wheel of the right-hand-drive car. Turning the ignition key, he listened with satisfaction as the motor immediately fired to life.

"We'll be back shortly," he said, waving to the man out of the window.

Pitt reversed the car, then turned down the back row of show cars, hoping to avoid Sunglasses. The assailant stepped around the last car in line and spotted Pitt behind the wheel just as the Delahaye pulled forward. Pitt gently mashed the throttle, trying to keep the rear wheels from spinning on the slick grass as the car lurched ahead. Sunglasses hesitated, then yelled for him to stop. Pitt promptly ignored the plea as the tires found their grip and the old car accelerated quickly, leaving the man in his tracks.

Pitt could hear additional shouting over the whine of the engine, then Loren called out a warning ahead. The Topkapi thief in the blue shirt appeared along the row of cars a dozen yards ahead.

"He's got a gun," Loren yelled as the accelerating car drew them closer.

Pitt could see that the man had produced a handgun, which he tried to obscure by holding it flat against the side of his leg. He stood near the back of a Peugeot wood-paneled wagon, waiting for the Delahaye to draw alongside.

With the motor screaming at high revolutions, Pitt popped the French car's tiny dash-mounted shifter into second gear. Just a few feet ahead, the blue-shirted man raised his arm holding the pistol.

"Duck down," Pitt shouted, then floored the accelerator.

The triple-carbureted engine spurted power, throwing Pitt and Loren back into their seats. The sudden acceleration threw off the gunman's timing as well, and he quickly struggled to aim the weapon toward the windshield. Pitt refused to give him the chance.

Yanking the steering wheel hard to the right, Pitt aimed the Delahaye's curved prow directly for the startled gunman. Blocked by the back of the Peugeot, the man had only one way to move. Furiously backpedaling, he abandoned making a precise shot in order to avoid becoming a hood ornament.

The Delahaye's front fender scraped along the Peugeot's bumper before creasing the gunman's leg, knocking him away from the car. Two shots rang out from his pistol before he crumpled alongside the Peugeot, writhing in agony. Both shots flew high, one shredding through the canvas roof, the other catching air.

Pitt hurriedly cranked the steering wheel back to avoid ramming the remaining row of cars. Fishtailing across the lawn, the Delahaye nearly struck a farmer's pickup truck entering the park loaded with melons. Shocked visitors scattered from their path as Pitt pounded on the horn in warning. Stealing a glance in the rearview mirror, he spotted Sunglasses and the Persian approaching the downed gunman, but neither had a weapon drawn.

Loren peeked up from beneath the dash, the color drained from her face. As they wheeled toward the park exit, Pitt gave her a reassuring wink.

"That fellow was right," he said with a slight grin. "She is a demon."

Pitt made as if he knew where he was going, bursting out of the park and turning left down the main road, which headed south along the Bosphorus toward Istanbul. The park gunmen showed no hesitation in making pursuit, quickly commandeering the farmer's idling truck at gunpoint. Shoving their injured accomplice in first, the other two men hopped into the vehicle and roared out of the park while melons flew off the truck bed like fired cannon shot.

Despite the Delahaye's age, Pitt and Loren had the advantage in vehicles. The French car's roots had been in racing, with Delahayes competing successfully in the pre-war Le Mans races. Hidden beneath the streamlined bodies custom-built for rich and famous Parisians were high-performing motor machines. A taut suspension and high-revving engine, by 1950s standards, gave Pitt ample opportunity to drive fast. The narrow, winding road, sprinkled with afternoon traffic, would prove to be an equalizer, however.

Screaming through the curves with the pedal to the floor, Pitt quickly shifted through the Cotal transmission. With the use of electromagnetic clutches, the transmission allowed Pitt to change gears by simply flicking the small gear lever mounted on the dash. He was well versed in driving old cars, having his own collection of antique vehicles housed in an airport hangar near Washington, D.C. It was a passion akin to his love of the sea, and he found he was actually enjoying himself, if not the circumstances, in pushing the old Delahaye to its limits.

Loren kept a resolute eye out the convertible's rear window as they squealed through a tight S-turn. She noticed Pitt frowning as he glanced at the instrument panel.

"Something wrong?"

"The fuel gauge is tickling empty," he replied. "I'm afraid a test-drive to Istanbul isn't in the cards."

An uptick in traffic began to impede their headway, and on a straight section of road Loren spotted the truck behind them playing catch-up at high speed.

"We need to find a busy place to lose them," she suggested.

There were few options on the small road, which traveled through an area filled with stately mansions. More cars clogged the roadway as they approached the village of Buyukdere, and Pitt passed the slower vehicles at every opportunity. Aided by the traffic, the pickup truck had steadily closed to within a quarter mile, with just a handful of interceding cars in between.

Pitt considered entering the populated portion of the village to the west, but slow-moving traffic clogged the artery into town. Skipping the cutoff, he clung to the coastal road, which suddenly spurted over the water on a lengthy bridged section. Finding a letup of oncoming traffic, Pitt accelerated hard, passing a line of cars slowed by a lethargic dump truck. He shook free of most of the traffic as the road touched land again, winding past the Bosphorus version of Embassy Row, where numerous foreign consulates occupied opulent summer retreats along the waterside.

"How's our melon truck holding up?" Pitt asked, his eyes glued to the road ahead.

"Just passing that dump truck, about a half mile back," Loren reported, before the vehicles behind them disappeared in a sweeping curve.

The green Delahaye tore past the ornate grounds of the British Summer Embassy when Pitt was suddenly forced to downshift while braking hard. Up ahead, a large moving van was unsuccessfully trying to back into a private drive, blocking both lanes of traffic in the process.

"Get out of the way!" Loren found herself yelling.

The truck driver never heard her, but it wouldn't have mattered. He casually inched the truck forward for a second try, ignoring the blare of car horns honking from the other direction.

Pitt quickly scanned the road for an out and found only one. Dropping the car into low gear, he sped forward and turned into the open gate of a walled estate to his right. The paved road turned to crushed gravel as they entered the grounds of an aging wooden mansion once owned by the Danish Royal Family. A sweeping circular drive divided a vast overgrown garden before looping past the steps of the salmon-colored main residence.

A gardener tending roses in the center island looked on incredulously as the old French sports car entered the grounds, appearing as if it was an original inhabitant of the estate. He watched curiously as the Delahaye slowed to a stop behind some thick shrubs rather than continuing on to the manor's front steps. A few seconds later, he realized why.

Preceded by the screech of skidding tires, the weathered pickup truck suddenly barreled through the front gate. The driver took the turn too fast, and the truck's tail drifted into a stone entry pillar, clipping the left rear fender. A few surviving melons popped out of the truck bed and disintegrated against the side of the pillar, leaving a trail of sticky orange flesh dripping to the ground.

The driver quickly regained control and charged toward the Delahaye, which sat idling straight ahead. Pitt intentionally baited the truck, not wanting it to stop and blockade the gate. He quickly stomped on the gas and popped the clutch, spewing a cloud of gravel and dust as the car shot forward. The truck closed fast, but not before Pitt reached the semicircular portion of the drive that curved past the residence. He accelerated hard as he turned left, blowing past the manor and into the opposite curve.

In the truck a dozen yards behind, the Persian leaned out the passenger window with a Glock automatic and began firing at the French car. Because of the angle of the curve, he had to reach out in front of the truck's windshield to aim, handicapping his accuracy. A few shots tore through the Delahaye's trunk, but the passengers and car mechanicals went unscathed.

By now, Pitt was drifting the car through the second curve, feathering the throttle to maintain momentum. At the outer edge of the turn, a large statue of Venus stood off the drive, with one raised arm pointing to the heavens.

"Look out," Loren shrieked as the speeding Delahaye drifted toward the marble statue.

Pitt held the wheel firm and eased his foot harder on the accelerator. As a succession of gunshots whistled over the roof, the car continued to slide toward the edge of the drive and the imposing Venus. The car's tires spun, then slowly bit into the loose gravel as the vehicle's momentum gradually shifted forward. Loren gripped the dashboard with white knuckles as the Delahaye's prow slipped onto the grass, heading for the bulk of marble. But the rear tires found their grip, shoving the front of the car just past the statue before nosing back onto the drive. Pitt and Loren heard a sharp scraping sound as the rear fender skimmed Venus's base, which ceased when all four wheels regained the gravel.

"You tore her arm off," Loren remarked, peering out the back window at the statue.

"I certainly hope that the Delahaye's owner carries collision insurance," Pitt said without looking back.

As the Delahaye charged toward the front gate, it was the truck's turn to navigate the second curve. The Persian still had his pistol dangling out the passenger door, lofting shots at the Delahaye while urging the driver to go faster. But with a higher center of gravity and balding tires, there was no way the truck could match the French convertible's slalom through the curve. Attempting to match speed, the ungainly vehicle almost immediately lost traction and began a sideways slip in the direction of the statue. Panicking as they started to drift off the driveway, Sunglasses stomped on the brakes, which only served to exacerbate the lateral drift.

The groundskeeper stared with his jaw open as the old truck smashed into Venus at a hard angle. The mangled artwork disappeared in a cloud of dust as the truck bounded forward and into a spin. Sliding back across the gravel drive, the truck spun three times before plowing into a thicket of small willows. The vehicle continued to slide, finally jarring to a halt against a thick chestnut tree as the three occupants were hurled against the dashboard.

Sunglasses slumped back into his seat, rubbing a fat lip obtained from kissing the steering wheel. Beside him, the man in the blue shirt was stemming the flow of blood from a mashed nose. Only the Persian escaped the collision unscathed, having braced himself with his free arm.

Listening to the engine idling without damage, he turned to the driver.

"Let's keep after them."

Sunglasses shook off his daze and reversed gear, roughly bouncing the truck back onto the drive. Hitting the brakes, a loud clattering arose from behind the cab. The Persian glanced out the rear window to see the decapitated head of Venus rolling about the truck bed with a clatter.

By the time they got back onto the drive, Pitt had already exited the estate. As he had hoped, the diversion had allowed sufficient time for the moving truck to sort itself out, and the coastal road was now clear. Pitt quickly pushed the old car up to high speed on the paved road.

"We might have bought a little time," he said, "but we're about out of gas."

Loren leaned over to see the fuel gauge needle flicker directly above the *E*.

"Maybe they'll stay in the clutches of Venus," she said hopefully.

Speeding past the Austrian Summer Embassy, the road opening up, they could see another shoreside village up ahead. A large car ferry was visible at the town dock, loading passengers and vehicles for a run down the Bosphorus.

"That ferry might be our best bet," Pitt said as the road dropped sharply to the waterfront.

"Yes, for that peaceful, relaxing cruise you were telling me about," Loren muttered.

A roguish grin crossed Pitt's lips. "Peaceful, perhaps, for someone," he replied.

They drove past a sign proclaiming the town of Yenikoy, and made their way through light traffic to the dock. Pitt pulled up behind an open truck loaded with oriental carpets waiting to board the ferry. He quickly scanned the dockside, eyeing a row of waterfront bars and restaurants similar to those in Sariyer.

"There's the truck," Loren suddenly blurted.

Pitt looked back up the road, catching a glimpse of the truck approaching the town a half mile away. He turned to Loren and motioned up a side street with his thumb.

"I want you to slip up to that restaurant with the green awning and order me a beer," he said.

"The dingy place with the darkened windows?" she asked, looking past a number of clean, respectable establishments.

Pitt nodded.

"What about our cruise?"

"We're going to give our seats up for our friends. Stay put until I get there. Now, go," he directed, giving her a quick kiss.

He watched as she climbed out of the car and high-tailed it up the street, then tentatively entered the scruffy bar. A few seconds later, he spotted the pickup truck in his rearview mirror rumbling up to the dock. Pitt noted with some amusement that the truck's front fender was mashed flat and streaked with white marble dust. A demolished front headlight left a vacant cavity that now resembled an empty eye socket. There was no doubt that the assailants had spotted the French car as the battered truck took its place in line to board the ferry three cars behind Pitt.

Pitt noticed the carpet truck in front of him dawdle as the ramp to the ferry cleared free and he quickly revved the Delahaye and jumped past the big vehicle, eliciting an angry honk from the driver. The truck offered a slight buffer of concealment, which Pitt hoped would hide the fact that he was the lone occupant in the car.

Pitt paid the toll attendant and drove onto the car deck of the covered ferry, pulling up behind a small sedan packed with young kids. He quickly jumped out of the car and looked behind him. The carpet truck was stuck idling alongside the toll attendant, blocking the other vehicles as its driver fished in his pockets for fare money. If any of the gunmen had hopped out of the pickup truck, they weren't yet visible. Pitt turned around and surveyed the ferryboat.

It was a double-decker, with the covered lower deck carrying the vehicles while passengers sat topside. He started to step toward a staircase when he spotted a vendor selling popcorn to the kids parked in front of him. The man was almost Pitt's height and build, with similar dark wavy hair.

"Excuse me," Pitt called to the man. "Would you be kind enough to watch my car while I go to the restroom?" He pulled a ten-lira Turkish bill out of his wallet as he asked the question.

The vendor spotted the note and nodded profusely. "Why, yes, of course," he answered.

Pitt stuffed the bill into the man's hand, then guided him to the driver's door.

"Please sit inside," Pitt requested. "Nobody will bother my car if it is occupied."

The man set down his rack of popcorn and eagerly jumped inside, excited to sit in the stylish old car.

"I'll be right back," Pitt said with a wink, then hurried toward the staircase.

He climbed to the upper deck and melded through the passengers as he made his way to the stern. The pickup truck was just coming up the ramp as he peered over the side, spotting all three figures sitting inside the cab.

The pickup was the last vehicle to board, and the dock crew soon pulled away the car ramp while the ferry crew raised a collapsible gate across the stern. Pitt felt the engine rumble belowdecks, then three blasts of the horn announced the ferry's imminent departure. Making his way to the stern rail, he waited for the ferry's prop to engage, then glanced forward.

At the head of the center stairwell, he saw Sunglasses appear, searching the crowd in frantic haste. Pitt could only imagine the look in the gunmen's faces when they had approached the Delahaye only to find a popcorn vendor sitting behind the wheel. He had little time to consider the amusement, though, as the deck suddenly swayed beneath his feet and a surge of boiling water arose off the ferry's stern.

He quickly climbed over the rail, creating a minor stir among the surrounding passengers that immediately drew Sunglasses' attention. The gunman started running across the deck, but Pitt disappeared from sight. He lowered himself from a rail stanchion until he hung by outstretched arms and then dropped himself to the lower deck. Landing in a tuck, he sprang to his feet and vaulted over the lower deck stern gate, then leaped from the transom in a furious lunge for the dock.

The ferry had pulled a few feet away when he jumped, and Pitt just managed to catch a foot on the edge of the auto ramp and roll forward. Tumbling down the ramp, he regained his balance and slowly stood up. The accelerating ferry was moving quickly into the channel, already putting nearly twenty feet between itself and the dock.

Pitt looked up to see Sunglasses rush to the ferry's upper rail and stare dismally at the growing distance between ship and shore. The assailant turned his gaze to Pitt, instinctively reaching a hand toward the holster he wore beneath a light jacket before abandoning the notion.

Pitt studied the figure, then threw him a jovial wave as if he were an old friend. Sunglasses stood impervious, staring back at Pitt with a face of chilled granite, as the ferry slowly made its way down the strait.

13

The setting sun cast a golden hue on the Mediterranean's westerly breakers as they crashed against the Israeli shoreline. Sophie gazed at the blue horizon thankful that the heat of the day had finally passed, then turned and stepped into the artifact tent. Professor Haasis was hunched over a papyrus scroll, his face aglow as he attempted to decipher the ancient script. Sophie smiled to herself, thinking how he resembled a wide-eyed kid in a candy shop.

"Give your brain a rest, Professor," she said. "They'll still be here in the morning."

Haasis looked up with a sheepish grin. On a long table before him were spread over a dozen of the ceramic boxes, each housing an assortment of the small papyrus scrolls. He reluctantly rolled up the scroll he was examining and placed it back in one of the boxes.

"Yes, I suppose I should take a break to eat," he said. "I just can't help myself. It is such an amazing wealth of data. This last scroll, for example," he said, tapping the box for emphasis, "it describes how an Anatolian merchant ship loaded with grain from Egypt was forced to seek safe harbor here when its mast shattered. Little gems like that make my heart beat faster."

"That doesn't exactly sound on par with the Dead Sea Scrolls," Sophie replied with a chuckle.

"Well, the average man on the street may not care

about this," he replied, "but for those who make history their life's work, it's like discovering a window to the past that used to be shuttered."

Haasis pulled off a pair of white gloves. "I really need to get these transferred to the university lab for proper analysis and conservation, but I just can't resist taking a first look."

He had examined all but three of the boxes by the time he stood and stretched.

"What's become of Dirk?" he asked. "I haven't seen him since he delivered the final box."

Sophie shrugged her shoulders, trying to appear indifferent. But the same question had been lingering in her head. Dirk's earlier dinner invitation had given her a rush all afternoon. She even sneaked off to wash up and to brush her hair, angry for once in her life that she hadn't carried any makeup with her. She felt her heart stop when a figure suddenly entered the tent behind them. Spinning around, she looked in disappointment to see that it was only Sam.

"You guys ready for dinner? The mess tent is featuring spaghetti and meatballs," he announced. A smear of red sauce on his chin revealed that he had already made a first pass through the chow line.

"Sounds great," Haasis replied. "Come along, Sophie, let's eat."

The antiquities agent moved slowly toward the exit, trying hard to hide her disappointment.

"Sam," she asked, "are we set up for tonight?"

Her assistant nodded. "Raban and Holder will be arriving within the hour. I told them we'd run surveillance till about midnight."

"Professor Haasis has offered us a tent, so I think I will stay the night. You can hitch a ride home with the boys, if you'd rather."

"I think I will. Sleeping on the ground isn't as much fun as it was when I was thirteen," Sam replied, rubbing his back.

They walked out of the tent to find Dirk standing outside with a beach towel draped over his arm like a waiter. He was dressed in khakis and a polo shirt, and Sophie couldn't help but think how nicely he had cleaned up. She fought hard to suppress a smile.

"I believe we had a dinner date," he said to her with a slight bow.

"I almost forgot," she lied.

He took her arm and escorted her behind Sam and Haasis as the group walked to the mess tent nearby. Sophie turned to follow the two men into the tent but felt Dirk suddenly tug her in the opposite direction.

"We're not eating with the others?" she asked.

"Not unless you have a craving for spaghetti that comes out of a can," he replied.

"No, not particularly," she replied, shaking her head.

"Good. Then it's off to Cape Pitt."

He guided Sophie down to the shoreline, where they walked along the beach a short distance. When they reached a rocky ledge that jutted into the sea, Dirk turned and helped her climb over the boulder-strewn surface.

"This was the site of a Roman palace," Sophie said, recalling the prior excavation of a large structure that featured Greek columns and a decorative pool.

"Many believe it was King Herod's, built after he

constructed the harbor," Dirk replied, showing he had studied up on Caesarea.

"I don't remember there being a restaurant located here," Sophie said, with a playful grin.

"It's just behind that last wall."

They climbed through the ruins to the tip of the promontory. Just past a crumbled stone wall, they reached a sheltered recess that offered a commanding view of the sea. Sophie laughed when she spotted an ice chest parked beside a small hibachi, its charcoal embers glowing red-hot.

"King Herod's Café, open for business. Hope you don't mind eating alfresco," Dirk said, spreading out the towel on a sandy spot. He quickly produced a bottle of white wine from the cooler and poured them each a glass.

"To damn fools," he said, clinking his glass against hers. Sophie blushed, then quietly sipped her wine.

"What's on the menu?" she asked, trying to change the subject.

"Fresh sea bass, snared by yours truly this afternoon. Grilled in lemon and olive oil, and accompanied by a vegetable kabob, organically grown on a kibbutz up the road." He held up a pair of skewers loaded with peppers, tomatoes, and onions.

"I'm sure glad I passed on the spaghetti," Sophie replied.

Dirk threw the kabobs and a pair of fish fillets onto the small grill and quickly had dinner served. Sophie found the fresh food tasted delicious and hungrily devoured her entire plate.

"It was terrific," she said, setting down her empty plate. "You sure you're not a professional chef?"

Dirk laughed. "Far from it. Put me in a kitchen, and I don't get much past peanut butter and jelly sandwiches. But show me a hot grill, and I'll happily run amok."

"You run amok with nice results," she said with a smile.

As he sliced up a small melon for dessert, she asked how he liked working at NUMA.

"I couldn't ask for a better job. I'm able to work in and around the sea, virtually anywhere in the world. Most of our projects are both interesting and fundamentally important to preserving the health of our oceans. And on top of that, I get to work closely with my family."

He noticed a faint look of alarm cross Sophie's face at the mention of his family.

"My father is the Director of NUMA," he explained. "And I have a twin sister named Summer who is a NUMA oceanographer. It's actually on account of my father that I was able to come to Israel. He relieved me on a survey project we've been working on along the coast of Turkey."

"Professor Haasis told me that he has several old friends at NUMA and holds the organization in high regard."

"He has certainly done some fine work here himself," Dirk replied.

"So your time in Caesarea is short?"

"I'm afraid so. Two more weeks, then I must head back to Turkey."

He passed her a plate of sliced melon, then asked, "Okay, now it's your turn. How did you come to be an archaeologist with a gun?"

Sophie smiled. "An interest in geology and history, instilled by my father from an early age, I suppose. I love archaeology and digging up the past, but I have always felt pain at seeing our cultural treasures being looted for profit. Working at the Antiquities Authority, I feel like I can help make a difference, although we are vastly outnumbered by the bad guys."

Dirk waved a hand toward the coastline. "Caesarea has been pretty well picked through over the centuries. You think the professor's small diggings here are really at risk?"

"Your discovery today proved that there are still cultural riches to be found. I was actually more concerned about the grave site, which a local reporter foolishly publicized in the press. The presence of someone masquerading yesterday as an antiquities agent doesn't help my radar any, either."

"Well, at least we haven't uncovered any gold or treasure. Any looter ransacking our site is apt to be sorely disappointed."

"You'd be surprised at the varied desires of the high-end artifact collector. Many collectors value cultural antiquities as much as treasure, to everyone's detriment. Those scrolls of yours would fetch a small fortune on the black market. I know I'll feel a lot better when Professor Haasis has all of the artifacts safely transported to the University of Haifa." She glanced at her wristwatch.

"I really should get back and coordinate our evening reconnaissance."

Dirk poured her a half glass of wine.

"How about a small one for the road?"

Sophie nodded and took the glass as Dirk sat close beside her with his own glass. The surf pounded the rocks around them as a deep blue twilight settled over their heads. It was a relaxing romantic moment, the kind that had escaped Sophie's life for quite some time. She turned to Dirk and whispered, "I'm sorry I yelled at you today."

He leaned over and kissed her softly, letting their lips linger.

"You can make it up to me another time."

Snuggling close, they finished the wine before Sophie forced herself to end their time together. Holding hands, they retraced their steps across the beach and up the hill toward camp. A generator-powered string of lights swayed over the assembly of tents, illuminating the campsite in a chalky glow. Sam was settled on a rock wall to one side, speaking to two men in dark clothes.

"I'm in the last tent on the left," Dirk said to Sophie. "Make sure the grave robbers don't disturb my sleep, will you?"

"Good night, Dirk."

"Good night."

Dirk watched Sophie join her colleagues, then turned toward the row of tents. Before turning in, he stepped over to the large artifact tent, which was still ablaze with light. Haasis was back at it, hunched over a scroll of papyrus with a magnifying glass in one hand.

"Uncover any secrets for the ages?" Dirk asked.

Haasis looked up momentarily, then gazed back at the papyrus.

"Nothing that weighty here, but still fascinating. Come take a look, I think you will appreciate this."

Dirk stepped closer, looking over Haasis's shoulder at the thin layer of fibered paper lined with a bold flowing script.

"It's all Greek to me," he said with a smirk.

"Oh, sorry," Haasis replied. "I'll give you a rough translation. This scroll provides a description of port activity sometime around A.D. 330, I believe. There is a brief description of a damaged Cypriot marauder that was captured adrift by an imperial Roman *trireme*. The vessel was subsequently towed to Caesarea, where the port authorities discovered that its decks were covered in blood and that a small cache of Roman armament was aboard. Many of the crew bore evidence of fresh wounds from an earlier battle."

"They were pirates?" Dirk said.

"Yes, apparently so. The incident created a stir, it says, as the personal armaments of a centurion named Plautius were found aboard. He was identified as a *Scholae Palatinae*, whatever that was."

"Probably didn't result in a nice consequence for the Cypriot crew."

"No, it didn't," Haasis replied. "The vessel was impressed into service as an imperial merchant ship, while the crew were summarily executed."

"Swift justice, indeed," Dirk said, picking up one of the ceramic boxes. "Do all of the scrolls contain such gripping accounts?"

"Only to an antiquities voyeur like me," Haasis said with a grin, then rolled up the scroll and put it back in one of the boxes. "I've reviewed most of the scrolls, and they are primarily bureaucratic records of port revenues and the like. Nothing too astounding individually, but collectively they will provide an important snapshot of daily life here nearly two millennia ago."

He wrapped the box in a loose cloth and placed it on top of a filing cabinet, then turned off an adjacent overhead light. The other boxes had all been carefully wrapped and stored in plastic bins for transport to the university.

"I'll leave something to look at in the morning," he said with a yawn. "You think you found everything in the chamber?"

"I believe so," Dirk replied, "but I'll borrow one of your trowels and take a second look, just to be sure."

"I never thought inviting a marine engineer to a field dig would generate such an abundance of work for me," Haasis said as he guided Dirk out of the tent.

Up the hill, they both spotted Sophie walking along the perimeter with one of her agents.

"Coming to Caesarea, I never thought there were such dazzling discoveries to be made," Dirk replied with a wink, then strolled toward his tent for the night.

14

The rattle of automatic gunfire sent Dirk bolt upright in his cot.

The shots sounded dangerously close. Dirk heard some shouting and then the return fire from a handgun. He quickly slipped into a pair of shorts and sandals, then staggered out of his tent as a cascade of gunfire from multiple weapons erupted above the camp. His first clouded thoughts were of Sophie, but he had little time to react. He heard, then spotted two figures charging down the trail, brandishing assault rifles.

Dirk immediately ducked behind the side of his tent, then scurried to a low retaining wall a short distance to the rear. He silently slipped over the wall and followed its cover away from the tents. To the rear of the camp were the crumbled remnants of several buildings that had once served the ancient port city. He threaded his way through the mounds of weathered debris, following a slight rise to a small corner partition. The darkened stone barrier provided a tight point of concealment by which he could observe the entire camp.

While his quick reaction had allowed for his escape, his fellow camp mates were not so fortunate. Sophie had been the next to react, bursting out of her tent near the trail with gun in hand. But one of the gunmen stood just a few feet away and quickly trained his assault rifle on her before she could shake the cobwebs from her eyes. Staring down the gun barrel, she had no choice but to reluctantly drop her weapon to the ground. The gunman responded by viciously jabbing the rifle into her shoulder, knocking her hard to her knees.

"What's going on here?" Professor Haasis shouted, emerging from his tent half dressed.

"Shut up," the other gunman ordered, swinging his rifle stock into the professor's ribs. Haasis sprawled forward, emitting a pained gasp as his body struck the ground. Sophie crawled over and helped him to his feet, both swaying weakly under the overhead lights. Another thug appeared on the trail and took over guarding Sophie and Haasis, while the other gunmen herded the archaeology students from their tents. Sophie gazed toward Dirk's tent, reacting with muted surprise when one of the gunmen found it empty.

Up the trail, there was a noisy commotion before several figures came into view. One of the antiquities agents, his right arm a bloody mess, staggered down the trail while struggling to support Sam. Sophie's deputy had a nasty gash across his forehead and shuffled his feet in a dazed state. Two more gunmen marched from behind, prodding the wounded men into camp.

"Sam, are you all right?" Sophie cried, moving cautiously toward the two agents. She grabbed hold of Sam and helped him sink to the ground beside the other seated captives. One of the female students assisted the agent named Raban, wrapping a torn shirt around his wounded arm, while Sophie held a palm to Sam's bleeding forehead.

"Where's Holder?" she whispered to Raban.

The agent gave her a grim look and shook his head.

Recovering from his blow, Haasis stood and shouted at his captors.

"What do you want? There's nothing here worth killing for."

Sophie studied the group of armed assailants for the first time. They appeared to be Arabs, each wearing a black headdress that covered his lower face. Yet they weren't the typical dirt-digging grave robbers looking for a few shekels from an old pot or two. They wore dark military-style fatigues and black boots that appeared nearly new. And they carried modern AK-74 assault rifles, updated versions of the venerable Kalashnikov AK-47. Sophie wondered for a moment if they might be a militant commando group that had stumbled onto their camp by mistake. But then one of them replied to Haasis's query.

"The scroll. Where is it?" barked the gang's obvious leader, a heavy-browed man who bore a deep scar along his right jawline.

"What scroll?" Haasis replied.

The man reached beneath his jacket and retrieved a small holstered SIG Sauer pistol. Casually aiming it at Haasis's thigh, he squeezed the trigger once.

The gun's report elicited a scream from one of the students as Haasis collapsed to the ground, grabbing his leg above the bloody wound. Sophie quickly spoke up.

"They're in the large tent," she said, pointing the way. "There is no need for further shooting."

One of the gunmen ran into the tent and rummaged around a few minutes before emerging with a ceramic box in one hand and a papyrus scroll in the other.

"There are many scrolls. Secured in plastic bins, more than a dozen of them," he reported.

"Do not leave any behind," the leader barked. Then he nodded toward the captives.

"Take them down to the amphitheater," he ordered two of his other men.

The pair of gunmen motioned with their weapons for the captives to stand and move. Sophie helped Sam to his feet while a pair of students helped up Dr. Haasis. With prods and shoves, the captives were herded along the path that led down to the beach. The scar-faced leader walked over to the artifact tent and grabbed the scroll from his subordinate's fingers. He studied it under one of the hanging lights for several minutes, then grabbed the ceramic box and ordered the man to retrieve a truck parked outside the grounds.

Dirk watched from his hiding spot until Sophie and the others had been marched out of the camp. He then quietly crept through the ruins, making his way toward the beach on a parallel track to the captives. His mind raced to try to develop a rescue plan or find something to use as a weapon, but his options were few against men armed with automatic assault rifles.

There was little ambient lighting once he moved from the camp, and he struggled to keep his footing over the rocky ground. He kept his eyes on the beam of a flashlight that danced to his right, carried by the guard leading the group. The hillside leveled briefly as Dirk crossed what had once been a stone-paved road. The flashlight beam disappeared behind a wall less than fifty feet to his side, but he could still track the shuffling steps of the captives making their way down the path. Wary of the sound of his own footsteps, he stopped and crouched low for a minute or two until the procession moved well ahead, then he made his way to the back side of the wall. Loose gravel crunched underfoot as he approached the barrier. Feeling along its sides, he moved to the end, then peered around the edge to find the meandering beam of light.

A cold ring of steel suddenly jabbed into the side of his throat, nearly blocking his windpipe. Dirk jerked his head to see one of the scarf-clad Arabs materialize from the other side of the wall, pressing an assault rifle farther into his neck. Even under the dim light, Dirk could detect the malicious hostility in the man's dark eyes.

"Do not move or you are dead," he whispered.

15

The rifle's muzzle never left the back of Dirk's neck as he was marched up the trail into camp. He was forced into the artifact tent, where one of the Arabs was busy stacking up the plastic bins for removal. The man had let his scarf slip, allowing Dirk to observe his small, ferretlike facial features. A second later, the terrorist leader entered the tent.

"Cover your face," he barked to the man in Arabic. The subordinate immediately retied his scarf with a quiet look of indignation. The leader then turned toward Dirk and the other guard.

"Why did you bring this man here?" he demanded.

"I counted the occupied tents, and we were a body short. I spotted him trailing his friends down to the beach." He held up a pair of night vision goggles that had proved Dirk's undoing.

The leader nodded in acknowledgment as he looked Dirk over.

"Shall I kill him here or put him with the others?" the guard asked.

The leader shook his head. "Tie him up and put him in the truck. A hostage might be useful until we are clear of here." He pulled out his pistol and leveled it at Dirk, allowing the other man to follow his directive.

Cutting some rope from the tent awning, the guard

tightly bound Dirk's wrists and arms behind his back. Jabbing again with his rifle, he prodded Dirk out the tent and up the hillside. A hundred yards along the trail, they passed the body of the antiquities agent named Holder, lying facedown in a pool of blood. Parked nearby was a dilapidated utility truck that had been backed from the parking lot to the side of the path.

The guard led Dirk to the back of the truck and gave him a hard shove, propelling him facedown onto the truck bed. Before Dirk could roll over, the guard climbed up and quickly tied his ankles together with a spare piece of rope.

"Do not try to leave the truck, my tall friend, or I shall kill you," the guard said. He then gave Dirk a swift kick to the ribs before jumping off the back of the truck.

Dirk shook off the sting as he watched the guard turn and walk back to the camp. He struggled with his wrist bindings, but they were tied too tightly to try to work free. Sliding around the back of the truck, he felt around for a loose tool or object but only bumped into a short stack of artifact bins. He then slithered around until he faced the open back of the truck.

The vehicle had folding double doors, leaving a straight drop to the ground. Dirk looked over the lip of the truck bed and eyed the rear bumper, a rusty plate of curved steel covered in flaking white paint. The inner edge of the bumper was thin and corroded but could serve as a cutting edge.

Reaching the bumper with his hands behind his back required a delicate balancing act, and he almost rolled out of the truck at first. But straining against one end of the bumper, he was able to press the rope against the ragged edge and work it back and forth. He'd barely begun to fray the rope when he heard steps along the path and he quickly slid back onto the truck bed with his hands beneath him.

The earlier guard, along with the ferret-faced man, appeared, carrying plastic artifact bins, which they placed on the back of the truck. Ferret-face then hopped in and stowed the bins near the cab, taking the opportunity to do his cohort one better by kicking Dirk in the back of the head as he passed by.

Dirk exaggerated the pain from the blow, groaning loudly and writhing as if in severe pain. The Arab chuckled at the result, jabbering to his comrade as they returned to camp. Dirk immediately resumed his position against the bumper, grating against the wrist ties. After one frenzied stroke, the rope frayed, and he felt the serrated edge scratch his wrist. He quickly worked the rope free, unraveling it from his wrists and arms. Rolling to an upright position, he attacked the rope around his ankles with his freed hands. But he hesitated when a crunching sound of footsteps on gravel sounded down the path. A stubborn knot was holding the line tight. He quickly relaxed the tension in his legs and worked the knot free. As the rope fell slack, he slid back into the truck, loosely wrapping the line around his ankle, then lying down with his arms behind him.

There was only one Arab on the trail, which Dirk recognized as Ferret-face. Dirk smiled to himself when he saw that the man was carrying an armload of artifact bins and no weapon. Like before, he placed the bins on the truck bed, then climbed inside to position them near the cab. Dirk resumed his artificial moans while writhing about to better position himself. He waited until the bins were stacked and the Arab turned to give him the obligatory kick. But the second Ferret-face's foot was raised, Dirk sprang forward, rolling his body forcefully into the man's other ankle.

Standing on one foot, the man was immediately thrown off balance by the impact. As he was falling down, Dirk jumped up, grabbed the foot that had been thrust at his chest, and shoved it skyward. The startled assailant crashed to the truck bed, landing on his head and shoulders while sending a trio of artifact bins flying. One of the bins turned over at Dirk's feet, releasing the ceramic box inside. Dirk reached down and grabbed the box, then lunged at Ferret-face. The Arab was struggling to his knees as Dirk smashed the box against the man's temple. The box shattered, sending him sprawling on the bed unconscious.

"Sorry about that, Dr. Haasis," Dirk muttered as he collected a mangled roll of papyrus in his hand and stuffed it in a bin. He then quickly tied Ferret-face into the same configuration as he himself had been bound, then jumped off the truck.

The trail was still quiet as Dirk moved to the front of the truck, checking but failing to find the vehicle's ignition keys. He continued across the parking lot, moving quietly and methodically, before slipping down into an adjacent field at a run. Leery now of the gunmen's night vision goggles, he figured his best chance at avoiding detection was to just get quickly out of sight.

He started down the hillside toward the beach, sticking to low-lying gullies and washes that offered the most concealment. He contemplated running out of Caesarea Park and trying to obtain outside help but knew that by the time any police would respond, the thieves would be long gone. And so might Sophie, Haasis, and the others.

He staggered across the stony remnants of a two-thousand-year-old residence and then past an ancient garden until he reached a bluff that overlooked the beach. Below and to his left rose the shadow of a Roman amphitheater. It was one of the best-preserved structures at Caesarea, a towering semicircle of stone seats that stood mostly intact and was still utilized for outdoor concerts and theater performances. With dramatic flair, the Romans had positioned the open end along the beach, offering theatergoers a spectacular view of the Mediterranean Sea as a stage backdrop.

Dirk worked his way along the bluff until he could see over the high stands of the amphitheater. A crossed pair of flashlight beams on the ground illuminated the group of captives, huddled in a mass on the beach behind the stage. Dirk could make out the two armed gunmen striding back and forth in the light, jabbering to each other over the crash of the nearby waves. He could also see that they were positioned in a difficult spot to approach undetected, with wide beachfront on either side and the flat expanse of open stage in front.

He watched as a silver-tipped breaker crashed onto the beach, rolling to within twenty yards of the group before dissipating away. It was nearly high tide, he observed. Watching another wave roll high onto the beach, he made up his mind. Guarding the captives, the gunmen had their backs to the sea and wouldn't expect an attack from that direction. A seaward approach was his only chance.

He gazed up the beach, barely making out the spit of land angling into the sea where he had discovered the ancient scrolls. Mentally searching for a tactic, he cursed that most of his dive equipment was back in his tent. But there was the pit excavation, which was still incomplete. There was a good chance that some digging tools were still nearby. And there was also his generator and water jet.

He thought for a moment, then twisted his face into a grimace.

"Well, a mad plan is better than no plan," he muttered to himself, then hastily descended the bluff toward the sea.

16

Sophie felt the eyes of the gunman stare at her incessantly. Stalking back and forth like a hungry tiger, the shorter of the two gunmen aimed his bloodshot eyes at her with nearly every step. She intentionally avoided making eye contact, tending to Sam and Raban or looking away toward the sea. This only served to frustrate the guard, and he finally demanded her attention.

"You," he said, waving his gun at her. "Stand up."

Sophie rose slowly to her feet but kept her eyes focused on the ground. The gunman poked his rifle beneath her chin, forcing her to raise her head.

"Leave her alone," Raban cried in a weakened voice.

The gunman stepped over and thrust a boot at the agent, striking him on the side of the jaw. Raban crumpled over, lying on the sand in an open-eyed daze.

"Coward," Sophie said, finally looking the Arab in the eye with contempt.

He slowly moved close to her. Easing his rifle up, he gently poked her in the cheek and jaw with the weapon's muzzle.

"Mahmoud, you like that one?" his partner said, watching the confrontation with amusement. "She is pretty, for a Jew. And even prettier for an antiquities agent," he added with a laugh.

Mahmoud said nothing, his eyes boring salaciously into

Sophie's. He eased the gun barrel down the side of her neck, then followed the border of her open-collared shirt, pressing the cool metal against her skin. When the barrel reached the top button of her blouse, he held it there, straining against the clasp. When it failed to give, he slowly pulled the barrel to one side, attempting a glimpse of her left breast.

Sophie wanted to knee him in the groin but opted for a quick kick to the shin, hoping it would lessen the likelihood of him killing her. Mahmoud jumped back, grunting in pain as he hopped about on one foot. His partner laughed aloud at the scene, heaping further humiliation on the gunman.

"You have a spirited one there. I think she is too brazen for you," he taunted.

Mahmoud shook off the blow and marched over to Sophie. He stood so close that she could smell the dank odor of his breath.

"We shall see who is spirited," he hissed, a rabid glare to his eyes.

He turned to hand his rifle to his partner when the loud whine of a generator erupted down the beach. A few seconds later, a pounding splash of cascading water echoed over the waves. All eyes turned that direction, and a faint silvery arc could be seen shooting over the horizon.

"Mahmoud, go and see what that is," the partner ordered, his demeanor suddenly serious.

Mahmoud leaned toward Sophie and whispered in her ear, "I shall have fun with you when I return."

Sophie eyed him with daggers as he turned and marched down the beach, his rifle at the ready. She then collapsed onto the sand, trying to hide her hands that trembled with fright. Trying to calm herself, she thought again of Dirk and wondered whether he might have had anything to do with the commotion.

As the figure of Mahmoud disappeared into the darkness, the other gunman paced nervously in front of the captives. He scanned down either stretch of beach, then stepped around the captives and surveyed the empty seats of the amphitheater with a flashlight. Finding nothing amiss, he resumed his position along the beachfront.

Lying on the sand, Sam rolled to a sitting position, finally regaining his bearings after an earlier blow to the head.

"How are you feeling, Sam?" Sophie asked him.

"Okay," he answered in a slurred voice. He looked around at his fellow captives, slowly reorienting himself. His gaze shifted toward the gunman, and he raised an unsteady arm in his direction and asked, "Who's that?"

"One of several terrorists holding us hostage," Sophie replied bitterly. But she nearly choked on her last words as she glanced toward the guard and realized that wasn't who Sam was asking about.

A dozen yards behind the Arab, a shadowy figure had emerged from the surf and was making a quick beeline toward the guard. He was tall and thin and carried a blunt object in his arms. Sophie's heart nearly pounded out of her chest when she recognized the owner of the profile.

It was Dirk.

The gunman stood with his back to the sea, his eyes focused on the area around the amphitheater. Just a turn of the head would expose Dirk's approach, leaving him quick fodder for the assault rifle. Sophie realized she had to hold the guard's attention so that Dirk could approach unseen.

"What . . . what is your name?" she stammered.

The gunman gave her a quizzical look, then laughed.

"My name? Ha. You can call me David, the boy shepherd tending to my flock."

He was proud of his joke and gazed at Sophie with beaming eyes. Sophie tried not to look past him as the shadowy figure moved closer.

"What will you do with the artifacts, David?" she asked, struggling to keep the man engaged.

"Why, turn them into cash, of course," he replied with a chuckle. It was then that he detected movement behind him, but he turned too late.

The flat blade of a shovel struck him in the side of the head as he turned. The blow stunned him, dropping him to his knees, as he fumbled to train his gun. Dirk quickly reversed his swing, leveling a second blow to the other side of the man's head, which knocked him down and out.

"Everybody here all right?" Dirk asked, catching his breath as the salt water dripped off his body.

Sophie jumped up and grabbed his arm, relieved at his presence.

"We're okay, but there's another gunman who just walked down the beach."

"I know. I set off the water jet to lure him away."

As he spoke, they could hear the distant generator sputter to a halt, the cascading waterfall dying with it.

"He'll be coming right back," she said in a low tone.

Dirk quickly surveyed the small group of captives. Sam

sat with a dazed look in his eye, leaning against the blood-ied agent Raban. Dr. Haasis was lying down with his leg wrapped in a shirt bandage, looking as if he was in a state of shock. The remaining students—three women and two men—sat looking at him with hopeless anxiety. Dirk could plainly see that the collected group would be unable to make a speedy escape. He gazed at the sleeping gun-man, then turned to Sophie.

"Help me get his jacket off."

Dirk lifted the man's torso off the ground while Sophie stripped off his loose black jacket. Holding him under the arms, Dirk dragged the man around to the back side of the captives.

"Bury his legs in the sand, then sit in front of his upper body," he told the two male students. They quickly shoved sand over his feet and legs, then tried to conceal the rest of his body by sitting cross-legged in front of it.

Dirk yanked off the gunman's scarf and wrapped it around his head, then slipped into the black jacket. He ran back around to the front of the group and picked up the assault rifle.

"He's coming," someone whispered in a frightened voice.

"Sit back down," Dirk said to Sophie as he checked the weapon. It was a mass-produced AK-74, likely smuggled into the country through Egypt. Dirk was vaguely familiar with the gun, having fired a similar version at a shooting range one time. He felt along the left side of the receiver to ensure that the fire selector switch was on automatic, then pulled back on the charging lever. He quickly raised the weapon and faced the group as if standing guard.

Mahmoud appeared along the beach and trudged up to the captives with an annoyed scowl.

"Someone made a water fountain with a generator," he muttered. "Shot fifty feet into the sky."

Dirk kept his back toward the man, waiting for him to step closer. When he felt him draw near, he slowly wheeled around, casually leveling the AK-74 at Mahmoud's chest.

"You take good care of the girl while I was gone?" the Arab asked. Then he froze.

It dawned on him that his silent partner had suddenly grown taller, was sporting a wet pair of short pants, and gazed bitterly at him through a pair of green eyes. Then there was the Kalashnikov rifle pointed in his direction.

"Drop your weapon," Dirk ordered.

Sophie repeated the command in Arabic, but it was unnecessary. Mahmoud knew exactly what Dirk meant. The Arab looked at Sophie and the students, then back to Dirk. Amateurs, he thought. His partner, Saheem, might have been duped, but he wouldn't be.

"Yes, yes," he said with a nod, extending his weapon toward the ground. But with a sudden move, he dropped to one knee and pulled the rifle stock to his shoulder while taking aim at Dirk.

The AK-74 in Dirk's hands barked first. Four slugs tore into Mahmoud's chest, throwing him backward, before he had a chance to squeeze the trigger. A heaving gasp dribbled from his lips, but his dying words were drowned by a frightened scream from one of the students. Sophie jumped to her feet and stepped close to Dirk.

"He was a filthy pig," she said, eyeing the dead man.

Dirk took a deep breath to calm his pounding pulse, then walked over to Mahmoud and picked up his rifle. Up the hill, the horn on the utility truck suddenly blared, echoing down to the beach.

"A probable call to arms," Dirk said. "We need to get everyone away from here and out of sight."

He walked over to the group and called to one of the students, a wiry man with long legs.

"Thomas, we need you to go get us some help. There's a housing development less than a mile up the beach. Find a phone, and see if you can get some police here pronto. Just be sure to tell them what they'll be up against."

The young man stood up and looked hesitantly at his friends, then turned and took off down the beach at a sprint. Dirk quickly scanned the area around them, then stood before the remaining group.

"We need to move before they come looking for their friends. Let's see if we can get around the back side of the amphitheater, for starters," he said.

"This one is stirring," replied one of the students, motioning toward the prone figure of Saheem.

"Leave him be," Dirk replied. He stepped over to Sophie and handed her one of the assault rifles. "Did you serve in the Israel Defense Forces?" he asked.

"Yes, I did my two years," she said. Israel's mandatory military conscription also applied to women. She took the gun without hesitation.

"Can you cover our retreat?" he asked.

"I can try."

Dirk leaned over and kissed her forehead. "Stay close to us."

He walked over and helped Dr. Haasis to his feet. The professor's eyes were dull and his skin pale from the shock of his wound. With help from the other male student, Dirk hauled him across the sand. With the others in tow, he led them over the amphitheater's stage and toward the far edge of the tiered seats. Sophie followed the group a few paces behind, peering through the darkness for any approaching figures.

Gasping for breath, Dirk muscled the deadweight of Haasis to the rear of the towering structure. Nearby was a storage shed that had been constructed to house concert equipment and was positioned against the side of the theater. Dirk dragged Haasis behind the shed and gently laid him on the ground. The other students and the wounded agents fell in alongside the professor as Sophie brought up the rear.

"We'll hold up here and wait for the police to arrive," Dirk said, finding the corner a manageable defensive position.

"Dirk, I see lights coming down the trail," Sophie reported quietly.

They peered around the side of the shed toward a pair of faint lights that bobbed down the hill. The beams slowly made their way along the beach, accompanied by an occasional shout of a name. One of the beams sprayed upon Saheem, who had managed to stand up but was staggering about in a daze. The dead body of Mahmoud was soon discovered, amplifying a frenzied murmur of voices. One of the lights turned and fanned across the interior of the amphitheater. Dirk wrapped an arm around Sophie and jerked her back from the edge.

"Sorry," he whispered, relaxing his grip only slightly. "They have night vision goggles."

Sophie slipped an arm around Dirk's torso and squeezed back. They clung to each other for a minute before Dirk attempted another peek. To his relief, both light beams were proceeding down the beach and could soon be seen bounding up the hill. A few minutes later, the faint rumble of the utility truck was heard making its way out of the park.

A wail of sirens and flashing lights arrived at the park just ten minutes later. Dirk and Sophie hiked up to the camp as a patrol of armed police with high-beamed flashlights and barking German shepherds burst down the trail. They led the police to the amphitheater, where Haasis and the injured agents were quickly evacuated by ambulance. Dirk noted with curiosity that the body of Mahmoud had disappeared, dragged up the hill by his comrades and carted off with the stolen artifacts.

After extensive questioning by the police, Dirk took a look inside the artifact tent. As he expected, all of the scroll boxes had been removed. What he didn't expect to find were the storehouse artifacts, which were still scattered about the tables in varying states of analysis and conservation. He exited the tent to find Sophie approaching from the parking lot. Under the overhead lights, he could see her eyes were red, and she appeared to be trembling. Dirk stepped over and grabbed her hand.

"They just took Arie away," she said, referring to agent Holder. "Shot dead over some stupid artifacts."

"They were as apt at stealing as they were at killing.

They heisted only the scrolls, didn't even bother with the other artifacts," he replied, nodding toward the tent.

Sophie's face seemed to harden. "The phony antiquities agent tipped them off. The young student, Stephanie, thought he was one of the gunmen here tonight."

"Any idea who would use such commando tactics to acquire black market antiquities?"

Sophie nodded. "I would have to suspect the Mules. A gang of Lebanese smugglers with suspected ties to Hezbollah. They're mostly known for transporting weapons and drugs, but they've drifted into antiquities before. They're the only ones I know of who would kill for artifacts."

"I wouldn't think those scrolls would be very easy to pawn."

"They've probably already been paid for. This was likely a contract job for a wealthy collector. One who knows no bounds."

"Catch them," Dirk said quietly.

"For Holder's sake, I will," she replied firmly. She gazed at the sea for a while, then looked at Dirk with a softened expression.

"I'm not sure any of us would be alive if you hadn't showed up on the beach."

Dirk smiled. "I just wanted to make sure I got a second date."

"That," she said, standing and giving him a peck on the cheek, "I can almost guarantee."

17

Pitt stood in the terminal waiting area and let out a slow sigh of relief. Looking out the window, he watched Loren's plane back away from the gate and head toward a line of jets awaiting takeoff from Atatürk International Airport. At last he could relax, knowing his wife was out of danger.

It had been an uneasy interval since he had stood on the dock of Yenikoy and watched the would-be assassins sail off on the Bosphorus ferry. He and Loren had quickly hailed a cab and raced back to Istanbul, sneaking into the rear entrance of their hotel and quietly checking out. They crisscrossed the city to ensure they weren't being followed, then checked into a modest hotel near the airport for the night.

"We probably should have gone to the U.S. Mission and reported the whole thing," Loren complained as they entered their bland room. "They could have at least provided us security at a nice hotel."

"You're right," Pitt conceded. "After thirty-seven briefings with a dozen bureaucrats, they'd probably find a safe place for us by a week from Thursday." He wasn't surprised that she hadn't pushed for diplomatic aid earlier. Despite her years in Congress, she rarely used her status to press for special treatment.

"The State Department is going to hear about it all the

same," she replied. "Those creeps need to be put behind bars."

"Just do me a favor and wait until you are safely home before you blow your horn."

Rebooking their flights, he saw her off on the first departure to Washington. With time to kill before catching his flight to Chios, he ate breakfast at an airport café, then tried phoning Dr. Ruppé. He was surprised when the archaeologist answered the number in Rome he had given Pitt.

"You calling from the airport?" Ruppé asked as a highly amplified boarding announcement blared from a speaker above Pitt's head.

"Yes, I just saw Loren off and I'm waiting for my flight out."

"I thought you two were staying another day."

Pitt filled him in on their adventure up the Bosphorus.

"Thank goodness you two are safe," Ruppé said, shocked at the story. "Those guys must certainly be well connected. Have you reported this to the police?"

"No," Pitt replied. "I was a bit leery after they discovered our whereabouts so quickly."

"Probably a wise move. The Turkish police have had a reputation for corruption. And based on my spate of bad news, you were probably right to think that way."

"What happened?"

"I got a call from my assistant at the museum. Apparently, someone broke into my office and tossed the place during daylight hours. The good news is, they didn't find my safe, so your gold crown is still safe."

"And the bad news?"

"They took the coins and some of my papers, which included your charts showing the location of the wreck. I can't say for sure, but it would seem to me there has to be a connection with all these events. Nothing like this has ever happened to me before."

"Another by-product of the leaky Turkish police?" Pitt asked.

"Might well be. My assistant already reported the crime, and they are conducting an investigation. But like the Topkapi robbery, they claim to be working without any leads."

"They ought to have a bushelful by now," Pitt lamented.

"Well, I guess there's not much more to be done. I'll try to have an interpretation of your crown when I get back to Istanbul."

"Take care, Rey. I'll call in a few days."

Pitt hung up the phone, hoping that his involvement with the Topkapi thieves was at an end.

But deep down, he had a feeling that it wasn't.

18

The Moroccan-styled villa commanded an arresting view of the Mediterranean from its rocky perch along the Turkish coastline. While not as gargantuan as some of the moneyed estates situated near the sea, it was built with a discerning eye for detail. Exquisitely glazed tiles covered every external wall, while miniature spires capped each roofline. Yet functionality superseded opulence, and a high premium was placed on the resident's privacy. A high stone wall encircled the landward perimeter, obscuring the interior compound from the eyes of locals and tourists alike who traveled along the coastal road to the nearby beach resort of Kuşadasi.

Ozden Celik stood at a large picture window, staring beyond the shimmering blue sea toward the faint outline of Samos, a Greek island fifteen miles away.

"It is a travesty that the islands off our own shore have been taken by another nation," he said bitterly.

Maria sat at a nearby desk, reviewing a stack of financial documents. The sunlit room was decorated similarly to the Bosphorus office, with tribal rugs on the floor and collectible artifacts from the Ottoman era gracing the walls and shelves.

"Do not antagonize yourself over the failings of men long dead," she said.

"The land was still ours when Suleiman ruled. It was

the great Atatürk who sacrificed our empire," he said in a sarcastic tone.

Maria ignored the comment, having heard her brother rail against the founder of modern-day Turkey many times before. Celik turned to his sister, his eyes ablaze with intensity. "Our heritage cannot be forgotten nor our rightful destiny denied."

Maria nodded quietly. "The Sheikh's wire transfer has cleared," she said, holding up a bank transmittal.

"Twenty million euros?" he asked.

"Yes. How much did you promise the Mufti?"

"I told him to expect twelve million, so let's give him fourteen, and we'll keep the remainder as before."

"Why so generous?" she asked.

"It's important to maintain his trust. Plus, it will allow me greater influence as to where the money is spent."

"I assume you have a strategy for that?"

"Of course. Attorneys and judicial bribes will absorb a large portion, to ensure that the Felicity Party, with Mufti Battal atop the ticket, appears on the ballot come Election Day. The remaining funds will be used for traditional political expenses; organized rallies, promotion and advertising, and additional fund-raising."

"His coffers must be filling fast, given the squeeze he's putting on his mosques, not to mention his general rising popularity."

"All of which we can take credit for," Celik replied smugly.

It had taken Celik several years to find and cultivate the right Islamic leader to front his goals. Mufti Battal had just the right mix of ego and charisma to lead the movement while still being malleable to Celik's designs. Under Celik's carefully choreographed campaign of bribes and threats, Battal had consolidated pockets of fundamentalist Islamic support throughout Turkey and gradually built it into a national movement. Working behind the scenes, Celik was about to turn the religious movement into a political one. Smart enough to realize his own aspirations would meet public resistance in some quarters, he hitched his wagon to the populist Mufti.

"It appears from the media reports that public outrage is still high over the Topkapi theft," Maria said. "It is being viewed as a very visible affront to the Muslim faithful. I would be surprised if it didn't raise the Mufti's popularity a percentage point or two."

"Exactly the intent," Celik replied. "I must ensure that he releases a public statement strongly condemning the heinous thieves," he added with a wry smile.

He stepped over to the desk, noting an array of coins in a felt box beside a stack of research journals and a nautical chart. They were the objects stolen from Dr. Ruppé, taken by Maria when she ransacked the archaeologist's office while visiting the museum dressed as a tourist.

"A bit risky, returning to the scene of the crime?" he asked.

"It wasn't exactly the Topkapi Privy Chamber," she replied. "I thought there was an outside chance our second bag of Muhammad relics might have ended up there, until I heard otherwise from the police. It was a quick and easy job to access his office."

"Anything of interest beyond the coins?" he asked,

admiring one of the gold pieces he pulled from the container.

"An Iznik ceramic box. There's a note by the archaeologist that says it dates to the Age of Suleiman, along with the coins. They apparently all came from the shipwreck discovered by the American."

Celik's brow rose in interest. "So it is a Suleiman shipwreck? I wish to know more."

There was a knock on the office door, which opened a second later to reveal a large man in a dark suit. He had a light complexion and gray, hardened eyes that had clearly witnessed the darker side of life.

"Your visitors have arrived," he said in a coarse voice.

"Show them in," Celik ordered, "and return with another Janissary."

The term *Janissary* dated back many centuries and referred to the personal guards and elite troops of the Ottoman sultans. In an odd twist of loyalty, the original Janissaries who served the Islamic palace typically were not Muslim themselves but Christians from the Balkans area. Conscripted as young boys, they were schooled and groomed as servants, bodyguards, and even Army commanders in service to the Sultan's empire.

In a similar fashion, Celik's Janissaries were Christian recruits from Serbia and Croatia, mostly former military commandos. In Celik's case, however, they were hired strictly as bodyguards and mercenaries.

The Janissary disappeared for a moment, then returned with a companion, who escorted three men into the room. They were the assassins who had chased Pitt and Loren up the Bosphorus. They shuffled in with a noticeable hint of apprehension, all avoiding direct eye contact with Celik.

"Did you eliminate the intruders?" Celik asked without greeting.

The tallest of the three, who had worn the mirrored sunglasses, spoke for the group.

"The man named Pitt and his wife apparently detected our presence and fled on a ferryboat to Sariyer. We established contact with them, but they escaped."

"So you failed," Celik said, letting the words hang in the air like an executioner's sword. "Where are they now, Farzad?"

The man shook his head. "They checked out of their hotel. We don't know if they are still in the city."

"The police?" he asked, turning to Maria.

She shook her head. "Nothing has been reported."

"This man Pitt. He must be lucky, if not resourceful."

Celik walked over to the desk and picked up the gold coin from Ruppé's office.

"He will no doubt return to his shipwreck. An *Ottoman* shipwreck," he added with emphasis. He walked close to Farzad and looked him in the eye. "You have failed once. I will not tolerate a second failure."

He stepped back and addressed all three men. "You will be paid in full for your work. You can collect your wages on the way out. Each of you is to remain underground until called for the next project. Is that clear?"

All three men nodded quietly. One of the Janissaries opened the door, and the men made a quick retreat for the exit.

"Wait," Celik's voice suddenly boomed. "Atwar, another word with you. The others may go."

The man who had worn the blue shirt stood where he was while Farzad and the Persian left the room. The first Janissary stayed in the room, closing the door then moving behind Atwar. Celik stepped close to the Iraqi.

"Atwar, you let this man Pitt subdue you during the Topkapi theft. As a result, we lost the Holy Mantle of the Prophet that was in our hands. Now yesterday, you let him elude you again?"

"He caught us all by surprise," Atwar stammered, looking to Maria for support.

She said nothing as Celik pulled open a desk drawer and retrieved a three-foot-long bowstring. As with his Ottoman ancestors, it was his favored tool for execution.

"Unlike Farzad, you have failed me twice," Celik said, nodding at the Janissary.

The guard stepped up and grabbed Atwar in a bear hug from behind, pinning the man's arms to his side. The Iraqi tried to struggle, but the Janissary was too powerful to break the grip.

"It was her fault," he cried, motioning his head toward Maria. "She ordered us to abduct the woman. None of this would have happened if we had let her go."

Celik ignored the words, slowly stepping closer until he was inches from the struggling man's face.

"You will not fail me again," Celik whispered in his ear. Then he flung the cord around Atwar's neck and tightened it with a lacquered wooden cylinder.

The man screamed, but his voice was quickly snuffed out as the cord tightened around his throat. His face turned blue and his eyes bulged as Celik twisted the block, applying greater pressure to the cord. A perverse look of delight filled Celik's eyes as he stared into the face of the dying man. He held the twisted cord tight well after his victim's body fell limp, seeming to savor the moment. He finally unraveled the garrote, taking his time removing it from the dead man's throat before returning it to the desk drawer.

"Take his body offshore after dark and dump it into the sea," he said to the Janissary. The guard nodded, then dragged the stiffening body out of the room.

The act of murder seemed to invigorate Celik, and he paced the room with nervous energy. The gold coin was back in his hand, fondled like a child's toy.

"You should never have brought in these imbeciles to do our work," he barked at Maria. "My Janissaries would have not failed at the task."

"They have served us well in the past. Besides, as you have just shown, they are expendable."

"We can't have any mistakes going forward," he lectured. "The stakes are too high."

"I will personally lead the next operation. Speaking of which, are you certain you wish to proceed in Jerusalem? I'm not sure the benefits are worth the risk."

"It has the potential to create a massive unifying impact. Beyond that, with a bit of inflated Zionist fright, it will be good for another twenty million euros from our Arab backers." Celik stopped pacing for a moment then gazed at his sister. "I realize it is not without danger. Are you committed to the task?"

"Of course," she replied without batting an eye. "My

Hezbollah contact has already made arrangements with a top operator who will assist with the mission for the right price. And should there be any difficulties, they will offer the necessary culpability."

"Hezbollah was not opposed to the nature of the mission?"

"I didn't provide them all of the details," Maria replied with a sly smile.

Celik walked over to his sister and gently stroked her cheek. "You have always proven to be the best partner a man could ask for."

"We have a destiny," she replied, echoing his earlier words. "When our great-grandfather was exiled by Atatürk in 1922, the first Ottoman Empire ended. Our grandfather and father spent their lives as outcasts, failing to fulfill the dream of restoration. But by the grace of Allah, a renewed empire is now within our fingertips. We have little choice but to act, for the honor of our father and all those before him."

Celik stood silent as teardrops welled in his eyes, his hand squeezing the gold coin until his fist shuddered.

PART II
The Manifest

19

The lemon yellow submersible slipped beneath the sloshing waters of the moon pool and rapidly disappeared from sight. The pilot descended quickly, not wishing to loiter about the mother ship while fierce currents matched wits with a Force 7 wind.

The frigid waters off the Orkney Islands northeast of the Scottish mainland were seldom mild. North Atlantic storm fronts routinely pounded the rocky islands with towering waves, while gale force winds seemed to blow without relief. But a hundred feet beneath the raging waters, the submersible's three passengers quickly turned a blind eye to the violent surface weather.

"I was a bit afraid of the descent, but this is actually much calmer than that rolling ship," stated Julie Goodyear from the rear seat. A research historian from Cambridge University on her first dive, she had been fighting the ill effects of seasickness since boarding the NUMA research vessel *Odin* in Scapa Flow three days earlier.

"Miss Goodyear, I guarantee that you are going to enjoy this flight so much, you're not going to want to go back to that bouncing tub," replied the pilot in a Texas drawl. A steely-eyed man with a horseshoe mustache, Jack Dahlgren toggled the diving controls with a surgeon's deft touch as he eased their descent.

"I believe you may be correct. That is, unless the claustrophobia in here gets the better of me," Julie replied. "I don't know how you two manage the confinement in here on a regular basis."

Though Julie was a tall woman, she still gave up a few inches to both Dahlgren and the woman seated in the copilot's seat. Summer Pitt turned and flashed her a comforting smile.

"If you focus your vision on the world out there," she said, motioning toward the submersible's forward viewing port, "then you tend to forget how cramped it is in here."

With long red hair and bright gray eyes, Summer posed a striking figure even in her grease-stained dive jumpsuit. Standing six feet tall in her bare feet, the daughter of NUMA's Director, and the twin sibling to her brother, Dirk, she was well accustomed to tight quarters. Employed as an oceanographer for the underwater agency, she had spent many an hour studying the seafloor from the constricted confines of small submersibles.

"How about I shed a little light on the matter," Dahlgren said, reaching up and flicking a pair of overhead toggle switches. Twin banks of external floodlights suddenly came on, illuminating the dark green sea surrounding them.

"That's better," Julie said, peering nearly forty feet into the depths. "I had no idea that we would be able to see so far."

"The water is surprisingly clear," Summer remarked. "It's much better visibility than we had in Norway." Summer and the crew of the *Odin* were returning from a three-week project off the Norwegian coast where they had monitored temperature changes in the sea and its impact on local marine life.

"Depth of one hundred seventy feet," Dahlgren reported. "We should be nearing the bottom."

He adjusted the submersible's ballast tanks to neutral buoyancy as a sandy brown bottom appeared in the depths beneath them. Engaging the vessel's electric motor, he applied forward thrust, making a slight course correction as he eyed a gyrocompass.

"We're near high water, and the current is still ripping through here at about two knots," he said, feeling the push against the submersible's outer hull.

"Not a fun place to go free diving," Summer replied.

They glided just a short distance before a large tubular object filled the view port.

"Mark one funnel," Dahlgren said as they hovered over the huge tube.

"It's so large," Julie said excitedly. "I'm used to looking at the funnels in proportion to the ship on grainy old black-and-white photographs."

"Looks like it came down pretty hard," Summer remarked, noting one end of the thin rusting funnel was twisted and crushed flat.

"Eyewitness reports claim that the *Hampshire* stood on her bow and actually flipped over as she sank," Julie said. "The funnels would have popped out at that point, if not earlier."

Summer reached to a console and engaged a pair of high-definition video cameras.

"Cameras rolling. Jack, it looks like there's the beginning of a debris field to our left."

"I'm on it," Dahlgren replied, guiding the submersible across the current.

A short distance beyond the funnel, a scattering of dark objects poked from the sand. They were mostly undecipherable debris long on corrosion that had fallen from the ship as it tilted and sank to the bottom.

Summer noted a brass shell casing and a ceramic plate mixed with unidentifiable bits and pieces as the concentration of objects intensified. Then a towering black figure slowly materialized in the water directly ahead of them. Inching closer, they saw it was the unmistakable form of a massive shipwreck.

A near century underwater had taken its toll on the World War I British cruiser. The vessel appeared as a tangled mass of rusted steel, sitting upright on the bottom with a heavy lean to starboard. Sections of the ship were nearly buried in sand, due to the effects of a scouring current. Summer could see that the superstructure had long since collapsed, while the teak decking had eroded away decades ago. Even sections of the hull plating had fallen in. The grand cruiser and survivor of Jutland was sadly just a shadow of her former self.

Dahlgren guided the submersible over the *Hampshire*'s stern, hovering above it like a helicopter. He then piloted it across the ship's length until reaching the bow, which was partially buried in the sand, the ship having augered into the seabed by her prow. He turned and guided the submersible several more times across its length, a video camera capturing digital footage while a secondary still camera snapped images that would later be pieced into a mosaic photo of the entire wreck.

As they returned to the stern, Summer pointed to a jagged hole cut into the exposed deck plate near an aft hold. Beside the hole was an orderly pile of debris that stood several feet high.

"That's an odd hole," she remarked. "Doesn't look like it had anything to do with the ship's sinking."

"The pile of debris alongside tells me that some salvors have been aboard," Dahlgren said. "Did somebody get inside her before the government protected the wreck site?"

"Yes, the wreck was first discovered by Sir Basil Zaharoff in the nineteen thirties and partially salvaged," Julie said. "They were after some gold rumored to have been aboard. Due to the treacherous currents, they reportedly didn't salvage a great deal off the ship. Nobody seems to believe they found much gold, if any at all."

Dahlgren guided them over the curved surface of the stern hull until he found a pair of empty drive shafts protruding from below.

"Somebody got her big bronze propellers, anyway," Dahlgren noted.

"The British government didn't secure the wreck site until 1973. No one has legally been allowed to dive on the wreck since. It took me three years to obtain approval simply to conduct a photographic survey, and that only happened because my uncle is an MP."

"Never hurts to have family in high places," Dahlgren remarked, giving Summer a wink.

"I'm just glad your agency offered the resources to help," Julie said. "I'm not sure I could have obtained the grant money necessary to hire a commercial submersible and crew."

"We had the help of a couple of Cambridge microbiologists on our Norway project," Dahlgren replied. "Brought some Old Speckled Hen with them. Darn nice people, so we were only glad to reciprocate."

"Old Speckled Hen?" Julie asked.

"An English beer," Summer said with a slight roll of her eyes. "The fact of the matter is, once Jack heard there was a shipwreck involved, there was no way we weren't going to help."

Dahlgren just smiled as he powered the submersible along a few feet above the cruiser. "Let's see if we can find out where they struck that mine," he said finally.

"Was it a mine or a torpedo that sank the *Hampshire*?" Summer asked.

"Most historians believe she struck a mine. There was a fierce gale blowing the night she sank. The *Hampshire* attempted to sail with several escort destroyers, but they couldn't keep pace in the rough seas so the cruiser continued on without them. An explosion occurred near the bow, which supports a collision with a mine. The German submarine U-75 was in the area and had reported releasing a number of mines farther up the coast."

"It sounds as if it was a terrible tragedy," Summer remarked.

"The ship sank in less than ten minutes. Only a handful of lifeboats were lowered, and they were either crushed against the ship or capsized in the heavy seas. Those men that were able to stay afloat were still doused by the frigid water. Most of the crew died of exposure long before reaching shore. Of the six hundred and fifty-five crewmen aboard, only twelve men survived."

"Lord Kitchener not being one of them," Summer said quietly. "Did they find his body?"

"No," Julie replied. "The famed field marshal didn't take to the lifeboats but went down with the ship."

A reflective silence filled the submersible as the occupants pondered the sunken war grave visible just beneath them. Dahlgren steered along the port hull near the main deck, which had collapsed in some areas by several feet. As they neared the bow, Dahlgren detected some buckling along the hull plates. Then the underwater lights fell upon a gaping cavity near the waterline that stretched almost twenty feet across.

"No wonder she sank so fast," Dahlgren remarked. "You could drive a pickup truck through that hole."

He angled the submersible until its lights were pointed inside the blast hole, revealing a twisted mass of metallic carnage that spread over two decks. A large haddock emerged from the interior, staring curiously at the bright lights before disappearing into the darkness.

"Are the cameras still shooting?" Julie asked. "This will make for some great research footage."

"Yes, we're still rolling," Summer replied. "Jack, can you move us a little closer to the impact?" she asked, staring intently out the view port.

Dahlgren tweaked the propulsion controls until they hovered just a foot or two from the gouged section of hull.

"Something in particular catch your eye?" Julie asked.

"Yes. Take a look at the blast edge."

Julie scanned the jagged rust-covered steel without

comprehension. In the pilot's seat, Dahlgren's eyes suddenly widened.

"I'll be. The lip of that mangled steel looks to be shoved outward," he said.

"Appears to be the case around the entire perimeter," Summer said.

Julie looked from Dahlgren to Summer in confusion.

"What are you saying?" she finally asked.

"I think she's saying that the Germans got a bum rap," Dahlgren replied.

"How so?"

"Because," Summer said, pointing to the hole, "the blast that sank the *Hampshire* appears to have come from inside the ship."

Ninety minutes later, the trio sat in the wardroom of the *Odin* reviewing video footage of the *Hampshire* on a large flat-screen monitor. Dahlgren sped through the wreck's initial footage, then slowed the viewing speed as the camera approached the port-side hole. Julie and Summer sat alongside with their noses to the screen, carefully studying the images.

"Stop right there," Summer directed.

Dahlgren froze the video on a close-up image of the shattered hull plate.

"That view shows it quite clearly," Summer said, pointing to the serrated steel edge that flared out like flower petals. "The force of the blast that created that had to come from within the ship."

"Could it have been caused by Zaharoff's salvage team?" Julie asked.

"Not likely," Dahlgren replied. "Though they probably made use of explosives here and there, they probably cut their way into the interior spaces they were seeking. They would have had no reason to create such a massive entry point, especially this close to the main deck." He hit the "Play" button on the video controls as he spoke. "We saw evidence of an internal explosion all around the opening, which wouldn't be the case if Zaharoff had just tried to enlarge the existing hole."

"How about an internal munitions explosion that might have been triggered by a mine or torpedo attack?" Summer asked.

"Not big enough," Dahlgren replied. "From what we could view inside, there was plenty of internal damage, but it was all focused near the hull. If the ship's munitions had gone off, it would have blown away major sections of the ship."

"Then that leaves an internal explosion," Julie said. "Perhaps there is something to the old rumors after all."

"What rumors would those be?" Summer asked.

"The death of Lord Kitchener in 1916 was a momentous event. He had been the hero of Khartoum in the Sudan two decades earlier and was considered a key architect for the eventual defeat of Germany in World War One. Of course, he may have been best known for his iconic recruiting poster, which displayed his image pointing an outstretched finger, urging you to join the Army. When his body was never found, wild conspiracy theories took root, suggesting that he had survived the sinking or that a double had been sailing in his place.

Others claimed that the IRA had planted a bomb aboard the ship when it was overhauled in Belfast a few months earlier."

"I guess this throws a new wrench into your biography," Summer remarked.

"Is that why you wanted to survey the *Hampshire*, because of Kitchener?" Dahlgren asked.

Julie nodded. "Documenting the state of the *Hampshire* was actually suggested by my dean, but the driving force was certainly my biography of the field marshal. I guess I'll have to return to Kitchener's old estate near Canterbury and take another look at his archives."

"Canterbury?" Summer asked. "That's not too far from London, is it?"

"No, less than a hundred miles."

"London is my next stop after we return to Yarmouth."

"Yarmouth is our next port of call after we drop you at Kirkwall," Dahlgren explained to Julie. "We're going to resupply there, then some of us are headed to Greenland for another project," he added, giving Summer an envious look.

"I will be flying to Istanbul next week to join my brother on a project in the Mediterranean."

"Sounds sunny and warm," Julie said.

"You're telling me," Dahlgren grunted.

"Maybe I can help you with your research for a few days, before my flight leaves London," Summer offered.

"You'd do that?" Julie asked, surprised at the offer. "Diving into some dusty old books is not the same as diving into a shipwreck."

"I don't mind. I'm curious to know myself what happened with the *Hampshire*. Heck, it's the least I can do since we helped open this can of worms."

"Thank you, Summer. That would be marvelous."

"No problem," she replied with a smile. "After all, who doesn't love a mystery?"

20

The shop marked "Solomon Brandy—Antiquities" was situated on a quiet side street in Jerusalem's Old City, not far from the Church of the Holy Sepulchre. Like the seventy-four other licensed dealers in the country, Brandy was officially sanctioned by the State of Israel to sell and trade in antiquities, providing that the artifacts at hand were not stolen goods.

The legal stipulation was a minor impediment to most dealers, who simply reused legitimate tracking identification numbers to sell nebulous items that came in the back door. Israel's antiquities laws strangely enough created a huge demand in Holy Land relics, and forgeries, by allowing the legal trade of artifacts, a practice banned by most other nations. Antiquities were often actually smuggled into Israel from neighboring countries, where they could be legitimized and sold to other dealers and collectors around the world.

Sophie Elkin stepped into Brandy's well-lit shop, cringing at the sound of a loud buzzer that activated with the opening door. The small interior was empty of people but crammed with artifacts that overflowed from glass cases fronting all four walls. She moved to a center island case filled with small clay pots tagged with the label "Jericho." Sophie's trained eye could tell that they were all forgeries, which would soon be treasured heirlooms for unknowing tourists making their once-in-a-lifetime pilgrimage to the Holy Land.

A stumpy man with pancake eyes emerged from the back room, wearing a dusty apron over rumpled clothes. He set a small clay figurine down on the counter, then looked up at Sophie with unease.

"Miss Elkin, what a surprise," he said in a flat tone that indicated her appearance was not quite welcomed.

"Hello, Sol," Sophie replied. "No tourists in yet?"

"It's still early. They see the sights in the morning, then shop in the afternoon."

"We need to talk."

"My license is current. I've filed my reporting in a timely manner," he protested.

Sophie shook her head. "What can you tell me about the theft and shootings at Caesarea?"

Brandy visibly relaxed, then shook his head.

"A sad tragedy. One of your men was killed?"

"Thomas Raban."

"Yes, I remember him. Very loud and vociferous. He threatened to wrap a shovel around my neck once, as I recall," he said with a smirk.

Sophie had caught Brandy in a sting operation two years earlier, accepting a large quantity of artifacts stolen from Masada. She'd dropped the charges when he agreed to secretly cooperate with the prosecution of the actual artifact thieves. But the antiquities agent used the old case to occasionally press him for information on other field investigations. Brandy would usually evade most of her inquiries, but in all her dealings with him he had never outright lied to her.

"I want the man who killed him," Sophie said.

Brandy shrugged his shoulders. "I'm afraid I can't help you."

"You hear things, Solomon. Was it the Mules?"

Brandy gazed nervously toward the window, looking for any lingering strangers. "They are a dangerous organization, the Mules. Terrorists operating within our own borders. You don't want to get too close to them, Miss Elkin."

"Were they responsible?"

Brandy looked her in the eye. "There are suspicions," he said in a low voice. "But I cannot say with certainty any more than you can."

"I know of no others who steal artifacts at the point of a gun and are not afraid to pull the trigger."

"Nor do I," Brandy admitted. "At least not in our country."

"Tell me, Solomon, who would have hired such a team?"

"Certainly not a dealer," he spat indignantly. "I don't have to tell you how things work in the black market. The preponderance of illegal excavating is done by dirt-poor Arabs who are paid a pittance for their discoveries. The artifacts are then passed through a series of middlemen— sometimes dealers, sometimes not—until finding a home with a public or private collector. But I can tell you that no dealer in Israel is going to jeopardize his livelihood by purchasing artifacts with blood on them. There's just too much risk."

Though Sophie had few doubts that half the artifacts in Brandy's store were acquired from illegal excavations, she knew that he was right. The quality of the best dealers' inventories was based on secret, shadowy deal making that entailed trust by both parties. There was too much potential exposure to trade with the wrong elements. Killing for artifacts just seemed far beyond the realm for the dealers that Sophie knew.

"I believe that no *smart* dealer would knowingly involve himself with such butchers," she said. "Have you heard of any attempts to sell Roman papyrus scrolls from the fourth century?"

"So, that is what they stole from Caesarea," he replied with a comprehending nod. "No, I am not aware of any effort to pawn such articles."

"If the goods are not on the market, then it must have been a job for a private collector."

"That's how I would see it," Brandy agreed.

Sophie stepped to the counter and picked up the small clay figurine. It was in the crude shape of an ox with a gilded yoke. She studied the shape and design closely.

"First Temple period?" she asked.

"You have a keen eye," he replied.

"Who's it for?"

Brandy stammered a bit. "A banker in Haifa. He specializes in early Israelite earthenware. He has a small but quite impressive collection, actually."

"Any papyrus scrolls in his possession?"

"No, not his area of interest. He's more of a hobbyist than a dire fanatic. The few collectors I know that are into papyrus are focused on particular texts or content. None are what you'd call a high roller."

"Then tell me, Sol, who would be passionate about

these scrolls and also have the means to go to this extreme?"

Brandy gazed at the ceiling in thought.

"Who's to say? I know wealthy collectors in Europe and the U.S. who are willing to go to great lengths to acquire a specific artifact. But there are certainly dozens of other collectors in the same league that I've never even heard of."

"Knowledge of the Caesarea scrolls was but a day old," Sophie said. "It doesn't seem likely to me that a Western collector could have responded so quickly. No, Solomon, I think that this was instigated by a regional source. Any local names fit the profile?"

Brandy shrugged and shook his head. Sophie expected little else. She knew that the high-dollar collectors were the gravy train for dealers like Brandy. He probably had no clue who was behind the Caesarea attack, but he certainly wasn't going to raise suspicions about any of his major clients.

"If you hear anything, anything at all, you let me know," she said. She started to leave, then turned and faced him with an admonishing glare.

"When I find these murderers—and I will—I won't treat kindly any accomplices, whether it's by act or knowledge," she stated.

"You have my word, Miss Elkin," Brandy replied impassively.

The buzzer sounded as the front door was opened, and a lean man with a stiff upright posture walked in. He had a square handsome face, sandy combed-back hair, and roving blue eyes that glistened in recognition of Sophie.

Dressed in worn khakis and a Panama hat, he cut a dashing figure laced with just a hint of snake oil.

"Well, if it isn't the lovely Sophie Elkin," he said with an upper-crust British accent. "Is the Antiquities Authority here to expand its biblical artifact collection beyond those acquired by confiscation?"

"Hello, Ridley," she replied coolly. "And, no, the Antiquities Authority is not in the artifact-collection business. We prefer that they remain where they are, in proper cultural context."

She glided over to the case of Jericho pots. "I'm just here to admire Mr. Brandy's latest batch of forgeries. Something you should know a thing or two about."

It was a stinging rebuke to Ridley Bannister. A classically trained archaeologist from Oxford, he had become a high-profile authority on biblical history in print and on television. Though many of his fellow archaeologists viewed him as a showman rather than an academic, no one denied that he had a remarkable understanding of the region's history. On top of that, he seemed perpetually blessed with good luck. His peers marveled at his uncanny ability to produce exciting discoveries from even the most obscure digs, locating royal graves, important stone carvings, and dazzling jewelry from overlooked sites. Equally savvy at promotion, he exploited book and film deals on his discoveries to attain a comfortable wealth.

His luck had run thin, however, when an underling brought him a small stone slab with an Aramaic inscription that dated to 1000 B.C. Bannister authenticated the marker as a possible cornerstone from Solomon's Temple, never suspecting that the carved stone was a forgery designed to earn the digger a fat bonus. Bannister took the fall, however, in a crushing embarrassment that his professional colleagues happily fostered. His reputation tainted, he quickly fell out of the limelight and soon found himself working limited excavations and even hosting guided tourist trips through the Holy Land.

"Sophie, you know as well as I that Solomon here is the most reputable antiquities dealer in all of Israel," he said, redirecting the conversation.

Sophie rolled her eyes. "Be that as it may, it's probably not a wise move for a reputable archaeologist to be seen hanging around a dealer's shop," she said, then stepped toward the door.

"Ditto, Miss Elkin. It was lovely seeing you again. Let's do have a drink together sometime."

Sophie gave him an icy smile, then turned and walked out of the shop. Bannister watched her through the window as she made her way down the street.

"A beautiful lass," he muttered. "I've always wanted to cultivate that relationship."

"That one?" Brandy said, shaking his head. "She'd sooner throw you behind bars."

"She might be worth the trip," Bannister agreed with a laugh. "What was she doing here?"

"Investigating the theft and shooting at Caesarea."

"An ugly incident, indeed." He looked at Brandy closely. "You didn't have anything to do with that, did you?"

"Of course not," he replied, angry that Bannister would even insinuate his involvement.

"Do you know what was stolen?"

"Elkin mentioned some papyrus scrolls, fourth-century Roman."

The description seized Bannister's attention, but he fought to maintain a disinterested demeanor.

"Any idea of their content?"

Brandy shook his head. "No. I can't imagine they'd contain anything astounding from that time period."

"You're probably right. I wonder who financed the theft?"

"Now you are starting to sound like Miss Elkin," Brandy said. "I really haven't heard anything about it. Maybe you should ask the Fat Man?"

"Ah yes. The very reason for my visit. You received the amulets from my associate Josh?"

"Yes, with a message that I was to hold them until we talked." Brandy stepped to the back room, then returned with a small box. He opened it up and laid out two green stone pendants, each featuring a carved ram motif.

"A nice matched pair of amulets from the Canaanite period," Brandy said. "Did these come from Tel Arad?"

"Yes. A former student of mine is leading a dig there for an American university."

"That boy could get himself into trouble for looting an antiquities dig."

"He's quite aware of that, but it's an exceptional case. The boy is actually straight as an arrow. He inadvertently trenched into a grave site and came away with some sterling artifacts. They actually dug up four identical amulets. One went to the university and one was donated to the Israel Museum. Josh sent me the other two as gifts for helping him in his career over the years."

Brandy raised his brow while asking, "You want me to sell them?"

Bannister smiled. "No, my friend. While I realize they would garner a pretty penny, I don't really need the cash. Take one for yourself and do with it what you wish."

Brandy's eyes lit up. "That is a very generous gift."

"You've been a valuable friend over the years, and I may need your help in the future. Take it with my blessings."

"Shalom, my friend," Brandy replied, shaking Bannister's hand. "May I ask what you are going to do with the other amulet?"

Bannister scooped it up and eyeballed it for a second, then slipped it into his pocket as he headed toward the door.

"I'm taking it to the Fat Man," he said.

"Wise idea," Brandy replied. "He'll pay you top dollar for it."

Bannister waved good-bye and stepped into the street smiling to himself. He was banking that the Fat Man would pay him for the amulet all right, but in something much more valuable than cash.

21

Julie Goodyear strolled past a monstrous pair of long-silenced fifteen-inch naval guns pointed toward the Thames, then walked up the steps to the entrance of the Imperial War Museum. The venerated national institution in the London borough of Southwark was housed in a nineteenth-century brick edifice originally constructed as a hospital for the mentally ill. Known for its extensive collection of photographs, art, and military artifacts from World Wars I and II, the museum also contained a large archive of war documents and private letters.

Julie checked in at the information desk in the main atrium, where she was escorted up two floors in a phone-booth-sized elevator, then climbed an additional flight of stairs until reaching her destination. The museum's reading room was an impressive circular library constructed in the building's high central dome.

A bookish woman in a brown dress smiled in recognition as she approached the help desk.

"Good morning, Miss Goodyear. Back for another visit with Lord Kitchener?" she asked.

"Hello again, Beatrice. Yes, I'm afraid the field marshal's enduring mysteries have drawn me back once more. I phoned a few days ago with a request for some specific materials."

"Let me see if they have been pulled," Beatrice replied,

retreating into the private archives depository. She returned a minute later with a thick stack of files under her arm.

"I have an Admiralty White Paper inquiry on the sinking of the HMS *Hampshire* and First Earl Kitchener's official war correspondence in the year 1916," the librarian said as she had Julie sign out the documents. "Your request appears to be complete."

"Thanks, Beatrice. I should just be a short while."

Julie took the documents to a quiet corner table and began reading the Admiralty report on the *Hampshire*. There was little information to be had. She had seen earlier accusations against the Royal Navy by residents of the Orkneys, who claimed the Navy dithered in sending help to the stricken ship after its loss had been reported. The official report clearly covered up any wrongdoings by the Navy and brushed aside rumors that the ship sank by means other than a mine.

Kitchener's correspondence proved only slightly more illuminating. She had read his war correspondence before and had found it mostly mundane. Kitchener held the post of Secretary of State for War in 1916, and most of his official writings reflected his preoccupation with manpower and recruiting needs of the British Army. A typical letter complained to the Prime Minister about pulling men from the Army to work in munition factories on the home front.

Julie skimmed rapidly through the pages until nearing June fifth, the date of Kitchener's death on the *Hampshire*. The discovery that the *Hampshire* had sunk from an internal explosion compelled her to consider the possibility that someone may have actually wanted him dead. The notion led her to an odd letter that she had seen months before. Thumbing through the bottom of the file, her fingers suddenly froze on the document.

Unlike the aged yellowing military correspondence, this letter was still bright white, typed on heavy cotton paper. At the top of the page was embossed "Lambeth Palace." Slowly, Julie read the letter.

Sir,

At behest of God and Country, I implore you a final time to relinquish the document. The very sanctity of our Church depends upon it. For while you may be waging a temporal war with the enemies of England, we are waging an eternal crusade for the salvation of all mankind. Our enemies are wicked and cunning. Should they seize the Manifest, it could spell the demise of our very faith. I strongly submit there is no choice but for you to accede to the Church. I await your submittal,

—Randall Davidson

Julie recognized the author as the Archbishop of Canterbury. In the margins, she noticed a handwritten notation that said "Never!" It was written in a script that she recognized as Kitchener's.

The letter struck her as perplexing on several levels. Kitchener, she knew, had been a churchgoing religious man. Her research had never revealed any conflicts with the Church of England, let alone the head of the Church himself, the Archbishop of Canterbury. Then there was the reference to the document or Manifest. What could that possibly be?

Though the letter seemed to have no possible bearing on the *Hampshire*, it was intriguing enough to stir her interest. She made a photocopy of the letter, then worked her way through the rest of the folder. Near the bottom, she found several documents related to Kitchener's trip to Russia, including a formal invitation from the Russian Consulate and an itinerary while in Petrograd. She copied these as well, then returned the folder to Beatrice.

"Find what you were looking for?" the librarian asked.

"No, just an odd kernel here and there."

"I've found that the key to discovering historical treasures is to just keep on kicking over the stones. Eventually, you'll get there."

"Thank you for your assistance, Beatrice."

As she left the museum and made her way to her car, Julie reread the letter several times, finally staring at the Archbishop's signature.

"Beatrice is right," she finally muttered to herself. "I need to kick over some more stones."

She didn't have far to go. Barely a half mile down the road sat historic Lambeth Palace. A collection of ancient brick buildings towering over the banks of the Thames River, it served as the historical London residence of the Archbishop of Canterbury. Of particular interest to Julie was the presence on the grounds of the Lambeth Palace Library.

Julie knew that the palace was not typically open to the public, so she parked on a nearby street and walked to the main gate. Passing a security checkpoint, she was allowed to proceed to the Great Hall, a Gothic-style red brick building accented with white trim. Contained inside the historic structure was one of the oldest libraries in Britain, and the principal repository for the Church of England's archives, dating back to the ninth century.

She stepped to the entrance door and rang a bell, then was escorted by a teenage boy to a small but modern reading room. Approaching the reference desk, she filled out two document request cards and handed them to a girl with short red hair.

"The papers of Archbishop Randall Davidson, for the period of January through July 1916," the girl read with interest, "and any files regarding First Earl Horatio Herbert Kitchener."

"I realize the latter request may be a bit unlikely, but I wish to at least attempt an inquiry," Julie said.

"We can perform a computerized search of our archives database," the girl replied without enthusiasm. "And what is the nature of your request?"

"Research for a biography of Lord Kitchener," Julie replied.

"May I please see your reader ticket?"

Julie fished through her purse and handed over a library card, having utilized the Lambeth archives on several occasions. The girl copied her name and contact information, then peered at a clock on the wall.

"I'm afraid we'll be unable to retrieve these documents before closing time. The data should be available for your review when the library reopens on Monday."

Julie looked at the girl with disappointment, knowing that the library would still be open for another hour.

"Very well. I will return on Monday. Thank you."

The red-haired girl clutched the document request

cards tightly in her hand until Julie left the building. Then she waved the teenage boy to the counter.

"Douglas, can you please watch the desk for a minute?" she asked in an urgent tone. "I need to place a rather important phone call."

22

Oscar Gutzman was his real name, but everyone called him the Fat Man. The origin of the moniker was evident at first sight. Carrying well over three hundred pounds on a five-foot frame, he appeared nearly as wide as he was tall. With a clean-shaven head and unusually large ears, he resembled an escapee from a traveling carnival. Yet his appearance belied the fact that Gutzman was one of the richest men in Israel.

He grew up a ragtag urchin in the streets of Jerusalem, digging up coins from the hillside tombs with orphaned Arab boys or bumming free meals from Christian soup kitchens. His exposure to Jerusalem's diverse religions and culture, along with a hustler's ability to survive the streets, served him well as an adult businessman. Building a tiny construction firm into the largest hotel developer in the Middle East, he became a self-made man of huge riches who floated freely with the power brokers of the entire region. His personal drive for wealth and success was surpassed, however, by his passion for antiquities.

It was the death of his younger sister at an early age, in a traffic accident outside a synagogue, that had altered his life. Like others who suffer a tragic personal loss, he began a private search for God. Only his quest migrated from the spiritual to the tangible as he sought to prove the truth of the Bible through physical evidence. A small collection of biblical-era antiquities had grown exponentially with his accumulated wealth, turning an early hobby into a life-long passion. His artifacts, numbering in the hundreds of thousands, were now stored in warehouses spread over three countries. In his late sixties, Gutzman now devoted his full time and resources to his personal quest.

Ridley Bannister entered an upscale boutique hotel situated on a prime parcel of Tel Aviv beachfront. The lobby was decorated in a minimalist contemporary style, with a number of uncomfortable-looking black leather chairs sitting starkly on a bright white-tiled floor. Bannister considered the design well executed, though he normally detested the look. A matronly hotel clerk greeted him warmly as he stepped to the front desk.

"I have an appointment with Mr. Gutzman. My name is Bannister," he said.

After a confirming phone call, he was escorted by a burly security guard to a private elevator and whisked to the top floor. Stepping off the elevator, the door to the penthouse was immediately thrown open by the Fat Man, a large cigar dangling from his lips.

"Ridley, come in, my boy, come in," Gutzman greeted in a wheezy voice.

"You're looking well, Oscar," Bannister replied, shaking hands before entering the apartment.

Bannister still found himself marveling at Gutzman's apartment, which resembled a museum more than a residence. Shelves and display cases were crammed everywhere, stuffed with pottery, carvings, and other relics, all thousands of years old. Gutzman led him down a hallway lined with ancient Roman mosaics, taken from a public bath in Carthage. They passed under a stone arch from the ruins of Jericho and entered an expansive living room that overlooked the sands of Tel Aviv's Gordon Beach and the sparkling Mediterranean beyond.

Taking a seat in an overstuffed leather chair, Bannister was surprised to find the residence empty but for a lone servant. On his prior visits, he had always found a throng of antiquities dealers milling about, hoping to hawk their latest prized artifact to the rich collector.

"The heat . . . I find it more oppressive all the time," Gutzman said, gasping from the walk to the front door. He then sank into an adjacent chair.

"Marta, some cold drinks, please," he shouted to his servant.

Bannister removed the pendant from his pocket and placed it in Gutzman's hand.

"A gift to you, Oscar. It's from Tel Arad."

Gutzman studied the pendant, a broad smile slowly forming across his face.

"This is quite nice, Ridley, thank you. I have a similar specimen from Nahal Besor. Early Canaanite, I would say."

"You are correct, as usual. Is this new?" Bannister asked, pointing to a small glass plate on the coffee table that had a molded rim.

"Yes," Gutzman said, his eyes perking up. "I just acquired it. Excavated from Beth She'an. Second-century molded glassware, probably manufactured in Alexandria. Look at the polishing on it."

Bannister picked up the plate and studied it closely.

"It's in beautiful condition."

The servant Marta appeared, delivering two glasses of lemonade, before disappearing into the kitchen.

"So, Ridley, what is the latest buzz in the world of legal archaeological discovery?" Gutzman asked with a chuckle.

"There appear to be relatively few new projects slated to take the field next year. The Israel Museum will be sponsoring a dig on the shores of Galilee in search of an early settlement, while Tel Aviv University has approval for new exploration work at Megiddo. Most of the academic efforts appear to be directed at the continuation of existing field projects. There are, of course, the usual assortment of foreign theologically sponsored digs, but, as we know, they seldom amount to much."

"True, but at least they show more imagination than the academic institutes," Gutzman said with derision.

"I've been looking at two sites that I think you will be interested in. One is at Beit Jala. If Bathsheba's tomb exists, I think it would be there, in the town of her birth, which was then called Giloh. I've already formulated a site summary and excavation plan."

Gutzman nodded for him to continue.

"The second site is near Gibeon. There's an outside chance of proving King Manasseh's palace is located there. This one needs more research but has great potential, I believe. I can obtain the necessary excavation paperwork as before under the auspices of the Anglican Church, if you are agreeable to sponsorship."

"Ridley, you have always delivered exciting finds, and I have found much joy in collaborating with your field digs. But I'm afraid my days of field sponsorship have come to an end."

"You have always been most generous, Oscar," Bannister replied, suppressing his anger at losing the support of a longtime benefactor.

Gutzman gazed out the window with a distant look in his eye.

"I have spent most of my personal fortune collecting artifacts that support the narratives of the Bible," he said. "I own mud bricks allegedly from the Tower of Babel. I have stone footings that may have supported Solomon's Temple. I have a million and one objects from the biblical era. Yet there is an element of doubt about each and every one of my pieces."

He suddenly fell into a wheezing fit, coughing and gasping for air, until he settled himself with a drink of lemonade.

"Oscar, do you need help?"

The Fat Man shook his head. "My emphysema has been getting the better of me lately," he gasped. "The doctors are not hopeful."

"Nonsense. You're as strong as David."

Gutzman smiled then slowly rose to his feet. The act seemed to give him renewed strength, and he stepped briskly over to a cabinet, then returned carrying a small plate of glass.

"Take a look at this," he said, handing it to the archaeologist.

Bannister took the glass, observing that it was actually two sealed plates compressing a document in the middle. Holding it up to the light, he could see the protected document was a rectangular piece of papyrus with clear horizontal writing.

"A fine example of Coptic script," he noted.

"Do you know what it says?"

"I can make out a few words, but am a bit lost without my reference materials," he acknowledged.

"It's a harbormaster's report from the Port of Caesarea. It details the capture of a pirate vessel by a Roman galley. The pirates had in their possession armaments from a Roman centurion, one belonging to the *Scholae Palatinae.*"

"Caesarea," Bannister said with a raised brow. "I understand that some papyrus artifacts were taken as part of the recent theft there. Along with the occurrence of at least one murder."

"Yes, most unfortunate. The document clearly dates to the early fourth century," Gutzman said, brushing off the inference.

"Interesting," Bannister replied, suddenly feeling uneasy with his host. "And the significance?"

"I believe it offers potentially confirming evidence of the Manifest, as well as an important clue to the cargo's disposition."

The Manifest. So that's what it was all about, Bannister thought. The old goat was staring down the Grim Reaper and was making a desperate play for divine evidence before his time ran out.

Bannister chuckled to himself. He had pocketed a lot of money from both Gutzman and the Church of England trying to hunt down the legend of the Manifest. Perhaps there was still more to be gained.

"Oscar, you know I've searched extensively both here and in England and have come up empty."

"There must be another path."

"We both came to the conclusion that it probably no longer exists, if it ever did in the first place."

"That was before this," Gutzman said, tapping the glass plate. "I've been at this game a long time. I can smell the link here. It is real and I know it. I've decided to devote myself and my resources to this and nothing else."

"It is a compelling clue," Bannister admitted.

"This will be," the Fat Man said in a tired voice, "the culmination of my life's quest. I hope you can help me reach it, Ridley."

"You can count on me."

Marta appeared again, this time reminding Gutzman of a pending doctor appointment. Bannister said good-bye and let himself out of the apartment. Leaving the hotel, he contemplated the papyrus scroll and whether Gutzman's assumptions could possibly be correct. The old collector did know his stuff, he had to admit. Of more concern to Bannister was formulating a means to profit from the Fat Man's new pursuit. Deep in thought, Bannister didn't notice a young man in a blue jumpsuit waiting beside his car.

"Mr. Bannister?" the youth inquired.

"Yes."

"Courier delivery, sir," he replied, handing Bannister a large, thin envelope.

Bannister slid into his car and locked the doors before opening the letter. Shaking out the contents, he just sat and shook his head when a first-class airline ticket to London plopped into his lap.

23

"Summer, over here!"

Stepping off the train from Great Yarmouth with a travel bag over her shoulder, Summer had to scan the crowded platform a moment before spotting Julie standing to one side, waving her hand in the air.

"Thanks for meeting me," she said, greeting the researcher with a hug. "I'm not sure I'd find my way out of here alone," she added, marveling at the massive covered rail yard of Liverpool Street Station in northeast London.

"It's actually pretty simple," Julie replied with a grin. "You just follow all the other rats out of the maze."

She led Summer past several station platforms and through the bustling terminal concourse to a nearby parking lot. There they climbed into a green Ford compact that resembled an overgrown insect.

"How was the voyage down to Yarmouth?" Julie asked as she navigated the car into the London traffic.

"Miserable. We caught a northerly storm front after leaving Scapa Flow and faced gale force winds during our entire run down the North Sea. I'm still feeling a little wobbly."

"I guess I should be thankful I was able to fly back from Scotland."

"So what's the latest on the mystery of the *Hampshire*'s

sinking?" Summer asked. "Have you established any connection with Lord Kitchener?"

"Just a very few loose threads, quite tenuous at best, I'm afraid. I checked the Admiralty's official inquiry into the sinking of the *Hampshire*, but it was a banal White Paper that simply blamed destruction on a German mine. I also examined the claim that the IRA may have planted a bomb on the ship, but it seems to be without merit."

"Any chance that the Germans could have planted a bomb?"

"There's absolutely no indication from known German records, so that seems unlikely as well. It was their belief that a mine from U-75 caused the sinking. Unfortunately, the U-boat's captain, Kurt Beitzen, didn't survive the war, so we have no official German account of the event."

"So that's two brick walls. Where are those loose threads that you were talking about?" Summer asked.

"Well, I carefully reviewed some of my documents on Kitchener and rechecked his military war records. Two unusual documents cropped up. In the late spring of 1916, he made a special request to the Army for two armed bodyguards for an unspecified reason. In that age, bodyguards were something of a rarity, reserved for perhaps only the King. The other item was a strange letter I found in his military files."

Stopping at a red light, she reached into a folder on the backseat and handed Summer a copy of the letter from Archbishop Davidson.

"Like I said, they are two flimsy items that probably mean nothing."

Summer quickly scanned the letter, wrinkling her brow at its contents.

"This Manifest he refers to . . . Is it some sort of Church document?"

"I really haven't a clue," Julie replied. "That's why our first stop is the Church of England's archives at Lambeth Palace. I've ordered up the Archbishop's personal records in hopes we might find something more substantial."

They crossed the River Thames over the London Bridge and drove into Lambeth, where Julie parked the green Ford near the palace. Summer absorbed the beauty of the ancient building that fronted the water, with Buckingham Palace visible across the river. They made their way to the Grand Hall, where they were escorted to the library's reading room. Summer noticed a thin, handsome man smile at them from a copy machine as they entered.

The archivist had a thick stack of folders waiting when Julie approached the desk.

"Here are the Archbishop's records. I'm afraid we had nothing on file related to Lord Kitchener," the young woman declared.

"Quite all right," Julie replied. "Thank you for searching."

The two women moved to a table and split the files and then began poring through the documents.

"The Archbishop was a rather prolific writer," Summer noted, impressed with the volume.

"Apparently so. This is his correspondence for just the first half of 1916."

As she attacked the file, Summer noticed the man at the copy machine gather some books and take a seat at the table directly behind her. Her nose detected a dose of cologne, musky but pleasing, which wafted from the man's direction. Taking a quick glance over her shoulder, she noticed he wore an antique-looking gold ring on his right hand.

She flipped through the letters quickly, finding them mostly dry pronouncements on budget and policy directed at the subordinate Bishops around Britain, along with their in-kind replies. After an hour, the women had both weeded through half of their piles.

"Here's a letter from Kitchener," Julie suddenly announced.

Summer peered anxiously across the table. "What does it say?"

"It appears to be a response to the Archbishop's letter, as it is dated just a few days later. It's short, so I'll read it to you:

> *Your Excellency,*
>
> *I regret that I am unable to comply with your recent request. The Manifest is a document of powerful historic consequence. It demands public exposure when the world is again at peace. I fear that in your hands, the Church would only bury the revelation, in order to protect its existing theological tenets.*
>
> *I beg of you to recall your subordinates, who continue to persecute me ceaselessly.*
>
> *Your obedient servant,*
> *H.H. Kitchener*

"Whatever could this Manifest be?" Summer wondered.

"I don't know, but Kitchener clearly held a copy of it and felt it was important."

"Obviously the Church did, too."

Summer heard the man behind her clear his throat, then turn and lean over their table.

"Pardon me for overhearing, but did you say Kitchener?" he asked with a disarming smile.

"Yes," Summer replied. "My friend Julie is writing a biography of the field marshal."

"My name is Baker," Ridley Bannister lied, obtaining introductions in return. "Might I suggest that a better source of Lord Kitchener historical documents may be found at the Imperial War Museum?"

"Kind of you to say, Mr. Baker," Julie replied, "but I've already exhaustively searched their materials."

"Which brings you here?" he asked. "I wouldn't expect a military hero's influence to stretch very far into the Church of England."

"Just tracing some correspondence he had with the Archbishop of Canterbury," she replied.

"Then this would indeed be the place," Bannister said, smiling broadly.

"What is the nature of your research?" Summer asked him.

"Just a bit of hobby research. I'm investigating a few old abbey sites that were destroyed during Henry VIII's purge of the monasteries." He held up a dusty book entitled *Abbey Plans of Olde England*, then turned again toward Julie.

"Have you uncovered any new secrets about Kitchener?"

"That honor belongs to Summer. She helped prove that the ship he was sunk on may have had a planted explosive aboard."

"The *Hampshire*?" he said. "I thought it was proven that she had struck a German mine."

"The blast hole indicates that the explosion originated inside the ship," Summer replied.

"Perhaps the old rumor of the IRA planting a bomb aboard may have been true," he said.

"You know the story behind that?" Julie asked.

"Yes," Bannister replied. "The *Hampshire* was sent to Belfast for a refit in early 1916. Some believe a bomb was inserted into the ship there and detonated months later."

"You seem to know a lot about the *Hampshire*," Summer commented.

"I'm just an obsessive World War One history buff," Bannister replied. "So, where is your research taking you from here?"

"We'll be going to Kent for another pass through Kitchener's personal papers housed at Broome Park," Julie said.

"Have you seen his last diary?"

"Why, no," Julie said, surprised at the question. "It has always been presumed to have been lost."

Bannister looked down at his watch. "Oh my, look at the time. I'm afraid I must run. It was a delight to meet you ladies," he said, rising from the table and offering a faint bow. "May your quest for historical knowledge meet with profound fulfillment."

He quickly returned his book to the librarian, then waved good-bye as he left the reading room.

"Quite a handsome fellow," Julie gushed with a grin.

"Yes," Summer agreed. "He was certainly knowledgeable about Kitchener and the *Hampshire*."

"That's true. I wouldn't think too many people would be aware that Kitchener's last diary went missing."

"Wouldn't it have gone down with him on the ship?"

"Nobody knows. He traditionally captured his writings in small bound books that covered the period of a single year. His writings from 1916 were never found, so it's always been presumed that he carried it with him on the *Hampshire*."

"What do you make of Mr. Baker's claim that the IRA may have bombed the *Hampshire*?"

"It's one of many outlandish assertions that arose after the sinking that I've found has no historical justification. It's difficult to believe that the *Hampshire* would have been carrying a bomb aboard for over six months. The IRA, or Irish Volunteers as they were known at the time, certainly wouldn't have known that far in advance that Kitchener would set foot on the ship. They didn't actually become a very militant group until the Easter Rising in April of 1916, well after the *Hampshire* had left Belfast. More telling is the fact that they never actually claimed responsibility for the sinking."

"Then I guess we keep digging," Summer said, opening up a new folder of the Archbishop's papers.

They worked for another hour before the stacks grew thin. Nearing the bottom of her last folder, Summer suddenly sat upright when she read a short letter from a Bishop in Portsmouth. She read it a second time before passing it over to Julie.

"Take a look at this," she said.

"'The parcel has been delivered and the messenger sent away,'" Julie said, reading the letter aloud. "'The item of interest shall cease to be a concern within 72 hours.' Signed, Bishop Lowery, Portsmouth Diocese."

Julie set the letter down and gave Summer a blank look. "I'm afraid I don't see the relevancy," she said.

"Look at the date."

Julie gazed at the top of the letter. "June 2, 1916. Three days before the *Hampshire* sank," she said in a surprised voice.

"It would seem," Summer said quietly, "that the plot has thickened."

24

After exiting the library, Ridley Bannister made his way across the Lambeth Palace grounds to a small brick building adjacent to the main living quarters. Entering through an unmarked door, he stepped into a cramped office, where a handful of men in security uniforms stared at video surveillance monitors or worked at desk computers. Ignoring the quizzical look from a man seated near the door, Bannister stepped toward a private office in the rear and walked through its open door.

A falcon-eyed man with greasy hair was seated at a desk watching a live video feed on his computer. Bannister could see the figures of Julie and Summer seated at a table in the reading room. The man looked up, shooting Bannister a disappointed look.

"Bannister, there you are. You were supposed to check in with me before the ladies arrived. Now you've blown your cover."

Bannister slid into a wooden chair facing the desk. "Sorry, old boy, they forgot my wake-up call at the Savoy this morning. I do want to thank you for the airline tickets, though. Glad you remembered first class this time."

The Archbishop of Canterbury's chief of security ground his teeth in contempt.

"You did purge the files before they were turned over

to them?" he asked, motioning toward his computer screen.

"I've been through those files before, Judkins," Bannister said, picking a piece of lint off his jacket. "There's nothing incriminating in those files."

Judkins's face turned red. "You had orders to review and clean those files."

"Orders? Orders, you say? Have I unknowingly been conscripted into the Archbishop's private army?"

There had been an immediate dislike between the two men the instant they had met, and the feelings only festered over time. But Judkins was Bannister's appointed contact, and there was little either man could do about it. The archaeologist pushed the line with Judkins as far as he dared without jeopardizing his contractual arrangements with the Church.

"You are an employee of the Archbishop and you will obey his requests accordingly," the security chief responded, his eyes aglow.

"I am nothing of the sort," Bannister retorted. "I am a simple mercenary for historical truth. While it may be true that the Archbishop has enlisted my services from time to time, I am under no obligation to 'follow orders' or even bow or curtsy in the esteemed Archbishop's general direction."

Judkins withheld responding, staring silently at Bannister while he waited for his blood pressure to decrease. When his face finally lost its red bluster, he spoke in a direct tone.

"While it certainly wouldn't be my choice, the Archbishop has elected to retain your services to inform and advise him of historical discoveries, particularly in the Middle East, that may have a bearing on existing Church doctrine. This alleged Manifest, and its prior association with the Church, has been deemed extremely sensitive. We, I mean the Archbishop, needs to know why this Cambridge researcher is inquiring into the records of Archbishop Davidson and at what risk to the Church."

Bannister smiled thinly at Judkins's forced deference.

"Julie Goodyear is a historian from Cambridge who has written several highly regarded biographies on leading figures of the nineteenth century. She is currently writing a bio on Lord Kitchener. Miss Goodyear and the American woman, Summer Pitt, have apparently discovered that Kitchener's ship, the *Hampshire*, was destroyed by an internal explosion. They seem to think there may be some remote connection to the late Archbishop Davidson."

Judkins physically paled at the news.

"My dear Judkins, is there something wrong?"

"No," the security chief replied with a violent shake of his head. "What about this Manifest?"

"The Archbishop knows that I made a diligent search for the document several years ago. At a considerable cost, I might add," he said with a wink. "I am relatively certain that it vanished along with Kitchener on the *Hampshire*."

"Yes, that is the Archbishop's understanding. However, there may be some related historical events that could prove, shall we say, troublesome to the Church and embarrassing to the Archbishop. I want you on those two women now."

"You want me?" Bannister replied, raising a brow.

"The Archbishop wants you," Judkins replied angrily. "Track them closely and extinguish things if you have to before they become a problem."

"I'm an archaeologist, not an assassin."

"You know what to do. Just handle it. You've got my number."

"Yes. And you've got my number?" Bannister asked, rising to his feet. "The number of my Bermuda bank account, that is?"

"Yes," Judkins grumbled. "Now, get out."

The security chief could only shake his head as Bannister bowed to him gracefully, then marched out of his office like he owned it.

25

The bright morning Mediterranean sun had already begun baking the *Aegean Explorer*'s deck when Rudi Gunn stepped into the sunlight with the day's first mug of coffee. He was startled to see an unfamiliar stretch of Turkish coastline just a mile or two off the ship's side railing. He heard the whir of an outboard motor in the distance and squinted until he spotted the ship's Zodiac bounding over the waves toward shore.

His groggy mind suddenly focused on the research project at hand, and he scurried to the stern of the ship. Making his way past a white submersible, he was disappointed to find the autonomous underwater vehicle lying securely in a padded rack. A large torpedo-shaped device, the robotic AUV contained a variety of sensors used to sample the water as it ran free of the ship. When he had staggered to bed six hours earlier, the *Explorer* was tracking the AUV as it surveyed a large grid ten miles from shore.

Gulping a large swallow of coffee, he turned and made his way forward, then climbed two flights of stairs to the bridge. There he found Pitt studying a coastal chart with the ship's captain, Bruce Kenfield.

"Good morning, Rudi," Pitt greeted. "You're up early."

"I could feel the engines throttle down from my bunk," Gunn replied. "How come we pulled off-line?"

"Kemal received word that his wife was in a traffic accident. It's apparently not serious, but we put him ashore so that he could go check on her."

Kemal was a marine biologist with the Turkish Environment Ministry who had been assigned to the NUMA vessel to monitor and assist with the water-sampling project.

"That's unfortunate," Gunn said. "After the Zodiac returns, how long will it take us to return to the grid and resume operations?"

Pitt smiled and shook his head. "We technically can't resume the survey until Kemal or a replacement is on board the ship. Our invite from the Turkish government specified that a representative from the Environment Ministry must be aboard at all times while we are conducting survey work in Turkish waters. At this point, it looks like we might be down for three or four days."

"We are already behind schedule. First our sensor flooded and now this. We may have to extend the project in order to complete the areas we agreed to survey."

"So be it."

Gunn noticed that Pitt seemed to share none of the frustration that he was feeling. It was uncharacteristic for a man that he knew hated to leave things unfinished.

"Since you returned from Istanbul, we've only had two full days of surveying on the new grid," Gunn said. "Now we go idle again, and you're not even upset. What gives?"

"It's simple, Rudi," Pitt replied. "Halting work on the algae bloom project means resuming work on an Ottoman shipwreck excavation," he said with a wink.

*

Less than four hours after the Zodiac was hoisted back aboard, the *Aegean Queen* reached Chios, dropping anchor a hundred yards from the site of the Ottoman shipwreck. Little time had been spent examining the site after Pitt and Giordino's initial dive, barely allowing the ship's underwater archaeologist, Rodney Zeibig, the chance to stake an aluminum grid over the exposed portions of the wreck.

Zeibig hastily trained a handful of scuba-qualified scientists in the art of underwater survey and documentation, then coordinated a careful examination of the wreck. Pitt, Giordino, and even Gunn took a hand in the dive rotation, photographing, measuring, and excavating test pits at various locations around the site. A small amount of artifacts, mostly ceramics and a few iron fittings, were retrieved as skeletal fragments of the wreck were exposed.

Pitt stood near the stern rail of the *Aegean Explorer* eyeing a growing pattern of whitecaps that dotted the sea under a stiffening westerly breeze. An empty Zodiac bounced wildly on the waves, moored to a nearby buoy that was fixed to the wreck site. A pair of divers suddenly poked to the surface, then bellied their way into the inflatable boat. One of the men released the mooring line while the other started the outboard engine, then they quickly raced to the side of the research ship. Pitt lowered a cable over the side and helped hoist the Zodiac onto the deck with the two men still seated in it.

Rudi Gunn and Rod Zeibig hopped out and began stripping off their wet suits.

"It's turned a bit bouncy out there," remarked Zeibig, a buoyant man with bright blue eyes and salt-and-pepper hair.

"I've passed the word that we're halting dive operations until the winds settle down," Pitt said. "The weather forecast indicates that things should be calm by morning."

"A good idea," the archaeologist replied, "although I think Rudi will be on pins and needles until he gets back to the wreck."

"Find something of interest?"

Gunn nodded with an excited look in his eyes. "I was digging in grid C-1 and touched a large carved stone. I only uncovered a small corner of it before our bottom time ran out. I think it may possibly be some sort of monolith or stele."

"That could add a clue to the ship's identity," Pitt said.

"I just hope we don't have to share in her discovery," Zeibig said, nodding toward the starboard rail.

Pounding over the waves just over two miles away was a high-performance motor yacht headed directly for the *Aegean Explorer*. It was Italian built, with wraparound smoked-glass windows and a large open stern deck. A red Turkish flag with white crescent and star flew from a mast, along with a smaller red flag that featured a single gold crescent. Though it was far smaller than a Monte Carlo show yacht, Pitt still could see that it was an expensive luxury boat. The three men watched as the yacht closed to within a half mile before slowing to a halt, where it bobbed on the unsettled waters.

"I wouldn't be too concerned about your wreck, Rod," Gunn said. "They don't exactly look like they're here to perform excavation work."

"Probably somebody just nosing about to see what a research ship is doing parked out here," Pitt said.

"Or perhaps we're blocking the view of someone's villa on shore," Gunn muttered.

Pitt assumed that no one besides Ruppé knew of the location of the wreck site. Perhaps he had already notified the Turkish Ministry of Culture, he considered. But then he remembered that Ruppé's office had been burglarized and his chart to the site stolen with the artifacts. His concern was diverted when he heard his name shouted from the forward part of the ship. He turned to see Giordino hanging his torso out of a work bay door beneath the bridge.

"Some info from Istanbul just came in for you over the wire," Giordino shouted.

"Speak of the devil," Pitt muttered. "Be right there," he yelled back, then turned to the other two men.

"I bet that is Dr. Ruppé's analysis of our earlier artifacts from the wreck."

"I'd like to see his results," Zeibig said.

The two divers quickly changed clothes, then met up with Pitt and Giordino in the small bay, which housed several computers linked to a satellite communications system. Giordino handed Pitt a multipage printout, then sat down at one of the computers.

"Dr. Ruppé also e-mailed a couple of photographs with the report," he said, tapping at a keyboard to open an electronic file. A close-up image of a gold coin filled the computer screen.

Pitt quickly scanned the report then passed it to Zeibig.

"Are we still looking at an Ottoman wreck?" Gunn asked.

"Almost certainly," Pitt replied. "Dr. Ruppé found a representative coin from a mint in Syria that he believes is identical to one of the coins in Al's lockbox. It dates to around 1570. Unfortunately, Ruppé says he had to base the comparison on memory, since the coins were stolen from his office."

"I'd have to agree with him," Giordino said. "It looks like the same coin to me."

"The mint marks were known to have been used between 1560 and 1580," Zeibig said, reading from the report.

"So we know the wreck is no older than 1560," Gunn said. "A shame the whole box of coins was taken, as that might have zeroed things in a bit more."

"The other dating clue was the ceramic box that held the crown," Pitt said. "As Loren and I discovered at the Blue Mosque, the particular design indicates the tiles came from the kilns of Iznik."

Giordino clicked to the next few photographs, which showed a number of known tile samples from Iznik.

"Unfortunately, the ceramic box was also taken from Ruppé's office, so again we're working from memory."

"His report indicates that the tiles incorporate patterns and colors that were popular with Iznik ceramics in the late sixteenth century," Zeibig noted.

"At least we have some consistency," Giordino noted.

"I can also attest that from what I saw of the wreck's framing, it corresponds with known sixteenth-century vessel construction in the Mediterranean," Zeibig added, looking up from the report.

"That's three for three," Gunn said.

"Which brings us to King Al's crown," Pitt replied with raised inflection.

Giordino pulled up a new photograph, which showed a detailed image of the gold crown. The seabed encrustations had all been cleaned from it, leaving a sparkling headpiece that looked as if it had just left the goldsmith.

"Thank goodness my baby was kept safe in Dr. Ruppé's vault," Giordino said.

"Dr. Ruppé calls this one of the most significant finds in Turkish waters, as well as one of the most mysterious," Pitt said. "Despite considerable research, he was unable to utilize the crown's shape and size as a clue in identifying its provenance. However, after a thorough cleaning, he clarified the faint engraving on the inside of the band."

Giordino brought up an enlarged photo of the crown while Zeibig thumbed to the description in the report.

"The engraving is in Latin," Zeibig reported with a quizzical look. "Ruppé translated the inscription as follows: 'To Artrius, in gratitude for capturing the relic pirates. —Constantine.'"

"Ruppé found records of a Roman Senator named Artrius. It so happens that he lived during the rule of Constantine," Pitt said.

"Constantine the Great?" Gunn blurted. "The Roman Emperor? Why, he lived a thousand years earlier."

The room fell silent as everyone stared at the photographic image. Nobody had expected such a disconnect with the shipwreck's other artifacts, particularly by something as remarkable as the gold crown. And yet there was no clue as to why it was aboard. Pitt inched away from the monitor and stood up, finally breaking the silence.

"I hate to say it," he said with a grin, "but I guess this means that King Al has been transferred to the Roman Legion."

26

Broome Park was a characteristic old English manor. Purchased by Kitchener in 1911, it featured a towering Jacobean-style brick house built during the rule of Charles I, surrounded by 476 acres of lush, parklike grounds. During his short occupancy, Kitchener labored extensively to upgrade the estate's gardens, while commissioning an elaborate fountain or two. But like top hat and tails or horse and carriage, Broome Park's original grace and charm was now mostly reserved for an earlier age.

Sixty miles southeast of London, Julie turned off at Dover and followed the short road to the estate. Summer was surprised to see a foursome playing golf on a stretch of grass just beyond a sign welcoming them to Broome Park.

"It's an all-too-familiar tale around Britain," Julie explained. "Historic manors are passed down from generation to generation until one day the heir wakes up and realizes he can't afford the taxes and maintenance. First the surrounding acreage is sold off, then more desperate measures are eventually taken. Some are converted to bed-and-breakfasts, others leased to corporations for conferencing or used as outdoor concert venues."

"Or even converted into golf courses," Summer said.

"Precisely. Broome Park has probably suffered the worst of all fates. Most of the manor has been sold off as a time-share and overnight lodging, while the surrounding grounds have been converted into a golf course. I'm sure Horatio Herbert is looking down in horror."

"Is the estate still in the hands of Kitchener's heirs?"

"Kitchener was a lifelong bachelor, but he bequeathed the estate to his nephew Toby. Toby's son Aldrich now runs the place, though he's getting on in years."

Julie parked the car in a wide lot, and they walked to the main entrance, passing an ill-kept rose garden along the way. Summer was more impressed when they entered the main foyer, which showcased a large cut-glass chandelier and a towering oil painting of the old man himself, his stern gray eyes seemingly imposing their will even from the flat canvas.

A wiry white-haired man was seated at a desk reading a book, but he looked up and smiled when he noted Julie coming in.

"Hello, Miss Goodyear," he said, springing up from the desk. "I received your message that you would be coming by this morning."

"You're looking well, Aldrich. Keeping the manor full?"

"Business is quite nice, thank you. Had a couple of short-term visitors check in already today."

"This is my friend Summer Pitt, who's helping me with my research."

"Nice to meet you, Miss Pitt," he said, extending a hand. "You probably want to get right to work, so why don't you follow me on back?"

He led them through a side door into a private wing that encompassed his own living quarters. They walked through a large sitting area filled with artifacts from North Africa and the Middle East, all acquired by Kitchener during his Army years stationed in the region. Aldrich then opened another door and ushered them into a wood-paneled study. Summer noticed that one entire wall was lined with tall mahogany filing cabinets.

"I would have thought you'd have all of Uncle Herbert's files memorized by now," Aldrich said to Julie with a smile.

"I've certainly spent enough time with them," Julie agreed. "We just need to review some of his personal correspondence in the months preceding his death."

"Those will be in the last cabinet on the right." He turned and walked toward the doorway. "I'll be at the front desk, should you require any assistance."

"Thank you, Aldrich."

The two women quickly dove into the file cabinet. Summer was glad to see the correspondence was of a more personal and interesting nature than the records at the Imperial War Museum. She slowly read through dozens of letters from Kitchener's relatives, along with what seemed an endless trail of correspondence from building contractors, who were being cajoled and pushed by Kitchener to complete refurbishments on Broome Park.

"Look how cute this is," she said, holding up a card of a hand-drawn butterfly sent from Kitchener's three-year-old niece.

"The gruff old general was quite close with his sister and brothers and their children," Julie said.

"Looking at an individual's personal correspondence is

a great way to get to know him, isn't it?" Summer said.

"It really is. A shame that the handwritten letter has become a lost art form in the age of e-mail."

They searched for nearly two hours before Julie sat up in her chair.

"My word, it didn't go down on the *Hampshire*," she blurted.

"What are you talking about?"

"His diary," Julie replied with wide eyes. "Here, take a look at this."

It was a letter from an Army sergeant named Wingate, dated a few days before the *Hampshire* was sunk. Summer read with interest how the sergeant expressed his regret at being unable to accompany Kitchener on his pending voyage and wished the field marshal well on his important trip. It was a brief postscript at the bottom of the page that made her stiffen.

"'P.S. Received your diary. Will keep it safe till your return,'" she read aloud.

"How could I have missed it?" Julie lamented.

"It's an otherwise innocuous letter, written in very messy handwriting," Summer said. "I would have skimmed past it, too. But it's a wonderful discovery. How exciting, his last diary may indeed still exist."

"But it's not here or in the official records. What was that soldier's name again?"

"Sergeant Norman Wingate."

"I know that name but can't place it," Julie replied, racking her brain.

A high-pitched squeak echoed from the other room, slowly growing louder in intensity. They looked to the doorway to see Aldrich entering the study pushing a tea cart with a bad wheel.

"Pardon the interruption, but I thought you might enjoy a tea break," he said, pouring cups for each of them.

"That's very kind of you, Mr. Kitchener," Summer said, taking one of the hot cups.

"Aldrich, do you happen to recall an acquaintance of Lord Kitchener by the name of Norman Wingate?" Julie asked.

Aldrich rubbed his brow as his eyes darted toward the ceiling in thought.

"Wasn't he one of Uncle Herbert's bodyguards?" he asked.

"That's it," Julie said, suddenly remembering. "Wingate and Stearns were his two armed guards approved by the Prime Minister."

"Yes," Aldrich said. "The other fellow . . . Stearns, you say his name was? He went down on the *Hampshire* with Uncle Herbert. But Wingate didn't. He was sick, I believe, and didn't make the trip. I recall my father often lunching with him many years later. The chap apparently suffered a bit of guilt for surviving the incident."

"Wingate wrote that he had the field marshal's last diary in his possession. Do you know if he gave it to your father?"

"No, that would have been here with the rest of his papers, I'm certain. Wingate probably kept it as a memento of the old man."

A faint buzzer sounded from the opposite end of the house. "Well, someone is at the front desk. Enjoy the tea," he said, then shuffled out of the study.

Summer reread the letter then examined the return address.

"Wingate wrote this from Dover," she said. "Isn't that just down the road?"

"Yes, less than ten miles," Julie replied.

"Maybe Norman has some relatives in the city that might know something."

"Might be a long shot, but I suppose it's worth a try."

With the aid of Aldrich's computer and a Kent Regional Phone Directory, the women assembled a list of all the Wingates living in the area. They then took turns phoning each name, hoping to locate a descendant of Norman Wingate.

The phone queries, however, produced no leads. After an hour, Summer hung up and crossed out the last name on the list with a shake of her head.

"Over twenty listings and not even a hint," she said with disappointment.

"The closest I had was a fellow who thought Norman might have been a great-uncle, but he had nothing else to offer," Julie replied. She looked down at her watch.

"I suppose we should go check into our hotel. We can finish the files in the morning."

"We're not staying at Broome Park?"

"I booked us in a hotel in Canterbury, near the cathedral. I thought you'd want to see it. Besides," she said, her voice dropping to a whisper, "the food here isn't very good."

Summer laughed, then stood and stretched her arms. "I won't tell Aldrich. I'm wondering if we might be able to make one stop along the way first."

"Where would that be?" Julie asked with a quizzical look.

Summer picked up the letter from Wingate and read the return address. "Fourteen Dorchester Lane, Dover," she said with a wry smile.

The motorcyclist slipped on a black helmet with matching visor, then peeked around the back end of a gardener's truck. He patiently waited as Julie and Summer stepped out the front door of Broome Park. Careful not to let himself be seen, he watched as they climbed into their car across the parking lot and then drove down the road to the exit. Starting his black Kawasaki motorcycle, he eased toward the lane, keeping a wide buffer between himself and the departing car. Watching Julie turn toward Dover, he let a few cars pass, then followed suit, keeping the little green car just ahead in his sights.

27

Modern Dover is a bustling port city best known for its ferry to Calais and its world-famous white chalk cliffs up the easterly coastline. Julie drove into the historic city center before pulling over and asking for directions. They found Dorchester Lane a few blocks from the waterfront, a quiet residential street lined with old brick row houses constructed in the 1880s. Parking the car under a towering birch tree, the women walked up the cleanly swept steps of number fourteen and rang the bell. After a long pause, the door was pulled open by a disheveled woman in her twenties who held a sleeping baby in her arms.

"Oh, I'm terribly sorry to bother you," Julie whispered. "I hope we didn't wake the baby."

The woman shook her head and smiled. "This one could sleep through a U2 concert."

Julie quietly introduced the two of them. "We're seeking information on a man who lived at this address quite some time ago. His name was Norman Wingate."

"That was my grandfather," the woman replied, perking up. "I'm Ericka Norris. Wingate was my mother's maiden name."

Julie looked at Summer and smiled in disbelief.

"Please, won't you come in?" Norris offered.

The young woman led them into a modest yet warmly

decorated family room, easing herself into a rocking chair with the sleeping baby.

"You have a lovely home," Julie said.

"My mum grew up in this house. I think she said grandfather bought it just before World War One. She lived here most of her life, as she and Dad purchased the home from him."

"Is she still alive?"

"Yes, although we had to move her into the old folks' home a few months back so she could receive proper nursing care. She insisted that we move in here when the baby was on the way. More room for us, at least."

"Your mum might still be able to help us out," Julie said. "We're looking for some old records from the war that your grandfather might have had in his possession."

Norris thought for a moment. "Mum did end up with all of my grandparents' belongings," she said. "I know she got rid of most of it over the years. But there are some old books and photographs in the nursery that you are welcome to have a look at."

She cautiously led them up a flight of stairs and into a pale blue room with a wooden crib on one wall. She gently laid the baby in the crib, eliciting a slight whimper from him before he drifted back to sleep.

"Over here are my grandfather's things," she whispered, stepping to a high wooden shelf. Old clothbound books filled the shelves, fronted by black-and-white photographs of men in uniform. Julie picked up one photograph showing a young soldier standing next to Kitchener.

"Is this your grandfather?"

"Yes, with Lord Kitchener. He headed up the entire Army during the war, did you know?"

Julie smiled. "Yes. He's actually the reason we are here."

"Grandfather often spoke about how he would have died along with Kitchener on his ship that sank during a voyage to Russia. But his father was gravely ill, and Kitchener had excused him from the trip."

"Ericka, we found a letter from your grandfather indicating that Kitchener had sent him his personal diary for safekeeping," Julie said. "We're hoping to locate that diary."

"If grandfather kept it, it would be here. Please, have a look."

Julie had read Kitchener's earlier diaries, which had been kept in small hardbound books. Scanning the shelves, she froze when she spotted a similarly bound book on the top shelf.

"Summer . . . can you reach that small blue book up high?" she asked nervously.

Stretching to her toes, Summer reached up and pulled the book down and handed it to Julie. The historian's heart began to beat faster when she noticed there was no title printed on the spine or front cover. Slowly opening the cover, she turned to a lined title page. In neat hand-written script was written:

Journal of HHK
Jan. 1, 1916

"That's it," Summer blurted, staring at the page.

Julie turned the page and began reading the first entries, which described efforts by the author to boost compensation for new military recruits. She soon flipped to the last written entry, located halfway through the book, which was dated June 1, 1916. She then closed the book and looked hopefully at Norris.

"This lost diary has long been sought by historians of Kitchener," she said quietly.

"If it means that much to you, then go ahead and take it," Norris replied, waving her hand at the book as if it were of no consequence. "No one around here is likely to be reading it anytime soon," she added, smiling toward her sleeping baby.

"I will donate it to the Kitchener collection at Broome Park, if you should ever change your mind about that."

"I'm sure Grandfather would be thrilled to know that there are still people around with an interest in Kitchener and 'the Great War,' as he used to call it."

Julie and Summer thanked the young mother for the diary, then tiptoed down the stairs and out of the house.

"Your detour to Dover certainly produced an unexpected bit of good luck," Julie said with a smile as they stepped to her car.

"Persistence leads to luck every time," Summer replied.

Excited with their discovery, Julie was oblivious to the black motorcycle that followed them off Dorchester Lane and onto the road to Canterbury, holding a steady pace several cars behind. As Julie drove, Summer skimmed through the diary, reading passages of interest out loud.

"Listen to this," she said. "'March third. Received an

unexpected letter from the Archbishop of Canterbury requesting a private viewing of the Manifest. The cat has finally escaped the bag, though how, I do not know. The late Dr. Worthington had assured me his secrecy in life, but perhaps he has failed me in death. No matter. I declined the Archbishop's invitation while risking his ire, in hopes that the matter can be deferred until the time when we are once again at peace.'"

"Dr. Worthington, you say?" Julie asked. "He was a well-known Cambridge archaeologist around the turn of the last century. He carried out several high-profile excavations in Palestine, if my memory serves."

"That would seem an odd connection," Summer replied, skimming more pages. "Kitchener was right about upsetting the Archbishop, though. Two weeks later, he has this to say: 'Called upon this morning by Bishop Lowery of Portsmouth, on behalf of Archbishop Davidson. He eloquently expressed a strong desire for me to donate the Manifest to the Church of England for the good of all mankind. He failed to elaborate, however, on the Church's intended use of the document. From the earliest moments, my kindred hopes were for a benevolent quest for the truth. It is now regrettably apparent that my Church is reacting in fear, with suppression and concealment their primary aim. In their hands, the Manifest might disappear for all posterity. This I cannot allow, and I informed Bishop Lowery as much, to his extreme disappointment. Though now is not the time, I believe that at the conclusion of this great conflict, a public release of the Manifest will offer a spark of hope for all mankind.'"

"He certainly makes this Manifest sound profound," Julie said. "And now Bishop Lowery has made an appearance. His cryptic letter to Davidson in June suddenly becomes more interesting."

"Kitchener doesn't provide much detail, but his anguish with the Church keeps growing," Summer said. "In April, he writes, 'Plans for the summer offensive in France are nearly complete. The constant harassment from the Archbishop's minions is becoming overwhelming. P.M. has approved my request for a security detail. Thankfully, I didn't have to specify why.'"

"So our friends Wingate and Stearns finally appear on the scene," Julie noted.

Summer thumbed faster through the pages as they approached the outskirts of Canterbury.

"In his April and May passages, he is bogged down with war planning and an occasional weekend away with relatives at Broome Park. Wait, though, listen to this. 'May fifteenth. Received another threatening call from Bishop Lowery. With his nefarious manner, I believe the country would be better served if he headed the Directorate of Military Intelligence rather than the Portsmouth Diocese.' A day later, he writes, 'Caught in a streetside confrontation by an anonymous C of E member who demanded the Manifest. Corporal Stearns disposed of the renegade without further incident. I'm beginning to regret ever discovering the blasted thing back in 'seventy-seven . . . or letting Dr. Worthington decipher it last year. Who would have imagined that an old slip of papyrus sold by a beggar during our survey of Palestine would have such consequence?'"

Summer turned to the next page. "Does that date mean anything to you?"

Julie contemplated her earlier writings on Kitchener. "That was well before his famous heroics in Khartoum. In 1877, I believe he was stationed in the Middle East. That's about the time that he took over an Army survey party in northern Palestine, as part of the Palestine Exploration Fund established by Queen Victoria."

"He worked as a surveyor?"

"Yes, and he took over the field survey team when its commander fell ill. They did quite top-notch work, despite being threatened on several occasions by local Arab tribesmen. Much of the Palestine survey data was in fact still being utilized as recently as the nineteen sixties. But as for Kitchener, he was traveling throughout the Middle East at that point, so there's no telling where he specifically may have acquired it. Unfortunately, he didn't begin keeping a diary until many years later."

"It must be very old if it is a papyrus document." Summer neared the end of the diary and halted at a late May entry.

"Julie, this is it," she gasped. "He writes, 'Another dire warning received from the Archbishop. I daresay they seem to be stopping at nothing in obtaining their desired wants. I have little doubt they haven't already slipped into Broome Park for a look around. My response will hopefully put them at bay. I told them that I am taking the Manifest to Russia and placing it on loan with the Orthodox Church in Petrograd for safekeeping until the war's end. Imagine their chagrin if they knew I actually safeguarded it with Sally, under the watchful eyes of Emily, till my return.' "

"So he didn't take it to Russia," Julie said, her voice crackling with excitement.

"Apparently not. Listen to this. On June first, he writes, 'My last entry for now. Prying eyes seem to be everywhere. I feel an uneasy dread about the trip at hand, but it is vital that the Russians stay with us and not negotiate a unilateral armistice with Germany. Will pass this diary to Corporal Wingate for safekeeping. H.H.K.'"

"I've read other accounts that he was uneasy when he departed and seemed to be dreading the trip," said Julie. "He must have had a premonition."

"Probably so or he wouldn't have left the diary behind. But the bigger question is, who was Sally?"

"She must have been someone trustworthy, but I don't believe I've ever run across anyone named Sally in my research on Kitchener."

"Not an old secretary, or perhaps the wife of a fellow officer?" Summer asked.

Julie shook her head.

"How about a pet name for one of his aides?"

"No, I should think there would be references in his correspondence somewhere, but I don't recall seeing it."

"It doesn't seem right that he would trust a casual acquaintance with the document. How about the other name, Emily?"

Julie thought for a moment as she waited to enter a traffic roundabout that led to downtown Canterbury.

"I can recall two Emilys, actually. Kitchener's maternal grandmother was named Emily, though she was long dead by 1916. Then there was his oldest brother, who had a granddaughter named Emily. I'll have to check my genealogy records when we get to the hotel to see when she was born. Her father, Kitchener's nephew, was named Hal. He used to visit Broome Park rather regularly."

"So the younger Emily would actually be a cousin to Aldrich?" Summer asked.

"Yes, that would be correct. Perhaps we can talk to Aldrich about her in the morning."

Julie had reached the city center and drove Summer slowly past Canterbury's famed historic cathedral. A few blocks away, she turned into the Chaucer Hotel, one of the city's modest old inns. After checking into neighboring rooms, the women met for dinner in the hotel restaurant. Summer devoured a large plate of fish and chips, not realizing how hungry the day's excursion had made her. Julie nearly matched her appetite, pushing away a plate cleaned of pasta.

"If you'd like to walk the meal off, we can take a stroll over to the cathedral," Julie offered.

"I appreciate the tour-guide offer," Summer replied, "but, to be honest, I'd like to spend some more time analyzing Kitchener's diary."

Julie beamed at the reply. "I was hoping you'd say that. I've been anxious to study the writings since we checked in."

"There's a quiet lounge off the lobby. How about we order some tea and take another pass through the diary there? I'll take notes while you read this time," she added with a smile.

"That would be lovely," Julie agreed. "I'll go get the diary and a notebook from my room and meet you there."

She climbed the stairs to the second floor and entered her room, then hesitated when she noticed her work papers strewn across the bed. The door suddenly slammed shut behind her as the lights were flicked off. A shadow approached as she started to scream, but a gloved hand quickly covered her mouth before her voice could resonate. Another arm slipped around her waist and pulled her tight against the assailant, who seemed to be wearing padded clothing. Then a deep voice grunted in her ear.

"Don't make a sound or you'll never live to see the dawn."

28

Summer waited in the lounge twenty minutes before phoning Julie's room. Receiving no answer, she waited another five minutes, then went upstairs and knocked on her door. Her concern heightened when she noticed a "Do Not Disturb" sign dangling from the doorknob. She saw a night maid was working her way down the corridor turning down beds and convinced her to check Julie's room. Opening the door and turning on the light, the maid gasped in shock.

Julie was seated on the floor with her arms behind her back and tied to the bed frame with a sheet. Another sheet was wrapped around her ankles, while a pillowcase covered her head. A desperate wiggling of her arms and legs revealed that she was very much alive.

Summer burst past the maid and ripped the pillowcase off Julie's head. Julie's wide eyes looked at Summer in relief as the American untied a knotted stocking that was wrapped around Julie's head in a gag.

"Are you hurt?" Summer asked, moving on to untie the sheet binding Julie's arms.

"No . . . I'm okay," she stuttered, fighting back tears of fear and relief rolled into one. "Just a little scared."

She quickly regained her composure while finding a steady voice.

"He was actually quite gentle. I don't think he meant to harm me."

"It was just one man?"

Julie nodded.

"Did you see what he looked like?"

"No, I'm afraid not. I think he was hiding in the bathroom, and I walked right past. He turned the lights off, then threw that pillowcase over my head. I don't have a clue what he looked like. I just remember that his clothes seemed lumpy or padded."

The hotel manager soon arrived, followed by a pair of Canterbury police officers. They carefully searched the room, then took a detailed report from Julie, Summer, and the maid. The historian had left her purse in the room, but it wasn't taken by the thief. Julie looked at Summer with dread when she realized that the only item missing from the room was Kitchener's diary.

"Typical hotel burglary attempt," Summer heard one of the officers tell the hotel manager out in the corridor. "She obviously surprised him in the room, and he decided to tie her up before fleeing. I don't have to tell you that there's a slim chance of catching the bugger."

"Yes, unfortunately I've seen it before," the manager replied. "Thank you, Detective."

The hotel manager returned to the room and apologized profusely to Julie, promising to have increased security on the floor all night. After he left, Summer offered to let Julie sleep in her room.

"Yes, if you don't mind, I think I'd be much more comfortable," she said. "Let me grab my toothbrush."

Julie walked into the bathroom, then suddenly called to Summer.

"What is it, Julie?" she said, rushing in.

Julie stood with a grim look on her face, pointing to a small vanity mirror next to the sink. The room thief had left her a warning, written in her own pink lipstick, on the mirror. Pointed and succinct, it said simply, "Let K be."

29

Julie awoke the next morning after a fitful night's sleep. Her sense of fear and anxiety had gradually evolved into a feeling of indignant violation. Rising early, she found herself burning with anger.

"Who could have known that we discovered the diary?" she said, pacing the floor of the hotel room. "We had only just found it ourselves."

Summer was in the bathroom, fixing her hair. "Perhaps he didn't actually know about the diary," she replied. "He might have just been trying to find out what you knew and got lucky."

"I suppose it's possible. But why the warning? What is it about Kitchener's death nearly a century after the fact that someone would still be afraid of?"

Summer sprayed on a touch of perfume, then joined Julie in the bedroom. "I'd say one thing is certain. It has to be someone who knows more than we do about either the Manifest or the sinking of the *Hampshire*."

"Or both," Julie concurred. She caught a whiff of Summer's perfume. "That's a lovely fragrance," she said.

"Thank you. It was a gift from a friend of mine in British Columbia."

"The cologne," Julie suddenly blurted. "I nearly forgot. The intruder who tied me up last night had the scent of men's cologne. I'm sure it was the same fragrance as worn by that fellow we met at Lambeth Library."

"You mean Mr. Baker? Do you think it was him?"

"I'm not sure about anything at the moment, but I think it could have been him. Don't you remember? He asked us about the diary. I thought it was a bit odd, at the time."

"You're right. We'll check with the library when we get back to London," Summer said. "I'm sure there's a good chance the librarian will be able to identify him."

Julie was slightly relieved, but the revelation only fueled her inquisitiveness.

"In the meantime, I say we get on over to Broome Park and see what Aldrich knows about his cousin Emily."

They ate a quick breakfast at the hotel, then hopped in the car and drove to Broome Park. Two miles outside of Canterbury, the car sailed through a deep dip in the road.

"Something doesn't feel right," Julie said, detecting a sharp vibration through the steering column.

The car struck another small rut in the road, and the passengers felt a sudden jerk followed by a wail of screeching metal. Summer looked out the window in shock to see the right front wheel bounding ahead of the car and onto the shoulder of the road. The car immediately veered sharply to the right into the oncoming lane. Julie yanked the steering wheel hard left to compensate, but there was no reaction.

The wheel-less right hub ground into the asphalt amid a spray of sparks as the car careened counterclockwise. The vehicle's three remaining tires smoked and squealed as the car spun around and then slid off the road backward. Bounding over the shoulder, the car skidded across a patch of grass before slamming into a low embankment. As the dust cleared, Julie shut off the idling motor, then turned to Summer.

"You okay?" she asked breathless.

"Yes," Summer replied, taking a deep breath herself. "Quite a jolt. I'd say we were a bit lucky."

She saw that Julie looked pale and still had her hands clenched tightly to the steering wheel.

"It was him," she said quietly.

"Well, if it was, he'll have to do a lot better than that to take us down," Summer replied defiantly, trying to lift Julie's spirits. "Let's see if we can get back on the road."

As she opened her door, a black motorcycle came blazing up the road. The rider slowed slightly, giving the damaged car a long gaze. Then he applied a heavy throttle and roared on down the road.

"Don't bother helping us," Summer spat as the black shape disappeared around the bend.

She hiked over to the road and found the stray wheel lying on the shoulder. Standing it upright, she rolled it back to the car. Julie had climbed out but was sitting on a large rock, her hands still shaking. Summer opened the trunk and retrieved the jack, then worked it under the front bumper. The ground was hard and mostly level, which enabled her to raise the hub off the ground. Despite some deep scoring on the hub, she was able to mount the wheel, fastening it down with a trio of lug nuts cannibalized from the other wheels. She made sure the lugs were tightened all the way around, then stowed the jack back in the trunk.

"Summer, you handled that with ease," Julie complimented. She had regained her demeanor and finally stopped shaking. "I thought we would have to ring the auto club."

"My father has been teaching me how to work on antique cars," she said with a proud grin. "He always says that any girl ought to be able to change a tire."

Julie surveyed a slight crease to the rear bumper, then handed the car keys to Summer.

"Do you mind driving the rest of the way? My nerves are shot."

"Not at all," Summer replied. "As long as you don't mind some slow going through any potholes."

Taking the keys, she hopped into the right-hand seat and started the car, then eased back onto the road. They felt no more ill effects from the car, and soon pulled into the parking lot at Broome Park. The two women entered the manor, finding Aldrich laying out croissants and tea in the garden atrium. Julie made no mention of their auto accident as she pulled him aside for a moment.

"Aldrich, I wonder if I could ask you about Emily Kitchener?"

The old man's eyes lit up immediately. "Why, Emily was a lovely lady. I was just telling a guest about her last night. She used to love walking the gardens here in the evening to hear the nightingales sing. Hard to believe she's been gone ten years now."

"She used to live here at the estate?" Summer asked.

"Oh yes. My father took her in when her husband was killed in a railway accident. That must have been around 1970. She lived in what's now the Windsor Suite, on the top floor."

"Do you by chance recall her having any friends or associates named Sally?" Julie asked.

"No, I don't recall anyone named Sally," he replied with a shake of his head.

"Did she ever mention being given any documents or papers from Lord Kitchener?" Summer queried.

"She never made any mention to me of such. Of course, she would have been quite young when the Earl died. You are welcome to take a look at her things, if you like. I have a few boxes of her possessions down in the basement."

Summer gave Julie a hopeful gaze.

"If it wouldn't be an imposition," Julie said to Aldrich.

"Not at all. I can take you down right now."

Aldrich led them to his private quarters and through a locked door to a corner stairway. Down the steps, they reached a dimly lit basement, which was little more than a broad corridor that extended beneath a fraction of the whole residence. Aged wooden crates and dust-covered furniture were stacked high along both walls.

"Much of this old furniture was the Earl's," Aldrich explained as he led them down the corridor. "I really must arrange for another auction one of these days."

At the end of the corridor, they reached a heavy door sealed with a dead bolt.

"This was originally a surplus pantry," he said, reaching for the bolt before realizing it had already been pulled aside. "They sealed it up tight to keep out the rats."

He flicked on an exterior light switch, then grabbed a pull handle and yanked the heavy door aside, revealing a ten-foot-long compartment lined with shelves on either side and a wooden cabinet at the far end. The shelves were jam-packed with cardboard boxes, mostly filled with documents and estate records.

"Emily's things should be right down here," he said, stepping to the rear and pointing at a waist-high shelf where three boxes were marked "E.J. Kitchener."

"Emily Jane Kitchener," Aldrich said. "Might be easiest for you to simply look through the boxes in here. Will you need an escort back upstairs?"

"Thank you, Aldrich, but that won't be necessary," Julie replied. "We'll lock things up and find our way out."

"I hope you both can join us for dinner tonight. We're having a fish fry in the garden." The old caretaker then turned and shuffled out of the pantry.

Summer smiled as she watched him leave. "He is the cutest little fellow," she said.

"An old-fashioned gentleman," Julie agreed, pulling two of the boxes to the front of the shelf. "Here you go, one for you and one for me."

Summer stepped over and flipped open the top of the box, which she noted was not sealed shut. The contents were a disheveled mess, as if someone had hastily thrown the items in the box or it had subsequently been rifled through. She smiled to herself as she pulled out a baby blanket and laid it on an empty shelf. Next to that she laid some children's dresses, a large doll, and several porcelain figurines. At the bottom of the box, she found some costume jewelry and a book of nursery rhymes.

"Box number one is filled with childhood memories," she said, carefully repacking the items. "Nothing of relevance, I'm afraid."

"I'm not faring much better," Julie replied, setting a

pair of sequined boots on the shelf. "Mostly shoes, sweaters, and a few evening gowns here." From the bottom, she pulled out a flat tray of dinnerware. "And some tarnished silverware," she added.

The women replaced the two boxes, then jointly opened the third box.

"This looks more promising," Julie said, retrieving a thin packet of letters.

As she began scanning the letters, Summer inventoried the rest of the box. Most of the contents were prized books of Emily's, along with a few framed photos of herself and her husband. At the bottom of the box, Summer found a large envelope that was stuffed with old photographs.

"No luck here," Julie said, finishing the last letter and inserting it back into its envelope. "These are all old letters from her husband. No mention of our mystery girl. I guess the secret of Sally just isn't meant to be revealed."

"It was an admitted long shot," Summer replied, pulling the photographs out of the envelope and spreading them across the shelf for Julie to see. They were all sepia-tinted images from nearly a century before. Julie held up one photo of a young woman in a riding outfit, holding the reins of a horse.

"She was a pretty young woman," Summer remarked, noting a delicate face set with penetrating eyes similar to her famous uncle.

"Here's one with Kitchener," Julie said, pointing to an earlier photo in a garden setting. Kitchener stood in his uniform next to a couple with their young daughter, clutching a large doll, between them. Summer recognized the toddler as a younger version of Emily from the horse picture.

"She looks about four years old there," Summer said, picking up the photo and flipping it over to see if a date was written on the back. She nearly choked when she read the inscription.

"April, 1916. Uncle Henry and Emily with Sally at Broome Park."

She shoved the photo in Julie's face. Julie read the inscription, then flipped it over and studied the image with a wrinkled brow.

"But that's Emily with her parents. Her mother's name was Margaret, I believe."

Summer looked at her and smiled. "Sally is the doll."

By the time the lightbulb clicked on in Julie's head, Summer was already tearing through the first box of Emily Kitchener's possessions. In an instant, she pulled out a porcelain-faced blond doll that was dressed in a checkerboard apron. Holding the doll up in the air, Summer compared it to the one in the photograph.

It was the same doll.

"He said the Manifest was safeguarded with Sally," Julie muttered. "And Sally is a doll?"

The two women studied the doll, whose clothes and extremities were well worn from the attentive play of a young girl nearly a century earlier. With tentative fingers, Summer turned the doll over and pulled off its checkerboard apron and matching calico dress. A heavy seam was visible along the doll's back, which kept the stuffing inside. Only the stitching was crude and uneven, not matching the workmanship of the rest of the doll.

"This doesn't look like the work of an expert seamstress," Summer noted.

Julie rummaged through one of the other boxes until producing a tarnished silver dinner knife.

"You care to perform the surgery?" she asked nervously, handing Summer the knife.

Summer laid the doll facedown on the shelf and began sawing at the topmost stitch. The dull-edged knife was a poor match for the tough catgut thread, but she eventually cut through the first few stitches. Setting the knife aside, she pulled apart the remaining seam, opening up the back side of the doll. Inside was a compressed mass of cotton wadding.

"Sorry, Sally," she said, carefully pulling out the wadding as if the doll were an animate object. Julie peered anxiously over Summer's shoulder, but slumped when she saw that the doll's torso was filled with nothing but cotton. She closed her eyes and shook her head as Summer pulled out a large ball of it.

"Silly idea," she muttered.

But Summer wasn't through. Peering inside the cavity, she felt around with her fingertips.

"Wait, I think there may be something in here."

Julie's eyes popped open as she watched Summer reach into the doll's left leg and grab hold of an object. Summer worked it back and forth until pulling out a linen-wrapped tube several inches long. Julie leaned closer as Summer set the object on the shelf and gently unwrapped the linen. Inside was a thick piece of parchment rolled into a scroll. Summer held the top edge down, then carefully unrolled it across the shelf as both women held their breath.

The parchment proved to be blank. But they soon saw it was protecting a smaller scroll rolled inside. It was a bamboo-colored papyrus leaf with a single column of script running down its center.

"This . . . this must be the Manifest," Julie uttered quietly, her eyes locked on the ancient document.

"It appears to be written in some sort of ancient script," Summer noted.

Julie stared at the lettering, finding it familiar. "It appears similar to Greek," she said, "but it's nothing that I've seen before."

"That would most likely be Coptic Greek," thundered a male voice behind them.

The women jumped at the unexpected assertion. Spinning their heads toward the door, they were shocked to find Ridley Bannister standing in the entry. He was dressed in a thickly padded black leather jacket and pants favored by dirt-track motorcycle racers. But neither woman noticed his unusual attire. Their attention was focused instead on the snub-nosed revolver he held in his hand, aimed squarely at their chests.

30

"You are the one that attacked me in my hotel room," Julie blurted, finally recognizing the leather outfit.

"Attack is rather a harsh description," Bannister replied casually. "I prefer to think that we were just sharing research information."

"Stealing, you mean," Summer said.

Bannister shot her a hurt look. "Not at all," he said. "Strictly borrowing. You'll find that the diary has found a new home with the rest of Kitchener's private papers upstairs."

"Oh, a penitent thief," Summer replied sarcastically.

Bannister ignored the cut.

"I must say, I am quite impressed with your sleuthing abilities," he said, eyeing Julie. "The leather diary was a marvelous discovery, though the Earl's comments were less than startling. But then identifying Sally on top of that. Quite an encore."

"We weren't quite as sloppy as you," Summer remarked.

"Yes, well, I had limited time to peruse Emily Kitchener's possessions. Be that as it may, a job well done. I searched ten years ago myself without such success." He raised the pistol and motioned with it.

"Would you ladies be so kind as to move to the rear of this compartment? I'll be needing to leave with the Manifest."

"To borrow?" Julie asked.

"Not this time, I'm afraid," Bannister replied with a sharklike smile.

Julie peered at the scroll before slowly stepping away.

"Tell us first. What is the significance of the Manifest?" she asked.

"Until it has been authenticated, no one can say for sure," Bannister said, creeping over to retrieve the parchment with the papyrus inside. "It's just an old document that some seem to think could rattle the theological powers that be." He picked up the scroll with his free hand and gently placed it in an inside pocket of his jacket.

"Was Kitchener deliberately killed because of it?" Julie asked.

"I would assume so. But that's one you'll have to take up with the Church of England. It's been nice chatting with you ladies," he said, backpedaling toward the door, "but I'm afraid I have a plane to catch."

He stepped out of the pantry and began closing the door behind him.

"Please don't leave us in here," Julie begged.

"Not to worry," Bannister replied. "I'll be sure and phone Aldrich in a day or so and let him know there's a pair of lovely lasses locked in his basement. Good-bye."

The door slammed shut with a whoosh followed by the sound of the dead bolt sliding home. Then Bannister flicked off the pantry's lights, plunging it into blackness. He quietly crept upstairs to Aldrich's quarters, stopping to replace the unloaded Webley pistol in a glass cabinet of Kitchener's military artifacts, where he had borrowed it minutes before. Waiting until the lobby cleared, he slipped out of the manor unseen and quickly hopped upon his rented motorcycle.

Three hours later, he called the Lambeth Palace head of security from a phone at Heathrow Airport.

"Judkins, it's Bannister."

"Bannister," the security man replied with an acid tongue. "I've been waiting for you to report. You've tracked this Goodyear woman?"

"Yes. She and the American have been down at Broome Park digging up Kitchener documents. Still there, as a matter of fact."

"Are they going to prove problematic?"

"Well, they are a bit suspicious and have certainly been barking up the right tree."

"But do they have anything damaging to us?" the security man asked impatiently.

"Oh, no," Bannister replied, patting his chest pocket with a wide grin. "They have nothing. Nothing at all."

31

The sealed pantry was as black as a cave. Summer placed a hand on the shelf for balance as she waited a moment for her eyes to adjust to the sudden darkness. But without a source of light, there was nothing to see. She remembered her cell phone and pulled it out of her pocket, the device emitting a dull blue glow.

"No phone signal down here, I'm afraid, but at least we've got a night-light," she said.

Using the cell phone as a flashlight, she stepped to the door, pushing it first with her shoulder, then applying a few firm kicks with the heel of her foot. The thick door didn't budge at all, and she knew that even a sumo wrestler wouldn't have been able to snap off the heavy dead bolt. She eased back over to Julie, flashing the phone toward her to find a scared look on her face.

"I don't like this one bit," Julie said in a shaky voice. "I think I want to scream."

"You know, Julie, that's a good idea. Why don't we?"

Summer tilted her head toward the ceiling and let out a loud scream. Julie immediately joined in, yelling repeatedly for help.

Muffled by the thick pantry door, the screams registered only faintly upstairs. The few guests who detected the faraway cries assumed it was somebody with an iPod cranked too high. The sound didn't register at all in Aldrich's aged ears.

The women took a short break, then tried yelling again. As more minutes ticked by without a response, they resigned themselves to the fact that they couldn't be heard. The screaming had served as a release, though, helping to expel the anxiety of their imprisonment. Julie, in particular, seemed to regain the composure that she had been close to losing.

"I guess we might as well get comfortable if we're going to be in here awhile," she said, pulling a large box onto the floor and using it as a chair. "Do you think he'll actually call Aldrich?" she asked somberly.

"I suspect so," Summer replied. "He didn't act like a trained killer, nor seem psychotic to me." Deep down, she wasn't so certain.

"Personally, I'd rather not wait for Aldrich," she added. "Maybe there's something in one of these boxes that can help us get out of here."

Under the dim glow of her cell phone, she began cracking open some of the other boxes. But it became readily apparent that there was nothing but papers, clothes, and a few odd personal belongings packed away in the former pantry. Soon growing discouraged, she pulled a box down alongside Julie and took a seat.

"It would seem we have little more than a nice wardrobe to help us escape."

"Well, at least we have something to wear in case we get cold," Julie said. "Now, if only we had something to eat."

"I'm afraid the pantry is bare in regards to food," Summer replied. Then she thought for a moment, contemplating her own words. "Aldrich said that this was built as a secondary pantry, didn't he?" she asked.

"Yes," Julie confirmed. "And thank goodness for the rat-proofing."

"Julie, do you know where the main kitchen is located in the manor?"

The researcher thought for a moment. "I've never set foot in it, but it's located off the main dining hall, along the west side of the residence."

Summer visualized the orientation of the estate. "We're on the west side, aren't we?"

"Yes."

"So the kitchen would be located roughly above us?"

"Yes, that would be right. What are you driving at?"

Summer rose to her feet and circled the room, studying the walls behind the storage boxes with her cell-phone light. She slowly made her way to the rear of the pantry, examining a bank of four wooden cabinet doors now visible behind a stack of boxes. She passed the phone to Julie to hold for her.

"If you were Kitchener's chef and you needed a sack of flour from the pantry, would you go lugging it through the house?" she asked, moving the stack of boxes aside. Then she reached up to the top two cabinet doors and tried to open them. But they were sealed shut.

"They're faux doors," Julie said, holding up the light while Summer dug her nails under the doors' edges to no avail. "Try the bottom doors."

Julie shoved a box on the floor aside so that Summer could try the lower doors. Tugging at the edges, she was surprised when both doors flew open effortlessly. Behind them appeared to be an empty black compartment.

"Move the light in," Summer requested.

Julie shoved the cell phone past the doors, illuminating a large tray at the base of the compartment that was affixed to a rear rack. A pulley wheel was visible to one side with a tight loop of rope around it that then ascended past the upper cabinet. Julie turned the cell light upward, revealing a long vertical shaft.

"It's a dumbwaiter," Julie said. "Why, of course. How did you know?"

Summer shrugged her shoulders. "A lifelong aversion to doing things the hard way, I suppose."

She surveyed the shelf for a moment. "It's a little tight, but I think it will suffice as an elevator. I'm afraid I'm going to have to borrow that light back."

"You can't go up that thing," Julie said. "You'll break your neck."

"No worries. I think I can just fit."

Summer took the cell phone and corkscrewed her long legs into the opening, then wormed the rest of her body in until she sat cross-legged on the tray. A pair of frayed ropes dangled beside the pulley used to hoist the tray, but she dared not test her weight on them. Placing the phone in her lap, she instead surveyed a thin link of bicycle chain that spooled around the actual pulley. She then leaned her head back into the pantry.

"Wish me luck. Hopefully I'll meet you at the front door in five minutes," she told Julie.

"Do be careful."

Summer grabbed the chain with both hands and pulled

down hard. The tray immediately rose off its base, and Summer rose up into the chute. Julie quickly grabbed a boxful of clothes and emptied it on the base as a cushion, should Summer lose her grip and fall.

But the athletic young oceanographer didn't fall. Summer was able to pull herself up ten feet before her hands and arm muscles began to weaken. She then found she could tilt the tray forward and wedge her feet against one side of the chute while pressing her back against the opposite side. Supporting her weight in this manner, she could temporarily free her hands from the biting edge of the pulley chain. Resting a few minutes, she then pulled herself up several more feet before pausing again.

She spotted the upper pulley just a few feet above her head and made one more effort to rise to the top. With her hands and arms aching, she muscled herself even with the pulley, scrunching her head beneath the top of the chute. The back side of a cabinet door appeared in front of her, and she quickly pushed on it with her feet. But the door didn't budge.

She could feel her arms weakening as she pushed with her feet again, this time detecting a hairline movement to the door. She was positioned too high and close to the pulley to wedge herself against the chute for relief and she could feel her hold on the chain waning. Realizing she was seconds from losing her grip, she pushed herself backward as far as she could, then rocketed forward, jamming her feet against the door with all her might.

She heard a horrendous crash as the cabinet door burst open, sending a wave of bright light into the cavernous chute. Summer was momentarily blinded by the sudden change in light as she slid through the door, letting go of the chain as her momentum carried her across a smoothly polished surface.

Her vision clearing, she found herself lying on a large teak buffet. It sat in a small but brightly lit lounge that had been constructed from an original section of the manor's kitchen. Summer was startled to see a half dozen elderly couples seated around the room having tea. They all silently stared at her as if she was an alien from Ursa Minor.

Slowly sliding off the buffet and onto her feet, she surveyed the source of the loud crash. Scattered about the floor were spoons, teacups, and saucers from a large formal tea set that had been sent flying when she kicked open the door.

Summer ruefully brushed herself off, hiding her grease-stained hands as she smiled at the collected gawkers.

"I do hate to miss teatime," she said apologetically, then quickly scurried from the room.

She ran into Aldrich in the hall as he rushed toward the commotion and redirected him to help Julie. Together, they dashed down the stairs and unlocked the pantry door. A relieved Julie smiled at the sight of Summer.

"I heard a terrible crash. Is everything all right?" she asked.

"Yes," Summer grinned, "but I might owe Aldrich a new tea set."

"Poppycock!" the old man grunted. "Now, tell me again who locked you in here."

Julie described Bannister and his motorcycle attire.

"Sounds like that fellow Baker," Aldrich said. "Checked out this morning."

"What do you know of him?" Summer asked.

"Not much, I'm afraid. Said he was a writer living in London who was down for a golf holiday. But I vaguely remember him visiting before, must be four or five years ago. I recall letting him into the archives. He's quite knowledgeable about the Earl. In fact, he was the one who also inquired about Emily."

Julie and Summer looked at each other knowingly, then Summer stepped back into the pantry.

"Would you like me to call the police?" Aldrich asked.

Julie thought for a moment. "No, I don't suppose that will be necessary. He has what he came looking for, so I don't think he'll be bothering us again. Besides, I'm sure he gave you a phony name and address in London."

"He's going to get more than a piece of my mind if he shows up here again," Aldrich huffed. "You poor dears. Please, come upstairs and have some tea."

"Thank you, Aldrich. We'll be right along."

As Aldrich strutted off, Julie sat down on a Queen Anne bench beside some covered furniture and breathed heavily. Summer exited the pantry a second later, noting a paleness in Julie's face.

"You all right?" Summer asked.

"Yes. Didn't want to admit it, but I am a bit claustrophobic. I don't care to experience that feeling again anytime soon."

Summer turned and closed the heavy door behind her.

"No need for either of us to set foot in there again," she said. "Where's Aldrich?"

"He went upstairs to make us some tea."

"I hope he can find some cups."

Julie shook her head with a disappointed grimace.

"I can't believe it. We had the clue to Kitchener's death right in our hands and it was plucked away by that thief before we had the chance to figure out what it all meant."

"Don't look so depressed. All is not lost," Summer replied consolingly.

"But we have so little left to go on. We'll probably never find out the true meaning of the Manifest."

"To quote Aldrich, poppycock," Summer replied. "We've still got Sally," she added, holding up the doll.

"What good is that?"

"Well, our friend may have stolen the left leg, but we've still got the right."

She held the flayed doll toward Julie, yanking away a small piece of cotton stuffing. Peering inside, the historian could make out the tip of yet another scroll of paper, this one in the right leg.

She said nothing, her eyes ablaze, as Summer gently worked the object free from the doll's interior. As Summer laid it on the bench and carefully unrolled it, they could both see that it was not a sheet of parchment or papyrus like the other scroll. Instead, it was simply a type-written letter, with the heading "University of Cambridge Archaeology Department" emblazoned across the top.

32

"Divers are still down," Gunn announced.

Standing on the bridge of the *Aegean Explorer*, he peered through a pair of binoculars at an empty Zodiac tied to a drop line that ran down to the Ottoman shipwreck. Every few seconds, he spotted a dual set of air bubbles breaking the surface a few feet from the buoyed line. Gunn swung the glasses past the Zodiac, refocusing the lenses on the large blue Italian yacht that was stationed close by. He noted curiously that its bow was facing him, which put the yacht perpendicular to the current. A partial glimpse of the rear deck showed some men scurrying about in activity, but Gunn's view was quickly obscured by the vessel's superstructure.

"Our nosy friend is still perusing the neighborhood," he said.

"The *Sultana*?" Pitt said, having earlier deciphered the Italian yacht's name.

"Yes. Looks like she's crept a little closer to the wreck site."

Pitt looked up from the chart table, where he was examining some documents.

"He must be rather hard up for entertainment."

"I can't figure out what he's up to," Gunn said, setting down the binoculars. "He's got his side thrusters on, positioning himself crossways to the current."

"Why don't you call him on the radio and ask him?"

"The captain tried a number of friendly calls last night. Couldn't even get a response."

Gunn stepped over and took a seat at the table opposite Pitt. Lying on the table were two tiny ceramic canisters that had been recovered from the wreck site. Pitt was comparing the items with an archaeological assessment of a merchant ship excavated by famed underwater archaeologist George Bass.

"Any luck dating these?" Gunn asked, picking up one of the canisters and eyeing it closely.

"They're very similar to some pottery found on a merchant ship that sank near Yassi Ada in the fourth century," Pitt said, showing Gunn a photograph from the report.

"So Al's Roman crown isn't a phony?"

"No, it would appear legitimate. We've got an Ottoman-era wreck that for some reason is carrying Roman artifacts."

"A nice find any way you slice it," Gunn said. "I wonder where the items originated?"

"Dr. Zeibig is assessing some grain samples that were embedded in one of the potsherds, which may indicate the vessel's point of origin. Of course, if you'd have let us uncover the rest of your monolith, we might already have an answer."

"Oh no you don't," Gunn protested. "That's my find, and Rod said I could recover it with him on our next dive. You just keep Al away from it. Which reminds me," he said, looking at his watch. "Iverson and Tang should be back up anytime now."

"Then I better go rouse Al," Pitt said, rising from the table. "We're scheduled for the next dive."

"I think I saw him napping next to his new toy," Gunn said.

"Yes, he's been anxious to test-dive the *Bullet*."

As Pitt made his way across the bridge, Gunn gave one last warning.

"Now, remember. You two keep your hands off my monolith," he cried, waving a finger at Pitt as he departed.

Pitt retrieved a dive bag from his cabin, then stepped to the rear deck of the ship. In the shadow of a white, aerodynamically shaped submersible, he found Giordino napping on a rolled-up wet suit. Pitt's approaching presence was enough to wake Giordino, and he cocked open a lazy eyelid.

"Time for another trip to my soggy royal yacht?" he asked.

"Yes, King Al. We've been assigned to examine grid C-2, which appears to be a ballast mound."

"Ballast? How am I to add to my jewelry collection from the ballast mound?" Sitting up, he began slipping into his wet suit while Pitt unzipped his dive bag and followed suit. A few minutes later, Gunn came rushing up with a concerned look on his face.

"Dirk, the divers were due up ten minutes ago, but they've yet to surface."

"They might be taking a cautious decompression stop," Giordino suggested.

Pitt gazed toward the empty Zodiac moored a short distance away. Iverson and Tang, the two men in the water, were both environmental scientists who Pitt knew to be experienced divers.

"We'll take the chase boat and have a look," Pitt said. "Give us a hand, Rudi."

Gunn helped lower a small rigid inflatable that was barely big enough to hold both men and their dive gear. Pitt quickly strapped on his tank, mask, and fins as Giordino started the outboard motor and drove them at full throttle toward the Zodiac. There was no sign of the two divers when they pulled alongside the larger inflatable boat.

The chase boat was still slowing when Pitt rolled over the side and into the water. He quickly swam over to the drop line, then descended alongside the rope. He expected to find the two men hanging on to the line ten or twenty feet beneath the surface in decompression, but they were nowhere to be seen. Pitt cleared his ears as he approached the fifty-foot mark, then kicked harder, pushing to reach the bottom. In the depths below, he could faintly make out the yellow aluminum excavation grid pegged into the sandy bottom. He flicked on an underwater flashlight as he approached the base of the drop line, where the visibility dimmed to a greenish murk.

He briefly searched the perimeter around the anchored line, then swam over the grid, following the length of the shipwreck. He hesitated as he crossed over the fourth grid box, noting that there was a large indentation in the sand where Gunn's beloved stone monolith had previously rested. Scanning ahead, he spotted a blue object near the ballast pile. Thrusting his fins sharply, he quickly kicked over to the prone figure of one of the divers.

The body was wedged beneath the aluminum grid, with a number of ballast stones rolled onto the chest. A glance into the wide unblinking eyes behind the mask told Pitt that the NUMA scientist named Iverson was quite dead.

Pitt searched the man's equipment and noticed he seemed to be missing his regulator. A few yards away, Pitt spotted it on the seabed, a clean cut in the line indicating that it had been severed.

Pitt noticed a light above him and was thankful to make out the stout figure of Giordino descending upon him. Approaching within a few feet, Giordino motioned toward the body of Iverson. Pitt responded by shaking his head, then held up the severed regulator, showing where it had been cut. Giordino nodded, then pointed toward the stern of the wreck, and Pitt joined him in swimming aft.

They found the body of Tang drifting above the sea-floor with a finned foot caught in the grid holding him anchored. He had drowned like Iverson, though he appeared to have flailed more wildly in his last moments of life. His mask, weight belt, and one fin had been torn away, and his severed regulator was visible in the nearby sand. Pitt drew his flashlight to the dead man's face, revealing a large purple welt on the right cheekbone. The scientist had probably seen what happened to Iverson and tried to defend himself, Pitt thought. Only the assailants had been too powerful or too many. Pitt turned the light to the deep around them, but the waters were empty. The attackers had already returned to the Italian yacht.

Grabbing hold of Tang's buoyancy compensator, he gave the corpse a tug upward as Giordino motioned that he would retrieve Iverson's body. Pitt ascended slowly with his dead companion, kicking toward the drop line as he rose. Nearing the surface, he detected the low rumble of engines come to life. As the sound increased in intensity, he rightly figured that it was the yacht, throttling up, as it proceeded to flee the scene.

While Pitt's hunch was correct, he never envisaged the yacht's path. Rising to the surface, he realized too late that the engines' roar had grown significantly louder and that a surface shadow was rapidly approaching. He broke the water alongside the Zodiac and chase boat, looking up to see the imposing hull of the yacht screaming toward him at high speed just twenty feet away. The large blue hull slapped against the surface while a fountain of white water sprayed from its churning propellers off the stern.

In an instant, the yacht burst upon the two small boats, instantly crushing the Zodiac with its battering hull and dicing propellers while batting the small chase boat across the waves like an insect. The demolished Zodiac quickly sank to the bottom as the yacht broke toward the horizon, surging like a bolt of lightning.

In the yacht's wake, the drop-line buoy slowly found its way back to the surface after being pummeled to the depths. Cut free from its line, it bobbed gently amid a foaming boil of sea that was colored crimson with human blood.

33

Giordino saw the shadow of the yacht pass overhead and surfaced a few yards from the buoy, the body of Iverson still in tow. He manually inflated the dead man's buoyancy compensator as he watched the mangled remains of the Zodiac sink nearby. In the distance, he spotted the partially deflated chase boat drifting rapidly away with the aid of a light breeze. He quickly scanned the waters around him but saw no sign of Pitt. It was then that he noticed a dark spot in the water near the drifting buoy.

Fearing the worst, he let go of Iverson and swam toward the buoy, intending to submerge and search for Pitt underwater. Reaching the buoy, he felt his stomach drop when he realized the darkened water nearby was created by human blood that pooled bright red. The center of the pool was suddenly disrupted by the rising presence of a wet suit-clad body. The body floated facedown, its head and extremities submerged, concealing its identity. The torso clearly displayed the source of the blood in the water. Sliced and mangled like it had been run over with a lawnmower, the body's back side was a gruesome mix of shredded flesh and neoprene, mutilated by the yacht's churning propellers.

Giordino fought back his revulsion and swam hurriedly to the body. Dreading what he would find, he gently grabbed the torso and eased the head out of the water.

It wasn't Pitt.

He nearly jumped out of his wet suit when he immediately felt a firm tap on his shoulder. Spinning around, he came face-to-face with Pitt, who had surfaced right behind him. Giordino noticed a faint streak of white paint on Pitt's hood and shoulder.

Spitting out his regulator, Giordino asked, "You okay?"

"Yes, I'm fine," Pitt replied, though Giordino could see a tint of anger in his friend's eyes.

"You and Tang were in the way of that freight train?" Giordino asked.

Pitt nodded. "Tang saved my life."

When he'd surfaced in the path of the speeding yacht, Pitt had just seconds to react. He quickly tucked an arm through Tang's buoyancy compensator and pulled the dead man to his chest, then leaned back and attempted to submerge. By then, the yacht was already upon them, slapping down hard onto Tang, and Pitt beneath him. Together, they were pummeled beneath the hull until they passed the wildly spinning propellers. Pitt had just been able to keep Tang above him, and the dead man's body bore the brunt of the slicing blades.

Pitt felt revulsion and anger at having to use the scientist's body as a human shield, but he knew that he would have otherwise been cut to ribbons.

"They killed him twice today," Giordino said somberly.

"They . . ." Pitt muttered, gazing toward the receding profile of the yacht racing toward the horizon. His mind was already churning over the question of who would commit murder over an old shipwreck, and why?

"We better get him out of here before every shark in

the Mediterranean shows up for lunch," Giordino said, grabbing hold of Tang's arm.

The *Aegean Explorer* had already weighed anchor and was creeping up to the men in the water. A group of deckhands lowered a crane and quickly hoisted the dead men aboard, then helped pull up Giordino and Pitt. The ship's captain and doctor scurried to the scene, followed closely by Gunn. The NUMA Deputy Director had a dazed look about him as he held an ice pack to his head.

"They both died in the water," Pitt said as the doctor kneeled down and quickly examined each man. "Drowned."

"Both accidental?" the captain asked.

"No," Pitt said as he stripped off his wet suit. He pointed to a severed air hose extending from Iverson's dive tank.

"Somebody cut their air lines."

"The same people that tried to iron us with the bottom of their rich Italian hull," Giordino added.

"I knew they were lying when they came aboard," Captain Kenfield said, shaking his head. "But I certainly didn't suspect they would resort to murder."

Pitt noticed a lump on Gunn's head that he was rubbing with the ice pack.

"What happened to you?"

Gunn grimaced as he lowered the pack.

"While you were down, the yacht sent over a small launch filled with armed thugs. Claimed they were with the Turkish Ministry of Culture."

"Policing the high seas in a luxury yacht?" Giordino asked skeptically.

"I asked for their identification, but was shown the stock of a rifle instead," Gunn said, repositioning the ice pack to the knot on his head.

"They told us in no uncertain terms that we had no authority to be working on a shipwreck of the Ottoman Empire," the captain said.

"Interesting, that they knew what the wreck was," Giordino noted.

"What else did they want?" Pitt asked.

"They demanded all of the artifacts that we had removed from the wreck," Kenfield said. "I told them to get off my ship, but that didn't go over too well. They marched Rudi and me onto the bridge wing and threatened to kill us. The crew had no choice but to acquiesce."

"Did they take everything?" Giordino asked.

Gunn nodded. "They cleared out the lab, then beat it back to their yacht just before you guys surfaced."

"But not before ordering us off the site and threatening us to stay off the radio," Kenfield added.

"I hate to tell you they didn't just take all our artifacts, Rudi," Pitt said. "They also dug up your monolith from the wreck site."

"That's the least of our losses," he said grimly. "They've got Zeibig."

The captain nodded. "They asked who was in charge of the wreck excavation. Dr. Zeibig happened to be in the lab, and they forced him to go with them."

"After what they did to Iverson and Tang, we know they won't hesitate to kill him, too," Giordino said quietly.

"Have you tried contacting anyone yet?" Pitt asked the captain.

"I just got off the satellite phone with the Turkish Ministry of Culture. They confirmed that they possess no yachts and have no policing resources assigned to this region. I also contacted the Turkish Coast Guard. Unfortunately, they don't have any vessels in the immediate area, either. They have directed us to their base at Izmir to file a report."

"In the meantime, the bad guys are able to disappear completely with Zeibig," Pitt said.

"I'm afraid there isn't much else we can do," the captain said. "That yacht is at least twice as fast as the *Aegean Explorer*. There's no way we could try pursuing them with any hopes of catching up. And once in port, we can alert our own government authorities as well."

Giordino loudly cleared his throat as he stepped forward. "I know something that could keep pace with that yacht."

He turned toward Pitt and gave him a confident wink.

"You sure she's ready?" Pitt asked.

"She's as ready," Giordino said, "as a hungry alligator in a duck pond."

Previously prepared for launch, it took only a few minutes to check that all systems were operational before Giordino's new submersible was lowered over the side. Seated at side-by-side controls, Giordino performed a quick safety check while Pitt radioed the bridge of the *Aegean Explorer*.

"*Explorer*, please give me a current fix on our target," he asked.

"Radar shows she's holding on a steady course of zero-one-two degrees," replied the voice of Rudi Gunn. "She's now approximately ten miles north of us."

"Roger, *Explorer*. Please follow at speed while we go try to catch the fox. *Bullet* out."

Pitt was wary of the notion of playing chase in a submersible. Normally reliant on battery power for propulsion, research submersibles were historically slow, plodding vehicles designed for limited range. But the *Bullet* had broken the rules of submersible development.

Named for the vessel's speed rather than shape, the *Bullet* was based on a design by Marion Hyper-Subs. The NUMA prototype mated a steel submersible cabin to a high-performance powerboat hull. As a submersible, the *Bullet* was capable of diving to depths of a thousand feet. On the surface, separate propulsion motors in a pressurized engine compartment along with a 525-gallon fuel tank allowed the *Bullet* to travel long distances at high speed. The design permitted the sub to reach remote dive sites without the need for an accompanying support vessel.

"Ready to engage surface drive," Giordino announced, then reached over and pressed the starter buttons for a pair of turbocharged diesel engines.

A deep rumble echoed behind them as the twin 500-horsepower motors churned to life. Giordino visually checked several gauges on the instrument panel, then turned to Pitt.

"We're ready to roll."

"Let's see what she can do," Pitt replied, easing back the throttle controls.

They were immediately pushed back into their seats as

the powerful diesels shoved the submersible ahead. In just a few seconds, the vessel was riding high on its sleek white hull, racing across the waves. Pitt felt the sub pitch and roll through the choppy seas, but as he gained a feel for its stability he gently added more throttle. With the control cabin perched near the forward edge of the vessel, he felt like they were flying over the water.

"Thirty-four knots," he said, eyeing a navigation screen readout. "Not too shabby."

Giordino nodded with a wide smile. "I figure she can do well over forty on a flat sea."

They blasted north across the Aegean Sea, bounding for nearly twenty minutes before they spotted a speck on the horizon. They pursued the yacht for another hour, drawing slowly closer as they passed north of the Dardanelles, weaving around a pair of large oil tankers sailing from the Black Sea. The large Turkish island of Gökçeada soon loomed before them, and the yacht altered course to the east of the island.

Pitt followed on a zigzag course so as not to appear to be directly following the yacht, then eased back on the throttles when they approached within a few miles. The yacht slowly turned away from Gökçeada and angled toward the Turkish mainland, hugging close to the coastline as it gradually reduced speed. Pitt turned and followed on a delayed parallel tack, holding well out to sea while staying within visible range of the luxury boat. Skimming low in the water, from a distance the *Bullet* appeared to be just a small pleasure craft out for an afternoon cruise.

The yacht traveled several more miles up the Turkish west coast, then suddenly slowed and veered into a semiprotected cove. As they sped past offshore, Pitt and Giordino could make out a few buildings and a dock with a small freighter moored alongside. Pitt held their course until they were a mile or two north of the cove and well out of sight, before dropping his own throttle to an idle.

"Seems like we've got two choices," Giordino said. "We can put ashore somewhere and make for the cove on foot. Or we can wait until dark and take the *Bullet* into the cove through the basement."

Pitt eyed the craggy coastline a half mile away.

"I'm not sure there are a whole lot of good spots to run aground around here," he said. "Plus, if Zeibig or anyone else should get injured, hiking back out could be problematic."

"Agreed. Then into the cove it is."

Pitt glanced at his orange-faced Doxa dive watch. "Dusk will be here in about an hour. We can start heading in then."

The hour passed quickly. Pitt radioed the *Aegean Explorer* with their position and instructed Rudi to bring the research vessel to a holding spot ten miles south of the cove. Giordino used the time to retrieve a digital marine chart of the coastal area and program a submerged route into the center of the cove. Once underwater, an autopilot system would drive the submersible to the specified location using computer-enhanced dead reckoning.

As darkness approached, Pitt guided the *Bullet* to within a half mile of the cove entrance, then shut off the surface diesels. Giordino sealed and pressurized the engine compartment, then opened a pair of hull gates that allowed water to be pumped into the ballast chambers. The bow chamber flooded first, and the submarine was soon diving beneath the surface.

Pitt deployed a set of dive fins, then engaged the electric thrusters for propulsion. He fought the urge to turn on the vessel's exterior floodlights as the watery world beyond the acrylic bubble faded to black. He eased the sub forward at low speed until Giordino told him to release the controls.

"The autopilot will do the driving from here," he said.

"You sure that thing won't impale us on a submerged rock or obstruction?" Pitt asked.

"We're equipped with high-frequency sonar that reads out a hundred meters in front of us. The autopilot will make course corrections for minor obstacles or give us a warning if something substantial is blocking our course."

"Kind of takes the fun out of flying blind," Pitt remarked.

While Pitt had no aversion to computers, he was old-school when it came to piloting. He could never be completely comfortable letting a computer operate the controls. There was a nuanced feel to the pilot's controls, both in the air and underwater, which even the best computers could not sense. Or so he told himself. With his hands free, he carefully noted their progress, standing ready to take the controls at a moment's notice.

The *Bullet* submerged to a depth of thirty feet, then automatically engaged its electronic thrusters. The submersible moved slowly along its programmed path, compensating for a light current as it eased into the entrance of the cove. Giordino noted that the sonar screen remained clear as they crept to the cove's center. A light flashed on the monitor, and the electric motors ceased whirring as they reached their designated end point.

"That concludes the automated portion of the program," Giordino announced.

Pitt's hands were already on the controls.

"Let's go see if we can find a parking space," he replied.

Purging the ballast chambers in tiny increments, they slowly ascended until just the top few inches of the cabin's acrylic bubble broke the surface. Overhead, they could see that the sky was in its last vestiges of twilight while the water around them appeared black. Giordino shut off all interior lights and unnecessary display panels, then goosed the ballast tanks a final time to elevate them a few more inches.

Rising out of their seats, the two men gazed at the shoreline. They could see that the circular cove was populated on the northern shoreline by only three buildings. The structures fronted a wooden pier that stretched perpendicular to shore. The blue Italian yacht was clearly visible, docked to the right side of the pier behind a small workboat. On the opposite side of the pier was a large rusty freighter. A wheeled crane on the pier was busy loading cargo onto the freighter under the blaze of some fixed overhead lights.

"You think Rod is still aboard the yacht?" Giordino asked.

"I think we should assume so, for starters. What do you say we double-park alongside her and take a look? They shouldn't be expecting us."

"I say surprise is a good thing. Let's move."

Pitt took a course bearing, then submerged the *Bullet* and crept toward the dockyard. Giordino activated the sonar system, helping guide them to within a few yards of the yacht. Easing gently to the surface again, they arose in its shadow just off its port beam. Pitt started to pull along-side the yacht when he noticed a commotion on the stern deck.

A trio of armed men came bursting from the interior and turned toward the dock. A second later, a fourth man came into view, being pushed across the deck by the others.

"It's Zeibig," Pitt remarked, catching a brief glimpse of the scientist's face.

From their low position in the water, they could just barely see Zeibig, who had his hands tied behind his back. Two of the gunmen roughly hoisted him up onto the dock, then prodded him toward shore. Pitt noticed one of the gunmen return to the boat and take up a casual position on the stern.

"Scratch one yacht," Pitt said quietly. "I think it's time to go invisible."

Giordino had already opened the ballast chambers, and the *Bullet* quickly vanished into the inky depths. They reconnoitered the cove once more, then crept in and surfaced just behind the stern of the freighter, tucking in right against its transom. It was an optimally concealed spot, obscured from shore by the freighter while mostly hidden from the pier by an adjacent stack of fuel drums. Giordino quietly climbed out and attached a mooring line to the pier, Pitt shutting down the power systems and joining him.

"Won't be a pretty scene if that big boy fires up his engines," Giordino said, eyeing the submersible floating just above the freighter's propellers.

"At least we've got his license plate number," Pitt replied, looking up at the ship's stern. In broad white letters was painted the ship's name, *Osmanli Yildiz*, which meant "Ottoman Star."

The two men crept along the pier until they reached the shadow of a large generator sitting across from the freighter's forward hold. Ahead of them was a handful of dockworkers occupied with loading large wooden crates into the freighter with the high crane. The blue yacht, with its armed gunman still pacing the deck, was moored just a few feet in front of it. Giordino gazed ruefully up at the bright overhead lights that illuminated the path ahead.

"I'm not so sure it's going to be easy to pass Go and collect our two hundred dollars from here," he said.

Pitt nodded, peering around the generator to survey the dockyard. He could see a small two-story stone building onshore flanked by a pair of prefabricated warehouses. The interior of the right-hand warehouse was brightly illuminated, highlighting a pair of forklifts that hauled crates out of an open bay door for the crane to transfer. In contrast, the left-hand warehouse appeared dark, with no visible activity around it.

Pitt turned his attention to the stone building in the center. A bright porch light illuminated its front façade, clearly revealing a gunman standing guard outside the front door.

"The stone building in the middle," he whispered to Giordino. "That's where Zeibig has to be."

He peered again, spotting the headlights of a car that was approaching from the surrounding hillside. The vehicle bounded down a steep gravel road, then turned onto the dock and pulled up in front of the stone building. Pitt was surprised to recognize the car as a late-model Jaguar sedan. A well-dressed man and woman climbed out of the car and entered the building.

"I think we need to make our play pretty quickly," Pitt whispered.

"Any thoughts on how to get off this pier?" Giordino asked, sitting perched on the side of a ladder tilted against the generator.

Pitt looked around, then gazed at Giordino for a moment, a small grin spreading across his face.

"Al," he said, "I think you're sitting on it."

34

Nobody paid any attention to the two men dressed in faded turquoise jumpsuits walking down the pier with their heads hanging down and carrying an aluminum ladder. They were obviously a pair of crewmen from the freighter returning the borrowed equipment to shore. Only they were members of the crew that nobody had ever seen before.

The men working on the dock were busy securing a crate marked "Textiles" to the crane and paid no heed as Pitt and Giordino passed by. Pitt had noticed the guard on the yacht glance at them momentarily before turning away.

"Which way do we go, boss?" Giordino asked as he stepped off the pier, holding the front end of the ladder.

The illuminated warehouse was nearly in front of them, its open bay door, just a few yards to their right.

"I say we avoid the crowds and go left," Pitt replied. "Let's shoot for the other warehouse."

They turned and walked along the waterfront, passing the narrow stone building. Pitt guessed it had originally been built as a fisherman's house but now served as an administrative office for the dock facility. Unlike the gunman on the yacht, the man guarding the front door eyed them suspiciously as they passed by the courtyard in front of the house. Giordino attempted to trivialize their presence by casually whistling "Yankee Doodle Dandy" as they passed, figuring the Turkish gunman would be unfamiliar with the tune.

They soon reached the second warehouse, a darkened building with its large waterfront drop-down door sealed shut. Giordino tried the handle on a small entry door alongside and found it unlocked. Without hesitating, he led Pitt inside, where they deposited the ladder against a work desk illuminated by a flickering overhead light. The rest of the building's interior was empty, save for some dusty crates in the corner and a large sealed container near the rear loading dock.

"That was easy enough," Pitt said, "but I don't think waltzing in the front door of the building next door looks as promising."

"No, that guard watched us like a hawk. Maybe there's a back door?"

Pitt nodded. "Let's go see."

Picking up a wooden mallet he noticed lying on the desk, he walked across the warehouse with Giordino. Adjacent to the loading dock was a small entry door, which they slipped through. They quietly made their way to the back side of the stone building only to find it had no rear or side doors. Pitt approached one of the lower-level windows and tried to peek in, but the blinds had been tightly drawn. He stepped away and studied the second-floor windows, then tiptoed back to the warehouse to confer with Giordino.

"Looks like we're back to the front door," Giordino said.

"Actually, I was thinking of trying an upstairs entry," Pitt replied.

"Upstairs?"

Pitt motioned toward the ladder. "Might as well put that thing to use. The windows were dark upstairs, but they didn't appear to have the blinds drawn. If you can create a distraction, I could climb up and enter through one of the windows. We can try to surprise them from above."

"Like I said, surprise is a good thing. I'll go get the ladder while you work on that distraction."

As Giordino padded across the warehouse, Pitt stuck his head out the back door and searched for a means to create a diversion. An option appeared in the form of a flatbed truck parked behind the opposite warehouse. He ducked back inside as Giordino approached with the ladder, but then he suddenly looked past him curiously.

"What's up?" Giordino asked.

"Look at this," Pitt said, stepping closer to the steel shipping container sitting nearby.

It was painted in a desert-khaki-camouflage scheme, but it was some black-stenciled lettering that had caught Pitt's attention. Several points around the container were marked, in English, "Danger—High Explosives." Beneath the warning was stenciled "Department of the U.S. Army."

"What the heck would a container of Army explosives be doing here?" Giordino asked.

"Search me. But I'd be willing to bet the Army doesn't know about it."

Pitt walked to the front of the container and slid across the dead bolt, then swung open the heavy steel door. Inside were dozens of small wooden crates with similar warnings stenciled on their sides, each tightly secured to metal shelves. Near the doorway, one of the crates had been pried open. Inside were several small plastic containers the size of bricks.

Pitt pulled one of the containers out and peeled off the plastic lid. Inside was a small rectangular block of a compressed clear powdery substance.

"Plastic explosives?" Giordino asked.

"It doesn't look like C-4, but it must be something similar to it. There's enough here to blow this warehouse to the moon and back."

"You think that stuff might be helpful in creating a distraction?" Giordino asked, raising an eyebrow in a sly arch.

"I know so," Pitt replied, resealing the container and handing it carefully to his partner. "There's a truck parked in back of the other warehouse. See if you can make it go boom."

"And you?"

Pitt held up the hammer. "I'll be knocking on the door upstairs."

35

Zeibig had not feared for his life. He was certainly distressed at being abducted at gunpoint, handcuffed, and locked in a cabin on a luxury yacht. Reaching the cove, he had his doubts as he was roughly herded ashore and into the old stone building, where he was directed to sit in an open conference room. His captors, all tall, pale-skinned men with hardened dark eyes, were certainly menacing enough. Yet they had not yet proven to be abusive. His feelings changed when a car pulled up in front and an austere Turkish couple emerged and entered the building.

Zeibig noted the guards suddenly assume a stiff, deferential posture as the visitors stepped inside. The archaeologist could hear them discussing the freighter and its cargo with a dock foreman for several minutes, surprised that the woman seemed to be making most of the demands. Finishing their shipping business, the couple strolled into the conference room, where the man glared at Zeibig with angry contempt.

"So, you are the one responsible for stealing the artifacts of Suleiman the Magnificent," Ozden Celik hissed, a vein throbbing out from his temple.

Dressed in an expensive suit, he looked to Zeibig to be a successful businessman. But the red-eyed anger in the man bordered on psychotic.

"We were simply conducting a preliminary site investigation under the auspices of the Istanbul Archaeology Museum," Zeibig replied. "We are required to turn over all recovered artifacts to the state, which we were intending to do when we returned to Istanbul in two weeks."

"And who gave the Archaeology Museum ownership of the wreck?" Celik asked with a furl of his lips.

"That you'll have to take up with the Turkish Cultural Minister," Zeibig replied.

Celik ignored the comment as he moved to the conference table with Maria at his side. Spread across the mahogany surface were several dozen artifacts that the NUMA divers had retrieved from the wreck site. Zeibig watched them peruse the items, then he suddenly became wide-eyed himself at the sight of Gunn's monolith lying at the far end of the table. Curiosity caused him to crane his neck, but it was too far away to make out the inscription.

"To what age have you dated this shipwreck?" Maria asked. She was dressed in dark slacks and a plum-colored sweater but unstylish walking shoes.

"Some coins given to the museum indicate that the wreck sank in approximately 1570," Zeibig said.

"Is it an Ottoman vessel?"

"The materials and construction techniques are consistent with coastal merchant vessels of the eastern Mediterranean in that era. That's as much as we know at the moment."

Celik carefully reviewed the collection of artifacts, admiring fragments of four-hundred-year-old ceramic plates and bowls. With the experienced eye of a collector, he knew that the wreck had been accurately dated, confirmed by the coins now in his possession. Then he approached the monolith.

"What is this?" he asked Zeibig, pointing to the stone.

Zeibig shook his head. "It was removed from the wreck site by your men."

Celik carefully studied the flat-sided stone, noticing a Latin inscription on its surface.

"Roman garbage," he muttered, then examined the remaining artifacts before stepping back over to Zeibig.

"You will never again plunder that which belongs to the Ottoman Empire," he said, his dark eyes staring madly into Zeibig's pupils. His hand slipped into his coat pocket and retrieved a thin leather cord. He twirled it in front of Zeibig's face for a moment, then slowly pulled it taut. Celik moved as if stepping away from Zeibig, then turned and whipped the strap over the archaeologist's head as he whirled behind him. The cord immediately constricted around Zeibig's neck, and he was jerked to his feet by a firm upward yank.

Zeibig twisted and tried to drive his elbows into Celik, but a guard stepped forward and grabbed his cuffed wrists, pulling his arms forward as the cord tightened around his neck. Zeibig could feel the cord bite into his thorax, and he struggled for air while the blood pounded in his ears. He heard a loud pop and wondered if the sound was his eardrum bursting.

Celik heard the sound as well but ignored it, his eyes ablaze with bloodlust. Then a second blast erupted nearby, shaking the entire building with the accompanying force of a thundering boom. Celik nearly lost his balance as the floor vibrated and window glass shattered upstairs. He instinctively released his grip on the leather garrote.

"Go see what that was," he barked at Maria.

She nodded and quickly followed the foreman out the front door to investigate. Celik immediately tightened his grip on the leather strap as the guard remained stationary, holding firm to Zeibig's wrists.

Zeibig had managed to suck in a few breaths of air during the interlude and renewed his efforts to break free. But Celik jabbed a shoulder into his back, turning as he pulled on the leather strap and nearly pulling the archaeologist off his feet.

Turning red and feeling his head pounding as he gasped for air, Zeibig gazed into the eyes of the guard, who smiled back at him sadistically. But then a puzzled look crossed the guard's face. Zeibig heard a muffled thump, then felt the leather strap suddenly slip free from his neck.

The guard let go of Zeibig's wrists and quickly fumbled inside his jacket. In the fuzzy, oxygen-deprived recesses of Zeibig's brain, he knew the man was reaching for a gun. With a sudden impulse that felt like it was happening in slow motion, Zeibig leaned forward and grabbed the guard's sleeve. The guard hastily tried to shake the hand free before finally shoving the archaeologist away with his free arm. As he gripped his handgun in a shoulder holster, an object whizzed by and struck him in the face. He staggered a bit until a second blow hit home and he crumpled unconscious to the floor.

Zeibig turned with blurry vision to see a man standing beside him, holding a wooden mallet in his hand, a grim look of satisfaction on his face. Coughing and sputtering for air, Zeibig smiled as his senses revived and he could see that it was Pitt.

"You, my friend," he said, wheezing out the words in pain, "have arrived like a breath of fresh air."

36

Nearly the entire dock crew had flocked to the rear of the warehouse to watch the smoldering remains of the truck light up the night sky. Giordino's handiwork could not have produced a better diversion. And it was all so simple.

Sneaking to the side of the truck, he'd quietly opened the cab door and peeked inside. The interior reeked of cigarette smoke, with dozens of butts littering the floor amid smashed cans of soda pop. A notebook, some tools, and the bony remains of roasted chicken wrapped in brown paper sat on the bench seat. But it was a thin, ragged sweat-shirt stuffed under the seat that caught Giordino's eye.

Giordino grabbed the shirt and easily ripped off a sleeve, then searched the dashboard until he found the cigarette lighter and pushed the knob in. He then made his way to the rear of the truck and unscrewed the gas cap. He carefully dangled the sleeve in the tank until it was partially saturated with gasoline, then pulled it up and laid the dry end over the side of the gas tank. He left the fuel-soaked end just inside the filler tube and rested the cap on top of it to seal in the vapors. When he heard a popping sound, he scurried to the cab and retrieved the cigarette lighter, then hurriedly ignited the dry end of the sleeve before the lighter turned cold.

He barely had time to run to the rear of the stone build-ing before the small flame crept up the sleeve to the fuel-soaked section of the cloth. The flames quickly ran to the filler, igniting the vapors in an explosion that blew apart the fuel tank.

But it was the charge of plastic explosives, positioned on top of the fuel tank, which did the real damage a second later. Even Giordino was surprised by the massive blast that blew the truck entirely off the ground and incinerated its back end.

Pitt had done his best to coordinate his break-in with the sound of the blast. Perched on the ladder outside one of the darkened second-story windows, he shattered the glass with his mallet as the building itself shook before him. He quickly climbed in, finding himself in the guest bedroom of the comfortably appointed living quarters. He was sneaking down the stairs when he heard Zeibig's struggling gasps and sprang with his mallet to lay down Celik and the guard.

Regaining his strength, Zeibig stood and looked down at the unconscious Celik, who had a large bump on the side of his head.

"Is he dead?"

"No, just napping," Pitt replied, noticing the prone figure beginning to stir. "I suggest we get out of here before they wake up."

Pitt grabbed Zeibig by the arm and started to lead him toward the front door, but the archaeologist suddenly stopped in his tracks.

"Wait . . . the stele," he said, stepping over to Gunn's stone slab.

Pitt gazed at the excavated stone, which stood nearly four feet high.

"Too big to take as a souvenir, Rod," he said, urging their departure.

"Let me study the inscription for just a moment," Zeibig pleaded.

Rubbing the surface with his fingers, he quickly read the Latin several times, pressing himself to memorize the words. Satisfied that he had it down, he looked at Pitt with a weak smile.

"Okay, got it."

Pitt led the way to the front entrance and flung open the door only to be met by an attractive woman with dark hair on her way in. Pitt knew he had seen her face before, but the evening clothes she wore obscured the context. Maria, however, recognized Pitt immediately.

"Where did you come from?" she demanded.

The harsh voice immediately came back to Pitt as the one that had threatened him in the Yerebatan Sarnici cistern in Istanbul. He was startled by her sudden appearance here but then realized it all made sense. The Topkapi thieves had ransacked Ruppé's office, which had led them to the wreck site.

"I'm from the Topkapi vice squad," Pitt said in a wry tone.

"Then you will die together with your friend," she snapped in reply.

Looking past them, she caught a glimpse of her brother and the guard lying on the floor of the conference room. A twinge of fear and anger crossed her brow, and she quickly backpedaled across the porch and turned toward the warehouse to yell for help. But her words were never heard.

A burly arm appeared from the shadows and wrapped around her waist, joined by a hand that gripped tightly over her mouth. The fiery woman kicked and flailed, but she was like a child's doll in the powerful grip of Al Giordino.

He carried her back up to the doorway and into the foyer, as he nodded pleasantly at Zeibig.

"Where would you like this one?" he asked, turning to Pitt.

"In a fetid Turkish prison cell," Pitt replied. "But I guess we'll have to make do with a closet for the moment."

Pitt located a small broom closet off the stairwell and opened the door, and Giordino deposited Maria inside. Zeibig brought over a desk chair, which Pitt wedged beneath the handle after Giordino slammed the door shut. A deluge of muffled sounds and angry kicks immediately ensued from within.

"That one's a devil," Giordino remarked.

"More than you know," Pitt replied. "Let's not give her a second chance at us."

The three men scurried out of the building and onto the darkened waterfront. The burning truck still had everyone's attention, though a few dockworkers returned to loading the freighter. The armed guards were nervously securing the area around the blast as the trio quickly made their way onto the pier. Pitt found a discarded gunnysack and draped it over Zeibig's hands to disguise the fact that he was still wearing handcuffs.

They moved by the extended crane, stepping as quickly as they dared without drawing attention. Keeping close to the freighter, they turned a shoulder toward the yacht and the idling workboat as they moved past, Pitt and Giordino shielding Zeibig as best they could. They relaxed slightly as they distanced themselves from the brightly illuminated section of the pier and saw no workers ahead of them. The shoreline remained quiet, and Pitt figured they were home free as they approached the stern of the freighter.

"Next stop, the *Aegean Explorer*," Giordino muttered quietly.

But the hopeful feelings vanished as they reached the end of the pier. Stepping to the edge, Pitt and Giordino looked down at the water, then scanned the area around them in disbelief.

The *Bullet* was nowhere to be seen.

37

Celik came to slowly, with a pounding ache in his head and a loud thumping in his ears. Rising unsteadily first to his knees and then to his feet, he shook off the fog and realized the thumping originated well beyond his ear canal. Detecting his sister's muffled voice, he stepped to the closet and kicked away the chair. Maria practically flew out, her face glowing red with anger.

Taking one look at the dazed appearance of her brother, she quickly calmed down.

"Ozden, are you all right?"

He rubbed the bump on his head with a slight wince.

"Yes," he replied coarsely. "Tell me what happened."

"It was that American from the research vessel again. He and another man set off an explosion in one of the trucks, then came in here and freed the archaeologist. They must have followed the yacht here."

"Where are my Janissaries?" he asked, weaving slightly back and forth.

Maria pointed to the prone guard lying beneath the conference table.

"He must have been attacked with you. The others are investigating the explosion."

She took Celik's arm and led him to a leather chair, then poured him a glass of water.

"You had better rest. I will alert the others. They cannot have gotten far."

"Bring me their heads," he spat with effort, then leaned back in the chair and closed his eyes.

Maria stepped onto the porch as two of the guards approached.

"The fire has been extinguished," reported one of the men.

"Intruders have attacked us and taken the captive. Search the dock and waterfront immediately," she ordered, "then launch the yacht and scour the cove. They must have a boat with them."

As the men ran off, Maria stared into the blackened cove, sensing that the intruders were still close at hand. A thin smile crossed her lips, her anger dissipating as she contemplated her revenge.

38

At that particular moment, the men from NUMA had neither boat nor submersible.

Giordino peered into the water, trying to determine if the *Bullet* had sunk at her mooring. Then he stepped over to examine a black iron bollard he had used to tie the craft up. There was no sign of the mooring line.

"I'm sure I tied her securely," he said.

"Then someone sank her or moved her," Pitt replied. He peered down the dock a moment in quiet thought.

"That small workboat. Wasn't she ahead of the yacht when we went ashore?"

"Yes, you're right. She's idling in back of the yacht now. We couldn't see much of her on the way back because of the generator. Perhaps she towed the *Bullet* somewhere."

A female voice was suddenly detected yelling loudly on the shore, followed by the shouts of several men. Pitt peeked around the stern of the freighter and saw several gunmen running toward the pier.

"Looks like the party is over," he said, glancing toward the water. "I think it's time we think about getting wet."

Zeibig held up his cuffed wrists.

"It's not that I'm afraid of the water, mind you," he said with a crooked grin. "But I don't particularly relish the idea of drowning *per se*."

Giordino put a hand on his shoulder.

"Right this way, my friend, for some dry patio seating."

Giordino led Zeibig to the wall of empty fuel drums stacked along the edge of the pier. He quickly rolled several drums aside, hoisting them like beer cans, until creating a small recessed space.

"Pier-side seating for one," he said, waving a hand toward it.

Zeibig took a seat on the pier, scrunching his legs together.

"Can I order a Manhattan while I'm waiting?" he asked.

"Just as soon as the entertainment ends," Giordino replied, wedging a drum against the archaeologist. "Don't you go anywhere until we get back," he added, then stacked several more drums around Zeibig until he was fully concealed.

"Not to worry," Zeibig's muffled voice echoed in reply.

Giordino quickly rearranged a few more drums, then turned to Pitt, who was gazing down the pier. At the far end, a pair of guards could be seen heading across the waterfront toward the pier.

"I think we better evaporate now," Pitt said, stepping to the end of the pier, where a welded-steel ladder trailed down into the water.

"Right behind you," Giordino whispered, and together the two men scrambled down the ladder, sliding quietly into the dark water.

They wasted no time working their way back toward shore, swimming between the pier's support pilings while safely out of view from above. Pitt was already formulating an escape plan but faced a dilemma. Stealing a boat seemed their best hope, and they had a choice between the workboat and the yacht. The workboat would be easier to commandeer, but the faster yacht could easily run them down. He braced himself for the daunting task of capturing the yacht without weapons when Giordino tapped him on the shoulder. He stopped and turned to find his partner treading water alongside.

"The *Bullet*," Giordino whispered. Even in the darkness, Pitt could see the white teeth from his partner's broad smile.

Gazing ahead through the pilings, Pitt looked at the workboat and the yacht just beyond. But sitting low in the water behind the workboat, he now noticed the crest of the submersible. They had walked right by it when they crossed the pier. Obscured by the generator, it had gone unseen when the men were trying to conceal Zeibig from any probing eyes aboard the yacht.

The two men quietly worked their way closer, observing that the submersible's mooring line was attached to the stern of the workboat. It had indeed been the suspicious guard on the back of the yacht who had strolled down the pier after Pitt and Giordino walked by and discovered the strange vessel astern of the freighter. Enlisting the aid of the workboat's captain, they had towed it alongside the yacht in order to get a better look at it under the bright dock lights.

Pitt and Giordino swam forward until they were even with the *Bullet*. They could see the armed gunman standing on the stern deck of the workboat and another man in its wheelhouse.

"I think our best bet is to keep the towline and pull her

into the cove to submerge," Pitt whispered. A sudden fray of shouting came from shore as the Janissaries began extending their search down the pier.

"You jump on the *Bullet* and prep her for diving," Pitt said, not wishing to waste any more time. "I'll see what I can do with the workboat."

"You'll need some help with that armed guard," Giordino said with concern.

"Blow him a kiss when I get aboard."

Then Pitt took a deep breath and disappeared under the water.

39

The guard couldn't quite make out the commotion on shore, but he could see that some of his fellow Janissaries were headed down the pier. He had already tried radioing his discovery of the submersible to his commander, not knowing that the man was still lying unconscious in the stone building. He contemplated returning to the yacht but thought it better to safeguard the submersible from the stern of the workboat. He stood there, gazing toward shore, when he was startled by a voice calling from the water.

"Pardon me, boy, is that the Chattanooga Choo Choo?" wafted a gruff voice.

The guard immediately stepped to the stern rail and looked down at the submersible. A soggy Giordino stood on the *Bullet*'s frame, one hand placed on the acrylic bubble for support while the other waved cheerily at the startled gunman. He quickly jerked his weapon up and started to shout at Giordino when he detected the sound of some squishy footsteps approaching from behind.

Too late, he turned to find Pitt barreling into him like he was a blocking dummy. Pitt kept his elbows high, striking the man on the side, just beneath the shoulder. With legs pinned against the rail, the guard had no way to balance himself from the blow. With a warbled grunt, he flipped over the side, splashing hard into the water.

"Company," Giordino shouted to Pitt as he released the hatch and scurried inside the submersible.

Pitt turned to see two men walking down the dock, gazing at him with alarm. He ignored them, turning his attention to the boat's small wheelhouse. A middle-aged man with a chubby face and sun-baked skin stumbled out at the sound of the splash, then froze at the sight of Pitt on the deck.

"Arouk?" he called, but the guard was just gurgling to the surface.

Pitt's eyes were already scanning the stern deck. Clamped to the gunwale a few feet away was a six-foot-long gaff. He quickly lunged for it, gripped the base, and whipped the barbed iron hook toward the workboat's captain.

"Over the side," Pitt barked, waving the hook toward the water.

Seeing the determined look in Pitt's eye, the captain saw no reason to hesitate. With his hands raised, he calmly stepped to the rail and threw his legs over the side, slipping heavily into the water. On the other side of the boat, the guard named Arouk had surfaced and begun shouting to his cohorts down the pier.

Pitt didn't wait around to decipher the conversation. Dropping the gaff, he raced into the wheelhouse and yanked the workboat's throttle to its stops. The boat lurched forward, then faltered as the trailing towline drew taut with the submersible. The boat gradually regained momentum and accelerated at what seemed like a snail's pace to Pitt. He glanced at the pier in time to see the two guards step to the edge and train their weapons on him.

His reflexes still quick, he dove to the floor an instant before the guns opened fire.

The wheelhouse exploded in a hail of splintered wood and shattered glass as a pair of extended bursts ripped through the structure. Shaking away a blanket of splinters and shards, Pitt crawled to the helm and reached up to the wheel, pulling it three-quarters of a turn to starboard.

With just a few yards to spare, the workboat was quickly closing on the yacht moored directly ahead. While Pitt could have turned hard into the cove, he knew doing so would leave Giordino and the *Bullet* exposed to sustained gunfire. In the confusion, he had no idea whether Giordino had even entered the submersible before the shooting began. He could only hope to deflect attention until they could reach a safer haven out in the cove.

Spotting a seat cushion on the pilot's chair, he ripped it away and crawled to the blasted remnants of the port-side window. Tossing it into the air, he succeeded in drawing the gunmen's attention again as they finished reloading their weapons. Another volley of gunfire shredded the exterior of the wheelhouse with vicious effect. Inside, Pitt clung to the deck with the seat cushion over his head as more splinters and shards sprayed about the cabin. The bullets kept flying until the gunmen emptied their clips for a second time.

When the firing ceased, Pitt raised his head to see that the workboat was pulling alongside the yacht. He crawled to the wheel and eased it to starboard, then held it steady. As the boat approached the bow of the yacht, he kneeled and cranked the wheel hard over.

The old boat was now chugging along at eight knots

as its bow turned sharply away from the yacht and the pier. Pitt could hear more yelling, but his move had bought a few precious seconds of safety as the yacht obscured the aim of the gunmen. They would now have to either board the yacht or step down the pier to get a clear shot, by which time Pitt hoped to be out of accurate range.

He stood for a moment and peeked out the back of the wheelhouse, spotting the *Bullet* bounding merrily behind. A dull glow from some of the interior electronics told him that Giordino had made his way inside and was powering up the submersible. He looked beyond it to the yacht, where he noticed a bubble of diesel exhaust erupt from the stern waterline. Pitt had banked on escaping in the *Bullet* before the yacht could get under way, but his opponent was jumping the gun. To make matters worse, he spotted the two gunmen racing across the yacht's stern deck with their guns at the ready.

Pitt ducked down and tweaked the wheel, angling the workboat toward the center of the cove while taking the *Bullet* out of the direct line of fire. The rattling of machine guns preceded a spray of bullets, most of which scattered harmlessly into the transom. Pitt willed the boat to go faster, but the old tub had peaked out with the submersible in tow.

When Pitt guessed they were a hundred yards from the pier, he suddenly cranked the wheel hard to port, then eased back on the throttle. He held the wheel well over until the boat had drifted completely around, and the yacht rose ahead off the bow. As the boat bobbed in the cove under idle, Pitt stepped to the stern and quickly untied the towline to the *Bullet*. Tossing it toward the submersible, he leaned over the rail and yelled at Giordino.

"Wait for me here," he said, motioning with his hands for him to stay put.

Giordino nodded, then held a thumbs-up against the acrylic bubble where Pitt could see it. Pitt turned and ran back to the wheelhouse as more gunfire opened up from shore, now peppering the workboat's bow. Reaching the wheelhouse, Pitt jammed open the throttle and adjusted the wheel until he was bearing for the end of the pier.

"Stay where you are, big girl," he muttered aloud, eyeing the luxury boat.

Free of the submersible, the workboat squeezed out another few knots of speed. Pitt kept the bow aimed toward the deep end of the pier, not wanting to give away his hand just yet. To the gunmen on the yacht, it appeared as if the boat was stuck in a large counterclockwise circle. Pitt held the ruse until the boat was passing parallel to the yacht some fifty yards away, then he turned the wheel sharply once more.

Aligning the bow till it was aimed amidships of the yacht, he straightened the wheel, then wedged a life jacket into the bottom spokes to hold it steady. Ignoring a fresh spray of gunfire that raked the bow, he sprinted out of the wheelhouse and onto the stern deck, where he dove headfirst over the rail.

The yacht's captain was the first to realize they were about to get rammed and he screamed for help to release the dock lines. A crewman appeared on deck and scrambled onto the pier, quickly releasing the bow and spring lines. One of the gunmen tucked away his rifle and crossed the deck to the stern line. Rather than hopping onto the pier to release a shortly secured line, he attempted to unravel the opposite end, which was knotted tightly around a bollard on the yacht's stern.

The captain saw the bow and spring lines tossed free, then turned in horror to see the workboat bearing down less than twenty yards away. Panicking in self-preservation, he jumped to the helm and pressed down the twin throttles, hoping that the stern line was also clear.

But it wasn't.

The yacht's big diesel engines bellowed as the twin props dug into the water and thrust the vessel forward. But it surged only a few feet before the stern line grew taut, anchoring it to the pier. The guard tumbled backward with a scream, nearly losing several fingers as the line snapped tight.

The water churned and boiled off the stern as the yacht fought to break loose. Then suddenly the line slipped free, the crewman on the pier bravely unraveling the dock line and ducking for cover. The yacht burst forth like a rodeo bronco, churning ahead in a spray of foam. The captain glanced out the bridge window, then clutched the helm with white knuckles, realizing the attempted escape had failed.

The unmanned workboat plowed into the yacht, striking the starboard flank just ahead of the stern. The boat's blunt, heavy bow easily shattered the fiberglass shell of the yacht, mashing its opposite side into the pier pilings. The sound of grinding metal filled the air as the starboard driveline was crushed, mangling a score of fuel and hydraulic lines and high-spinning gears. The combined momentum swung the yacht's stern to the pier, where its spinning port propeller was knocked off by a piling. The yacht gamely lurched forward as a final gasp, breaking free of both the workboat and pier before its motors fell silent and it drifted aimlessly toward shore.

Pitt didn't bother watching the collision but instead swam hard underwater, surfacing only momentarily for a quick gulp of air. He pushed himself until his lungs ached, and his stroke count indicated he was close to where he had cut the *Bullet* loose. Easing to the surface, he gazed toward the pier while regaining his breath. The success of the attack was clearly evident. He could see the yacht drifting helplessly toward shore while the workboat, its motor still throbbing at high revolutions, pounded repeatedly into the pier as its mangled bow sank lower and lower into the water. Numerous people raced along the pier, surveying the scene and yelling in confusion. Pitt couldn't help but grin when his ears detected a female voice shouting amid the fray.

Secure for the moment, he turned and paddled into the cove, his eyes searching the surface of the water. He took a quick bearing from shore to convince himself he was in the right location, then slowly surveyed the waters around him. In every direction, all he could see was small, dark lapping waves, and he suddenly felt very alone.

For the second time that night, the *Bullet* had disappeared without him.

40

Rod Zeibig grimaced when he heard the first burst of automatic gunfire. Any hopes of a stealthy getaway seemed to vanish with the metallic clatter of spent shell casings spewing across the wooden pier. Of greater concern was the safety of Pitt and Giordino, who were clearly the target of the barrage.

Zeibig was surprised to hear the gunfire continue for several minutes unabated. Curiosity finally overcoming his fear, he leaned over the edge of the pier and peeked around the stack of fuel drums. Near the opposite end of the dock, he could just make out the superstructure of the yacht and a number of men yelling to shore. On the pier, he noticed a crewman furiously engaged with one of the mooring lines.

Zeibig ducked back into his hiding nook as more gunfire resumed. Seconds later, the gunfire ceased, and then a loud crash shook the pier, jiggling the fuel drums around him. More shouts erupted in the aftermath, but the gunfire remained silent. With a melancholy conjecture, the archaeologist quietly wondered if Pitt and Giordino had died in a last rebellious act.

Staring blankly into the cove while contemplating his own fate, he noticed a sudden disturbance in the water before him. A dull greenish glow appeared faintly in the depths, which gradually grew brighter. Zeibig looked on, unbelieving, as the transparent bubble of the *Bullet* quietly broke the surface directly in front of him. Seated at the controls was the burly figure of Al Giordino, an unlit cigar dangling from his lips.

The archaeologist didn't wait for a formal invitation to board but hastily lowered himself down a mussel-covered piling and into the water before the submersible finished surfacing. Swimming to its stern, Zeibig climbed up on one of the exterior ballast tanks, then crept to the rear hatch. Giordino immediately opened the hatch and ushered Zeibig inside, quickly resealing it behind him.

"Boy, am I glad to see you," Zeibig said, squeezing into the copilot's seat while trying not to drip water on any of the electronics.

"I wasn't relishing a swim home myself," Giordino replied, rushing to blow the ballast tanks and submerge the vessel as quickly as possible. Craning his neck upward, he scanned the pier around the fuel drums for sight of any observers.

"No one has bothered to expend much time at this end of the pier," Zeibig reported, watching the water rise up and over the top of the acrylic bubble. He then turned to Giordino with trepidation in his voice.

"I heard a big crash, and then the shooting stopped. Dirk?"

Giordino nodded. "He stole the workboat that had towed the *Bullet* to the other side of the pier. He cut me loose, then set off after the moored yacht."

"I think he was successful," Zeibig replied in a morose tone.

Eyeing a depth-gauge reading of thirty feet, Giordino

halted the ballast pumps, then gently backed the submersible away from the pier. Reversing thrust, he angled into the cove, then gave Zeibig a reassuring smile.

"Knowing Dirk, I don't think he rode the boat to the end of the line. As a matter of fact, I'd wager a month's salary that he's swimming laps in the middle of the cove this very moment."

Zeibig's eyes immediately perked up. "But how will we ever find him?"

Giordino affectionately patted the pilot console. "We'll trust the penetrating peepers of the *Bullet*," he said.

With his own eyes glued to a navigation screen, Giordino guided the submersible along a meandering track he had recorded at the point where Pitt had cut him free from the workboat. The dead reckoning system wouldn't return him to an exact position the way GPS would, but it would be very close.

Giordino followed the trail at a depth of thirty feet, gradually rising to just ten feet as he approached the original starting point. He then eased back on the propulsion controls until they hovered in a stationary position.

"Are we out of range of their gunmen?" Zeibig asked.

Giordino shook his head. "We were lucky not to take any fire earlier. They were all focused on stopping the boat. I don't think I'd like to give them a second chance."

He reached over and toggled on several switches beside an overhead monitor. "Let's hope the boss hasn't strayed too close to shore."

A grainy blank image appeared on the monitor as it displayed the readings from the submersible's sonar system. Giordino dialed up the system's frequency, which produced a more detailed image while reducing the range of the scan. Both men studied the screen intently, seeing only a flat display of mottled shadows. Giordino then feathered a side thruster, gently rotating the submersible in a clockwise direction. There was little change in the image as the forward-looking sensor scanned the center of the cove. Then Giordino noticed a small smudge at the top of the screen.

"There's something small about a hundred feet away," he said.

"Is it Dirk?" Zeibig asked.

"If it's not a porpoise, a kayak, or a million other potential items of floating debris," he replied.

He adjusted the thrusters and guided the submersible toward the target, watching it grow in size as they moved closer. When the shadow began to run off the top of the sonar screen, Giordino knew they were almost directly beneath the target.

"Time to take a look," he said, then gently purged the ballast tanks.

Pitt was floating on his back, conserving energy from his swim from the workboat and several minutes of treading water, when he felt a slight disruption in the water beneath him. He turned over to see the dim interior lights of the *Bullet*, rising fast just a few feet away. He swam closer, positioning himself directly above the acrylic bubble as it broke to the surface. Giordino was quick to cut the ascent, allowing only the top few inches of the *Bullet* to bob above the water.

Pitt lay prone on the bubble, spreading his arms wide for support. Beneath him, he could see Giordino looking up at him with a relieved smile, then motioning to inquire if he was okay. Pitt pressed his thumb and forefinger together and held it against the acrylic, then pointed toward the center of the cove. Giordino nodded in reply, then gestured for him to hang on.

Hugging the acrylic with his arms and legs, Pitt held tight as the submersible began moving forward. Giordino eased the thrusters ahead slowly until they were creeping along at just a few knots. Pitt felt like he was waterskiing on his belly. The small waves sloshed around his face, and he had to strain his neck skyward every few seconds to grab a breath of fresh air. When the dock lights receded to a safe distance, Pitt rapped his knuckles as hard as he could on the acrylic. The forward movement halted immediately, and a few seconds later the submersible rose fully to the surface amid a small surge of bubbles.

Pitt slid off the acrylic nose and onto the *Bullet*'s frame, then stepped to the rear hatch. He hesitated a moment, turning a last gaze toward shore. In the distance, he could just make out the workboat alongside the pier, sinking heavily by its bow. Nearby, some men in a Zodiac were trying to run a line from the pier to the yacht before it drifted aground. With some measure of relief, Pitt could see that hunting for the submersible appeared low on the shore crew's priorities. The hatch then popped open beside him, and Giordino welcomed him inside.

"Thanks for coming back to get me," Pitt said with a sideways grin.

"King Al leaves no man behind," Giordino puffed. "I trust you kept our shore hosts duly occupied?"

"Put a nasty scratch in their yacht, which should keep

them out of commission for the moment," he replied. "Nevertheless, since you have already retrieved the good Dr. Zeibig I see no point in loitering."

He followed Giordino to the pilot seats, where they quickly submerged the vessel. Silently, they crept out of the cove at a safe depth, ascending again once they were a half mile offshore. Giordino reconfigured the *Bullet* for surface running, and to Zeibig's astonishment they were soon charging across the black sea at better than thirty knots.

A quick radio call to the *Aegean Explorer* confirmed that she was standing off the southeast tip of Gökçeada. Thirty minutes later, the lights of the research vessel came into clear view upon the horizon. As they drew closer, Pitt and Giordino saw that a second, larger vessel was positioned on the opposite side of the *Explorer*. Giordino slowly eased back the *Bullet*'s throttles as it approached, guiding it alongside the starboard flank of the NUMA ship and an overhanging crane. Pitt recognized the second vessel as a Turkish Coast Guard frigate, which held station a short distance off the *Explorer*'s port beam.

"Looks like the cavalry has finally arrived," Pitt said.

"I'll gladly point the way to the guys in the black hats," Zeibig replied.

A pair of divers appeared in a Zodiac and attached a lift cable to the *Bullet*, then the sleek submersible was hoisted aboard. Rudi Gunn stood on the stern deck and helped secure the sub before stepping to the rear hatch. His downturned face brightened when he saw Zeibig climb out ahead of Pitt and Giordino.

"Rod, are you all right?" he asked, helping the archaeologist step to the deck.

"Yes, thanks to Dirk and Al. I could use a bit of help in losing these, however," he added, holding up his handcuffed wrists.

"The shipboard machine shop should be able to manage that," Gunn replied.

"Al's got the location of the yacht and its crew," Pitt said. "A little base of operations up the coast. We can pass the coordinates to the Turkish Coast Guard or run up there with them in the *Explorer*."

"I'm afraid that's not in the cards," Gunn replied, shaking his head. "We've been ordered to proceed to Çanakkale, a port town on the Dardanelles, as soon as we got you safely aboard."

He motioned toward the Turkish frigate, which had inched closer when the submersible appeared. Pitt gazed over and noticed for the first time that a row of armed sailors lined the frigate's rail, their weapons pointed at the NUMA research ship.

"What's with the threatening posture?" he asked. "We've had two crewmen murdered and another kidnapped. Didn't you radio the Coast Guard earlier?"

"I did," Gunn replied testily. "But that's not why they're here. It seems somebody else called them first."

"Then why the show of arms?"

"Because," Gunn said, his eyes red with anger, "we are under arrest for looting a submerged cultural resource."

41

Dusk had arrived in the eastern Mediterranean, casting a pale rosy tint to the sky as the *Ottoman Star* broached the entrance to the Port of Beirut, just north of the Lebanese capital. The old frigate had made a swift voyage from the Aegean, reaching the port city in less than forty-eight hours. Circling past a modern new containership terminal, the freighter turned west through the port complex, steaming in slowly to dock at an older general-cargo quay.

Despite the late hour, many of the local dockworkers stopped and stared as the freighter was berthed, smiling at the odd spectacle on her deck. Carefully wedged beside the forward hatch and resting on a hastily constructed wooden cradle sat the damaged Italian yacht. A pair of workmen in coveralls was busy cutting and patching the large gash in its hull inflicted by the now sunken workboat.

Maria sat quietly on one side of the ship's bridge, silently watching the captain deal with the small parade of port, customs, and trade representatives who filed aboard in search of paperwork and money. Only when the local textile distributor complained about his short shipment did she intervene.

"We were forced to accelerate our departure," she said bluntly. "You'll receive the difference with the next shipment."

The browbeaten distributor nodded, then left quietly, not wishing to tangle with the fiery woman who owned the ship.

The dockyard cranes were quickly engaged, and soon metal containers filled with Turkish textiles and produce were being rapidly unloaded from the ship. Maria stuck to her perch on the bridge, watching the work with disinterested eyes. Only when she spotted a dilapidated Toyota truck pull up and park alongside the gangway did she sit upright and stiffen. She turned to one of the Janissary guards that her brother had sent to accompany her on the voyage.

"A man I am to meet has just pulled up on the dock. Please search him carefully, then escort him to my cabin," she ordered.

The Janissary nodded, then stepped briskly off the bridge. He was mildly surprised to find the driver of the truck was an Arab attired in scruffy peasant clothes and wearing a ragged *keffiyeh* wrapped around his head. His dark eyes glared with intensity, however, deflecting attention from the long scar on the right side of his jaw, which he had acquired in a knife fight while a teen. The guard duly searched him, then showed him aboard, escorting him to Maria's large and stylishly appointed cabin.

The Turkish woman sized him up quickly as she offered him a seat, then dismissed the Janissary from her cabin.

"Thank you for coming here to meet me, Zakkar. If that is indeed your name," she added.

The Arab smiled thinly. "You may call me Zakkar. Or any other name, if it so pleases you."

"Your talents have come highly recommended."

"Perhaps that is why so few can afford me," he replied, removing the dirty *keffyeh* and tossing it onto an adjacent chair. Seeing that his hair was trimmed in a neat Western cut, Maria realized that the grubby outfit was simply a disguise. Given a shave and a suit, he could easily pass as a successful businessman, she thought, not knowing that he often did.

"You have the initial payment?" he asked.

Maria rose and retrieved a leather satchel from a cabinet drawer.

"Twenty-five percent of the total, as we agreed. Payment is in euros. The balance will be wired into a Lebanese bank account, according to your instructions."

She stepped closer to Zakkar but clung to the satchel.

"The security of this operation must be unquestioned," she said. "No one is to be involved who is less than completely trustworthy."

"I would not be alive today if conditions were otherwise," he replied coldly. He pointed at the satchel. "My men are willing to die for the right price."

"That will not be necessary," she said, handing him the satchel.

As he peered inside at its contents, Maria stepped to a bureau and retrieved several rolled-up charts.

"Are you familiar with Jerusalem?" she asked, laying the charts across a coffee table.

"I operate in Israel a good portion of the time. It is Jerusalem where I am to transport the explosives?"

"Yes. Twenty-five kilos of HMX."

Zakkar raised his brow at the mention of the plastic explosives. "Impressive," he murmured.

"I will require your assistance in placing the explosives," she said. "There may be some excavation work required."

"Of course. That is not a problem."

She unrolled the first chart, an antiquated map labeled, in Turkish, "Underground Water Routes of Ancient Jerusalem." Placing it aside, she displayed an enlarged satellite photograph of Jerusalem's walled Old City. She traced a finger across the eastern face of the wall to the hillside beyond, which descended into the Kidron Valley. Her finger froze atop a large Muslim cemetery perched on the hill, its individual white gravestones visible in the photo.

"I will meet you here, at this cemetery, at exactly eleven p.m., two nights from now," she said.

Zakkar studied the photo, noting the nearby cross streets, which were overlaid on the image. Once they were committed to memory, he looked up at Maria with a quizzical gaze.

"You will be meeting us there?" he asked.

"Yes. The ship will be sailing from here to Haifa." She paused, then added firmly, "I will be leading the operation."

The Arab nearly scoffed at the notion of a woman directing him on an assignment, but then he considered the handsome payoff he would receive for the indignity.

"I will be there with the explosives," he promised.

She moved to her bunk and pulled out a pair of wooden footlockers stored underneath. The heavy lockers had metal handles affixed to each end and were stenciled with the words "Medical Supplies," written in Hebrew.

"Here is the HMX. I will have my guards carry it to the dock."

She stepped to the Arab mercenary and looked him hard in the eye.

"One last thing. I want no cowardice over our objective."

Zakkar smiled. "As long as it is in Israel, I do not care what or whom you destroy."

He turned and opened the door. "Till Jerusalem. May Allah be with you."

"And also with you," Maria muttered, but the Arab had already slid down the corridor, the Janissary following close behind.

After the explosives were transported to the Arab's truck, Maria sat down and studied the photograph of Jerusalem once more. From the antiquated cemetery, she eyed the glistening target positioned just up the hill.

We'll shake up the world this time, she thought to herself, before carefully returning the photograph and charts to a locked cabinet.

42

Rudi Gunn paced the bridge like a nervous cat. Though the bump on his head had long since receded, a purple bruise still blemished his temple. Every few steps, he would stop and scan the weathered dock of Çanakkale for signs of relief. Finding none, he would shake his head and resume pacing.

"This is crazy. We're on our third day of impoundment. When are we going to be released?"

Pitt looked up from the chart table, where he was studying a map of the Turkish coast with Captain Kenfield.

"Our consulate in Istanbul has assured me that our release is imminent. The necessary paperwork is promised to be meandering through the local bureaucracy even as we speak."

"The whole situation is outrageous," Gunn complained. "We're placed in lockdown while the killers of Tang and Iverson are allowed to slip free."

Pitt couldn't argue with him, but he did understand the dilemma. Long before the *Aegean Explorer* had contacted the Turkish Coast Guard, the marine authority had been alerted by two earlier radio calls. The first reported that the NUMA ship was illegally salvaging a historic Turkish shipwreck protected by the Cultural Ministry. The second call reported two divers killed during the salvage operation. The Turks refused to identify the source of the calls but rightfully acted on them in advance of the *Aegean Explorer*'s request.

Once the NUMA ship was escorted to the port city of Çanakkale and impounded, the case was turned over to the local police, further compounding the confusion. Pitt immediately phoned Dr. Ruppé in Istanbul to document their approved presence on the wreck site, then he phoned his wife, Loren. She quickly badgered the State Department to push for their immediate release even after the police had searched the ship and, finding no artifacts, slowly realized there was no basis for arrest.

Rod Zeibig ducked his head through the doorway and broke the air of exasperation.

"You guys got a minute?"

"Sure," Gunn replied. "We're just busy here pulling our hair out of our heads one strand at a time."

Zeibig stepped in with a folder in his hand and headed to the chart table.

"Maybe this will perk you up. I've got some information on your stone monolith."

"Apparently, it's not mine anymore," Gunn mused.

"Did you manage to remember your Latin inscription?" Pitt asked, sliding over to allow room for Gunn and Zeibig to sit down.

"Yes. I actually wrote it down right when we got back to the ship but put it aside during all the commotion. I finally examined it this morning and performed a formal translation."

"Tell me it's the gravestone of Alexander the Great," Gunn said wishfully.

"That would be wrong on two accounts, I'm afraid.

The stone tablet is not a grave marker *per se* but a memorial. And there's no mention of Alexander."

He opened the folder, revealing a handwritten page of Latin that he had jotted down after viewing the monolith. The next page contained a typewritten translation, which he handed to Gunn. He read it silently at first, then aloud.

"In Remembrance of Centurion Plautius.
Scholae Palatinae and loyal guardian of Helena.
Lost in battle at sea off this point.
Faith. Honor. Fidelity.

—CORNICULAR TRAIANUS"

"Centurion Plautius," Gunn repeated. "It's a memorial to a Roman soldier?"

"Yes," Zeibig replied, "which adds veracity to Al's crown being of Roman origin, a gift from the Emperor Constantine."

"A *Scholae Palatinae* loyal to Helena," Pitt said. "The *Scholae Palatinae* were the elite security force of the later Roman emperors, as I recall, similar to the Praetorian Guard. The reference to Helena must be Helena Augustus."

"That's right," Zeibig agreed. "The mother of Constantine I, who ruled in the early fourth century. Helena lived from A.D. 248 to 330, so the stone and the crown would presumably date to that era."

"Any idea who this Traianus is?" Gunn asked.

"A *cornicular* is a military officer, typically a deputy position. I searched some Roman databases for a Traianus but came up empty."

"I guess the big mystery still remains: Where did the crown and monolith originate and why were they in an Ottoman wreck?"

He gazed past Zeibig, perking up at the sight of two men in blue uniforms who were making their way down the quay toward the ship.

"Well, well, the local constables have returned," he said. "I hope that's our parole papers they are carrying with them."

Captain Kenfield met the officers on the dock and escorted them aboard, where Pitt and Gunn joined them in the wardroom.

"I have your impoundment release here," the elder officer stated in clear English. He was a round-faced man with drooping ears and a thick black mustache.

"Your government was very persuasive," he added with a thin smile. "You are free to go."

"Where does the investigation of my murdered crewmen stand?" Kenfield inquired.

"We have reopened the case as a potential homicide. At present, however, we have no suspects."

"What about that yacht, the *Sultana*?" Pitt asked.

"Yes, we saw the boat nearly cut Dirk to shreds," Gunn pressed.

"We were able to trace that vessel to its owner, who informs us that you must be mistaken," the officer replied. "The *Sultana* is on a charter cruise off Lebanon. We received e-mail photos this morning of the vessel moored in the Port of Beirut."

"The *Sultana* was heavily damaged," Pitt said. "There is no way she could have sailed to Lebanon."

The officer's assistant opened a briefcase and pulled out several printed photographs, which he handed to Pitt. The photos showed bow and port-side views of the blue yacht moored at a dusty facility. Pitt didn't fail to notice that none of the photos showed the starboard flank, where he had rammed the yacht. The last photo showed a close-up of a Lebanese daily newspaper with the present date, the yacht appearing in the background. Gunn leaned over Pitt and studied the photos.

"That sure looks like the same boat," he said reluctantly. He could only nod when Pitt showed him the photo of a life ring that clearly showed the yacht's name. Pitt simply nodded, finding no evidence that the photos had been doctored.

"It doesn't belie the fact that one of our scientists was also kidnapped and taken to the yacht's facility up the coast," Pitt said.

"Yes, our department contacted the local police chief at Kirte, who sent a man to investigate the dock facility you described." He turned and nodded to his assistant, who retrieved a thick packet from his case and handed it to his supervisor.

"You may have a copy of the report that was filed in Kirte. I've taken the liberty of having it translated into English for you," the officer said, handing it to Pitt while giving him an apologetic look. "The investigator reported that not only were the ships you described absent from the harbor, there were in fact no vessels at all at the facility."

"They certainly covered their tracks quickly," Gunn remarked.

"The facility records indicate a large freighter similar to

the one you described was at the dock earlier in the day, taking on a shipment of textiles. However, the records indicate that the vessel left harbor at least eight hours before your alleged arrival at the facility."

The officer looked at Pitt with a sympathetic gaze.

"I'm sorry there is little else we can do at the moment, pending additional evidence," he added.

"I realize this has turned into a rather confusing incident," Pitt said, suppressing his frustration. "I wonder, though, if you can tell me who owns the shipping facility near Kirte?"

"It is a privately held company called Anatolia Exports. Their contact information is in the report." He looked at Pitt with a pensive gaze. "If there is any additional service I can provide, please let me know."

"Thank you for your assistance," Pitt replied tersely.

As the police officers left the boat, Gunn shook his head.

"Unbelievable. Two murders and a kidnapping, and nobody is at fault but us."

"It's a raw deal, all right," Captain Kenfield said.

"Only because we're playing against a stacked deck," Pitt said. "Anatolia Exports apparently bought off the Kirte police. I think our resident constable recognized that."

"I suppose the whole situation was a bit embarrassing for them, so perhaps they are just trying to save face," Kenfield said.

"They should be more concerned with doing their job," Gunn swore.

"I would have thought they'd be jumping through

hoops after you told them that you spotted the woman from the Topkapi theft," Kenfield said to Pitt.

Pitt shook his head. "I didn't tell them anything about her."

"Why not?" Gunn asked incredulously.

"I didn't want to endanger the ship anymore while we're in Turkish waters. We've seen firsthand what they're capable of doing, whoever 'they' are. Plus, I had a sneaking suspicion it would go nowhere with the local police."

"You're probably right about that," Kenfield said.

"But we just can't let them walk away," Gunn protested.

"No," Pitt agreed with a determined shake of the head. "And we won't."

The lines had been cast and the *Aegean Explorer* was inching away from the dock when a dilapidated yellow taxi came roaring into view. The rusty vehicle skidded to a stop at the water's edge, the rear door flew open, and a tall, slender woman jumped out.

Pitt was standing on the bridge when he spotted his daughter running along the dock.

"It's Summer," he shouted to the captain. "Hold the boat."

Pitt ran down to the main deck, ducking when a large duffel bag came flying through the air and landed at his feet. A second later, a thin pair of hands appeared on the side rail, followed by a bushel of red hair. Summer then swung her body over the side, landing on her feet on the forward deck. Pitt approached, holding her bag, and gave her a clenching hug.

"You know we were coming back to get you," he said with a laugh.

Realizing that the ship had reversed power and was returning to the dock, Summer gave her father a sheepish look.

"Sorry," she said, still catching her breath. "When I phoned the ship from London, Rudi told me you'd probably be here for another day or two. But when the taxi neared the dock, I saw you pulling away and panicked. I really didn't want to miss the boat."

Pitt turned and waved up to the bridge, indicating it was safe to depart. Then he casually escorted Summer to her cabin.

"I wasn't expecting to see you for another few days," he said.

"I took an earlier flight from London and figured it would be easier to catch you here in Çanakkale coming from Istanbul." Her face turned somber as she said, "I heard about your shipwreck . . . and what happened to Tang and Iverson."

"We've had our share of trouble and excitement," he replied as they entered her cabin and he placed her bag on the bunk. "Why don't we go grab a coffee in the wardroom, and I'll tell you all about it."

"I'd like that, Dad. Then I can tell you all about what I've been up to in England."

"Don't tell me you've got a mystery of your own?" he asked, smiling.

Summer gave her father an earnest gaze, then replied, "One bigger than you could ever imagine."

PART III
The Crescent's Shadow

The *Bullet*

43

"Sophie, I think I may have a hot one for you."

Sam Levine nearly tripped as he burst into the Director of Antiquities' office. The cuts and bruises on his face from the incident at Caesarea had mostly healed, but he still carried a large scar on his cheek from the encounter with the Arab thieves. Sophie was seated at her desk, studying a Tel Aviv police report on a grave looting, but looked up with interest.

"Okay, I'm listening."

"One of our network informants, an Arab boy named Tyron, reports a possible dig tonight in the Muslim cemetery at Kidron."

"Kidron? That's just over the wall from the Old City. Somebody's getting rather brazen."

"If it is even true. Tyron has had a spotty track record when it comes to tips."

"Who is supposedly turning the shovels?"

"I only got one name out of him, a petty thief named Hassan Akais," Sam replied, sliding into a chair opposite Sophie's desk.

"Doesn't ring a bell," Sophie replied after contemplating the name. "Should I know him?"

"We picked him up a few years ago on a raid at Jaffa. We didn't have enough on him to press charges, so he was let go. Seems to have kept his hands clean since then. He's been paying our informant to tend some sheep, and apparently the boy overheard talk of an operation tonight."

"It sounds like small fish to me."

"I thought so, too. But then there's this," Sam said, handing Sophie a computer printout. "I ran his name through the system and, lo and behold, the Mossad suspects him of having possible links to the Mules."

Sophie leaned forward and studied the paper with heightened interest.

"His links appear a bit tenuous, at best," Sam added, "but I thought you would want to know."

Sophie nodded as she finished reading the report but neglected to pass it back to Sam.

"I would like to talk to this Hassan," she finally replied in a measured tone.

"We're a bit thin for an operation tonight. Lou and the gang are in Haifa until tomorrow, and Robert is home sick with the flu."

"Then it will just have to be you and me, Sammy. Any objections?"

Sam shook his head. "If this guy had anything to do with Caesarea, then I want him, too."

They made their plans for the evening rendezvous, then Sam rose and left the office. Sophie had resumed reading the police report when she suddenly felt someone staring at her. She looked up in surprise to see Dirk, standing outside her doorway, holding a large bouquet of lilacs in his hand.

"Pardon me, I'm looking for the chief gunslinger around here," he said with a radiant smile.

Sophie practically leaped out of her chair.

"Dirk, I didn't think you'd be free until next week," she said, hopping over and giving him a peck on the cheek.

"The university suspended the excavation at Caesarea for the season, so I guess my work is through for now," he said, placing the flowers on her desk. He then grabbed her in a tight embrace and kissed her. "I missed you," he whispered.

Sophie felt her skin flush, then remembered her office door was open.

"I can take a short break," she stammered. "Shall we go have lunch?"

As soon as he nodded, she led him away from the prying eyes of the office and into a nearby courtyard.

"I know a beautiful spot to picnic in the Old City. We can grab something to eat along the way," she offered.

"Sounds perfect," he said. "I haven't seen much of Jerusalem. A walk in the streets is always the best way to capture the essence of an interesting city."

Sophie grabbed his hand and led him off the manicured grounds of the Rockefeller Museum. Just a short distance away stood Herod's Gate, one of a handful of entry points into Jerusalem's Old City. Roughly a mile square, the Old City is the religious heart of Jerusalem, containing the historical landmarks of the Church of the Holy Sepulchre, the Western Wall, and the Dome of the Rock. An imposing stone wall constructed by the Ottoman Turks over four hundred years ago runs in a complete perimeter around the historic section.

Walking through the gate and into the Muslim Quarter, Dirk admired the aged beauty of the cut limestone, which seemed to be the basis of every monument, business, and residence in the city no matter how shabby or dilapidated. But he was more amused watching the diverse population making their way through the narrow streets and alleys. Spotting an Armenian Jew waiting for a crossing light beside an Ethiopian in a white robe and a Palestinian wearing a *keffyeh*, he realized that he was treading on a patch of ground unique in all the world.

Sophie guided him down a dark and dusty alley that led to a bustling open-air market called, in Arabic, a *souk*. She expertly navigated their way past a throng of vendors, stopping to purchase some falafel, lamb kebabs, sweet cakes, and a bag of fruit from the assorted hawkers.

"You said you wanted some local flavor, so here it is," Sophie teased, making Dirk carry their ad hoc lunch.

She led him down a few more blocks, then crossed onto the grounds of St. Anne's Church. A graceful stone structure built by the Crusaders, its location in the heart of the Muslim Quarter represented one of the many peculiar juxtapositions to be found in the ancient city.

"A nice Jewish girl is taking me to a Christian church?" Dirk asked with a chuckle.

"We're actually headed to the grounds in back of the church. A place that I thought an underwater explorer might enjoy visiting. In addition to the fact," she added with a wink, "it's a lovely spot for a picnic."

They entered the property and made their way to the rear grounds, where they found an open area shaded by mature sycamore trees. A trail led a short distance to a fenced chasm that dropped away like an open mine. Remnants of brick walls, stone columns, and ancient arches rose from the dry base of the cavity.

"This was the original Pool of Bethesda," Sophie said as they peered down into the now-dusty depths. "It was originally a reservoir for the First and Second Temples, then baths were later constructed. Of course, it was better known as a healing center after it was written that Jesus cured an invalid here. There's not much water left, I'm afraid."

"Probably just as well," Dirk replied. "Otherwise, it would be wall-to-wall tourists vying to take a bath."

They found a secluded bench beneath a towering sycamore, where they sat down and attacked their lunch, passing the delicacies back and forth.

"Tell me, how is Dr. Haasis getting on?" she asked.

"Quite well, actually. I just visited him this morning before traveling to Jerusalem. He's resting at home but eager to get back to work. The leg wound didn't prove serious, so he should be free of his crutches in another week or two."

"The poor fellow. I feel so sorry for him."

"He told me he feels bad for you. He seems to think it was his fault that your agents were placed in such a dangerous situation."

Sophie shook her head. "That is ridiculous. He had no way of knowing an armed band of terrorists would attack any more than we did."

"He's a man with a generous soul," Dirk said, sampling a fresh fig from the bag of fruit. "By the way, the Israeli Security Agency grilled me pretty good over the last few days. I hope you can tell me that you're close to catching the bad guys."

"Shin Bet, as they are known, has taken the lead on the

investigation, but I'm afraid the trail of evidence has already turned cold. The assailants' truck was found to be a stolen vehicle. It was discovered driven into the sea near Nahariyya. Shin Bet thinks that the thieves likely crossed into Lebanon shortly after departing Caesarea. They are believed to be connected with a smuggling operation that has known ties to Hezbollah. I fear they will be difficult to identify, let alone capture."

"Any idea who they might have been working for?"

"Not really. I've made plenty of inquiries and have a few suspicions, but no hard proof. Sam and I are doing everything we can," she said, her voice drifting away as her thoughts turned to the dead agent Holder.

Dirk reached over and clasped her hand in his and squeezed tight.

"I never thought I'd have to deal with something like this," she continued, falling teary-eyed.

She looked into Dirk's eyes and squeezed his hand back. "I'm really glad that you are here," she said, then leaned over and kissed him.

They sat huddled for a long while, Sophie feeling safe again in the arms of Dirk. Staring at the empty pools of Bethesda, she eventually regained the will to face her job again. Taking a deep breath, she smiled through moist eyes.

"Can you smell the jasmine in the air?" she asked. "I've always loved the fragrance. It reminds me of when I was a child, and all the days were filled with happiness."

"They will be again," Dirk promised.

"I must be getting back," she finally whispered, though her arms retained their lock around Dirk.

"I'll be waiting for you," he replied.

She suddenly remembered the planned operation with Sam that night.

"We can have dinner, but I'm afraid I have to work tonight. A surveillance job. We received a tip about an artifact thief who might be connected to the Lebanese smugglers."

"May I come along?"

Sophie started to shake her head, then relented. "We are a bit shorthanded. It's just Sam and me, so we could use some extra support. But no heroics this time."

"A silent observer, that's me. I promise," he said, smiling.

They rose together and took a final look at the dry pools. Sophie felt a sudden hesitancy to leave, though she didn't know why. She finally gathered Dirk's hand and led him slowly away from the pools, fighting a swirl of emotions within her heart.

44

The *Ottoman Star* crept slowly into the Israeli Port of Haifa, the decrepit freighter relegated to a berth at the end of the quiet west terminal. With only a small quantity of remaining textiles to off-load, the Turkish crew could have easily emptied the ship's holds in a few hours. But they were under strict orders to procrastinate unloading so that work would not be completed until late in the evening.

Presenting a pair of fake passports at the port's customs office, Maria and one of the Janissaries then rented a car and made their way out of Haifa. Posing as a married couple on holiday, they could travel through most of the country with limited scrutiny. But in making their way to Jerusalem, they took no chances. Maria drove a circuitous route to avoid entering the West Bank and being subjected to additional security checkpoints, which might find the fanny pack under her seat containing a gun, cash, and a pair of night vision goggles.

Maria knew well that attempting to transport the HMX explosives into and through the country was another matter. Zakkar and his associates in the Mules could handle that risk, at a cost that was well worth the price. The Arab smuggler had carefully outlined to Maria how the explosives would be transported via truck, then on foot, even strapped to the bellies of a herd of sheep at one point, in order to reach the destination without being detected by the Israeli security forces.

But that was only half of the challenge. The Turkish woman had other equally important business to conduct in person. With the help of a tourist map, they entered the busy streets of Jerusalem, bypassing the Old City in making their way to one of the newer neighborhoods to the west. Locating the recently opened Waldorf Astoria Hotel, they parked their car on the street and walked to the next block south. Tucked into a row of trendy tourist shops, they found a tiny teahouse, with strings of beads shading the windows, and stepped inside.

At a corner table in the dimly lit café, Maria spotted a bearded man rise to his feet and smile in her direction, revealing a gold-plated front tooth. Maria approached him with her Janissary in tow.

"Al-Khatib?" she asked.

"At your service," the Palestinian replied, bending toward her in a slight bow. "Won't you join me?"

Maria nodded and sat down at the table with the Janissary beside her. Al-Khatib took a seat across from them and poured them each a cup of tea. Maria noticed that he had the sunbaked skin and callused hands of an old artifact plunderer, which was exactly what he was.

"Welcome to Jerusalem," he said by way of a toast.

"Thank you," Maria replied, gazing around the room to ensure there were no prying ears nearby.

"Have you succeeded with the task for which you were hired?" she asked in a low voice.

"Yes, with ease," the Palestinian replied, smiling again. "The aqueduct was exactly where you indicated it would be. It is an amazing historical validation. May I ask where you obtained the research data?"

It was Maria's turn to smile.

"As you know, the present wall around the Old City was constructed by Suleiman the Magnificent in the early fifteen hundreds. His engineers mapped the route in detail, incorporating the locations of existing obstructions. The maps, which we have acquired in Turkey, are replete with abandoned aqueducts and other features constructed back to the Age of Herod, which have since been lost or hidden."

"A marvelous discovery, and one that I would love to examine some time," al-Khatib said hungrily.

"I'm afraid I didn't bring the documents with me on this trip," she lied. "My family has an extensive collection of Ottoman artifacts, and the maps were part of a larger acquisition." She neglected to mention that they had all been stolen from a museum in Ankara.

"Historical documents of prized value, I should think. May I ask the purpose of the excavation?"

Maria brushed aside the inquiry. "You were able to expand the opening around the aqueduct?" she countered.

"Yes, I have done as you requested. I quietly enlarged the opening, then burrowed a meter or two into the hillside. The entrance is properly concealed by scrub brush."

"Excellent," Maria replied, then reached into her pack and retrieved an envelope filled with Israeli banknotes. Al-Khatib's eyes widened as she slid the fat envelope across the table.

"There is a bonus for your timely work," she said.

"I am most grateful," the Palestinian gushed, quickly stuffing the envelope into his pocket.

Maria finished her cup of tea, then said, "You will show us to the site now."

Al-Khatib looked at his watch with dismay. "It will be dark shortly, but there is a bright moon tonight."

Then he saw the cold, determined look in Maria's eyes and quickly backpedaled.

"Of course, if that is what you wish," he stammered. "Do you have a car?"

He paid the bill, then the trio made their way down the street to the rental. Following al-Khatib's directions, Maria drove around the southern end of the Old City, then turned north into the Kidron Valley. The Palestinian directed her to the fringe of an ancient Muslim cemetery, where Maria concealed the car behind an adjacent stone warehouse that was crumbling at the seams.

Their shadows disappeared under the approaching twilight as the Janissary removed a pickax and a bag filled with electric lanterns from the rear of the car. He and Maria then followed the Palestinian as he hopped over a low stone wall and wound his way through the dusty cemetery. The grounds were all but deserted at the late hour, but the group kept to the remote western section, well away from a mosque in the center and a side road to the east. The Janissary did his best to conceal the ax, hiding the business end under his arm as he walked.

To the east of them rose the Mount of Olives, dominated by a large Jewish cemetery and several churches and gardens. Rising from a hillside to their immediate west stood the towering stone wall that surrounded the Old

City. Just over the wall was the original Temple Mount, now occupied by the al-Haram ash-Sharif, or Noble Sanctuary. At the center of the holy grounds was the Dome of the Rock, a towering structure that housed the stone upon which Abraham had prepared to sacrifice his son. In Islamic tradition, that rock was also deemed the departure point for Muhammad's visit to heaven during his Night Journey, earmarked by his footprint in the stone. Maria could just make out the top of the Muslim shrine's large gold dome, the towering structure appearing maple brown in the fading light.

Al-Khatib reached the simple marker of a Muslim Emir who'd died in the sixteenth century, and turned left. Stepping to the end of an irregular row of grave sites, he began climbing the rocky hillside that rose sharply toward the Old City. Maria fumbled for a flashlight in her pack but kept it turned off, stumbling over rocks and scrub, until reaching a slight plateau, where al-Khatib slowed.

"We are close," he whispered.

Flicking on his own penlight, he led them higher up the hill, stopping finally beside a pair of desert shrubs. Panting for breath, Maria noticed that both plants were actually dead, their roots wedged into a small mound of stones. Behind the dead shrubs was an orderly stack of limestone rocks.

"It is behind here," al-Khatib said, waving his light toward the plants. He turned and nervously scanned up and down the hillside to ensure they were not being observed.

"There are occasional security patrols in this area," he cautioned.

Maria pulled out the pair of night vision goggles and carefully scanned the surroundings. The nearby sounds of the city wafted down the valley, and a blanket of lights twinkled across the surrounding hills. But all was empty in the cemetery below.

"There is no one about," she confirmed.

Al-Khatib nodded, then knelt down and began tossing the stones aside. When a small opening appeared, Maria ordered the Jannisary to assist. Together, the two men quickly cleared away a concealed entrance, exposing a narrow passageway almost five feet in height. After removing all of the obstructions, the Palestinian stood and rested.

"The aqueduct was actually quite small," he said to Maria, circling his hands together in a tight diameter. "A good deal of digging was required to enlarge it."

Maria looked at the man without pity as she considered the original construction history. The aqueduct opening found on the hillside was simply an outlet, she knew, for a much more elaborate engineering feat. Nearly two thousand years before, Roman engineers under Herod had constructed a series of aqueducts from the distant hills of Hebron, which brought fresh water to the town and the fortress of Antonia, built on the site of the Temple Mount. The aqueducts were all constructed by hand, by laborers much more fit than the pudgy Palestinian who stood before her, Maria thought.

She held her flashlight to the mouth of the passage and flicked it on. The light revealed a narrow tunnel that ran five feet into the hillside. In the rear, she could see the small aqueduct opening at floor level, which continued deeper into the dirt wall. The tunnel was cleanly carved, and Maria could see that al-Khatib had excavated it with some skill.

"You have done nice work," she told him, turning off her light. Then she took the pickax from the Janissary and handed it to the Palestinian.

"I need you to dig another two or three feet," she demanded.

The well-paid artifact hunter readily nodded, hoping for an additional bonus while curious as to the task at hand. Taking a lantern from the Janissary, he squeezed to the rear of the tunnel and began digging into the rocky wall. The Janissary stepped in behind him and with gloved hands began removing the loose dirt and chipped debris accumulating around al-Khatib's feet.

As Maria stood watch near the entrance, al-Khatib labored steadily, swinging the ax for nearly twenty minutes straight and carving away several more feet of soil. Breathing hard, he laid a heavy stroke into the hillside, feeling an odd lightness through the ax's handle. Yanking back the ax, he realized he had punched a hole through to an open space behind the wall of dirt. The startled Palestinian stopped and held up the lantern. He could see only a black expanse of emptiness through the small hole but marveled at the rush of cool air that flowed through it.

With renewed energy, he furiously attacked the barrier, quickly expanding the hole to man-size. Pushing the debris aside, he barreled through the opening with the lantern, stumbling into a wide, high-ceilinged cavern.

"Praise be Allah," he gasped, tossing the pickax aside as he gazed at the far walls.

They reflected alabaster white because of the electric lantern and revealed even rows of chisel marks. Al-Khatib's trained eye recognized the rock as limestone, showing where large blocks had been cut and removed by hand.

"A quarry, like Zedekiah's Cave," he blurted as Maria and the Janissary entered with another pair of lanterns.

"Yes," Maria replied. "Only this one was lost to history when the Second Temple was destroyed."

Beneath the walls of the Old City, less than a mile away, was another vast cave, carved by slaves who chiseled limestone for Herod the Great's many engineering projects. Its name was acquired from the last king of Judah, Zedekiah, who reportedly used it as a hiding place to escape the armies of Nebuchadnezzar.

With the added light, the trio could see that the quarry dispersed into multiple passages, extending like fingers of a hand into the darkness. Al-Khatib eyed a large main tunnel that stretched directly east as far as he could see.

"This must extend well under the Haram ash-Sharif," he said uneasily.

Maria nodded in reply.

"And the Dome of the Rock?" he asked, tension apparent in his voice.

"The Dome's sacred stone is itself situated on bedrock, but the main tunnel does underlie the structure. Another tunnel approaches the al-Aqsa Mosque, in addition to other points on the grounds. That is, if Suleiman's maps are accurate, which they have proven to be so far."

The Palestinian's face turned pale as his initial excitement turned to trepidation.

"I do not wish to tread beneath the site of the sacred rock," he said solemnly.

"That will not be necessary," Maria replied. "Your work is finished."

As she spoke, she reached into her pack and retrieved a compact Beretta pistol, which she leveled at the startled Palestinian.

Unlike her brother, Maria felt no rush or thrill at taking the life of another. In fact, she felt nothing at all. Committing murder was the emotional equivalent of changing her socks or eating a bowl of soup. They were at different ends of the sociopathic scale, products of abusive childhoods and genetic homogeneity, but they had both ended up as remorseless killers.

The pistol barked twice, sending a pair of slugs into al-Khatib's chest as the echo of the shots reverberated loudly through the chamber. The relic hunter dropped to his knees, a momentary look of incomprehension in his eyes, before he fell over dead. Maria calmly walked over and removed the envelope of banknotes from his pocket and stuffed it in her pack. Then she glanced at her watch.

"We have less than an hour before the explosives are to be delivered," she said to the Janissary. "Let us survey the quarry and select our sites."

Stepping over the dead man's body, she retrieved his lantern, then quickly scurried off into the dark.

45

It was nearing ten o'clock when Sophie pulled into a small dirt lot outside the northeast wall of the Old City and parked behind a closed dress shop. Across the road and down a short hill was the northern tip of the Muslim cemetery, which meandered south across a widening gulch as part of the Kidron Valley headlands. Shutting off the ignition, she turned to Dirk, who gazed at her from the passenger seat.

"Are you sure you want to do this?" she asked. "Most night operations turn out to be a boring exercise in futility."

Dirk smiled as he nodded his head. "I'm not one to waste the chance for a stroll in the moonlight with a beautiful girl."

Sophie suppressed a laugh. "You're the only one I know who could find something romantic in a stakeout."

But she had to admit to similar feelings. They had enjoyed an intimate dinner at a quiet Armenian café inside the Jaffa Gate, and as the evening progressed she developed a compelling desire to cancel the surveillance operation and invite him to her apartment instead. She quelled the notion, knowing the prospect of obtaining potential information about the killers of agent Holder was much too important.

"It's not like Sam to be late," she said, checking her watch, then gazing out the window for his vehicle.

A minute later, her cell phone vibrated, and she answered, speaking animatedly in Hebrew.

"It was Sam," she said after hanging up. "He was in an auto accident."

"Is he all right?"

"Yes. Apparently a van filled with Christian pilgrims missed a turn and drove into him. He's okay, but his car is wrecked. He thinks a few elderly tourists might be injured, so it's going to take a while to clean up. He doesn't think that he'll be able to get here for another hour."

"Then I guess we better start without him," Dirk replied, opening the door and climbing out of the car. Sophie followed him, opening the trunk and removing a pair of night vision binoculars, which she strung around her neck. Then she leaned over and opened a large leather case that was lying flat in the trunk. Inside was a weathered, government-issue Tavor TAR-21 assault rifle. Sophie slid in a fully loaded clip and chambered the first round, then slid the weapon over her shoulder.

"Armed for bear this time, I see," Dirk remarked.

"After Caesarea, I will always be better armed," she said, her voice filled with resolve.

"Why not let the Shin Bet handle the stakeout if you suspect the Lebanese smugglers are involved?"

"I considered that," she replied, "but the tip was rather flimsy. We're most likely dealing with some ragtag teenage pothunters who probably won't even show up."

"That would be all right with me," Dirk said with a wink as he grabbed her hand.

They crossed the road and hiked down the embankment that spilled into the cemetery. Sophie stopped and scanned the grounds with her binoculars.

"We need to move farther down," she said quietly.

They hiked another dozen yards down the slope, stopping at a low rise that offered an unobstructed view of nearly the entire cemetery. Around them, the Muslim flat stone graves glimmered white under the moonlight like an array of displaced teeth scattered about a sand-colored blanket. Sophie took a seat on a stone ledge and carefully surveyed the lower grounds with her night vision glasses. She spotted a few kids playing a late-night game of soccer on the other side of the Western Wall, but the cemetery itself appeared deserted. She was scanning toward the east when she felt Dirk's body slide in alongside her, his arm wrapping around her waist. She slowly lowered the binoculars.

"You are distracting me from my work," she protested lightly, then placed a hand around the back of his neck and kissed him passionately.

They embraced for several minutes until a faint shuffling sound disrupted their intimacy. Sophie quickly gazed down the hill again.

"Three men with large backpacks," she whispered. "Two of them appear to be carrying shovels or possibly weapons, I can't tell."

She put down the binoculars and looked up the hill. "We need Sam," she said with frustration.

"He's still a half hour away," Dirk said, glancing at his watch.

The sound of the three men's steps grew louder as they trudged up the center of the cemetery. Sophie unholstered her Glock pistol and handed it to Dirk.

"We'll make the arrest," she whispered. "Then I'll call the Jerusalem police to take them in."

Dirk nodded in agreement as he took the pistol, checking to see that it was loaded. They crept from their spot, moving slowly down the hill. They followed the larger grave markers for cover, which gradually carried them to their right. Approaching a raised tomb that offered concealment, they inched along its high back side, then kneeled down and waited.

The minutes ticked by slowly as the three purported grave robbers worked their way closer. Sophie quietly clipped her flashlight to the barrel of the Tavor, then held perfectly still as the men trudged by a few feet away. She nodded to Dirk, then suddenly sprang to her feet. Leaping behind the men, she clicked on the flashlight, then shouted in Arabic, "Stop! Hands in the air!"

The three men turned and froze at the sudden ambush, squinting as Sophie played the light's beam on their faces. Two of the men, each holding an AK-74 pointed at the ground, glared at her with menace. One of them was short, shabbily dressed, with droopy eyes, who Sophie recognized as Hassan Akais, the subject of the tip. The second was equally dirty, distinguished by a prominently bent nose. It was the third man, however, who sent a shiver down Sophie's spine. Clearly the leader of the trio, he calmly stared back at her with probing eyes that danced above a deep scar on the right side of his jaw. It was the same face that had glared at her in Caesarea, leading the assault that killed detective Holder.

Sophie's hands trembled in recognition, causing the flashlight's beam to flicker about the terrorist's face. Sensing her hesitation, Akais quickly and silently swung his weapon up to bear on Sophie. As his finger reached for the trigger, a loud shot echoed through the cemetery. A splotch of red materialized on the gunman's wrist as a 9mm slug tore through his forearm.

The man winced in pain, letting go of the trigger while grabbing his bloodied arm with his free hand. He looked up blankly at Sophie before spotting Dirk standing a few steps to her side, an automatic pistol extended in his hands at arms' length.

"Throw down your weapons or I shall aim a bit higher next time," Dirk commanded.

The other Arab, who wore a long, straggly beard, quickly shed his AK-74, but the wounded man didn't move. He stared at Dirk with hatred in his eyes. Then suddenly his face softened, and he gritted his teeth in a defiant smirk as his gaze shifted past Dirk's shoulder.

"I'm afraid it is you who shall throw down your weapons," came a hardened female voice from the darkness. "Place your hands in the air where I can see them."

Dirk turned toward the voice to find a short-haired woman standing directly behind Sophie with a pistol pointed to the back of her skull. He saw she was dressed in dark, casual clothes, but had her own night vision goggles perched on her forehead. Dirk felt another presence, and he craned his neck slightly to see the shadow of another man in the darkness with a raised gun aimed at his own head.

Sophie gave him an apologetic look as she lowered her Tavor to the ground. With little choice, Dirk smiled innocently at the Turkish woman, then gently tossed his pistol onto a nearby grave.

46

Dirk and Sophie were marched at gunpoint up the side of the hill and into the narrow passageway. Like the Arab terrorists who followed them, they were startled at the sight of the huge quarry that awaited on the other side, now illuminated by the pale glow of several lanterns. Sophie had visited Zedekiah's Cave on several occasions and was astonished to find another, equally expansive quarry situated beneath the Temple Mount. Her awe turned to fear when she spotted the bloodstained body of al-Khatib lying facedown beside one of the lanterns. Her fear was only enhanced at her recognition of the Arab terrorist leader.

"The tall one . . . he led the attack at Caesarea," she whispered to Dirk.

Dirk nodded, already aware that the well-armed contingent was after something more important than an old grave or two. The Janissary prodded them to a low stone ledge, where they took a seat, under gunpoint, near the dead Palestinian. Maria ignored them as she gathered the heavy backpacks from the three Arabs.

"This is the entire quantity?" she asked Zakkar.

"Yes, all twenty-five kilos are there, with fuzes and detonators," the Arab replied. He gazed up at the high ceiling. "Do you aim to blow up the Dome of the Rock?"

Maria looked at him coldly. "Yes, and the al-Aqsa Mosque. Do you have a problem with that?"

The Arab shook his head. "You will cause great anger in our lands. But perhaps it will result in the greater good of Allah."

"There will be a greater good," Maria replied sharply.

She knelt down and quickly inventoried the explosives, then rose to her feet. Noticing Sophie and Dirk observing her movements, her face quickly soured.

"You nearly exposed our mission," she hissed at Zakkar.

The Arab shook his head. "They are archaeological police looking for grave looters," he said without acknowledging his own recognition of Sophie and Dirk. "It was a random surveillance. Why don't we just kill them now?" he asked, tilting his head in their direction

"Israeli archaeologists, you say?" Maria mulled her own words over. "No, we shall not kill them. They shall die 'accidentally' in the blast," she said with a wicked grin. "They will make the perfect scapegoats."

She waved for the Janissary to approach, then turned again to Zakkar.

"Have your two men stand guard," she said, glancing at her watch. "It is time we set the explosives, which I wish to detonate at one o'clock."

She picked up a lantern as the Janissary hoisted up two of the backpacks. Zakkar addressed his two men, then picked up the other pack and a lantern and followed Maria as she disappeared down one of the passageways.

"Destruction of the Dome will unleash a horrific wave of bloodshed," Sophie whispered to Dirk.

"Silence!" barked the bearded Arab, briefly waving his gun in Sophie's direction.

His partner, the wounded man named Akais, sat on a nearby rock, cradling his arm. The gunshot had missed any major arteries, and he had stemmed the flow of blood with his *keffiyeh*, now wrapped tightly around his arm. Though he had walked easily up the hill and into the quarry under his own power, he was now suffering a moderate degree of shock from loss of blood. At times he would glare at Dirk with rage, then his eyes would glaze over into a thousand-mile stare.

Dirk methodically surveyed the quarry, searching for a means of escape that wouldn't garner a bullet in the back. But there appeared to be few avenues. Staring at the dead Palestinian for a few moments, he took note of the two remaining lanterns. One was lying on the floor near the dead man, some ten feet from his own position. The bearded gunman slowly circled the other lamp, perched on a stone across the cavern.

Dirk caught Sophie's attention and casually motioned toward the bearded guard. Then he rubbed the back of his hand across his mouth, whispering beneath it.

"The lantern . . . can you turn it off?"

Sophie eyed the lamp and the adjacent guard, then nodded faintly with a determined glare. She then carefully scanned the walls of the cavern, examining every cut and chisel mark that she could make out in the dim light. On a wall beyond the guard, she found what she was looking for, an irregular mark from which to build a story.

She stared at the spot with rapt fascination until the guard caught her gaze and turned to see what she was looking at. Keeping her eyes locked on the wall, she gently rose to her feet and took a step forward.

"Do not move," the Arab hissed, turning back toward her.

Sophie tried her best to ignore him without getting shot.

"This quarry is two thousand years old, directly beneath the Dome of the Rock," she murmured. "I think I see a sign of the Prophet over there."

The guard looked suspiciously at her, then at Dirk. The NUMA engineer gave him the best clueless and uninterested look he could muster. Grabbing the lantern, the Arab backed slowly to the wall, keeping his assault rifle leveled on the pair. Reaching the wall, he took several hasty glances at the carved limestone. A pair of parallel gouges ran lightly across the surface at eye level while a faded mark in charcoal was visible between the cuts. The gunman looked at the mark blankly, then focused on Sophie.

"Yes, that's it," she said, taking another tentative step forward. When the gunman didn't react, she continued walking toward him at a cautious pace.

"Any tricks, and your friend dies first," the Arab spat, keeping his gun aimed at Dirk. He then turned and yelled at his companion.

"Hassan, stay alert."

The wounded gunman responded by sluggishly nodding his head.

"Now, show me," the gunman continued, speaking to Sophie while backing away from the wall.

Sophie crept to the wall and placed a hand on the surface near the cuts and marking. She had seen similar cuts in the walls of Zedekiah's Cave and knew they were

379

nothing more than the preliminary markings for a limestone slab that for some reason was never cut by the quarrymen. The faded charcoal was likely a numerical marking or placeholder for the unused stone. Yet she played it for much more.

"Like his footprint in the Dome's sacred rock above, I believe this may be an indication of Muhammad's departure on the Night Journey," she said, referring to the visit to heaven atop a winged steed. "I can't quite make it out under the light, though. May I borrow the lantern?"

She never looked at the guard, instead pretending to be engrossed in the wall carving as she extended a hand out toward him. He reacted instinctively, tentatively passing the lantern while also shifting the muzzle of his rifle in her direction. Grabbing the lantern, Sophie held it up to the wall, her eyes still glued to the charcoal marking.

"See this here," she said quietly, pointing her free hand at the rock. She then casually let her hand slip to the base of the lantern, where her fingers groped for the power switch. Finding it with her index finger, she clicked the lamp off and froze.

Under the yellow glow of the far lamp, she was still quite visible to the Arab. He started to grunt a command at her, then noticed a sudden movement out of the corner of his eye.

Dirk had quietly been waiting for that moment. The instant Sophie's lantern went dark, he sprang from the ledge. He knew bullets would follow him immediately, so he took two steps and dove for the light.

He wasn't to be disappointed. The bearded gunman swung his weapon and fired instantly. But Dirk had already hit the ground, and the bullets whizzed high over his head. Extending an arm as he landed, he grabbed the lantern one-handed. Not bothering to fumble with the switch, he simply slammed the lantern against the ground, smashing the glass panes and bulb.

The cavern plunged into total darkness, which was quickly punctuated by bursts of fiery light from the muzzle of the Arab's assault rifle. The angered gunman fired several protracted rounds at Dirk, which echoed like thunder through the quarry as bullets ricocheted off the limestone walls.

The fire was aimed at Dirk's last position, but he had immediately rolled away from the lantern and scurried crablike across the floor toward the entry passage. After crawling twenty feet, he stopped and circled around, groping about the floor with his hands. The firing ceased as he found what he was looking for—the body of the dead Palestinian. Or, more precisely, the pickax that lay near the man's feet.

An uncomfortable silence fell over the cavern as the odor of gunpowder drifted through the air. The Arab gunman, confident that he had killed Dirk, turned and fired toward the spot where Sophie had been standing moments earlier. But under the glow of the muzzle flash, he saw that she was no longer there.

Running a hand along the wall for guidance, Sophie smartly had run toward and then past the gunman while he was firing at Dirk. When the shooting stopped, she froze, the lantern still clasped in her hand, as she willed her heart to stop beating so loudly.

"Hassan, do you have a light?" the Arab shouted.

The wounded gunman was slowly regaining his senses and rose to his feet unsteadily.

"I am here, by the entrance. Do not shoot this way," he pleaded in a weak voice.

"The light?" his partner barked.

"It is in my backpack, which I can't seem to locate," Akais replied, groping around his feet.

"The others took the backpacks," replied the other man angrily.

Dirk made the most of the distracting conversation to move in for the kill. Hoisting the pickax over his shoulder, he crept toward the entryway and the voice of the wounded gunman. In his unsteady state, he would be the easiest to take down. With a little luck, Dirk could swap the ax for an assault rifle and shoot the other man before he knew what happened.

As the conversation died, Dirk still stood several feet from the wounded man. He would have to take a blind swing at him, as he couldn't afford to reveal his position. Halting for a moment, he slid a foot forward silently, then slid again. But even in his diminished state, Akais detected a presence nearby.

"Salaam?" he suddenly asked.

The voice was close, Dirk realized, close enough to strike. He had taken another soft step forward and raised the ax to swing when a lantern suddenly came on across the cavern. He spun to see it was Maria, with a lantern in one hand and a pistol in the other. Staring at Dirk, she eased the pistol to her left until it was aimed at the heart of Sophie, who stood crouched against the wall just a few feet away.

"Drop the ax or she dies now," the Turkish woman said.

Sophie gave him a forlorn look as he reluctantly dropped the pickax to the ground. Looking at her eyes wide with fear was the last thing he remembered. Then Hassan smacked the stock of his rifle into the back of Dirk's head and he crumpled to the ground in a sea of darkness.

47

A well-traveled white taxi turned into the dirt lot and came to a stop alongside Sophie's car. Sam Levine quickly paid the driver, then hopped out. As the cab drove off into the night, Sam tried phoning Sophie. Not surprised that she didn't answer, he sent her a text message telling her where he was. When there was no response to that, he set off for the cemetery, knowing that she usually turned her phone off during a reconnaissance operation.

He crossed the street with a slight limp, his side and hip aching from the auto accident. In the confusion, he had left his night vision gear in the trunk of his damaged car, but he did have an automatic pistol holstered at his side. By moving slowly and quietly, he banked that Sophie would be able to spot him before he disrupted the surveillance.

Climbing down the embankment, he realized that he would have no problem moving slowly. He winced as a steep step sent a shooting pain through his leg, and he resorted to taking small, stuttering steps as he navigated the sloping grounds that led to the cemetery.

The cemetery appeared silent and empty as he crept past the ancient tombs. He stopped every few yards to look and listen, expecting Sophie to silently appear out of the dark and tap him on the shoulder. But she never materialized.

Hiking another few steps, he stopped again, this time at hearing a distant noise. It was the clacking sound of rocks being piled upon one another, emanating from the center of the cemetery. Sam quietly tiptoed a few yards closer, stopping behind a low retaining wall. The clattering continued from down the hill. As he peered cautiously over the wall, under the light of a half-moon, he could just make out several shadowy figures moving about a flat grave near a short stone lamp tower that had lost its illumination decades ago.

The antiquities agent pulled out his pistol, then sat and waited. Several minutes ticked by as he wondered where Sophie was and why she wasn't making an arrest. Perhaps she had abandoned the recon, he thought, but that didn't prevent him from doing his duty.

Climbing over the wall with a grimace, he hobbled downhill toward the grave robbers. The sound of rattling stones ceased, and he could make out several of the figures retreating toward the southern end of the cemetery. He tried to run, but the stinging pain in his joints quickly slowed him to a shuffle. With a rising sense of desperation, he stopped and shouted, "Halt!"

The demand had an inverse effect. Rather than stopping the intruders, it prompted them to flee quicker. Sam could hear their accelerated steps as they ran through the cemetery and past its southern boundary. Moments later, the sound of not one but two automobiles starting up disrupted the night, followed by the screech of tires as both cars quickly sped away.

Sam shook his head in dismay as he spotted the receding taillights. Then he thought again about his supervisor.

"Sophie, are you out there?" he shouted.

But he was only answered by the silence of the empty graveyard.

Ambling down to the light tower, he stepped to the adjacent grave site, expecting to find a hastily dug crater burrowed into it. Instead, he was surprised to see an orderly mound of stones covering the grave. It was unusual for robbers to conceal their handiwork, he knew. Curious, he lifted a few of the stones off the top of the mound. He nearly fell backward when a human hand appeared in the moonlight.

Working more hesitantly, he gently removed more of the stones until revealing the bloodied torso and head of the murdered Palestinian. Staring at the corpse with revulsion, Sam silently wondered what sort of twisted thieves had come to the graveyard to make a deposit.

48

A dull light seemed to burn through Dirk's eyes, though his lids were tightly closed. There was nothing dull, however, in the throbbing pain that surged through his head.

With a Herculean effort, he slowly forced open an eyelid, cringing as he slowly focused on a glowing lantern sitting inches from his face. Climbing back to full consciousness, he noticed the discomfort of the cold, hard limestone floor beneath his body. His arms stirred slightly as his hands groped along the surface, searching for support.

Taking a deep breath, he pressed with his arms, raising his torso while pulling up his legs, until he reached a sitting position. An explosion of stars swirled before his eyes, and he nearly passed out again, staving off slumber by breathing deeply. Resting a few minutes until the dizziness and nausea passed, he noticed a cool dampness on his back. Rubbing a hand across the back of his head, he felt a stinging knot that was caked with dried blood.

The gears in his mind slowly began churning as he recognized his surroundings. Sitting alone in the empty cavern, he immediately called out to Sophie in a weakened voice. Only silence countered his ringing ears. Grabbing the lantern, he painfully rose to his feet, the pounding in his skull rising to new proportions as he staggered about like a drunk.

He gradually regained his strength and steadiness as he searched around the cavern, then crawled out the passageway. The cemetery appeared dark and silent around him, so he quickly reentered the quarry.

He shouted for her again, this time in a stronger voice that echoed through the chamber. From deep inside one of the tunnels, he thought he heard a faint slap in reply. Though his hearing was far from optimal, the sound, if real, seemed to emanate from the large tunnel to his right. It was the same tunnel that Maria and her men had entered with the explosives.

Ducking slightly as he entered the six-foot-high tunnel, Dirk moved as briskly as his throbbing head would allow. Unbeknownst to him, the tunnel stretched more than two hundred yards into the hillside, bisecting the grounds of the Haram ash-Sharif several feet above his head. Of greater importance to the bombers was its proximity to the Dome of the Rock, burrowing beneath it to within a few yards of the revered rock itself.

The tunnel curved and twisted, occasionally passing through small chambers where pockets of limestone had neatly been quarried away. As Dirk rounded a tight bend, he detected a faint light glowing from the tunnel ahead. With the skip of a heartbeat, he forced himself to double his pace, ignoring the pounding ache that shot through his head with each labored step.

The distant light brightened as he jogged through a small, rectangular chamber, then into a straight section of tunnel. Chasing the beckoning rays, he staggered out of the tunnel and into a final chamber that curved around like a punch bowl. Parked in the center was one of the electric lanterns. To his right, Dirk saw a mass of clear puttylike material pressed onto the wall with several wire detonators dangling from its core. To his left lay Sophie, squirming and wriggling, a gag in her mouth and her feet and wrists bound with straps from a backpack. A large rock had been placed between her knees, effectively pinning her to the ground. When she gazed at Dirk, the terror in her glistening eyes quickly vanished.

"I see you're trying to have a blast without me," he said with a weary grin.

But he didn't give her the opportunity to reply. Heaving the rock from between her legs, he hoisted her over his shoulder, then grabbed both lanterns with his free hand. Finding renewed strength, he quickly shuffled back down the tunnel, careful not to bang her head against the low ceiling.

He carried her more than half the distance to the main cavern before dizziness reappeared in full force. Reaching the small chamber, he gently set her on the ground and removed her gag as he caught his breath.

"You look terrible," she said. "Are you badly hurt?"

"I'm fine," he grunted. "You were the one with the worries."

"What time is it?" she asked hurriedly.

"Five minutes to one," Dirk replied, gazing at his watch.

"The explosives. The woman said they were set to detonate at one a.m."

"Let 'em blow. Let's just get out of here."

"No."

Dirk was startled by the tone in her voice. It was less of a request than a demand.

"If the Dome and the mosque are destroyed, it will mean disaster for my country. War will ensue like no other we have seen."

Dirk looked into Sophie's dark eyes, seeing determination, hope, love, and despair. With the seconds ticking, he knew he couldn't hope to win a debate on the matter.

"I think I can disable the detonator," he said, untying her hands. "But you've got to get out of here. Here's an extra lantern. Untie your feet and head for the exit."

He turned to run back into the tunnel, but she grabbed his shirt and pulled him close for a quick but passionate kiss.

"Be careful," she said. "I love you."

His mind in a whirl, Dirk took off running. Her words seemed to extinguish all pain, and he found himself nearly sprinting through the tunnel. In a matter of seconds, he charged into the last chamber and approached the plastic explosives.

As a marine engineer, he had a rudimentary knowledge of explosives, having worked on salvage projects where underwater demolitions had been required. Though he was unfamiliar with the HMX explosives, the detonating technology in front of him was a common configuration. A single electronic timer fuze was wired to a string of detonator caps, which in turn were embedded in the explosives.

He glanced at his watch, seeing it was three minutes to one.

"Don't blow early," he muttered under his breath as he held the light to the wall.

He quickly searched the plastic explosives for additional fuzes, not realizing the quantity of HMX in front of him was enough to level a skyscraper. Finding only the one fuze, he grabbed hold of it and yanked it from the wall. The fuze, with its associated detonator caps, slipped freely from the HMX. With the blasting device dangling in his hand, Dirk took off running back down the tunnel.

He soon reached the now-dark and empty rectangular chamber, where he was thankful to see by her absence that Sophie had heeded his directions to flee. He stopped for a moment and hurled the fuze assembly against the far wall of the chamber, then dashed into the tunnel. With a sense of relief and fading adrenaline, he stepped into the main chamber, the pain in his head renewing its friendship. He made his way across the dark cavern, noticing for the first time that the body of the Palestinian was no longer there.

Squeezing through the entry tunnel, he welcomed the fresh air outside by sucking in several deep breaths, then glanced around for Sophie. Not spotting her or her light, he flicked off his own lantern momentarily, then called out her name. Neither her light nor her voice responded.

Then a sick feeling suddenly hit Dirk like a blow to the belly. The mosque. Sophie had said that the Dome and the mosque would be destroyed. There must be a second set of explosives for the mosque, and Sophie was inside trying to deactivate it.

Dirk shot back through the passageway like an arrow. Inside the main cavern, there were three small tunnels bored into the hillside to the left of the Dome tunnel. Dirk raced to the entrance of each, shouting out Sophie's name down the dark corridors. At the entrance to the last tunnel, he heard a garbled reply, and recognized her silky voice calling from the distance. He immediately burst into the tunnel, running at a sprint through the chiseled corridor.

He'd taken only a few steps when he heard a popping noise in the distance, like a short string of firecrackers exploding. It was the detonators that he had pulled free beneath the Dome, now igniting harmlessly in the rectangle chamber.

Dirk's heart pounded like a sledgehammer as he realized the second cache would detonate at any second.

"Sophie . . . get out of there . . . now!" he shouted between pounding breaths.

Ahead in the tunnel he could see a faint glimmer of light, and he knew he was getting closer. Then he heard another series of pops, and he dove to the floor with an agonized heart.

The explosion shook the ground like an earthquake, accompanied by an earsplitting boom. Seconds later, the expanding force of exploding gasses burst through the tunnel with a roaring gust, blowing a shower of dust and rock in front of it. Dirk felt his body lift off the ground and slam into the wall, knocking the breath out of him. Hammered by rock and buried in a blanket of choking dust, he felt the world around him once again turn to black.

49

Sam had been standing with his back to the hillside, examining the dead Palestinian, when Dirk briefly emerged from the passageway in search of Sophie. Hearing someone else call Sophie's name, the antiquities agent wheeled around in time to catch a glimpse of Dirk's lantern disappearing back into the passageway. Sam once more pulled out his phone and tried calling Sophie, then crept slowly up the hill.

He was only a few yards from the quarry entrance when the cache of explosives detonated. From his vantage, it was little more than a muffled bang followed by a slight rumble beneath his feet. Seconds later, a plume of smoke and dust came pouring out of the small passageway.

He approached the entrance and found a discarded lantern in the bushes while waiting for the air to clear. Turning on the lamp, he stepped cautiously through the passageway. He was stunned as he stepped into the main cavern, shocked that a huge quarry existed unrecorded beneath the Temple Mount.

The air was still thick with smoke and dust, and Sam kept a sleeve to his nose as he surveyed the interior. He poked a head into each of the four tunnels, hesitating at the last one, which spewed a heavy plume, and then he suddenly heard the clattering sound of rock on rock echoing from within.

Proceeding slowly into the tunnel, he detected the glow of another light far down the corridor. Accelerating his pace, he encountered a pile of debris shaken from the walls by the blast. Stepping carefully past the rubble, he moved farther into the depths of the hillside. The dark tunnel straightened for several yards, and Sam could suddenly see the lantern burning brightly ahead.

A nervous sweat poured down his face as he coughed away the dust that caked his nasal passages. Making his way past a jagged boulder, he staggered out of the tunnel and into a large chamber illuminated by the lantern set on a fallen rock. The chamber resembled an underground gravel pit, with mounds of rocks piled on the floor throughout. A large, irregular hole had been eaten out of the ceiling just over the worst of the debris, the handi-work of the blast. A thick white haze still hung over everything, obscuring visibility despite the light.

From the opposite side of the chamber, Sam detected a faint movement.

"Sophie?" he called, reaching uneasily for the grip of his handgun.

Like an apparition, a figure appeared through the haze. With a brief sense of relief, Sam recognized Dirk emerging from the gloom. The relief faded when he saw that Dirk held the limp body of Sophie in his arms.

"Is she all right?" he asked quietly.

Sam tentatively stepped closer, observing that Dirk had covered her head and torso with a light jacket. It was then that he noticed Sophie's dangling limbs appeared mis-shapen and coated with a thick layer of blood and dust.

He looked up at Dirk for an explanation and immediately shivered. Any hope for Sophie's well-being was immediately extinguished by Dirk's ragged appearance. Dirk stood staring at him with a battered and bloodied face, his eyes lost and soulless. The life seemed to be crushed out of him, and Sam knew at once that Sophie was dead.

50

The explosion beneath the Haram ash-Sharif was nearly suppressed before the smoke even cleared. The Dome of the Rock had been Maria's primary target, and it was there that she had planted the bulk of the explosives. But they went undetonated, rendered harmless when Dirk pulled out the blasting caps. It was a second, smaller cache, planted beneath the al-Aqsa Mosque, that did explode, though ultimately with minimal effect.

The ground beneath the eighth-century mosque shook and its windows rattled, but no fireballs erupted from the earth to consume it. Seconds before the explosives detonated, Sophie had removed a large block of them and tossed them down the tunnel before attempting to remove the fuzes in the remaining material. The diminished blast did little more than crack the foundation of a fountain behind the mosque. The Haram's Palestinian caretakers initially took little note, believing the explosion came from another part of Jerusalem.

Inside the quarry, Sam Levine had been fast to act. Police and paramedics arrived quickly, treating Dirk while removing Sophie's body to the morgue. Shin Bet security agents were equally prompt. The quarry was thoroughly searched, and the remaining explosives carefully secured and removed. The entire complex was then sealed off before the proprietors of Haram ash-Sharif even realized what had happened.

News of the attempted attack quickly spread through Jerusalem, creating an uproar. Local Muslims decried the assault, while the city's Jews were horrified at the potential desecration of the Temple Mount. Each faction blamed the other, and tempers soared on all sides. Publicly defensive while privately tightening security around the city, the Israeli government quietly brought Jerusalem's Muslim leaders to the quarry, where they jointly agreed to permanently barricade the site against future intrusion.

Anger in the street remained high, but outbursts were remarkably few, and violence was averted. Within days, the tensions abated, as no one stepped forward to claim responsibility for the attacks, while the real bombers disappeared without a trace.

General Braxton read the CIA report without uttering a word. Only a sporadic twitching of the National Intelligence Director's mustache revealed a hint of emotion. Across his desk, intelligence officer O'Quinn and an Israeli CIA specialist sat silently staring at their shoes. They quickly sat upright when they observed Braxton remove a pair of granny-style reading glasses from the tip of his nose.

"So let me see here," the general said in his gravelly voice. "Some nuts nearly blow up half of Jerusalem, and neither Mossad nor Shin Bet have a clue who did it? Is that the truth or is that just what the Israelis are telling us?"

"The Israelis clearly lack confidence in the investigation," the CIA man replied. "They believe a Lebanese weapons- and drug-smuggling ring known as the Mules are at least partially responsible. The Mules have known ties to Hezbollah, so it's possible they targeted Jerusalem in retaliation for Israel's continued problems in Gaza. The American involved in the incident identified one of the bombers as being involved in a recent terrorist incident at an archaeological dig in Caesarea."

"Is the American one of our agents?" Braxton asked.

"No, he's a marine engineer with NUMA. He's recovering from minor injuries at an Israeli Army hospital in Haifa."

"A marine engineer? What in blazes was he doing in Jerusalem?"

"Apparently he was romantically involved with the antiquities agent who was killed in the blast. He happened to accompany her on a routine stakeout and got caught up in the fray. A good thing, it turned out, as he was the one who prevented the main cache of explosives from detonating beneath the Dome of the Rock."

"Sir, we really dodged a bullet on that one," O'Quinn said. "There were enough explosives there to easily level the entire Dome structure, let alone a good chunk of the Old City. It would have ignited regional animosity like nothing we've seen. I'm certain that missiles would be flying over Israel today had the shrine been taken out."

Braxton grunted, boring his eyes into O'Quinn. "Since we're on the topic of explosives, I see you have some unsavory homegrown connections to add to the mix."

"We obtained a sample of the unexploded ordnance from the Israelis and confirmed in lab testing that it is in fact HMX. It was produced by a domestic manufacturer under contract with the U.S. Army," O'Quinn reported soberly.

"It's our own bloody explosives?" the general thundered.

"I'm afraid so. We've done some digging, and it appears that the Jerusalem sample matches up with a shipment of high-grade HMX that was secretly sold to Pakistan for use in their nuclear weapons program back in the early nineties. The Pakistanis have since confirmed that a container of HMX went missing a short time thereafter. Black market operatives in the military are believed to have sold it to buyers outside the country, but no evidence of its use has emerged until this year."

"An entire container of HMX. Unbelievable," Braxton said.

"The container would have housed approximately eight thousand pounds of the high explosive. It accounts for significant destructive power."

The general closed his eyes and shook his head. "I presume this attack is connected to the other recent mosque bombings?" he asked without opening his eyes.

"We know that the al-Azhar Mosque in Cairo and the Yeşil Mosque in Bursa were both hit with HMX. In both cases, nobody claimed responsibility for the attacks. And no evidence was found linking the blasts to any local factions. We appear to have a similar set of circumstances in Jerusalem."

"What of this dead Palestinian who was found in the graveyard?"

"He was a low-level artifact hunter with no known terrorist associations," the CIA man responded. "He may have had some involvement with the discovery of the quarry, but he is not believed to have been a player in the actual attack."

"Which takes us to the still unanswered questions of who and why."

O'Quinn gave the general a pained look. "Nobody has claimed responsibility for any of the attacks, and I'm afraid we just don't have a firm trail," he said. "As Joe can verify, the intelligence agencies are looking at suspects across the board, from fringe Christian and Jewish sects to al-Qaeda and other Muslim fanatic groups. We're reliant on the foreign intelligence agencies, and they don't have any strong connections at this point."

The CIA man nodded. "General, the targets have all been sites of theological importance in the Sunni Muslim world. We think there's a strong possibility that the attacks are originating from a Shia source. The possible Hezbollah link in the Jerusalem attack furthers the theory. I have to tell you, there is a growing contingency within the agency that believes it's the Iranians, trying to divert attention from their weapons program."

"It's a viable motivation," Braxton agreed, "but they'd certainly be playing with fire if they got caught with dirty hands."

O'Quinn quietly shook his head.

"I have to disagree, sir," he said. "These bombings don't have the earmark of the Iranians. It would certainly represent a new level of external extremism that we haven't seen before."

"You're not giving me much else to go on, O'Quinn," the general growled. "What about that Turk, Mufti Battal, that you were excited about?"

"He's entered the presidential race, as we feared. He and his party would certainly benefit from any outrage in the fundamentalist community that these bombings may incite. It raises the point that these attacks may be linked to specific political goals rather than general terrorist tactics. As for Battal, we're monitoring his activities closely, but we've yet to witness any pattern of coercive tactics so far. We certainly have no hard proof of a link, at this point."

"So you've got nothing there. Perhaps the question you

boys need to be thinking about is where they intend to strike next."

"The targets have clearly been growing in significance," O'Quinn said.

"And they've been denied in their latest outing, which ought to scare us all, in what they might be planning next."

"The Kaaba in Mecca might be a possible target. I'll see to it that the Saudis are advised to increase security," O'Quinn said.

"We've got analysts working overtime on the matter," the CIA man added. In the true Washington vernacular of helplessness, he added, "We're doing everything we can."

Braxton brushed off the comment with a glare. "Let me tell you what to do," he said, leaning forward over his desk while eyeballing both intelligence men with ire. "It's really a simple exercise to put a stop to this. All you have to do," he said, his voice rising to a fever pitch, "is find me the rest of those explosives!"

52

The *Ottoman Star* eased into the cove north of the Dardanelles late in the afternoon, docking at the long pier that now stood empty. Beneath the adjacent rippled waters, the sunken workboat still sat on the sandy bottom, waiting for the shore crane and a dive crew to raise it from the depths.

Standing on the ship's bridge, Maria was surprised to note her brother's Jaguar parked on the dock. Celik watched as the ship approached the pier, then emerged from the Jaguar's backseat as the mooring lines were secured. He briskly stepped down the quay with an attaché case tucked under his arm and boarded the ship.

"I wasn't expecting you to meet me here, Ozden," Maria said by way of a greeting.

"Time is short," he replied, gazing about the bridge with an agitated expression. The captain and helmsman caught his drift and quickly stepped off the bridge, leaving Celik alone with his sister.

"I heard that the police searched the facilities after we departed," Maria said. "Is it not dangerous for you to be here?"

Celik smirked. "The local police have been well paid to look after our interests. They paid a cursory visit and were kept away from the warehouses." The police investigators reminded him of the assault by the NUMA men, and he subconsciously rubbed the spot on his head where Pitt had clubbed him.

"Those Americans will pay for their intrusion," he said in a guttural tone. "But we have more important matters to address first."

Maria braced for the onslaught over the failure at Jerusalem, but the expected outburst never materialized. Celik quietly gazed out the forward window, eyeing the empty dock.

"Where is the *Sultana*?"

"I left it in Beirut to complete the repair work. The crew will bring her to Istanbul in a few days."

Celik nodded, then stepped close to his sister.

"Now, tell me, Maria, why did the mission fail?"

"I am uncertain myself," she replied calmly. "The primary charge failed to detonate. It was set with multiple fuzes, and I am positive it was staged properly. There must have been outside interference. Even the secondary charge should have produced more damage. I suspect the Israeli archaeologist who was killed may have somehow disabled some of the charges."

"The results were disappointing," Celik replied, suppressing his usual vitriol, "but I am thankful for your safe return."

"We put the Lebanese smugglers ashore in Tripoli on the voyage back, so the Israelis have nowhere to search and no trail to follow."

"You have always covered your tracks well, Maria."

Despite his unusually calm demeanor, she could see the distress in his face.

"How is the Mufti faring?" she asked.

"He is campaigning like a professional politician and has won the public support of some key members of the Grand National Assembly. But he is still trailing in the polls by at least five percentage points, and we have just days to go before the election." He looked at her with an admonishing gaze. "The Jerusalem attack failed to give us the boost that is necessary for us to win."

"Perhaps it is beyond our control," she said.

Maria's words suddenly released the anger that Celik had kept bottled up.

"No!" he shouted. "We are too close. We must not fail to seize the opportunity. The restoration of our family empire is at stake," he said, nearly tasting the power of his own planned ascension. The mad eyes were suddenly ablaze, and his face pulsed red with fury. "We cannot let this chance slip through our fingers."

"The Golden Horn?"

"Yes," he replied, opening his attaché case and pulling out a map. "The intercept must occur tomorrow night," he said, handing her a folder. "Enclosed is the target ship's schedule and route. Can you be ready?"

Maria looked at her brother with trepidation.

"Yes, I believe so," she said quietly.

"Good. There is a team of Janissaries waiting to board the ship who will act in support of the operation. I will be counting on you."

"Ozden, are you sure you want to do this?" she asked. "The risks are high. It will mean the death of a great many of our own countrymen. And I fear the repercussions if we don't succeed."

Celik stared at his sister with a gaze born of delusion, then nodded firmly.

"It is the only way."

53

Abel Hammet watched the rays of the setting sun sparkle like balls of fire atop the loafing waves of the Mediterranean. Standing on an open bridge wing, the Israeli ship captain watched the sun drop beneath the horizon, ushering in a welcome evening breeze. Sucking in deep breaths of the cool air, he swore he could detect the smell of Turkish pine trees from the shoreline ahead. Peering over the distant prow of his vessel, he could just begin making out a few twinkling lights along the southern Turkish coast. Temporarily refreshed, he stepped back onto the bridge of the *Dayan* to complete his watch.

At just under a hundred meters in length, the *Dayan* was a relatively small tanker, certainly minuscule in comparison to the supertankers that plied oil from the Persian Gulf. Though sharing most of the characteristics of the crude carriers, she had actually been purpose-built for a slightly different cargo: fresh water. Spurred by a recent trade agreement, the Israeli government had three identical vessels constructed to transport water to its dry and dusty shores.

Sitting two hundred and fifty miles across the Mediterranean from Israel, Turkey was one of the few countries in the arid region that actually possessed a surplus of fresh water. Controlling the headwaters of both the Tigris and Euphrates, as well as other rich highland rivers, it sat on a strategic resource that would only grow in importance in the coming decades. Tapping it as a new export, the country had agreed to sell a tiny fraction of its water to Israel in a trial trade deal.

Dayan carried just over a million gallons, and Hammet knew its contribution to Israel's water supply was a drop in the bucket, but the biweekly commutes across the Med ultimately added up. For him, it was easy sea duty, and he and his nine-man crew enjoyed the work.

Standing in the center of the wheelhouse, he studied the ship's progress on a navigation monitor.

"Engine back two-thirds," he ordered the helmsman. "We're forty miles from Manavgat. No use in us arriving before daybreak since the pumping facility won't be manned any earlier."

The helmsman repeated the order as the speed was reduced on the ship's single engine. Riding high on the sea with an empty hold, the tanker gradually slowed from twelve knots to eight. As midnight approached a few hours later, the executive officer appeared on deck to relieve the captain. Hammet took a final scan of the radar system before turning in.

"There's a vessel coming up behind us off our port flank, but otherwise the seas are clear," he told the exec. "Just keep us off the beach, Zev."

"Yes, Captain," the man replied. "No midnight swims tonight."

Hammet retired to his cabin a deck below and quickly fell asleep. But he awoke a short time later, feeling something amiss. Shaking away the cobwebs, he realized that the ship's engine was not throbbing and shuddering through the deck as usual when under way. He thought it odd that no one had come to wake him if there was a navigational problem or mechanical issue with the ship.

Slipping on a bathrobe, the captain exited his cabin and climbed a stairwell up to the bridge. Stepping into the darkened wheelhouse, Hammet froze in shock. A few feet in front of him, the executive officer was lying facedown in a small pool of blood.

"What's going on here?" he barked at the helmsman.

The helmsman stared back at him in wide-eyed silence. Under the dimmed lights of the bridge, Hammet could see that the young man had an ugly gash across the side of his face. The captain's vision was suddenly diverted out the forward window, where he noticed the lights of another vessel shining dangerously close to the tanker's port beam.

"Hard right rudder!" he shouted at the helmsman, ignoring a rustling behind him.

A tall figure emerged from the back wall, dressed in black, with an ebony ski mask covering his head and face. In his hands, he held an assault rifle, which he raised to shoulder height. The helmsman ignored Hammet's command, merely staring as the gunman stepped closer. Hammet turned and looked just in time to see the rifle whipping toward his face. He heard the crash of the gun's stock strike him on the side of the jaw an instant before a flash of pain surged through him like a bolt of lightning. He felt his knees buckle, and then the pain vanished as everything turned to black and he joined his executive officer flat on the deck.

54

"Ridley, my friend, come in, come in."

The Fat Man's voice sounded like sand in a mixer as he welcomed Bannister into his Tel Aviv apartment for the second time in as many weeks.

"Thank you, Oscar," the archaeologist replied, strutting in with an air of confidence that had been notably lacking on his last visit.

Gutzman led him to a sitting area, where a thin, well-dressed Arab sat at a nearby desk, reviewing some documents. He looked up, eyeing Bannister with a suspicious stare.

"That is Alfar, one of my curators," Gutzman said with a derisive wave of his hand. Catching a look of caution in Bannister's face, he added, "Do not worry. His ears are safe."

Gutzman reached his favorite sitting chair and tumbled into it without grace.

"Now, what is of such importance that you have called on me again so soon?" he asked.

Bannister spoke quietly, buttering up his victim for the kill.

"Oscar, you know as well as I that hunting for history is at best a speculative business. We may search for days, weeks, or even years for that one monumental discovery and still come up empty. Sure, along the way there may be important finds and occasionally the exciting piece that taps the imagination. Most of the effort usually ends up going for naught. But there is always the chance of that rare instance where the stars are in alignment and one is very, very lucky to find a singular gift from the heavens."

He leaned forward in his chair for effect and stared into the Fat Man's eyes.

"Oscar, I believe I may be on the verge of such a find."

"Well, what is it, my boy?" Gutzman wheezed. "Don't toy with me."

"I was just in London for a short visit and happened to call on an antiquities dealer I've known for a number of years. He recently acquired a cache of items stolen years ago from the Church of England's archives," he lied, pausing, again for effect.

"Go on."

"A portion of the material contained original artwork, jewelry, and artifacts liberated from the Holy Land during the Crusades." Bannister looked cautiously back and forth across the room, then added in a low voice, "Included in the works was an original copy of the Manifest."

Gutzman's eyes inflated like balloons.

"Are . . . are you serious?" he rasped. He tried to contain his excitement, but his face turned flush with exaltation.

"Yes," Bannister replied, producing an intentionally poor photocopy of the papyrus document. "I have not seen the original myself, but I've been assured that it is authentic."

Gutzman studied the page for several minutes without

uttering a word. Only the ruffling of the page in his unsteady fingers disturbed the silent room.

"It exists," he finally said in a hushed tone. "I cannot believe by God's good graces that it has come to be." The old man then looked at Bannister sternly. "This dealer, he will sell it to me?"

Bannister nodded. "Given the nature of his acquisition, he is forced to sell it quietly. That is why he has priced it at only five million pounds sterling."

"Five million pounds!" Gutzman cursed, propelling himself into a coughing fit. When he recovered his breath, he stared into Bannister's eyes.

"I will never pay that," he said, finding a strong voice.

Bannister paled slightly, not anticipating the response. "I suspect the price may be negotiable, Oscar," he stuttered. "And the dealer indicated he would have the document carbon-dated at his expense."

Having purchased artifacts from grave robbers to politicians, Gutzman knew how to get his price. More than that, he knew when he was being played, and the hesitation in Bannister's voice did not go undetected.

"Stay here," the Fat Man said, rising unsteadily from his chair and leaving the room.

He returned a moment later with a thick binder. Gutzman sat down and opened it, revealing a collection of photographs encased in plastic sleeves. Ancient artifacts of assorted age and style, large and small, appeared in the photographs. Bannister recognized statues, carvings, and pottery that he knew were worth hundreds of thousands of dollars. Gutzman flipped to the back of the binder, then removed several photos and handed them to Bannister.

"Take a look at these," the Fat Man huffed.

"Part of your collection?"

"Yes, from my storehouse in Portugal."

Bannister studied the photos. The first showed a small collection of rusty swords and spear tips. The second photo showed an iron military helmet that Bannister recognized as a Roman Heddernheim type. A thin bronze panel containing the image of an eagle, a scorpion, and several crowns appeared in the next photo. The final image was of an object undistinguishable to Bannister. It appeared to be a large, angular mass of metal that was twisted and warped on one side.

"A rare collection of Roman armament," Bannister said. "I'm guessing the eagle and scorpion reliefs are part of a battle standard?"

"Very good, Ridley. It's not just any standard, however, but the emblem for the *Scholae Palatinae*, the elite Roman guards of Constantine the Great. What do you make of that last object, my friend?"

Bannister studied the photograph again but shook his head.

"I'm afraid I don't recognize it."

Gutzman smiled in minor triumph. "It is the bronze ram from an imperial galley ship. Based on its size, it likely came from a Liburnian *bireme*."

"Yes, I see it now. The business end has been flattened by contact. Where on earth did you find this?"

"It was lodged in the hull of another vessel, a fourth-century Cypriot raider, if the story is to be believed. The damaged vessel ran aground and sank in a protected area of soft silt. A number of the artifacts were remarkably

413

preserved. It wasn't long before the wreck was picked over by local divers, well before the state archaeologists arrived on the scene. A wealthy collector snatched up most of the items before the authorities knew what had been removed."

"Let me guess who the wealthy collector was," Bannister said with a smirk.

Gutzman let out a gurgled laugh. "A fortunate tip that came my way, in this particular instance," he said, grinning.

"They are extremely nice pieces, Oscar. But why are you showing them to me?"

"I purchased these artifacts many years ago. And for many years, I have thought about the rumor of the Manifest. Is it true? Could the cargo possibly exist? Then, one night, I had a dream. I dreamt that I was holding the Manifest in my hands, much like I held your copy today. And, in my mind, I see Roman weapons and artifacts around me. But not just any artifacts. I see these artifacts," he said, pointing to the pictures.

"We often dream the reality we seek," Bannister said. "You really think there is a connection between the Manifest and these Roman relics? Couldn't they have come from any sea engagement?"

"Not just any sea engagement would involve the *Scholae Palatinae*. You see, they were the successors to the Praetorian Guard, who were wiped out by Constantine at the Battle of Milvian Bridge, when he routed Maxentius and consolidated the empire. No, it's clear to me that the Cypriot vessel tangled with a galley of imperial decree."

"Does the vessel itself date to the proper era?"

Gutzman smiled again. "The vessel, as well as the armaments and artifacts, all consistently date to approximately A.D. 330. Then there is this," he said, pointing to a weathered Roman shield in one of the photographs.

Bannister had missed it in his first viewing, but now noticed the shield beside the spear tips, featuring a faded Chi-Rho cross across its center.

"The cross of Constantine," Bannister muttered.

"Not only that but the papyrus from Caesarea adds weight to the theory," Gutzman said. "The dream is real, Ridley. If your Manifest is true, then I have already heard the voice of Helena through my own artifacts."

Bannister's eyes lit up with intrigue at the possibility of it all.

"Tell me, Oscar," he asked pointedly, "where was the shipwreck discovered?"

"The vessel was found near the village of Pissouri, on the southern coast of Cyprus. Perhaps it is not impossible that the actual cargo of the Manifest is buried in the vicinity?" he speculated with raised brows. "Now, *that* would be a gift from the heavens, would it not, Ridley?"

"Indeed," the archaeologist said, the wheels turning in his head. "It would be a discovery for the ages."

"But, alas, we are jumping the gun. I must examine the Manifest first and see if it is indeed authentic. You tell your London friend I'm willing to pay a hundred thousand pounds for it. But I will require the carbon dating and a personal examination first," he said, rising to his feet.

"A hundred thousand pounds?" Bannister replied, his voice the one now rasping.

"Yes, and not a penny more."

The old collector patted Bannister on the shoulder. "Thank you for coming to me first, Ridley. I believe that we are on the path to glorious things here."

Bannister could only nod in disappointment as he walked to the door. After he was safely down the elevator, Gutzman walked back to the living area and approached Alfar.

"You listened to our conversation?" the Fat Man asked.

"Yes, Mr. Oscar. Every word," the Arab replied in a course accent. "But I do not understand why you do not buy this Manifest."

"Very simple, Alfar. I am quite certain that it is Bannister who possesses the Manifest, not some London broker. He is trying to bilk me mightily for it and he yet might succeed."

"Then why tell him about your Roman artifacts?"

"To plant the seed. You see, he has a gift for discovery. He now leaves here disillusioned about selling the Manifest but also bewildered, as am I, about the possibility that the artifacts actually exist. I am certain that his ego will drive him there immediately. It may be a fool's gamble, but why not try? Bannister is resourceful and lucky. If it can be found, then he is the man to do it. So why not let him find it for us?"

"You are a smart man, Mr. Oscar. But how will you control Bannister?"

"I want you to contact Zakkar. Tell him I have a simple surveillance job for him, one that will pay very well."

"He left word that he does not want to set foot in Israel for several months, if possible."

"Feeling the heat, is he?" Gutzman said with a chuckle. "No matter. You tell him not to worry, the job won't be in Israel. It's Cyprus where he'll have to earn his pay."

55

Hammet winced under the glare of the bright fluorescent lights that welcomed his first efforts at opening his eyes. The discomfort was nothing in comparison to the searing pain that throbbed from the back of his head. Forcing his lids open once more, he fought to identify where he was. The first answer was: Flat on his back, staring into a bank of overhead lights.

"Captain, how are you feeling?" came the familiar voice of the *Dayan*'s executive officer.

"Like I was leveled by a locomotive," Hammet replied, raising his head to take in his surroundings.

As his vision cleared, he could see he was lying on a dining table in the ship's mess, a stack of linen napkins serving as a makeshift pillow beneath his head. Members of his crew circled around him, concern and fear evident in their faces. Suddenly feeling self-conscious at his position, he raised himself to his elbows and slid off the table, the executive officer helping him slump into a chair. Overcoming a wave of nausea, he peered at the exec and nodded in thanks.

For the first time, he noticed that the executive officer wore a bloodied bandage around his head and that his skin was two shades paler than normal.

"I feared you were dead," Hammet said.

"Lost a bit of blood, but I'll manage. You had us more worried, as you slept the night away."

The tanker captain gazed toward a nearby porthole, seeing the rays of the early-morning sun streaming in. He suddenly realized that the ship's engine was silent and that the ship was obviously moored in place. A few feet along the bulkhead, he was startled to see a pair of black-clad men sitting on either side of the entry door. They cradled automatic rifles on their laps while staring back at him with menacing glares.

"How'd they get aboard?" Hammet asked quietly.

"Not sure," the exec replied. "Must have been by small boat from that freighter. A group of armed men burst onto the bridge before we knew what was happening."

"Did you get off a distress call?"

The exec shook his head grimly. "No time."

Hammet took a headcount of his crew seated around him, noticing his third officer was absent.

"Where's Cook?"

"He was taken to the bridge early on. My guess is, they had him piloting the ship."

A short time later, the door to the mess was thrown open, and the third officer brusquely shoved inside by another gunman. Sporting a large bruise on his cheek, the young officer stepped to the table and approached Hammet.

"Glad to see you're okay, Captain," he said.

"What can you report?" Hammet asked.

"Sir, they had me pilot the ship at gunpoint. We tracked north at full speed all night, following a black freighter named the *Ottoman Star*. At around dawn, we docked alongside her in a small protected cove. We're still in Turkish waters, about ten miles north of the Dardanelles."

"Any idea who these people are?"

"No, sir. They spoke Turkish but made no demands. Can't imagine why someone would hijack an empty water tanker."

Hammet nodded in response, quietly wondering the same thing.

The Israeli tanker crew was held aboard the ship for another twenty-four hours, given access to the galley but little else. Several times Hammet approached the guards with questions or requests but each time was silently rebuked with the muzzle of a gun. Throughout the day and night, they could hear the sound of workers and machinery echoing from the forward deck. Sneaking a peek out the porthole, Hammet could glimpse a crane swinging crates from the freighter to the tanker.

They were finally taken off the ship late in the day when some additional guards arrived and they were ordered to help load the ship. Marched down the pier, Hammet was shocked to see what had been done to his vessel. The assailants had cut away a pair of huge holes in the forward deck. The tanker's twin forward storage tanks, which each held 150,000 gallons of water, were now exposed like a half-open can of sardines. The captain could see that the crates he had witnessed being off-loaded from the freighter now lined the perimeter bulkheads of each exposed tank.

"The idiots have converted our tanker to a cargo carrier," he cursed as they were led ashore.

His dismay only grew when the crew was marched into the south warehouse and directed to transport the small boxes of plastic explosives from the Army container.

They were guided back to the tanker, where they deposited the explosives in the center of the two open tanks. Hammet took a second to study the crates already loaded aboard, seeing they were filled with fifty-pound bags marked "Ammonium Nitrate Fuel Oil."

"They mean to blow up the ship," he whispered to his exec as they were marched back for a second load of HMX.

"With us in it, I imagine," the exec replied.

"One of us needs to try to slip away. We've got to find some help to stop this madness."

"As the captain, you'll be the first missed."

"With that bloody head wrap, you wouldn't be far behind," Hammet said.

"I'll try," came a voice from behind them. It was the tanker's helmsman, a diminutive man named Green.

"It's dark in the warehouse, Green," Hammet said. "See if you can get lost in the shadows."

But the guards were poised to prevent an escape and ordered Green back in line every time he lingered or tried to drift away from the others. Reluctantly, he joined the line of explosives haulers.

The crew continued their forced labor until the explosives in the container dwindled. Hammet curiously noted a dark-eyed woman in a jumpsuit monitoring their progress from the tanker's deck before taking a position up on the bridge. As they returned to the warehouse for what he knew would be the last load, Hammet turned to his helmsman.

"Try to stay behind in the container," he whispered.

The captain passed the word for his entire crew to

quickly crowd into the container before a guard yelled at them to slow down. But it gave Green the chance to slip to the back of the container. He quickly climbed to the top shelf, then stretched against the side of the wall, his bantam body barely visible from below. Hammet let the other crewmen carry out the last of the explosives, then walked out of the container with his palms up.

"No more," he said to the nearest guard, then followed the others across the warehouse.

Stepping quickly, he couldn't help craning his neck as the guard walked over and peeked into the container. Satisfied that it was empty, the guard turned and slammed the door shut. Hammet turned away, holding his breath as he prayed for silence. But his hopes vanished with the sound of the dead bolt sliding closed with a sickening thud that Hammet felt all the way down to his toes.

56

The tires of the commuter plane kicked up a cloud of dust as they touched down on the dry runway of Çanakkale Airport a short distance southeast of the Dardanelles. The plane turned toward its designated terminal, slowly pulling to a stop as its twin propellers fell quiet. Summer watched from behind a barricade as her brother stepped off the plane with the last passengers. He walked with a slight limp and sported a few small bandages but otherwise appeared healthy. But as he stepped closer, she could see that he carried the worst of his wounds internally.

"Still in one piece, I see," she said, giving him a hug. "Welcome to Turkey."

"Thanks," he replied in a low voice.

Gone was his usual positive energy and upbeat disposition. Even his eyes seemed darker, Summer thought. Not sad and mournful, as she might have expected, but cold and almost angry. It was a look she had never seen in her brother before. Gently grabbing his arm, she led him toward the baggage claim.

"We read the news about the attack on the Dome of the Rock, never imagining you were involved," she said quietly. "Then Dad heard through the grapevine that you were there and had prevented the explosion."

"I only stopped one of the charges from going off," he said bitterly. "The Israeli security forces kept me out of the news while they patched me up at an Army hospital. I guess they didn't want the presence of an American to muddy up the local politics."

"Thank goodness, you weren't severely injured." She paused and looked at him with concern. "I'm sorry to hear about your Israeli friend."

Dirk nodded but said nothing. They soon reached the baggage claim and found his luggage. Making their way to a small borrowed van in the parking lot, Summer said, "We've got one more pickup to make."

Driving to the opposite end of the airport, she found a dilapidated warehouse building marked "Air Cargo." Requesting a pickup for NUMA, she was handed a pair of overnight packages, and then two men wheeled out a small crate and loaded it into the rear of the van.

"What's in the crate?" Dirk asked as they pulled away.

"A replacement inflatable boat. The *Aegean Explorer* lost two of her dinghies during a melee over a shipwreck."

Summer filled Dirk in on what she knew about the discovery of the Ottoman wreck, the death of the two NUMA scientists, and the abduction of Zeibig.

"The Turks haven't busted the guys in the yacht?" Dirk asked.

Summer shook her head. "Dad's pretty livid over the response from the local authorities. The *Explorer* was impounded for a few days and blamed for the deaths of Tang and Iverson."

"Justice rules for those with power. That's tough news about Tang and Iverson. I've worked with them on other projects. Both good men," he said, his voice trailing away as the discussion of death directed his thoughts to Sophie.

"On top of that, the algae bloom survey has fallen to pieces. Our Turkish environmental representative, who is required to be on board, is absent with some kind of family need. Meanwhile, Rudi and Al have been having trouble with the new AUV." She wanted to add that Dirk's arrival would help cheer everybody up, but she knew that wouldn't be the case in his current condition.

Summer drove to Çanakkale's commercial docks and located the *Aegean Explorer* moored beside some large fishing boats. She led her brother aboard and to the ship's wardroom, where Pitt, Gunn, and Giordino were discussing their sailing schedule with Captain Kenfield. They warmly greeted the younger Pitt as he entered with his sister.

"Didn't your father teach you not to play with explosives?" Giordino joked, pumping Dirk's hand with a crushing grip.

Dirk forced a smile, then hugged his dad before sitting down at the table. "Summer tells me you've found an Ottoman shipwreck," he said. The tone in his voice made it clear his focus was elsewhere.

"One that's caused us a lot of trouble," Pitt replied. "She dates to around 1570, and came with some unusual Roman artifacts aboard."

"Unfortunately, all that's left of those artifacts is some photographs," Gunn added ruefully.

"Of course, it all pales in comparison to Summer's discovery," Pitt said.

Dirk turned toward his sister. "What was that?" he asked.

"You mean she didn't tell you?" Giordino said.

Summer gave Dirk a sheepish look. "We ran out of time, I guess."

"Such modesty," Gunn said, rifling through a stack of papers on the table. "Here, I made a copy from Summer's original," he said, handing a sheet of paper to Dirk.

He held up the page and studied it carefully:

University of Cambridge
Department of Archaeology

Translation (Coptic Greek):
Imperial Vessel *Argon*
Special Manifest for Delivery to Emperor Constantine
Byzantium

Manifest:
Personal items of Christ, including a small wardrobe with:
Cloak
Lock of hair
Letter to Peter
Personal effects
Large crypt stone
Altar—from Church of Nazarene
Contemporary painting of Jesus
Ossuary of J.

Assigned to 14th Legionaries, at Caesarea
Septarius, Governor of Judaea

"This is for real?" Dirk asked.

"The original is written on papyrus. I saw it briefly," Summer replied with a shake of her head, "so I know it exists. This was a translation performed by a well-known Cambridge archaeologist and etymologist in 1915."

"It's incredible," Dirk said, his attention fully grabbed by the document. "All of these items personally related to Jesus. They must have been collected by the Romans after his death and destroyed."

"No, far from it," Summer said. "They were obtained by Helena, mother of Constantine the Great, in A.D. 327. The items on the Manifest were sacred, and likely sent to Constantine to celebrate the Roman Empire's conversion to Christianity."

"I still can't believe you found it in England, of all places," Gunn said finally.

"All on account of our dive on HMS *Hampshire*," Summer explained. "Field Marshal Kitchener apparently obtained the papyrus document while conducting a survey of Palestine in the 1870s. Its meaning apparently wasn't understood until the translation was made decades later. Julie Goodyear, the authority on Kitchener who helped locate the Manifest, thinks that the Church of England may possibly have killed Kitchener because of it."

"I guess you could understand their fears," Giordino stated. "Finding an ossuary with Jesus' bones in it would certainly kick over a few apple carts."

"It's an interesting connection to the Roman artifacts we found on the Ottoman wreck, which also date to the time of Constantine and Helena," Gunn noted.

"So these Jesus artifacts were placed on a Roman ship leaving Caesarea?" Dirk asked.

Summer nodded. "Helena is known to have made a pilgrimage to Jerusalem, where she claimed to have discovered the True Cross. Fragments of the cross reside in churches all over Europe today. A common tale relates how the nails from the cross were melted down and incorporated into a helmet and bridle for Constantine. So Helena and the cross apparently made it safely to Byzantium. There is no mention of these items, however," she added, pointing to the list. "They must have been shipped separately and were apparently lost to history ages ago. Can you just imagine the impact if we could have seen a contemporary image of Jesus?"

The room fell silent as everyone's imagination conjured up a visual image of Christianity's namesake. Everyone, that is, except Dirk. His eyes remained focused on the bottom of the Manifest.

"Caesarea," he said. "It indicates that the shipment left Caesarea under the guard of Roman legionaries."

"That's just where you were working, isn't it?" his father asked.

Dirk nodded.

"They didn't happen to leave a sailing plan lying around etched in stone, did they?" Giordino asked.

"No, but we were fortunate in uncovering a number of papyrus documents from that era. The most interesting of them described the capture and execution of some Cypriot pirates. What was interesting was that the pirates had apparently battled a legionary force at sea sometime before they were captured. Dr. Haasis, whom I worked with at Caesarea, said the Roman legionaries were part of some group called the *Scholae Palatinae*, led by a centurion named Platus, as I recall."

Gunn nearly fell out of his chair.

"What . . . what did you say his name was?" he stammered.

"Platus, or perhaps it was Platius."

"Plautius?" Gunn asked.

"Yes, that was it. How did you know?"

"That was the name on my marker, er, the marker that was found on the wreck site. It was a memorial to Plautius, who apparently died in a sea battle."

"But you don't have any clue where the marker came from?" Dirk asked.

Gunn shook his head as Zeibig's face suddenly brightened.

"Dirk, you said the pirates were from Cyprus?" he asked.

"That's what the papyrus record indicated."

Zeibig rifled through some papers, pulling out a page of research data.

"The Roman Senator inscribed on the gold crown, Artrius? Dr. Ruppé sent some historical research which indicated that he served as Governor of Cyprus for a short while."

A thin smile crossed Pitt's face. "Cyprus, that's the clue we've been missing. If the Cypriot historical records are intact, I'll bet you'll find that Traianus, the name on the monolith, was also on Cyprus. Perhaps he even reported to Governor Artrius."

"Sure," Giordino agreed. "Traianus was probably ordered by the Governor to erect a memorial after the gold crown arrived in the mail."

"But what were the Roman crown and marker doing on an Ottoman wreck?" Dirk asked.

"I think I have a theory about that," Zeibig said. "As I recall, Cyprus historically remained under Venetian rule long after the fall of the Roman Empire. But the Ottomans came around and successfully invaded the island around 1570, which just happens to be the approximate date of our shipwreck. I'd speculate that the gold crown and stone tablet were simply antiquarian spoils of war that were being shipped back to the sitting Sultan in Constantinople."

"We can assume from the Manifest that Plautius was assigned to transport the religious relics on behalf of Helena," Gunn said. "The stele from the wreck, along with Dirk's papyrus discovery, confirms that he lost his life fighting pirates off of Cyprus. Is it possible that the events all occurred on the same voyage?"

"I would wager that members of this *Scholae Palatinae*, like the Praetorian Guard, would not be far from the Emperor's seat of power except in unusual circumstances," Pitt said.

"Such as guarding his mother while she traveled to Jerusalem," Summer said.

"Which would explain the gold crown," Giordino said. "It may well have been awarded to Artrius while he was Governor of Cyprus, sent from Constantine in appreciation for capturing the pirates who killed Plautius."

"The same pirates that stole the relics?" Gunn asked. "That's the real question. Who ended up with the relics?"

"I performed a cursory historical search on the Manifest items," Summer said. "While there are claimed fragments of the True Cross located in dozens of churches across Europe, I could find no substantive record of any of the items on the Manifest being exhibited today or in the past."

"So they disappeared with Plautius," Gunn said.

"The record at Caesarea stated that the pirates were captured and brought to port on their own ship," Dirk stated. "The vessel's decks were bloodied, and a number of Roman weapons were found aboard. While they had apparently battled Plautius, it wasn't clear what became of his ship. Or the relics, for that matter."

"Which probably means that the Roman galley of Plautius was sunk," Pitt said.

The others in the room noticeably perked up at the notion, knowing that if one man could find an important shipwreck, it was the lean fellow with the green eyes sitting in front of them.

"Dad, could we try to look for it after the completion of the Turkish project?" Summer asked.

"That may be sooner than you think," Gunn said.

Summer turned and gave him a puzzled look.

"The Turkish Environment Ministry informed us that they have discovered a significant amount of waste dumping by a large chemical plant in Çiftlik, a town near Chios," Pitt explained. "Rudi looked at the currents, and there seems to be a strong correlation with the dead zone we were mapping in the vicinity of the Ottoman wreck."

"Better than a ninety-five percent probability," Gunn confirmed. "The Turks have kindly asked us to come back in a year and do some sample testing, but at this point we no longer need to extend any of our survey work."

"Does that mean we go back to the Ottoman wreck?" Summer asked.

"Dr. Ruppé is organizing a formal excavation under the auspices of the Istanbul Archaeology Museum," Pitt said. "Until he has the necessary approvals from the Cultural Ministry, he has suggested that we avoid any further work on the site."

"So we can try for the Roman galley?" Summer asked excitedly.

"We're on the hook for assessing a small region just south of here," Pitt said. "We should be able to complete the work in two or three days. Providing, that is, that our AUV is operational," he said, shooting Gunn a sideways glance.

"That reminds me," Summer said. "I've got your spare parts."

She tossed the two overnight packages to Gunn, who quickly tore the seal off the first one and looked inside.

"Our replacement circuit board," he replied happily. "That should get us back in the water."

He looked at the other package, then slid it over to Pitt.

"This one's addressed to you, boss."

Pitt nodded, then looked around the table. "If we've got an operational AUV again, then let's go finish up our Turkey survey project," he said with a wry grin, "because it's a long voyage to Cyprus."

An hour later, the *Aegean Explorer* gently shoved off from the Çanakkale dock. Pitt and Giordino watched from the bridge as Captain Kenfield guided the vessel out the mouth of the Dardanelles, then south along the Turkish coastline. Once the *Explorer* was safely clear of the busy strait, Pitt sat down and opened the overnight package.

"Cookies from home?" Giordino asked, taking a seat across from Pitt.

"Not quite. I had Hiram do some digging on the *Ottoman Star* and the *Sultana*."

"Hiram" referred to Hiram Yaeger, NUMA's head of computer resources. From the NUMA headquarters building in Washington, Yaeger managed a sophisticated computer center that tracked detailed oceanographic and weather data around the globe. A skilled computer hacker, Yaeger had a nose for uncovering secrets, and didn't mind utilizing both authorized and unauthorized data sources when the need arose.

"Two vessels that I'd like to find at the bottom of the sea," Giordino said. "Was Yaeger able to find anything?"

"It appears so," Pitt replied, perusing several pages of documents. "Both vessels are apparently registered in Liberia, under a shell company. Yaeger was able to trace ownership to a private Turkish entity called Anatolia Exports, the same outfit the police mentioned. The company has a lengthy history of shipping Turkish textiles and other goods to trading partners throughout the Mediterranean. It owns a warehouse and office building in Istanbul, as well as a shipping facility on the coast near the town of Kirte."

"Ah yes, I know the latter quite well," Giordino said with a smirk. "So who runs this outfit?"

"Ownership records cite a couple named Ozden Celik and Maria Celik."

"Don't tell me . . . They drive a Jaguar and like to run over people with boats."

Pitt passed over a photo of Celik that Yaeger had gleaned

from a Turkish trade association conference. Then he shared a number of satellite photos of the Celiks' properties.

"That's our boy," Giordino said, examining the first photo. "What else do we know about him and his wife?"

"Maria is actually his sister. And data is somewhat scarce. Yaeger indicates that the Celiks are secretive types who keep a very low profile. He says he had to do some real digging to find any juice."

"And did he?"

"Listen to this. A genealogical trace puts both Celiks as great-grandchildren of Mehmed VI."

Giordino shook his head. "Afraid I don't know the name."

"Mehmed VI was the last ruling Sultan of the Ottoman Empire. He and his clan were kicked off the throne and out of the country when Atatürk swept into power in 1923."

"And now the poor boy has nothing to show for it but a mangy old freighter. No wonder he has a chip on his shoulder."

"He apparently has a lot more than that," Pitt said. "Yaeger believes the pair may be among the richest people in the country."

"I guess some of that explains the fanaticism over the Ottoman shipwreck."

"And the brashness of the Topkapi theft. Though there might have been another motivation."

"Such as?"

"Yaeger found a possible financial link to an Istanbul marketing organization. The organization is helping promote the candidacy of Mufti Battal in the upcoming presidential election."

Pitt set down the page he was reading. "Rey Ruppé in Istanbul told us about this Mufti. He has a large fundamentalist following and is viewed as a dangerous power in some circles."

"Never hurts to have friends with deep pockets. I wonder what's in it for Celik?"

"A question that might have an illuminating answer," Pitt said.

He set down the last of the report and pondered the wealthy Turk and his savage sister while Giordino took a look at the satellite photos.

"I see the *Ottoman Star* has returned to home port," Giordino said. "I wonder what a Greek tanker is doing alongside her."

He slid the photo across the table for Pitt to examine. Pitt took a look at the high overhead shot of the now-familiar cove, spotting the freighter at the dock. On the opposite side of the dock was a small tanker ship, its blue-and-white flag barely visible atop its mast. The flag caught his eye, and Pitt studied it a moment before grabbing a magnifying glass from behind the chart table.

"That's not a Greek flag," he said. "The tanker is from Israel."

"News to me that Israel has its own tanker fleet," Giordino said.

"Did you say something about an Israeli tanker?" Captain Kenfield asked, overhearing the conversation from across the bridge.

"Al found one parked in the cove of our Turkish friends," Pitt said.

Kenfield's face turned pale. "While we were in port,

there was an alert making the rounds about an Israeli tanker that went missing off the coast near Manavgat. It's actually a water tanker."

"I recall seeing one a few weeks back," Pitt remarked. "What's the size of the missing ship?"

"The ship was named the *Dayan*, I believe," he said, stepping to a computer and performing a quick search. "She's eight hundred gross tons and three hundred ten feet long."

He turned the computer monitor toward Pitt and Giordino so that they could see a photograph of the ship. It was a dead match.

"The photos are less than twenty-four hours old," Giordino said, noting a date stamp on the image.

"Captain, how's your secure satellite phone working?" Pitt asked.

"Fully operational. Do you want to make a call?"

"Yes," Pitt replied. "I think it's time we call Washington."

57

"O'Quinn, good of you to come by. Please, step inside and grab a seat."

The intelligence officer was startled that the Vice President of the United States greeted him in the second-floor foyer of the Eisenhower Executive Office Building and personally showed him into his office. Washington protocol surely dictated that a secretary or aide escort a lesser being into the sanctified lair of the Number Two. But James Sandecker was that rare breed who had little use for such pageantry.

A retired Navy admiral, Sandecker had been responsible for founding the National Underwater and Marine Agency decades earlier and building it into a powerhouse oceanographic unit. He surprised everyone by passing the reins to Pitt and accepting a vice presidential appointment, where he hoped to further the cause of protecting the world's oceans. A small but fiery individual with flaming red hair and goatee, Sandecker was known in the capital as a blunt and outspoken man who was nevertheless highly respected. O'Quinn had often been amused during intelligence briefings to see how quickly the Vice President could dissect an issue, or individual, in order to get to the heart of the matter.

Stepping into the large office, O'Quinn admired a collection of antique oil paintings, featuring old ships and racing yachts, which lined the paneled walls. He followed Sandecker to his desk and took a seat opposite of him.

"Do you miss the sea much, Mr. Vice President?"

"There's no shortage of days that I'd prefer to be sailing something other than a desk," Sandecker replied, reaching into a drawer and jamming a large cigar between his teeth. "Are you monitoring events in Turkey?" he asked pointedly.

"Yes, sir. That's part of my regional assignment."

"What do you know about a nutcase named Ozden Celik?"

O'Quinn had to think a moment. "He's a Turkish businessman who's been associated with members of the Saudi Royal Family. We think he might be involved in helping to finance the fundamentalist Felicity Party of Mufti Battal. Why do you ask?"

"He's apparently been up to a few other things. You're aware of the Israeli tanker ship that went missing two days ago?"

O'Quinn nodded, recalling mention of the incident in a daily briefing report.

"The vessel has been observed at a small shipping facility controlled by Celik a few miles north of the Dardanelles. I have reliable word that this Celik was behind the recent theft of Muslim artifacts at Topkapi." Sandecker slid a satellite photo of the tanker across his desk.

"Topkapi?" O'Quinn repeated, his brows rising like a pair of drawbridges. "We believe there may be a link between the Topkapi theft and the recent mosque attacks at al-Azhar and the Dome of the Rock in Jerusalem."

"The President is aware of that possibility."

O'Quinn studied the satellite photograph.

"If I may ask, sir, how did you acquire this information?"

"Dirk Pitt at NUMA. Two of his scientists were killed by Celik's men and a third kidnapped and taken to the same facility," Sandecker replied, pointing to the photo. "Pitt got his man out, and he discovered a container of plastic explosives at the facility. An Army supply of HMX, to be exact."

"HMX is the explosive compound identified from the mosque bombings," O'Quinn said excitedly.

"Yes, I recall that from your presidential briefing."

"Celik must be acting on behalf of Mufti Battal. It's clear to me that the anonymous mosque attacks, utilizing our explosives, are an attempt to incite fundamentalist outrage across the Middle East, and particularly in Turkey. Their goal must be to sway public opinion in order to sweep Battal into office."

"It's a logical motive. That's why this hijacked Israeli tanker is cause for concern."

"Have we contacted the Turkish government?"

"No," Sandecker replied with a shake of his head. "The President is worried that any action on our part could be construed as American meddling in the election outcome. Frankly, we don't know how deep Battal's tentacles may reach into the existing government. The stakes are simply too high, and the race too close, to risk a potential backlash that might throw the election to his party."

"But our analysts tell us that the Mufti stands an even chance of winning anyway."

"The President understands that, but he nevertheless

has ordered absolutely no U.S. involvement until after the election."

"There are backdoor channels we could use," O'Quinn protested.

"It's already been deemed too risky."

Sandecker pulled the cigar from his teeth and examined the chewed end. "It's the President's mandate, O'Quinn, not mine."

"But we can't simply look the other way."

"That's why I called you here. You have intelligence contacts in the Mossad, I presume?" he asked.

"Yes, of course," O'Quinn nodded.

Sandecker leaned over his desk, his bright blue eyes boring into the intelligence officer.

"Then I would suggest that you consider calling them and telling them where their missing tanker is located."

58

Rudi Gunn had completed repairs on the faulty AUV sensors by dusk, shortly before the *Aegean Explorer* reached its survey grid some twenty miles southeast of Çanakkale. The AUV was deployed, and the ship's crew resumed their round-the-clock tracking schedule. By the time the midnight shift went on duty, the bridge had emptied to just the ship's second officer and a helmsman.

The ship was cruising at a slow speed to the north when the helmsman suddenly gawked at the radar screen.

"Sir, a vessel has suddenly appeared off our port beam, less than a quarter mile off," he stuttered excitedly. "I swear, she wasn't there a minute ago."

The bridge officer glanced at the radar scope, seeing a small amoeba of yellow light nearly merge with the center point, which represented the *Aegean Explorer*.

"Where on earth did she come from?" he blurted. "Right twenty degrees rudder," he quickly ordered, fearful that the unknown vessel was on a perpendicular heading.

As the helmsman turned the ship's wheel over, the officer stepped to the port bridge window and peered outside. The moon and stars were concealed by low clouds, draping the sea in darkness. Expecting to clearly view the lights of the nearby vessel, the officer was surprised to see only black.

"The fool doesn't have her running lights on," he said, searching the sea unsuccessfully for a shadow. "I'll try her on the radio."

"I wouldn't advise that," barked a crisp voice with the hint of a Hebrew accent.

The officer turned in shock to find two men dressed in dark camouflage entering the bridge from the starboard wing. The taller of the two men stepped forward, exposing a lean face blunted by a lantern jaw. The intruder stopped a few feet from the officer, leveling a light machine gun at his chest.

"Have your helmsman resume his course," the commando said, a stern look from his dark eyes expressing his will. "There is no danger to your vessel."

The officer reluctantly nodded to the helmsman. "Resume original heading," he said. Turning to the commando, he stammered, "What are you doing on our ship?"

"I'm looking for a man named Pitt. Bring him to the bridge."

"There is no one aboard by that name," the officer lied.

The commando took a step closer.

"Then I will clear my men off and sink your vessel," he threatened in a low voice.

The officer wondered if it was an idle threat. But a gaze into the battle-hardened eyes of the commando left no doubt that it was a possibility. Nodding sullenly, the officer relieved the helmsman at the wheel so he could retrieve Pitt. The second commando immediately fell in step behind the helmsman as he exited by a rear stairwell.

A few minutes later, Pitt was marched onto the bridge, a look of anger searing his drowsy eyes.

"Mr. Pitt? I am Lieutenant Lazlo, Israeli Navy Special Forces."

"Excuse me if I don't welcome you aboard, Lieutenant," Pitt replied drily.

"My apologies for the intrusion, but we require your assistance on a sensitive mission. I have been assured that sources in your government at the highest level have approved your cooperation."

"I see. If that is the case, then were the midnight theatrics really necessary?"

"We are operating in Turkish waters without authorization. It is essential that we maintain our secrecy."

"Okay, Lieutenant, put down your guns and tell me what this is all about."

The commando reluctantly lowered his weapon, indicating for his partner to follow suit.

"We have been ordered to effect the rescue of the crew of the Israeli tanker *Dayan*. It has been reported that you are familiar with the facility where the ship is being held."

"Yes, the cove north of the Dardanelles. Is she still there?"

"Intelligence reports within the last ten hours confirm as much."

"Why not use diplomatic channels to get their release?" Pitt asked, baiting the man.

"Your government has provided information that there may be a connection between the hijackers and the recent attack on the Dome of the Rock in Jerusalem. The report of an explosives stockpile at the facility has our intelligence specialists fearing another attack."

Pitt nodded, understanding that pursuing Celik through

official channels might entail a dangerous delay. The Turk was clearly up to no good, and Pitt would like nothing more than to put him out of business.

"Very well, Lieutenant, I'll be happy to help." He turned and faced the second officer. "Rogers, please inform the captain that I've left the ship. By the way, Lieutenant, how did you get aboard?"

"We have a small inflatable tied up off the starboard flank. Our departure will be made easier if your vessel can temporarily slow."

Rogers obliged the request, then stood on the bridge wing and watched Pitt and several shadows slip over the rail and quietly vanish into the night. A few minutes later, the helmsman called him over to the radar scope.

"She's disappeared," the man said, gazing at the screen.

Rogers looked at the empty blue radar screen and nodded. Somewhere on the open sea, Pitt had disappeared from the surface along with the mystery vessel. It was, he fervently hoped, only a temporary vanishing act.

59

The *Tekumah* wasted no time returning to the stealthy depths. A Dolphin class submarine built at the HDW shipyards in Kiel, Germany, she was one of only a handful of subs operated by the Israeli Navy. Diesel-powered and relatively small in size, she was nevertheless packed with a sophisticated array of electronics and weaponry that made her a formidable underwater foe.

The inflatable had barely touched the side of her hull when waiting crewmen hoisted Pitt and the commandos onto the deck and hustled them down a hatch while the inflatable was stowed in a watertight compartment. Pitt had just taken a seat in the sub's cramped officers' mess when the dive command reverberated through the vessel.

Lazlo secured his weapons, then brought a pair of coffees to the table and sat down opposite Pitt. Reaching into a nearby folder, he laid out a satellite photo of Celik's shipping facility, similar to the one Pitt had received from Yaeger.

"We're going in with two small teams," the Israeli explained. "One will search the tanker and the other the shore facilities. Can you tell me about the buildings?"

"Provided I can go in with you," Pitt replied.

"I don't have authorization for that."

"Look, Lieutenant," Pitt said, staring coldly at the commando. "I didn't come along with you just to take a joyride

445

on a submarine. Celik's men killed two of my scientists and kidnapped a third. His sister abducted my wife at gunpoint. And sitting inside his compound is enough high-grade explosives to start World War Three. I understand that you want the *Dayan*'s crewmen back, but there's potentially a lot more at stake here."

Lazlo sat silent for a moment. Pitt was not the man he expected to find aboard the research vessel. Far from being some nebbish egghead scientist, Pitt was all substance.

"Very well," the commando replied quietly.

Pitt took the photo and carefully explained the layout of the two warehouses and the stone administrative building.

"Can you tell me about any security elements?" Lazlo asked.

"It's a functioning port facility first, but we encountered a number of armed personnel. I suspect that they were mostly Celik's personal security detail, but a number were probably assigned to the site. I would anticipate a small but heavily armed security presence. Lieutenant, are your men trained in demolitions?"

The commando smiled. "We are Shayetet 13. Demolitions are an important part of our training."

Pitt had heard of the Israeli Special Forces unit, which was similar in function to the U.S. Navy SEALs. They were called the "Bat Men," he recalled, on account of the batwing insignia they wore on their uniforms.

"Members of my government are very concerned about a container of HMX plastic explosives that we found sitting in this warehouse," Pitt said, pointing to the photo.

Lazlo nodded. "Our mission orders are for rescue only, but the elimination of those explosives would be of mutual interest. If they are still there, we will take care of them," he promised.

A short man in an officer's uniform ducked into the mess and stared at the two men with a humorless face.

"Lazlo, we'll be at the deployment zone in forty minutes."

"Thank you, Captain. By the way, this is Dirk Pitt, from the American research vessel."

"Welcome aboard, Mr. Pitt," the captain replied without emotion. He quickly turned his attention back to Lazlo. "You'll have approximately two hours of darkness to complete your mission. I'm warning you, I don't want to be on the surface at daybreak."

"Captain, I can make you a promise," the commando replied with cool arrogance. "If we're not back in ninety minutes, then you may sail without us."

60

Lazlo would be wrong about the mission's duration, but not in the manner that he expected.

Surfacing two miles northwest of the cove, the *Tekumah* quickly off-loaded its commando team for the second time that night. Dressed in nondescript black fatigues, Pitt joined the eight-man rescue team that climbed into a pair of inflatable boats and raced away from the sub. Stopping outside the entrance to the cove, the pilot of each boat shut off its outboard engine and resumed propulsion with a silent, battery-powered electric motor.

Gliding into the cove, Pitt took a disappointed look toward the pier, then whispered to Lazlo.

"She's gone."

The Israeli commando silently cursed as he saw that Pitt was right. Not only was the tanker gone but the entire pier was empty. The buildings on shore appeared dark and uninhabited as well.

"Alpha Team, revise landing to joint shore recon," he radioed to the other boat. "Assigned target is the east warehouse."

There was still a chance that the tanker crew was held captive ashore, but he knew it was false optimism. The success of any covert operation, he knew from years of experience, was always the quality of the intelligence. And this time, the intelligence appeared to have failed.

The two boats ran ashore simultaneously a few yards from the pier, their occupants scrambling ashore like silent ghosts. Pitt followed Lazlo's squad as they approached the stone building and then stormed in with a fury. Watching from the front courtyard, Pitt could tell by sound that the building was deserted, like the rest of the port facility. He made his way toward the west warehouse, hearing the light steps of Lazlo approach as he reached the door.

"We haven't cleared this building yet," the Israeli whispered in a hard tone.

"It's empty like the others," Pitt said, flinging open the door and stepping inside.

Lazlo saw that Pitt's words were true as he flicked on the interior lights, revealing a cavernous building that was empty save for a large metal container on the far side.

"Your explosives?" the commando asked.

Pitt nodded. "Let's hope it's still full."

They stepped across the warehouse to the container, where Pitt slid the dead bolt free. Pulling on the handle, he was suddenly confronted by a lunging figure from inside who swung a piece of broken crate. Pitt managed to sidestep the blow, then turned to throw a punch. But before he could strike, the toe of Lazlo's boot appeared out of nowhere, burying itself in the attacker's stomach. The startled assailant gasped as he was lifted off his feet and slammed into the side of the container. He meekly dropped his makeshift weapon as the muzzle of Lazlo's assault rifle was prodded into his cheek.

"Who are you?" Lazlo barked.

"My name is Levi Green. I am a seaman from the tanker *Dayan*. Please don't shoot," he pleaded.

"Fool," Lazlo muttered, pulling away his rifle. "We are here to rescue you."

"I . . . I'm sorry," he said, turning to Pitt. "I thought you were a dockworker."

"What are you doing in this container?" Pitt asked.

"We were forced to load its contents, boxes of explosives, on the *Dayan*. I hid in here in hopes of escaping, but they locked the door, and I was trapped."

"Where are the other crewmen?" Lazlo asked.

"I don't know. Back on the ship, I suppose."

"The tanker is no longer here."

"They modified the ship," Green said, his eyes still wide with fear. "Cut open the forward tanks and filled them with bags of fuel oil. We were forced to place the boxed explosives inside."

"What do you mean 'bags' of fuel oil?" Pitt asked.

"There were crates and crates of the stuff in fifty-pound bags. They were marked as some sort of fuel oil mixture. Ammonium something or other."

"Ammonium nitrate?" Pitt asked.

"Yes, that was the stuff."

Pitt turned to Lazlo. "Ammonium nitrate fuel oil, or ANFO. It's a cheap but highly effective blasting agent," he said, recalling the devastating effect a truckload of similar material had on the Murrah Federal Building in Oklahoma City back in 1995.

"How long have you been in the container?" Lazlo asked the seaman.

Green looked at his watch. "Just over eight hours."

"Which means they may have a hundred-mile head start," Pitt computed quickly.

Lazlo reached down and grabbed Green's collar, then yanked him to his feet.

"You're coming with us. Let's move."

Two miles to sea, the *Tekumah*'s captain was relieved to see the Bat Men approach the rendezvous point less than an hour after they had departed. But his sentiment turned when Lazlo and Pitt reported the disappearance of the *Dayan*. The submarine's radar records were hastily reviewed, and the *Dayan*'s Automatic Identification System signal was accessed, but neither provided any indication as to the tanker's whereabouts. The three men sat down and studied a map of the eastern Mediterranean.

"I will alert naval command," the captain said. "They might already be within hours of Haifa or Tel Aviv."

"I believe that's a wrong assumption," Pitt said. "If history repeats, they're looking to detonate that ship at a Muslim site, to make it look like an attack by Israel."

"If they were to strictly target a major population center, Athens appears closest," Lazlo noted.

"No, Istanbul is somewhat closer," Pitt said, eyeing the map. "And it's a Muslim city."

"But they wouldn't attack their own people," the captain said derisively.

"Celik has shown no shortage of ruthlessness to date," Pitt countered. "If he's already bombed mosques in his country and throughout the region, there's no reason to doubt he wouldn't kill thousands more of his own countrymen."

"The tanker is that dangerous?" the captain asked.

"In 1917, a French cargo ship carrying wartime explosives caught fire and blew up in Halifax Harbor. Over two thousand nearby residents were killed in the blast. The *Dayan* may be carrying ten times the explosive power of that French freighter. And if she's headed to Istanbul, she'll be sailing into a city center of over twelve million people."

Pitt pointed to the marine approach to Istanbul on the map. "At a speed of twelve knots, she would still be two or three hours from the city."

"Too far out of range for us or our boats to catch her," the captain said, "not that I would sail through the Dardanelles anyway. I'm afraid the best that we can do is alert the Greek and Turkish authorities while we remove ourselves from their territorial waters. In the meantime, we can leave it to the intelligence satellites to figure out exactly where she's headed."

"What about the crewmen?" Lazlo said.

"Lieutenant, I'm afraid there's nothing more we can do," the captain replied.

"Three hours," Pitt muttered quietly while studying the route to Istanbul. "Captain, if I'm going to have a chance at catching her, I need to get back to my ship at once."

"Catch her?" Lazlo asked. "How? I didn't see a helicopter aboard your ship."

"Not a helicopter," Pitt replied with a determined voice. "But something that's nearly as fast as a speeding bullet."

61

The *Bullet* tore across the water like a high-speed hydroplane. Steering with a firm grip on the yoke as the turbo diesels whined loudly under full power behind him, Pitt shot Giordino a quick glance from the pilot's seat.

"You were wrong about her top speed," he said, nearly yelling to be heard.

Giordino craned his head toward the navigation screen, where a small readout indicated that they were traveling at forty-three knots.

"Always better to under-promise and over-deliver," he replied with a thin smile.

Seated in the passenger seat behind them, Lieutenant Lazlo found no such mirth. The brawny commando felt like he was inside a blender, as the *Bullet* pitched and rolled over the waves. Struggling repeatedly to stay in his seat, he finally discovered the straps to a seat belt and buckled himself tightly in, hoping he could forgo a bout of seasickness.

Pitt had caught a break when the *Tekumah* returned him to the *Aegean Explorer*. The *Bullet* had already been fully fueled and prepped for launching. Rousing Giordino, they hurriedly deployed the submersible. When Lazlo realized that Pitt had a real chance of chasing down the tanker, he quickly insisted on joining them.

They soon found themselves screaming through the

busy Dardanelles Strait in the dead of night, dodging ships, in a desperate race toward Istanbul. It took all of Pitt's focus and energy to keep the *Bullet* on an even keel while slipping between the tankers and merchant ships traveling in both directions. A bright set of xenon headlights helped improve visibility while Giordino provided a second set of eyes to detect smaller vessels or debris in the water.

It wasn't the way Pitt would have preferred to travel through the historic waterway. With a love of history, he knew that both Xerxes and Alexander the Great had led their armies in opposite directions across the strait formerly known as the Hellespont. Not far from Çanakkale, on the southwest shore, stood Troy, site of the Trojan War. And farther north, on the opposite shore, were the landing beaches where the failed Allied campaign of Gallipoli originated in World War I. The beaches and barren hillsides were simply a blur to Pitt, whose eyes darted between the navigation screen and the black waves ahead that quickly vanished beneath the speeding bow.

The narrow passage of the Dardanelles soon opened into the broad waters of the Sea of Marmara. Pitt relaxed slightly, now that he had more room to maneuver about the scattered string of ships, and was thankful that the open water remained calm. Passing by the northern tip of the island named Marmara, he was diverted by the sound of Rudi Gunn's calm voice calling over the radio.

"*Aegean Explorer* calling *Bullet*," Gunn said.

"This is *Bullet*. What do you have for me, Rudi?" Pitt replied over a radio headset.

"I can give you a tentative confirmation. Hiram located

an updated sat image that appears to show the vessel in question entering the Dardanelles."

"Do you know what time that was?"

"Looks to be about twenty-three hundred hours local time," Gunn replied.

"You might want to give Sandecker a call back."

"I already have. He said he'll wake some people up over here."

"He better. There may not be much time. Thanks, Rudi."

"Be careful and stay afloat. *Explorer* out."

"Let's just hope Celik doesn't own the Turkish Navy and the Coast Guard, too," Giordino muttered.

Pitt wondered how far Celik's corrupt reach actually extended, but there was little he could do about it now. He glanced at the nav screen, noting that they were now traveling at forty-seven knots, the *Bullet* finding more speed as her fuel load was burned down.

"Can we catch them if we have to?" Lazlo asked.

Pitt looked at his watch. It was four a.m. A quick mental calculation told him that at their respective top speeds, both vessels would approach Istanbul in about an hour.

"Yes," he replied.

But he knew it would be close. Very close.

62

There would be no repeat of Jerusalem this time, Maria thought to herself. Working under the glow of the tanker's deck lights, she carefully inserted a dozen individual blasting caps into separate blocks of the HMX plastic explosive. She then wired each blasting cap to individual electronic timer fuzes. Glancing at her watch, she stood and gazed past the ship's bow. Ahead on the horizon was a blanket of twinkling white dots layered beneath a hazy black sky. The lights of Istanbul were now less than ten miles ahead. Kneeling down to the deck, she set each timer for a two-hour delay, then activated the fuzes.

Placing the charges into a small box, she climbed down into the opened section of the forward port water tank. The floor of the tank was packed tight with crates of ammonium nitrate fuel oil, and she had to snake her way past a maze of pallets to reach the center. In a cramped nook, she found a wide stack of wooden bins that held three thousand pounds of HMX. She proceeded to bury one of the charges deep into the middle bin, then stuffed four more of the charges in nearby crates of the ANFO. Making her way to the starboard-side tank, she repeated the process with the remaining charges, ensuring that they were all safely concealed.

She was climbing back to the ship's bridge when her

cell phone rang. She saw to no surprise that it was her brother calling.

"Ozden, you are up early," she answered.

"I am on my way to the office to personally witness the occasion."

"Don't stand too close to the window, there's no telling how powerful the blast will be."

Maria could hear her brother snicker. "I am sure there will be no disappointment this time. Are you on schedule?"

"Yes, we are operating to plan. The lights of Istanbul are already in view. I have arranged for the event to transpire in just under two hours."

"Excellent. The yacht is on its way; it should rendezvous with you shortly. Will you be joining me?"

"No," Maria replied. "I think it is better if the crew and I disappear with the *Sultana* for a short while. We will take the boat to Greece for safekeeping, but I will make my way back in time for the election."

"Our destiny is near, Maria. We shall taste the fruits of our labor shortly. Farewell, my sister."

"Good-bye, Ozden."

As she hung up the phone, she reflected briefly on their odd relationship. They had grown up together on an isolated Greek island and, by nature, had been close siblings, drawing nearer after their mother had died at a young age. Their demanding father had placed high expectations on them both, but he had always treated Ozden like waiting royalty. Perhaps that is why she had always been the tougher of the two, baring knuckles and fighting her way through her youth, more a second son to her father than a daughter. Even now, as her brother went to sit in his gilded office, it was she who commanded the ship and led the mission. She had always been the shadow fighter while her brother took the front seat. But it was all right with her, for she knew that Ozden was nothing without her. Standing on the bridge and peering over the broad bow of the tanker, she felt she was the one in power now, and she would enjoy every second of it.

But her shell of armor cracked slightly when the ship's radio suddenly blared.

"Istanbul Coast Guard to tanker *Dayan*. Istanbul Coast Guard to tanker *Dayan*. Come in, please."

An angry scowl crossed her face, then she turned and spat to the pilot.

"Assemble the Janissaries."

Ignoring the radio call, she turned and quietly studied the tanker's radar screen, mentally preparing for the coming engagement.

The emergency midnight diplomatic warnings from Israel and the U.S. were ultimately directed to the Turkish Coast Guard, whose Istanbul command base gave assurances that all approaching tankers would be stopped and searched well short of the city. A local fast patrol craft was scrambled, joined by an Istanbul police boat, to stand picket south of the Bosphorus.

Tensions heightened when a large, unidentified ship appeared on the radar screen, steaming north. Suspicions were immediately raised when the vessel's Automatic Identification System transponder was found to be deactivated. When repeated radio calls went unanswered, the smaller and speedier police boat was dispatched to go investigate.

Racing toward the ship, the police soon saw by its shadow and running lights that it was clearly a tanker the size of the *Dayan*. The police boat zipped down the tanker's high flanks, then circled around her stern. The police commander took note of the Israeli flag flying from the aft mast as he read the ship's name beaded in white letters across the transom.

"It's the *Dayan*," he said, transmitting to the Coast Guard patrol boat.

They were to be the last words he would ever speak.

63

The *Dayan*'s deck and running lights cut to black an instant before the fusillade erupted. A line of armed Janissaries materialized on the tanker's stern rail and simultaneously fired down on the small police boat. The small boat's captain was the first to die, cut down by a direct burst through the bridge windshield. Another police officer standing on the deck was gunned down an instant later, shot in the back before he knew what hit him. Another man on the deck, a veteran police sergeant, reacted quicker, diving behind the gunwale and returning fire with his service automatic. But he was killed when the boat drifted aside and he lost his cover, the Janissaries all concentrating fire on him.

The shooting fell quiet for a moment as the fourth and last man aboard the police boat climbed up from below. Seeing his dead comrades, he stepped onto the stern deck with his hands in the air. He was a young rookie, new to the force, and his voice quivered as he begged the gunmen not to shoot. But his plea was met by a short burst of fire, and he crumpled to the deck, joining his comrades in death.

The lifeless police boat meandered behind the tanker for several minutes like a lost puppy. In its wheelhouse, the radio sputtered with repeated hails from the Coast Guard vessel, calls that fell only on dead ears. The big tanker's wash finally nudged its bow aside, and the floating morgue motored aimlessly toward the western horizon.

The sound of gunfire was Hammet's call to action. The Israeli tanker captain had been in a state of anguish for hours, ever since he and his crew had been forced back into the mess room after loading the plastic explosives aboard ship and setting sail. He knew that the armed Turks, whoever they might be, had converted his vessel into a suicide bomb ship, and that the Israeli crew would likely be part of the blast.

The captain and his first officer had quietly discussed escape plans, but their options were few. The pair of guards watching them at the door appeared at a higher state of readiness than before and was rotated out for a fresh pair every two hours. Food had been cut off to the captives, and they were no longer allowed to approach the bulkhead and peer out the porthole.

At that late hour, the tanker's crew were mostly sprawled out on the floor asleep. Hammet was lying among his men, although sleep was the furthest thing from his mind. He feigned slumber, however, when the door opened, and a man whispered excitedly to the guards. The two men arose immediately and slipped out, leaving the Israeli crew temporarily unguarded.

Hammet instantly jumped to his feet.

"Everybody up," he said quietly, shaking awake his first officer and those around him. As the groggy crew staggered to its feet, Hammet assembled them near the door and quietly formulated a plan.

461

"Zev, take the men and see if you can get them off the aft escape raft without being detected," he ordered his exec. "I'm going to visit the engine room and see if I can disable the ship. You have my order to jettison without me if I can't catch up in ten minutes."

The exec started to voice a protest when the sound of gunfire echoed from the stern of the ship.

"Belay that," Hammet said quickly. "Take the men across the deck and try to deploy the port inflatable. You might have to just toss it over the rail since we're at speed."

"That's going to be a tough jump into the sea for some of the men."

"Grab some lines and life vests from the day locker, and they can lower themselves down. Now, move!"

Hammet knew they had only minutes, if not seconds, and he hurriedly prodded the men out of the mess room. As the last man hustled by, he stepped onto the deck and closed the door behind him. They stood near the base of the high stern superstructure facing the starboard rail. The exec quickly led the crew forward and across the facing of the superstructure, each man hugging the wall to avoid detection from the bridge high above. Hammet turned and moved the other direction, heading for an aft passageway to the engine room.

The sound of automatic gunfire still ripped through the air, and as he reached the rear of the superstructure he could see a half dozen armed men at the stern rail firing toward the water. Ducking down, he sprinted across to a side doorway that opened to a stairwell. With his heart pounding, he rushed down the stairs, passing three decks, before exiting into a wide passageway. A door to the engine room stood just ahead, which he approached cautiously before opening it slowly. He was met by a gust of warm air and a deep mechanical rumble as he stepped inside and carefully peered around.

Hammet had hoped that the hijackers didn't enlist a standby engineer for their one-way voyage, and he was correct. The engine room stood empty. He quickly climbed down a grated stairwell, then stood next to the tanker's huge diesel engine, pondering what to do. There were assorted means he could use to shut down the engine, but a sudden power failure would raise immediate alarm. He needed a delayed effect that would allow time for the crew to safely escape first.

Then he gazed past the engine toward two large fuel bunkers that sat forward like a fat pair of horizontal grain silos.

"Of course," he muttered to himself, quickly stepping forward with a glint in his eye.

64

In less than ten minutes, Hammet was back at the top of the stairwell, peering across the stern deck. The shooting had long since ceased, and Hammet did not see any of the Janissaries about, giving him an uneasy feeling. Beyond the stern rail, he spotted the shadow of a small boat, angling away from the tanker, which he rightly suspected was the target of the gunfire.

Stepping quickly, he made his way across the rear wall of the superstructure to the port-side deck. Peering around the corner, he was relieved to find it empty. A pair of ropes tied to the rail and dangling over the side gave him hope that the crew had already escaped. But his heart sank when he spotted the inflatable life raft still secured in its rack alongside the bulkhead. He cautiously moved closer, peering over the side to see if anyone was hanging from the ropes but saw only empty water below.

The shot rang out before he felt it, a single clap from a nearby pistol. A trickle of blood ran warm down his leg before a burning ache pulsated in his upper thigh. The leg quickly turned wobbly, and he fell to his other knee as a figure emerged from the bulkhead shadows.

Maria walked calmly over, keeping her pistol leveled at Hammet's chest as she drew closer.

"A bit late to be out for a stroll, Captain," she said coldly. "Perhaps you best join your comrades."

Hammet stared at her with disappointment in his eyes. "Why do this?" he cried.

She ignored the query as a pair of Janissaries ran up, alerted by the gunshot. At her orders, they grabbed Hammet and dragged him across the deck, depositing him in the ship's mess. There, he found his forlorn crew, seated on the floor with long faces, a guard pacing back and forth with his rifle at the ready.

The Janissaries roughly dumped the captain on the floor, then took up positions on either side of the door. The *Dayan*'s executive officer rushed over to help Hammet to a seated position while a crew medic attended to the leg wound.

"I was hoping not to find you here," Hammet said, wincing.

"Sorry, Captain. Those men at the stern stopped shooting just as we tossed our lines over the side. We were spotted before we even had a chance to deploy the inflatable."

Though the bleeding from his leg wound had been halted, Hammet could sense his body going into shock. He took several deep breaths, trying to relax.

"Any luck at your end?" the exec asked.

The captain looked down at his wounded leg, then forced a pained nod.

"I suppose you could say so," he replied, his eyes turning glassy as his voice wavered. "One way or another, I believe our voyage is about near its end."

65

Three miles to the north, the Turkish Coast Guard patrol boat repeatedly hailed both the *Dayan* and the police craft, but to no avail. When the sight of distant muzzle flashes was reported to the bridge, the patrol boat's captain ordered an immediate intercept of the tanker.

As the Coast Guard boat sped toward the big ship, its bow-mounted 30mm turreted gun was manned while a small boarding crew was readied. The boat made a quick sweep around the tanker, then drew up on the tanker's starboard flank when no police boat was spotted. The captain then hailed the *Dayan* over the loudspeaker.

"This is Coast Guard vessel SG-301. You are hereby ordered to heave to and prepare for boarding," he shouted.

As the Coast Guard captain waited to see if the *Dayan* would slow, his second officer called out to him.

"Sir, there's another vessel approaching from our starboard."

The captain looked over to see a dark-colored luxury yacht pull up abreast of the Coast Guard boat, then drop back behind it.

"Tell him to back off, if he doesn't want to get blasted out of the water," the captain ordered testily. His attention was quickly diverted back to the tanker, where a figure suddenly appeared above them at the rail.

The captain was surprised to see it was a woman, who

stood waving at the boat while attempting to shout something. The captain stepped to the bridge wing, then called back to his helmsman.

"Bring us in tight, I can't hear her."

Maria smiled to herself as the Coast Guard boat eased to within a few feet of the tanker's hull. Standing at the rail, she towered over the smaller vessel yet was easily able to look right at the bridge.

"I need your help," she shouted at the pair of officers, who both now stood on the wing.

Not waiting for a reply, she reached down to a small duffel bag at her feet and quickly tossed it over the rail. Her throw was nearly perfect, the bag arcing toward one of the officers, who easily plucked it out of the air. She waited a second to watch the officer open the bag, then she dropped to the deck and covered her head.

The ensuing explosion lit up the night sky with a bright flash followed by a thunderous roar. Maria waited for the flying debris to land before peeking over the side rail. The Coast Guard boat's bridge was a scene of annihilation. The blast had gutted the entire superstructure, vaporizing all of the men who stood there. Smoke billowed to the sky from a dozen small fires that were consuming the boat's electronic components. Around the rest of the boat, stunned and burned sailors were picking themselves up after having been knocked flat by the concussion.

Maria crept down the passageway on her own vessel, then yelled through an open doorway.

"Now!" she screamed.

Her small team of armed gunmen burst out of the door and sprinted to the rail, immediately spraying their weapons on the dazed sailors below. The firefight was short-lived, as the 30mm gun crew was quickly eradicated, followed by the boarding crew. A few of the sailors recovered quickly and returned fire. But they were forced to shoot at an awkward angle, which deprived them of cover. Within minutes they were overwhelmed, and the patrol boat's deck was a mass of dead and wounded men.

Maria called for her shooters to cease, then spoke into a handheld radio. Seconds later, the blue yacht came racing up alongside the patrol boat, then slowed and gingerly began nudging against the Coast Guard vessel's bow. It took just a few bumps before the patrol boat was scraping and banging against the side of the tanker. Without power, the patrol boat began losing momentum and slid back alongside the tanker's flank.

The yacht slowed as well, gradually slipping abreast of the patrol boat while keeping it pressed against the *Dayan* until the *Dayan*'s stern loomed up. Holding steady, the yacht waited until the tip of the boat's bow crossed the transom, then gave it a hard nudge with full bow thrusters. The boat pivoted left and surged across the flattened waters off the tanker's stern. A muffled bang arose from beneath the surface as the tanker's giant bronze propeller dug into the hull of the boat.

With its decks bloodied by the dead and wounded and its wheelhouse spewing smoke, the Coast Guard boat suddenly lurched and listed heavily to starboard. Only a scattering of screams pierced the night air as its bow nosed into the air, and then the entire ship rocked back onto its stern, disappearing beneath the waves as if she'd never been.

66

Both physical and mental fatigue were beginning to weigh on Pitt after two hours of running at high speed at night. They had traveled past the center of the Sea of Marmara, where they encountered larger swells that sent the *Bullet* airborne every few seconds. In the rear seat, Lazlo had finally calmed his stomach but had grown sore from the ceaseless pounding on the submersible's hull.

Their hopes were lifted when they picked up the radio traffic from the Coast Guard patrol boat on the international distress channel.

"I think I heard them call the *Dayan*," Giordino said, dialing up the volume on the VHF radio to hear over the roar of the *Bullet*'s engines.

They listened closely over the next few minutes as the repeated calls to the *Dayan* went unanswered. Then the radio fell silent altogether. A few minutes later, Giordino spotted a small white flash on the horizon.

"Did you see that?" he asked Pitt.

"I caught a glimpse of a flash dead ahead."

"It looked like a fireball to me."

"An explosion?" Lazlo asked, craning his neck forward. "Is it the tanker?"

"No, I don't think so," Pitt replied. "It didn't appear that large. But we're too far away to know for sure."

"It could be upward of ten miles away," Giordino

agreed. He gazed at the navigation screen, eyeing the entrance to the Bosphorus near the top of its digital map. "That would put them pretty close to Istanbul."

"Which means we're still about fifteen minutes behind," Pitt said.

The cabin fell silent in conjunction with the radio. Pitt, like the others, could only assume that the Turkish authorities had failed to stop the tanker. It might well be up to them to avert a catastrophic explosion that could kill tens of thousands. But what could three men in a submersible possibly hope to do?

Pitt shook the thought from his mind as he tapped the throttle levers, ensuring that they were fully against their stops, as he sighted a direct path toward the burning lights of Istanbul.

67

Maria paced the tanker's bridge with an anger that turned her features to cold stone.

"I was not expecting a challenge from the Coast Guard," she said. "How did they know we were approaching?"

A short, ashen-faced man piloting the tanker shook his head.

"The *Dayan* is known to be missing. It's possible a passing vessel identified us and reported it to the Coast Guard. Perhaps it is a good thing. The authorities will now know right away that the Israelis are responsible for the attack."

"I suppose that is true. Still, we cannot afford any further interference."

"The radio has been silent. I don't believe they had the opportunity to alert anyone," the captain said. "On top of which, the radar is clear of vessels ahead of us."

He glanced out the side window, noting the lights of the blue yacht visible just a few yards off the tanker's beam.

"The *Sultana*'s reported some minor damage during contact with the Coast Guard vessel," he reported, "but they are ready to take us off at any time."

"How long until we can evacuate?"

"I will slow the vessel as we enter the eastern channel

of the Bosphorus. You can prepare to evacuate as I align the ship toward the Golden Horn and set the automatic pilot. I would estimate that the ship will be in position in about fifteen minutes."

Maria looked at her watch. The electronic fuzes were timed to detonate in just over one hour.

"Very well," she said calmly. "Let us not delay."

68

Pale bands of crimson streaked across the dark gray sky as the sun prepared its daily climb over the eastern horizon. All across Istanbul, pious Muslims were arising early to partake in a large meal before daybreak. The *muezzins* would begin their warbled cries shortly, beckoning the faithful to mosque for dawn prayer. The mosques would be more crowded than usual, as the Islamic calendar showed it was the last week of Ramadan.

The name Ramadan refers to the ninth month of the Islamic calendar, when tradition dictates that the first verses of the Qur'an were revealed to Muhammad. Adherents focus on attaining a closer relationship with God during the month, which is fostered through a strict adherence to fasting during daylight hours. The act of self-purification is promoted not only by fasting but by an emphasis on good deeds toward others. Special food and gifts are given to friends and relatives while charity and aid are offered to the poor. But just a few miles from the city's historic mosques, Maria Celik was preparing to unleash her own brand of charity.

The Israeli tanker steamed into the mouth of the Bosphorus, hugging close to the Asian shoreline. When the Golden Horn slipped into view across the strait, the tanker's pilot reduced power.

"Now is the time," he said to Maria.

473

The swift current of the Bosphorus, flowing south from the Black Sea, quickly slowed the large vessel to a crawl. Maria gathered several men along the starboard flank and lowered a steel accommodation ladder over the side. The yacht cruised up immediately and held station off the foot of the stairs.

"Secure the prisoners and then get the rest of the men off," she ordered one of the Janissaries, then stepped onto the lowered stairway.

She made her way down the metal steps, then was helped aboard the yacht by a waiting crewman. Climbing up to the wheelhouse, she was met by her two Iraqi hired thugs. Even in the predawn darkness, the one named Farzad was wearing his trademark sunglasses.

"You have made the preparations in Greece?" she asked them.

"Yes," Farzad replied. "We can make a quiet entry through Thios. A secure covered berth has been reserved for the *Sultana*, and transportation has been arranged for you to Athens. Your return flight to Istanbul is booked in three days."

Maria nodded as they watched the remaining Janissaries climb down the stairway and hop onto the yacht. The guards watching the tanker crew had been quietly pulled, and the door to the mess room chained shut.

On the bridge of the *Dayan*, the pilot watched the last of the Janissaries step off, then he signaled the yacht that he was changing course. As the *Sultana* temporarily slipped away from the tanker's side, the pilot increased the engine's revolutions to half speed and eased the bow toward the west. Taking a bearing toward the

474

Süleymaniye Mosque, he programmed the automatic pilot and then engaged it.

He was about to step off the bridge when he noticed a flashing on the console. Glancing at the warning light, he simply shook his head.

"Nothing I can do about that now," he muttered, then scrambled down to the stairwell and leaped to the waiting yacht, leaving the massive *Dayan* to her own devices.

69

The *Bullet* spewed a rooster tail of white water from its stern as it tore into the entrance of the Bosphorus Strait. A few early-rising fishermen stared in awe at the hybrid submersible/speedboat as it zipped by in the gloomy light of dawn.

Pitt was scanning the horizon ahead when he spotted an approaching boat traveling at high speed.

"Kind of has a familiar profile to her," he remarked to Giordino.

As the Italian yacht powered south under speed, the two vessels raced by each other quickly, passing just a short distance apart.

"That's Celik's yacht, all right," Giordino confirmed.

"Leaving the scene of the crime, most likely."

"Probably an indication that there's not a whole lot of time left on the clock," Giordino replied, eyeing Pitt with a cautionary gaze.

Pitt said nothing, shoving aside the suicidal nature of approaching the bomb ship while he formulated a plan to stop it.

"That must be her up ahead."

It was Lazlo, raising an arm and pointing off the port bow. Two miles ahead, they could see the stern of a large tanker disappearing behind a rise on the western shoreline.

476

"They're sending her into the Golden Horn," Pitt said, any doubt about the tanker's mission fully erased.

The watery heart of Istanbul for over two thousand years, the famed harbor is surrounded by some of the most densely populated neighborhoods in the city. Directed at the Süleymaniye Mosque, situated just two blocks from the waterfront, the tanker's detonation would not only shatter the historic structure, but devastate the half million people who lived within a mile of the impact zone.

But the pilotless *Dayan* wasn't there yet. It had just narrowly missed colliding with an early-morning ferry when the *Bullet* approached from behind. Pitt noticed the ferryboat's captain shaking a fist and angrily tooting his horn at the tanker, oblivious to the fact that its wheelhouse was empty.

"No sign of anyone aboard," Giordino said, craning his neck at the tanker's high deck and superstructure.

Pitt throttled around the *Dayan*'s port flank, looking for a means of access, then shot around the tanker's bow to her starboard side. Giordino quickly pointed to the stairs extending off the rear flank.

"Beats climbing a rope," Giordino said.

Pitt guided the submersible close alongside the lowered steps.

"The helm's yours, Al," he said. "Stick around . . . but not too close."

"You sure you want to go aboard?"

Pitt nodded with a firm eye.

"Lazlo," he said, turning toward the commando. "With your expertise, we'll take a crack at defusing the

477

explosives. If that fails, I'll try to get her turned toward the Sea of Marmara, and then we can bail out."

"Don't do any unnecessary sightseeing," Giordino said as they made their way out the rear hatch.

"I'll dial you up on channel 86 if I need you," Pitt said before stepping out.

"I'll keep my ears on," Giordino replied.

Pitt crept along the port pontoon until reaching the lowered stairs, easily grabbing its handrail and pulling himself on. Lazlo followed right on his heels. Pitt raced to the top of the stairs, then leaped onto the tanker, gazing ahead at the huge forward deck. He immediately saw the two large steel cutouts that Green had described, housing the mixture of explosives materials.

"Give us time," he said to himself as Lazlo followed him at a sprint toward the storage tanks. "Just give us time."

70

The Janissary approached Maria tentatively, reluctant to intrude on her conversation with the yacht's captain. Noticing him gradually encroach on her space, she finally turned and snapped at him.

"What is it?"

"Miss Celik, the boat we just passed traveling in the opposite direction? I . . . I believe it may be the same vessel used by the intruders at the Kirte port facility."

Maria's jaw dropped, but only for a moment. Wheeling around, she peered out the back window, just catching a glimpse of the *Bullet* as it rounded the bluff into the Golden Horn.

Turning back to the yacht's captain, her eyes blazed with fury.

"Turn us around at once," she bellowed. "We're going back."

Pitt barely knew where to start. The forward port hold was like a rat's maze at eye level. Six-foot-high pallets filled with heavy bags of ANFO were stacked everywhere, loaded in apparent haste. Somewhere in the middle were hidden the powerful stores of HMX. And attached to that, Pitt hoped, would be a readily apparent fuze and blasting cap.

Pitt had told Lazlo that they had five minutes to locate

and defuse the explosives. Lazlo was simultaneously searching the starboard hold, after having given Pitt an on-the-fly explanation of what to look for. Half the allotted time had already been expended by the time Pitt had worked his way to the center of the hold and discovered dozens of blocks of the plastic explosive stacked in several wooden bins. With the seconds ticking by loudly in his head, Pitt hastily opened the bins one by one, tossing the explosives aside when no visible fuze was found inside. It wasn't until he reached the last bin that he found an electric timer wired to a small blasting cap pressed into a block of the plastic explosive. With a hopeful nod, he quickly yanked the mechanism from the HMX, then retraced his steps through the maze.

Five minutes had already elapsed when he climbed the ladder out of the hold and stepped onto the deck. Lazlo was just climbing out of the starboard hold and sprinted over to Pitt, carrying a pair of timers in his hand. Pitt held up his timer and blasting cap, handing it to Lazlo.

"I found this in the main cache of HMX," Pitt said.

"It's no good," Lazlo replied with a stern shake of his head. "They've got multiple charges hidden throughout the hold. I inadvertently found this one tucked into a crate of the ANFO," he said, holding up one of the timers. "I'm positive there are more."

He looked at Pitt's timer, then compared it to the two that he held.

"Fourteen minutes until she goes off," he said, turning and winging the timers over the side rail. "There's no way we can find them all."

Pitt digested his words.

"Try to find the crew," he ordered. "I'll get us turned back into the strait."

Pitt didn't wait for a reply, taking off at a sprint for the bridge. The deck beneath his feet rumbled and vibrated, and he suddenly felt the whole ship shudder. Reaching a side stairwell, he took a quick glance aft, then wished he hadn't.

Bearing down on the tanker from the east was the blue yacht of Ozden Celik.

71

Tailing off the stern of the tanker, Giordino had already spotted the hard-charging yacht bearing down in his direction. He flicked the marine radio to channel 86 and tried sending a warning call to Pitt, but there was no answer from the *Dayan*'s bridge. Accelerating the submersible, he eased away from the tanker, heading into the center of the channel while pulling parallel with the *Dayan*'s superstructure. He was too low in the water to see anyone on the bridge, but he did spot Lazlo working his way across the deck.

Peering behind him, he was surprised to note the yacht had altered course and was suddenly closing fast on the *Bullet*. He realized they must not have seen him drop Pitt and Lazlo at the tanker. Despite the early-morning gloom, he could make out two figures climbing to the yacht's forward rail. In their arms, he knew, were automatic weapons aimed at him.

Giordino immediately goosed the throttles to the submersible. The *Bullet* nearly leaped out of the water, surging quickly up to speed. Giordino tore past the bow of the tanker, then pulled close to the northern shoreline. A short distance ahead was the Galata Bridge, which he figured would provide some cover. But a quick glance behind revealed that the fast yacht was less than fifty yards behind, having closed the gap while the *Bullet* was accelerating.

Giordino cursed aloud as he spotted a small flash of yellow light erupt from the yacht's bow.

The burst of gunfire struck the water inches from the submersible's hull, though Giordino could neither see nor hear the bullets striking. He nevertheless whipped the steering yoke hard left, followed by a sharp turn to the right. The nimble submersible responded immediately, zigzagging across the water. The action was enough to temporarily disrupt the accuracy of the yacht's shooters.

The Galata Bridge suddenly loomed up, and in a flash Giordino passed under it. He banked hard once more, then he looked back to see the yacht burst from under the bridge and follow suit. The faster and more maneuverable *Bullet* was finally showing its legs, and the distance between the two vessels gradually began to increase. But that spurred only more shooting from the yacht.

Giordino kept up the zigzag pattern as he eyed another bridge, the Atatürk, less than a half mile ahead. A sudden banging above his head forced him to duck involuntarily, then he looked up to see that a trio of bullet holes had pierced the submersible's acrylic bubble. Any thoughts of ducking behind an obstacle and trying to submerge suddenly vanished, so he set his sights on the bridge.

Several thick footings arose from the channel to support the Atatürk, and Giordino targeted them for cover. Circling in and between the footings, he knew he could distract the yacht while avoiding a direct line of fire. But his concern for self-preservation diminished when he thought of Pitt and the explosives-laden tanker.

Just over a mile behind, the *Dayan* was surely on its final death march. He had to be available to get both men off the tanker, and most likely soon. Right now, he had no way of knowing if Pitt and Lazlo had any hope at all.

Then he turned and looked behind him and saw that the pursuing yacht had suddenly vanished.

72

Lazlo only had to follow his ears to locate the tanker's captive crewmen. Though in a weakened state from his gunshot wound, Captain Hammet had his men seeking an escape route the minute the guards left the mess room. The heavily wrapped chain locking the entry door was quickly deemed unbreakable, so the men turned their sights elsewhere. They were surrounded by steel bulkheads, and so there was in fact only one way to go and that was up.

Using butcher knives from the small galley, the crew began making their way through the ceiling panels and into an overhead duct, hoping to breach the deck above. Lazlo heard the clatter from a storeroom he was searching in an adjacent bay and immediately raced to the mess's door. Quickly unraveling the chain, which was tied in a simple knot, he kicked open the door. Several crewmen, standing on tabletops with knives in their hands, stopped what they were doing and stared at him in surprise.

"Who's in command here?" Lazlo barked.

"I'm captain of the *Dayan*," Hammet said. He was seated in a nearby chair with his leg resting on a stool.

"Captain, we have just minutes before the ship blows up. What is the quickest way to get you and your crew off?"

"The aft emergency lifeboat," Hammet replied, rising

to his feet with a grimace. "You can't disable the explosives?"

Lazlo shook his head.

"Every man to the lifeboat," Hammet ordered. "Let's move."

The crewmen quickly piled out the door, Lazlo and the executive officer helping Hammet out last. Stepping onto the deck, Hammet felt an unusual vibration beneath his feet, then looked over the rail. The Israeli captain was shocked to see the minarets of the Süleymaniye Mosque rising a short distance ahead of them.

"We're in the middle of Istanbul?" he stammered.

"Yes," Lazlo replied. "Come, we have little time."

"But we must get the tanker turned around and out of here," he protested.

"Someone is on the bridge attempting that."

Hammet started to follow the others toward the stern, then hesitated as the deck shuddered again.

"Oh, no," he groaned with a sullen frown. "I made her run dry of fuel."

73

Pitt had only just discovered that same fact. Racing onto the bridge, he had ignored a pair of flashing red lights on the main console as he searched for and found the control that disabled the auto helm. The tanker was just approaching the Galata Bridge, steaming toward its center span, as Pitt regained control of the helm. Glaring at a bridge support off his port bow, he realized there was insufficient room to cut the big ship around. He would have to cross under the bridge first, then make a sweeping turn around and back under to exit the Golden Horn.

As the bow began to slip under the bridge, Pitt saw that the span ahead appeared to be at nearly eye level, and he wondered whether the tanker's tall superstructure would fit beneath it. Waiting for it to approach, he finally looked down at the flashing red lights. With dismay, he saw they were low-fuel indicators for both the main and auxiliary fuel tanks. When Hammet had sneaked into the engine room, he had opened release valves on the bunkers that dumped fuel into the bilge, where it was then pumped over the side. The tanks were now dry, Pitt knew, as evidenced by the faltering engine that was drawing on the last remaining bit of fuel.

With a sudden certainty, Pitt knew he had no chance to guide the tanker back toward the Sea of Marmara, where it could explode without harm. Just sailing it safely away from the city was now a lost hope. Standing on the bridge of a ticking time bomb, one that was about to lose power, most men would have fallen prey to panic. They would have felt only the heart-pounding urge to flee, to get off the death ship and try to save their own skins.

But Pitt wasn't like most men. His pulse barely beat above normal, as he coolly surveyed the surrounding coastline. While his nerves were calm, his mind was in hyperdrive, exploring any and all remedies to the crisis at hand. Then a potential solution appeared across the harbor. Risky and foolhardy, he thought, but it was a solution all the same. Dialing the bridge marine radio to channel 86, he picked up the transmitter.

"Al, where are you?" he called.

Giordino's voice immediately crackled back through the speaker.

"I'm about a mile ahead of you. Been playing cat and mouse with the yacht, but I guess they got tired of my scent. Keep your eyes open, because they're screaming back in your direction. You and Lazlo ready for me to come fetch you off that ship?"

"No, I need you somewhere else," Pitt replied. "A large dredge ship, sitting off the southeast corner of the bridge."

"I'm there. Out."

The tanker's superstructure had just slipped under the bridge span when the engine shuddered again. Passing back into the morning light, Pitt saw the blue yacht bearing down on the tanker barely a hundred yards ahead. Ignoring the yacht, he applied full left rudder, then stepped to the rear window, wondering how Lieutenant Lazlo was making out.

74

The Israeli commando was helping carry Captain Hammet to the lifeboat when the sound of gunfire erupted a short distance away. A second later, shattered glass fell crashing to the deck from above. Lazlo peered up, seeing that the fire was concentrated on the windows of the bridge. He could just make out the radio masts of the yacht as it slid along the tanker's starboard beam.

"Quickly, into the boat," Lazlo urged the sailors.

Six of the crewmen had already climbed into the covered fiberglass lifeboat. It was positioned on a steeply angled pad just above the stern rail, its bow pointing to the water below. The executive officer and another man then assisted Hammet as he stumbled through the boat's rear entry. He fumbled with his seat belt and ordered his crewmen to fasten themselves in. Then he looked up at the entry just as Lazlo was about to close it from the outside.

"You're not coming with us?" Hammet asked with a shocked look.

"My work is not finished," Lazlo replied. "Launch yourself immediately and head to shore. Good luck."

Hammet tried to thank the commando, but Lazlo quickly shut the door and jumped off the boat. Seeing that his crew were all secured in their seats, the captain turned to his executive officer.

"Set us loose, Zev."

The exec pulled a lever that released an external clamp, sending the lifeboat sliding. The boat slipped off its ramp, then plunged to the water some forty feet below, its prow knifing several feet beneath the surface. The boat barely had time to right itself on the surface when the blue yacht appeared nearby, and the clatter of machine-gun fire erupted. Only this time, the gunfire didn't originate from the yacht.

Hiding on the stern, Lazlo let loose with two quick bursts from his M-4 assault rifle. Aimed at two armed men crouching on the yacht's bow, the burst killed one of the men outright, his limp body rolling over the side. The second gunman barely escaped injury and quickly retreated into the main cabin.

Standing on the bridge, Maria watched the incident with anger. Glancing at her watch, she shrieked at the yacht's captain.

"There is still time! Take us alongside the ramp."

"What about the lifeboat?" he asked.

"Forget them. We'll deal with them later."

The yacht surged forward, escaping Lazlo's view as it ran up to the lowered ramp. Maria quickly ordered two of her Janissaries up the steps.

"I'll go secure the bridge," volunteered the Iraqi Farzad. He retrieved a Glock pistol from a concealed shoulder holster, then stepped toward the cabin door.

Maria nodded. "See that the tanker runs ashore. Quickly!"

Lazlo had crossed the stern and just peeked over the rail as the yacht pulled away from the ramp. A spray of gunfire from a gunman on the yacht peppered the rail, forcing Lazlo to dive for the deck. Looking up, he cursed as he spotted the two Janissaries crest the ramp and dive onto the ship, taking cover behind a bulkhead near the superstructure.

Remaining prone, Lazlo rolled against the rail, then shimmied backward to a large scupper that drained the deck of seawater. He curled inside it, finding some cover behind a flat flange in front of the scupper. It was far from an optimal defensive position, but Lazlo didn't think he had been seen and might surprise the boarders.

He was right. The trained commando waited patiently as the two Janissaries attempted to move aft in tandem. When they both had revealed themselves on the deck, Lazlo raised his rifle and fired.

His initial aim was true, as his rifle pumped four rounds into the chest of the first man, dropping him dead instantly. The second man immediately dropped and rolled behind a stanchion before Lazlo's aim could catch up with him.

Both shooters now found themselves pinned down in their defensive positions. A protracted volley erupted back and forth, as each hoped a lucky shot would subdue his opponent.

On the bridge, Pitt tried to ignore the gunfire while keeping the tanker's rudder turned hard over. But he still maintained a wary eye on the yacht, tracking its roving position. It was while sneaking a peek out the rear window that he had spotted a third man climb aboard behind the Janissaries and disappear toward the forward deck, several moments before Lazlo started shooting.

As the firefight erupted below, Pitt searched the bridge

for a possible weapon of his own, digging through an emergency kit mounted above the chart table. Poking his head briefly out the side window, he saw that the surviving Janissary engaged with Lazlo was positioned almost directly below him. He quickly dashed back to the kit and returned with a large fire extinguisher. Hanging out the window, he took quick aim and let it fly.

The makeshift red missile missed the Janissary's head by inches, instead striking him on the back of the shoulder. The gunman gasped at the surprise blow, more from the shock than pain, and instinctively turned and craned his head upward to eye the source of the attack.

Twenty yards away, Lazlo locked in on the man through the sights of his carbine and squeezed the trigger. The quick burst produced no violent scream or splattering blood. The Janissary simply slumped forward in death, leaving a sudden, uncomfortable silence about the ship.

75

The tanker's bridge appeared to be empty when Farzad entered slowly from the rear stairwell. Noticing the shoreline of Sultanahmet sliding horizontally across the bow, he stepped to the helm to halt the sweeping turn. He lowered his pistol as he located, then reached for, the rudder controls.

"Let's not fiddle with that just now," Pitt said.

Pitt emerged from a crouched position behind a console by the port bulkhead. In his hand, he held a brass flare gun pinched from the emergency kit.

Farzad looked at Pitt with surprised recognition that quickly evolved to anger. But his ire turned to mirth when he gazed at Pitt's weapon.

"I have been anxious to meet again," Farzad said in a deep accented voice.

As he subtly tried to raise his pistol, Pitt pulled the trigger on the flare gun. The ignited flare burst across the bridge, striking Farzad in the chest with a cloud of sparks. His clothing promptly caught fire as the charge fell to the floor, then spun off into the corner like a rodent on fire. A second later, the starburst ignited, sending a shower of flame and smoke across the wheelhouse.

Pitt had already dived to the floor, covering his head, as the sparks blew quickly by. Farzad had been less reactive, patting down his incinerated clothes when the starburst sent a second wave of flames his way. He was enveloped in a cloud of smoke and sparks before stepping away from the eruption, coughing for air. Pitt immediately jumped to his feet and bounded forward, hoping to tackle the man before he could see to shoot. But the hired gunman was still aware of Pitt and turned the Glock in his direction.

A loud gunshot thundered through the bridge, but Pitt knew that Farzad hadn't pulled the trigger. The gunman's body was instantly thrown back toward the helm, then slid to the floor, leaving a bloody trail along the console.

Lazlo stepped quickly onto the bridge, his smoking rifle aimed at the prone and smoldering body of Farzad.

"You okay?" Lazlo asked, eyeing Pitt off to his side.

"Yes, just enjoying a small light show," Pitt replied, coughing because of the heavy smoke that lingered in the air. "Thanks for the timely entrance."

Lazlo passed over the now-dented fire extinguisher, which he had held tucked under one arm.

"Here, thought you might like this back. I appreciate the earlier aerial support."

"You just returned the favor," Pitt said, then applied the extinguisher to a scattering of small fires that the flare had ignited.

"I didn't notice this one slip aboard," Lazlo said, ensuring that Farzad was indeed dead.

"He quickly jumped on behind the first two."

"I imagine that they'll try again."

"Time's running short," Pitt replied. "But you might raise that ramp all the same."

"Good idea. What about us?"

"We might be cutting it close. I trust you can swim?"

Lazlo rolled his eyes, then nodded. "See you below," he said, then disappeared down the stairwell.

The smoke from the flare cleared quickly out of the shattered bridge windows as Pitt stepped to the helm and gauged their position. The *Dayan* was more than halfway through its wide U-turn, its bow inching slowly toward the southern span of the Galata Bridge. Pitt tweaked the rudder to guide the big tanker dangerously close to the shoreline as it completed its turn, then he nudged up the engine revolutions. The stuttering and hesitation from belowdecks was worse than before, and Pitt fought to squeeze as much speed out of the faltering engine as he could.

He quickly scanned the shoreline waters for signs of the *Bullet*, but it was nowhere in sight. After Pitt's earlier radio call, Giordino had raced at top speed toward the dredge ship and had already passed under the Galata Bridge. As if he knew Pitt was searching for him, Giordino suddenly hailed the tanker on the marine radio.

"*Bullet* here. I'm past the bridge and just pulling alongside the green cutter dredge. What do you want me to do?"

Pitt told him his plan, which evoked a low whistle from Giordino.

"I hope you had your Wheaties today," he added. "How much time do you have?"

Pitt glanced at his watch. "About six minutes. We should be along in about half that time."

"Thanks for bringing the powder keg my way. Just don't be late," he added, then quickly signed off.

By now, the *Dayan* had completed its turn, and the

south span of the Galata Bridge loomed ahead less than a quarter of a mile away. Pitt willed the ship to go faster, as he felt the seconds tick by, while the bridge seemed to hold its distance. The timing would be close, he knew, but there was little he could do about it now.

Then the unwanted sound of silence suddenly drifted from the tanker's bowels. The rumbling and stumbling beneath his feet vanished as the console in front of him lit up like a Christmas tree. The *Dayan*'s fuel-starved engine had finally given up its last gasp.

76

Tailing the *Dayan* a few dozen yards off its starboard flank, Maria gazed at it through a pair of binoculars. To her disappointment, the big tanker had continued to veer away from shore and was quickly approaching a return pass under the Galata Bridge. She realized why when she scanned the tanker's wheelhouse and caught a brief glimpse of Pitt at the helm.

"They have failed," she said, her voice nearly hoarse with anger. "Get my last men aboard quickly."

The yacht's captain looked at her nervously.

"Shouldn't we be getting clear?" he urged.

Maria stepped close so that no one else on the bridge could hear.

"We can part once the men are aboard," she whispered coldly.

Her last three Janissaries assembled on deck as the yacht raced over to the *Dayan*'s flank. As the yacht approached the tanker's accommodation ladder to off-load the gunmen, the stairway suddenly rose off the water. At the top of the steps, Lazlo stood at the hydraulic controls hoisting the ramp up.

"Shoot him!" Maria yelled, spotting the commando.

The startled Janissaries quickly aimed their weapons at Lazlo and fired. The Israeli commando had been watching the men's reaction and turned to step from the rail.

But he lingered a moment longer at the controls, wishing to keep the ramp out of reach. The hesitation proved costly, as a burst from one of the guns caught him in the shoulder.

He immediately lost his balance, falling forward onto the controls, before slipping to the deck to avoid further gunfire. His left arm was numb, and he felt a sharp pain in his shoulder, but his senses were still intact as he heard a loud crash from below. One-handing his rifle, he shimmied to the rail, then stood and peered quickly over the side.

To his disappointment, he saw that the lower end of the stairway swung out from the tanker and was positioned just over the yacht. Then he looked closer and realized that it was actually wedged into the yacht itself. Falling on the controls, he had inadvertently released the lower-end retracting cable. The heavy steel platform had shot toward the sea like an arrow. Only instead of striking water, it had crashed into the topside bow of the yacht, penetrating several feet through the deck.

Despite the damage and heightened angle, two of the Janissaries had already leaped onto the ramp and were attempting a fast climb to the top. Lazlo aligned his gun on the rail and fired a sustained round, sending both men flailing over the side and into the water.

Suddenly feeling dizzy from a loss of blood, Lazlo curled back onto the deck and rummaged for a medical kit in his combat pack. Fighting the urge to lay down and go to sleep, he told himself he only needed to keep the yacht at bay a few more minutes. Then he glanced up toward the bridge and wondered how much more time Pitt really needed.

*

Time was anything but an ally to Pitt now. The last time he checked, there were less than six minutes until detonation, but he tried not to think about it. His focus was simply on driving the tanker a short distance beyond the bridge.

Since the engine had quit, the tanker was sailing on pure momentum. Multiple shipboard generators provided auxiliary power for Pitt to turn the rudder, but the huge single propeller had spun its last turn. The Golden Horn's gentle current pushed lightly at his stern, and Pitt hoped it would be enough to keep up speed for a few more minutes. Given enough time, the current was ultimately capable of carrying the tanker safely to the Sea of Marmara. But time was going the way of the ship's fuel.

With agonizing slowness, the south span of the Galata Bridge grew larger in the forward bridge window, and Pitt was relieved to note that the *Dayan* was still gliding along at seven knots. Sporadic gunfire caught his attention again, and he dared a quick glance out the window. The yacht was so close to the tanker's side that he could see only a fraction of the boat. He spotted Lazlo, lying near the head of the stairway, and felt assured that the tanker was still secure for the moment.

The underside of the bridge soon loomed up, casting the deck and wheelhouse in a brief shadow. Pitt took to the helm and feathered the rudder controls with nervous fingers. The rest would be up to Giordino, he thought quietly.

"I just hope you can hold your end of the bargain, partner," he muttered aloud, then watched the shadow cast by the bridge gradually fall away.

77

At 454 feet in length, the *Ibn Battuta* was one of the largest dredge ships Giordino had ever seen. Owned and operated by the Belgian company Jan De Nul, it was one of just a handful of self-propelled cutter suction dredges in existence. Unlike a regular suction dredge, which slurped up mud and goo from the seafloor using a long, trailing vacuum tube, the cutter dredge also had a digging mechanism, or cutter head. In the *Ibn Battuta*'s case, the head was a six-foot-diameter ball faced with counter-rotating tungsten carbide teeth capable of chewing through solid rock. Affixed to a hull-mounted boom that could be lowered to the seafloor, the cutter head resembled the open jaws of a megalodon shark waiting to bite.

The dredger had been operating fifty feet from shore and was moored by a pair of huge support legs, called spuds, that protruded through the ship's forward hull. The ship was perpendicular to shore, with its stern facing the channel, which played directly into Pitt's hands.

Giordino, approaching the ship from the stern, spotted a heavy length of chain dangling over the dredger's starboard rail. He eased the *Bullet* alongside, then cut power. Quickly climbing out, he snared the chain, and attached it to the *Bullet* before it could drift away. Hoisting himself up the chain, he grabbed the ship's rail and pulled himself onto the deck.

As a potential hazard in the channel, the *Ibn Battuta*, named for a fourteenth-century Moroccan explorer, stood brightly illuminated by dozens of overhead lights. Giordino peered from one end of the ship's deck to the other and found it completely empty, the crew still asleep in their bunks. Only a lone seaman stood early-morning watch on the bridge, and he had been oblivious to Giordino's approach and boarding.

Giordino quickly moved aft, searching for the dredger's controls, which he prayed weren't located in the wheelhouse. In the center of the stern deck, forward of a large A-frame and well ahead of the cutter apparatus, he spotted a small, elevated shack with broad windows. Climbing up its steps, he entered it and took a seat in the rear-facing operator's chair. He was thankful to find that the dredging mechanism could be operated by a single man, but he cringed when he saw that the control panel was labeled in Dutch.

"Well, at least it isn't Turkish," he muttered while quickly scanning the board.

Finding a switch marked "Dynamo," he flicked it to the "Macht" position. A deep rumble shook the deck as the dredge's massive power generator fired to life. Up on the bridge, the seaman standing watch rushed to the rear window at the noise and quickly spotted Giordino's figure in the controls shack. His excited voice was soon blaring over a two-way radio affixed to the shack's wall. Giordino calmly reached over and turned the radio off before gazing to his left.

The high prow of the tanker was just emerging from beneath the Galata Bridge, barely a hundred yards away.

Giordino abandoned his efforts at trying to decipher the Dutch console and frantically started pushing buttons. One series initiated a grinding sound ahead of him, and he looked up with satisfaction to see the teeth of the cutter head rotating with a menacing whine. The supporting boom stretched horizontally off the dredger's stern, holding the head some twenty feet above the water. It was way too high for what Pitt had in mind.

"*Wat doe jij hier?*" a deep voice suddenly grumbled at Giordino.

Giordino turned to see a squat man with tousled hair climbing into the small controls house. The *Ibn Battuta*'s pump engineer, still wearing his pajamas under a dingy overcoat, stepped over and clamped a hand on Giordino's shoulder. Giordino calmly raised a finger and pointed out the window.

"Look!" he said.

The engineer glanced to the side and froze in shock at the sight of the *Dayan* bearing down on the dredge ship. He started to say something as he turned back toward Giordino only to be met with the balled fist of a right cross. Giordino's knuckles struck him on the button of his chin, and he wilted like a wet noodle. Giordino quickly caught the man in his arms and laid him gently on the floor.

"Sorry, my friend. It ain't the time for pleasantries," he said to the unconscious engineer before scrambling back to the console. He sensed the shadow of the high tanker blanket the controls shack as he hurriedly surveyed the console. Noticing a small lever to the side, he reached over and pushed it down. With great relief, he watched the end of the boom suddenly drop toward the water. He held the lever down until the cutter head was nearly submerged, its rotating teeth creating a foamy froth on the surface.

Releasing the lever, he glanced up the channel. The bow of the huge tanker was now less than twenty feet away. With a helpless feeling, he stood and watched it approach, knowing there was nothing else to be done.

78

Pitt knew it was a desperate gamble, but his options were nearly nonexistent. There had simply been no time to get the tanker safely to open sea, and with the engine now dead there was no chance of escaping the crowded shores of Istanbul. Even if the tanker detonated in the center of the Golden Horn, thousands would die. Pitt's only hope was to try to submerge at least some of the explosives and minimize their destructive force.

And that's where the *Ibn Battuta* came into play. With its rock-eating cutter head, Pitt knew the dredger had the ability to slice through the tanker like a can opener. But he had to put the tanker right on the money for it to work. If he came in too tight, he would rip the boom right off the back of the dredger. Approach too wide, and he would miss the head completely.

Gliding powerless under the Galata Bridge, he gazed ahead at the dredger off his bow. Though the cutter head was still elevated above the water, he could see its rotating teeth and knew that Giordino was at work. He lightly tapped the rudder control, then stepped to the starboard window and poked his head out. Riding high in the water, he couldn't quite see down the tanker's slab sides to the surface, which added to the difficulty of alignment. He tried not to focus on the fact that he had one, and only one, chance to succeed.

Quickly approaching the Belgian dredger, Pitt was relieved to see its stern boom drop, lowering the cutter head into the water. A few seconds later, he spotted Giordino standing near the stern rail, waving at him to edge the tanker in closer. Pitt sprinted back to the helm and turned a few degrees to starboard, then waited for the bow to respond. When the tanker inched in closer, Giordino raised his arms in the air, giving Pitt the thumbs-up.

Pitt left the helm and returned to the side window to watch the impact. Behind him, he suddenly noticed the roar of a high-revving engine, punctuated by the shrill scream of a woman's voice. He glanced down to see Lazlo still lying prone on the deck at the head of the stairway. This time, he noticed a small pool of blood on the deck near his chest. Beyond Lazlo, he saw the yacht alongside, wildly weaving back and forth, once even banging into the side of the tanker.

Pitt idly wondered why the yacht was even still hanging around. But it wasn't worth pondering now, he thought, as he turned and faced the dredger, and the moment of truth.

"Get us clear!" Maria screamed for at least the third time.

The normally controlled tyrant was flushed with panic as she repeatedly looked at her watch. There were just minutes to go.

Sweat ran down the yacht captain's brow as he swung its rudder to and fro, fighting to break free of the embedded ramp. He had waited until they cleared the Galata Bridge before reversing engines, bucking against the momentum of the tanker. Yet the ramp remained lodged in the yacht's deck like a barbed hook in the mouth of an angry marlin.

The yacht's engines howled as the captain applied full reverse power before trying to swing the boat wide. Unknown to the captain, the stairway's lower wheels and axle had caught around the anchor chain in the yacht's anchor locker and was now hopelessly entangled by the wrenching motion of the boat.

The stairway now was a twisted pretzel of steel, yet the platform refused to break apart. With its props churning a maddening boil of water off its stern, the yacht was dragged alongside the tanker like a puppy on a short leash. The captain looked ahead at the dredger, waiting for the *Dayan* to turn away from the Belgian ship. But as they drew closer, he came to the grim realization that the tanker wasn't going to move clear.

With desperate urgency, he swung the yacht hard side to side, slapping against the side of the tanker before pulling wide. But the stubborn platform refused to break free. The *Dayan*'s bow was now abreast of the dredger, but he could see that there was a narrow gap between the vessels, although a boom hung low in the water.

With Maria still staring him down, he nodded toward the dredger.

"The boom will break our tie to the ramp," he said. "We will be free shortly."

79

Pitt's alignment was less than perfect, but not by much.

The *Dayan*'s bow grazed several feet past the cutter head before the rotating teeth made contact with the tanker's hull. Though muffled somewhat by the water, the cutter emitted a screeching wail as its teeth ground against the steel hull plates. For several feet, the head simply forged a deep indentation into the tanker's side. Then the endless line of teeth caught a hull plate seam and ripped open a gaping hole.

Once breached, there was no going back. The rotating cutter ball ate through the hull like a hungry beaver, fed by the forward momentum of the 8,000-ton tanker. The tungsten teeth chewed past the hull and into the stainless steel tanks that held fresh water when the ship was under load. But instead of being fresh, it was now murky green, as the waters of the Bosphorus rapidly began filling the tanks.

From his high perch, Pitt could see water swirling around the bottom of the forward starboard tank. He could only hope that rising waters would spill over into the port tank and dilute the explosive force of both stock-piles. But time was not on his side.

Scanning the deck of the *Ibn Battuta*, he spotted Giordino already sneaking back to the NUMA submersible. He had been replaced at the stern rail by a handful of the dredger's crew. Awakened by the racket, they stood staring dumbfounded at the physical carnage their ship was inflicting on the huge tanker just a few feet in front of them.

As the cutter head bore even with the bridge, Pitt stepped to the helm and as a final gesture cut the rudder fifteen degrees to port. Already slowed by the incoming water, the tanker might travel another half mile, Pitt guessed, before exploding, and he wanted to ensure that she was headed to the center of the channel. The head was still grinding across the hull with a metallic din when Pitt abandoned the bridge, hurrying down the stairwell to grab Lazlo and get off the ship.

He didn't wait around to watch the fate of the yacht. With Maria still screaming in the *Sultana* captain's ear, the captain tucked the yacht up against the tanker's hull, hoping to avoid a direct collision with the dredger. He quickly noticed the subtle bank of the tanker as it eased to port, giving him a slim hope of escape. The turn allowed the yacht to pass just clear of the dredger's boom, as the cutter head was pulled free of the *Dayan*. But there was no room to escape the head itself.

The masticating ball reached the bow of the yacht, striking the starboard hull. Still being dragged like a rag doll, the yacht was pulled up and across the top of the cutter head. The cutter easily chewed a six-foot swath across the underside of the yacht's fiberglass hull before decapitating its whirling twin propellers. The yacht's thumping motors fell silent as the engine compartment flooded, and the yacht began settling by its stern.

The captain stood frozen in shock, his hands still glued

to the wheel. But Maria showed no such restraint. Retrieving a Beretta pistol from her purse, she stepped close to the captain, pressed the muzzle against his ear, and pulled the trigger.

Not waiting for his body to hit the floor, she scurried to the yacht's bow to free them from the tanker once and for all.

80

By the time that Pitt reached the main deck, the tanker had already developed a noticeable list. The cutter head had ripped a two-hundred-foot gouge down its length, slashing into every one of the starboard storage tanks. A full crew of men with pumps couldn't have staved off the flooding for long. It was exactly the effect Pitt had hoped for, but now he had to find a way off for Lazlo and himself.

As the tanker rapidly leaned to starboard, Pitt figured it would be either a short hop down the stairway or, if necessary, a jump from the rail. As he approached Lazlo, he was surprised to see the yacht still clinging alongside. From the angled position of the tanker's deck, he was able to peer right down onto the yacht and see the entangled stairway impaled in it. Of greater interest was the figure of Maria standing on the bow, wielding a pistol. She fired several shots into the twisted link of steel that held the ramp together, then spotted Pitt a short distance above her.

"Die with the ship!" she yelled, aiming the gun at Pitt and pulling the trigger.

Pitt was a hair faster, diving to the deck alongside Lazlo as the bullet whizzed over his head.

"Come on, Lieutenant, it's time we find another exit," he said to the commando.

Lazlo struggled to turn his way, looking at Pitt with glassy eyes that were barely open. Pitt suddenly realized the severity of his wound, seeing the bloody shoulder that Lazlo had managed to patch with a bandage. Every second counted now, though, so Pitt reached over and took a firm grip of the back of Lazlo's collar.

"Hang on, partner," he said.

Ignoring Maria, Pitt sprang to a crouch, then backpedaled up the inclined deck, dragging Lazlo behind him. Maria immediately fired, peppering a handful of shots in their direction. Her shots struck close but missed both men before Pitt had them safely out of sight. Regaining a touch of strength, Lazlo had Pitt pull him to his feet. The commando's jacket was soaked red, and a trail of blood had followed him across the deck.

The tanker suddenly lurched beneath their feet, listing almost thirty degrees to starboard. Pitt quickly realized that their most immediate danger wasn't from the pending explosives.

"Can you climb with me?" Pitt asked Lazlo.

The tough commando nodded, and with an arm around Pitt for support he took shaky steps up the deck.

Behind them, Maria continued shooting, her target again the battered stairway. Several more well-aimed shots at the ramp's joint finally weakened the metal, which had bent sharply with the sinking tanker. Stomping the ramp with her foot, its joint finally broke free, releasing the upper stairway to swing hard against the ship.

Free at last, Maria sneered at the tanker from the bow of the slowly sinking yacht. The tanker would drift well clear before exploding, and she might have time to make it back to the bridge for safety. At the very least, she thought, Pitt and Lazlo would die with the ship.

She might have been right, only she failed to account for the *Dayan*'s own bit of vindictive wrath.

81

From the twentieth floor of his high-rise office situated on the eastern shore of the Bosphorus, Ozden Celik watched the events unfold with increasing dread. He had barely been able to make out the shadow of the tanker when it first approached Istanbul under the faint light of dawn. But the slowly graying sky had expanded his panoramic view until the towering minarets of Süleymaniye Mosque were clearly visible across the waters of the strait.

With a tripod-mounted pair of high-magnification binoculars, he focused on the *Dayan* just as its emergency lifeboat was released off the stern. He watched in dismay as the tanker crossed under the Galata Bridge while the *Sultana* appeared alongside in an apparent gun battle. Celik could feel his heart pounding when he saw the tanker complete a wide turn and reemerge beneath the far end of the bridge.

"No, you are supposed to run ashore by the mosque!" he cursed aloud at the sluggish tanker.

His frustration mounted when repeated phone calls to Maria went unanswered. He lost sight of the yacht when the tanker turned, its high profile obscuring the smaller vessel. Holding his breath, Celik hoped that the yacht had turned and fled up the Golden Horn to escape the blast, which he knew was now imminent. But his eyes bulged in horror when the *Dayan* passed close to the dredge ship, then turned toward the channel, revealing that the yacht was still alongside its starboard flank.

Focusing the binoculars, he saw his sister on the yacht's bow, shooting a gun first at the tanker, then at the metal stairway. Celik couldn't help but notice the tanker listing precariously above her.

"Get away! Get away!" Celik shouted to his sister from two miles away.

The eyepieces dug into his brow as he watched the scene with horror. Maria at last succeeded in freeing the yacht from the stairway's clasp, but it didn't move far. Celik had no idea that the yacht had been stripped of its propellers and was itself sinking. Baffled by the sight, he couldn't understand why the yacht hung close to the heavily listing tanker.

From his vantage point across the strait, Celik could not hear the symphony of creaks and groans that emanated from the bowels of the tanker as its center of gravity was upset. The massive flooding across the *Dayan*'s entire length augmented the starboard list until the deck rose like a steep mountain. Crashing sounds erupted throughout the tanker as dishes, furniture, and equipment lost their fight with gravity and tumbled against the starboard bulkheads.

As the starboard rail touched the water, the hulking tanker wallowed completely up onto its side, holding the awkward position for several seconds. The *Dayan* could have broken up or simply sank on its side, but it instead held together and resumed its death roll with a flourish.

Still standing on the bow of the yacht, Maria felt the shadow of the tanker cross her body as the ship began to flip over. Drifting just a few yards from the bigger *Dayan*, the yacht was well within its reach. There would be no escaping its destructive blow.

Maria looked up and raised an arm, as if to ward off the blow of the giant tanker as it rolled over. Instead, she was flattened like an insect. The capsizing *Dayan* slammed the water's surface, engulfing the yacht while creating a ten-foot wave that crashed toward the shoreline, tossing the *Ibn Battuta* about like a rowboat. The dark, barnacle-encrusted hull of the tanker filled the horizon, its mammoth bronze propeller spinning idly in the morning sky. Muffled bangs from collapsing bulkheads mixed with rushing water echoed throughout the hull as the over-turned ship slowly began to settle by the bow.

Celik gripped his binoculars with trembling hands as he watched his sister die beneath the weight of the capsized tanker. Frozen in shock, he stared unblinking before his emotions brimmed over. Heaving the tripod across his office with a wail, he fell to the carpet, then covered his eyes and sobbed uncontrollably.

82

Celik wasn't the only one who watched in horror as the tanker capsized. Giordino was just climbing into the *Bullet* when he heard a crashing sound behind him and turned to see the *Dayan* turn turtle atop the yacht. He quickly sealed the rear hatch as the resulting wave barreled into the *Ibn Battuta*, carrying the submersible up and away from the dredge ship.

Giordino quickly fired up the diesel engines and motored toward the tanker. He thought anxiously of Pitt, who had waved at him from the bridge of the tanker just minutes before. The bridge was now far underwater, and all he could see was the cold, lifeless underbelly of the Israeli tanker.

Ignoring the danger that the tanker might explode at any time, he raced along its near side. Surprisingly little debris had floated away when the ship turned over, and he was able to speed quickly down its length to search for bodies in the channel. He knew that Pitt was like a dolphin in the water. If he had somehow survived the capsizing, there was at least a chance that he had swum clear.

Nearing the submerged bow, Giordino swung around and motored back close to the hull, either not knowing or not caring that the timed explosives would detonate in less than two minutes. The waters ahead of him remained empty as he passed the tanker's midsection and approached the stern. With a heavy heart, he reluctantly considered the notion that his old friend had not made it off alive.

Nudging the throttles higher, he started to turn away when he noticed a pair of ropes stretched over the hull. Oddly, the lines appeared to run from the ship's submerged port rail up the hull and over the keel, a short distance in front of the propeller. With a glimmer of hope in his eye, Giordino accelerated briskly, sweeping around the tanker's broad stern, which was now rising high into the air.

Reaching the tanker's opposite side, he spotted the ropes dangling high from the keel, but the hull was otherwise empty. Then barely fifty yards away in the water he spotted two objects. Turning instantly, he raced closer, seeing with joy that it was Pitt towing an injured Lazlo away from the ship.

Giordino sped in closer, then expertly reversed engines to quickly drift alongside. Pitt hoisted Lazlo onto a pontoon, then shouted at Giordino as the latter moved to open the hatch.

"No time," Pitt yelled. "Get us out of here."

Giordino nodded, then waited until Pitt climbed aboard and wrapped an arm around Lazlo before accelerating. The two men were tossed and splashed as the *Bullet* charged quickly ahead, bounding over the harbor waters. Giordino turned and sped toward the Galata Bridge, determining that it would provide the closest cover.

The *Bullet* was a hundred yards shy of the bridge when a deep thump sounded across the channel. Though a portion of the explosive material had fallen to the seabed when the *Dayan* capsized, nearly half of the fuel oil and most of the HMX remained lodged in the two forward storage tanks. But with the ship sinking by the bow, the flooded tanks were almost entirely underwater, greatly diluting the blast's impact.

A quick series of successive thumps sounded as the timed fuzes detonated, and then a huge explosion ripped open the tanker's hull. The concussion echoed across the hills and streets of Istanbul like a sonic boom. A fountain of white water blew from the tanker's underside, spraying chunks of steel and debris a hundred feet into the air. The jagged chunks fell to earth across a quarter-mile swath, raining down in a deadly hail from the heavens.

Yet the terrifying blast proved mostly benign. Due to the angle of the sinking tanker, the main force of the blast was centered ahead of it and toward the Bosphorus. Pitt's last-second course adjustment had diverted the impact away from shore and toward a wide patch of empty water.

As the steel and debris splashed into the bay, a loud creak echoed from the tanker as the perforated section of hull gave way. The decimated bow broke free and promptly sank quickly to the channel bottom while the remaining hull lingered on the surface a few moments before foundering.

Bobbing beneath a span of the Galata Bridge, Giordino climbed out of the *Bullet*'s cabin to check on his passengers.

"Thanks for the lift," Pitt said as he attended to Lazlo.

"You boys were cutting it a bit close there," Giordino replied.

"We got lucky. Maria Celik wanted to use us for target

practice on the starboard rail, so we hiked up the deck. Happened to find a pair of lines that had been lowered over the port side, and we were scrambling down them as the ship turned turtle. We managed to make it over the keel, then slid down the other side to avoid the yacht."

"You needn't have worried," Giordino said with a grin. "It got flattened like a pancake."

"Any survivors?"

Giordino shook his head.

"Lazlo needs medical attention," Pitt said. "We better get him to shore."

He and Giordino helped him inside the submersible, then they motored toward the southern shoreline.

"That was some blast," Giordino said to Pitt. "Could have been a lot worse."

Pitt simply nodded quietly, staring out the cockpit window.

Ahead of them, the massive remains of the Israeli tanker rose up high by its stern. The vessel stood near vertical in an almost defiant manner before plunging beneath the waves with a rush. Somewhere not far across the strait, the twisted dreams of a renewed Ottoman dynasty sank with it.

83

The tanker explosion rattled Istanbul more politically than physically. The confirmed loss of the police boat and Coast Guard vessel in conjunction with the attack put the country's military forces on high alert. When the tanker was identified as the *Dayan*, a flurry of high-level accusations between Turkey and Israel went flying across diplomatic channels. Protests by panic-stricken residents of the city nearly led to a military response. But fears of a Turkish/Israeli conflict were assuaged when the authorities found the *Dayan*'s rescued crewmen.

Interviewed publicly, the crewmen detailed their hijacking and captivity at the hands of the unknown gunmen. Turkish sentiment quickly turned when the men described loading the explosives at gunpoint and almost dying aboard the ship but for their last-minute rescue. Privately, after checking Lazlo into a hospital, Pitt and Giordino had informed Turkish authorities of their role in sinking the tanker.

When U.S. intelligence secretly provided evidence that the same HMX explosives were used in the mosque attacks in Bursa, Cairo, and Jerusalem, the Turkish forces were quick to act. Secret raids were immediately carried out against Celik's home, office, and port facilities, while the *Ottoman Star* was located in Greek waters and seized. As public pressure mounted to identify who committed the attack and why, the official investigation wasn't kept quiet for long.

With the release of their names, Ozden and Maria Celik became public pariahs and a source of national embarrassment. When it was later discovered that they had orchestrated the break-in at Topkapi, the national embarrassment and anger turned to outright rage. Investigators and journalists alike dove into the pair's concealed pasts, revealing their ties to the last Ottoman ruling family, as well as to underworld mobsters and drug runners who had kick-started Celik business holdings.

Inevitably, the Celiks' financial dealings with Arab royalty were uncovered, leading to the revelation that millions of dollars had been funneled to Mufti Battal. The objective of the Celiks' attacks became readily apparent, and public furor was directed to the Mufti and his Felicity Party. Although no evidence was found that the Mufti was involved or even aware of the terrorist attacks, the damage was done.

The final confirmation of the Celiks' guilt was confirmed when divers were sent to the bottom of the Golden Horn. The mangled remains of the *Sultana* were located not far from the shattered hull of the tanker. A salvage team brought the wreck to the surface, where it was left to a police forensics team to remove the crushed body of Maria Celik from the flattened deck of the yacht.

His name in ruin, his assets seized, and his dead sister's body held in the Istanbul city morgue, there was nothing left of Ozden Celik's empire but the man himself.

Yet he had apparently vanished into nothingness.

84

The Friday noon prayer, called *khutbah*, was typically the highest-attended Muslim service of the week. It was the time when the resident mosque Imam would offer a separate, faith-inspiring sermon before leading the assemblage in prayer.

At Istanbul's Fatih Mosque, the prayer hall remained oddly empty, despite the *muezzin*'s recent call to prayer. The *khutbah* was normally packed to the gills, with dozens of people spilling out of the prayer hall and into the courtyard, hoping to catch a glimpse of Mufti Battal while listening to his words of hope. But that was not the case today.

Barely fifty ardent followers stood in the open hall as Mufti Battal entered and stepped to a raised platform near the *mihrab*. The once-mighty Mufti looked like he had aged twenty years in the past week. His eyes were sunken and cold, his skin pale and lifeless. The swagger and conceit that had fueled his rise to power was completely absent. Gazing at the sparse crowd, he trembled slightly, suppressing the single emotion of rage.

Speaking in a subdued voice, he began his homily railing against the dangerous, unchecked powers of the establishment. In uncharacteristic fashion, he was soon rambling incoherently, targeting a litany of perceived ills and threats. The somber faces staring back at him in disillusionment finally checked his diatribe. Ending his sermon abruptly, he recited a short passage from the Qur'an dealing with redemption, then led the small audience in prayer.

Not wishing to mingle with his brethren, Battal quickly stepped to the side of the prayer hall and entered an anteroom where he kept a small office. He was surprised to find a bearded man in the room seated in front of his desk. He was dressed in the faded white shirt and trousers of a laborer, and wore a wide-brimmed hat that partially covered his face.

"Who let you in here?" Battal thundered at the man.

The stranger stood and raised his head to look Battal in the eye, then tugged on his fake beard.

"I let myself in, Altan," replied the haggard voice of Ozden Celik.

Beneath his commoner's disguise, his appearance was not far removed from that of Battal's. He had the same drawn, gaunt face and pasty skin. Only his eyes burned with a greater, somewhat crazed intensity.

"You have endangered me by coming here," Battal hissed. He quickly stepped to the back door and opened it cautiously, sticking his head out in surveillance.

"Come, follow me," he said to Celik, then slipped out the door.

He led him down a corridor, then entered a seldom-used storage room at the rear of the mosque. A washing machine was wedged into one corner, fronted by a cluster of old towels left to dry on a wire clothesline. As Celik followed him in, Battal closed the door behind him and locked it.

"Why have you come here?" he asked impatiently.

"I need your help to get out of the country."

"Yes, your life is finished in Turkey. As nearly is mine."

"I have sacrificed everything for you, Altan. My wealth, my property. Even my sister," he added, his voice quivering. "It was all done for the aim of making you President."

Battal stared at Celik with nothing but contempt.

"You have destroyed me, Ozden," he said, his face flush with anger. "I was crushed in the election. My benefactors have disappeared. My congregation has abandoned me. All because you have tainted my reputation. And now this."

He pulled a letter out of his pocket and winged it at Celik. The Turk ignored it, simply shaking his head as it fell to the floor.

"It is from the Diyanet. I have been relieved as Mufti of Istanbul." Battal's eyes flared as he sneered at Celik. "You have utterly destroyed me."

"It was all done to achieve our destiny," Celik replied quietly.

Battal could control his emotions no longer. He grabbed Celik by his shirt and flung him across the room. Celik fell against the hanging laundry, snapping the line as he dropped to the ground covered in towels. He struggled to get to his feet, but Battal was already on him. Grabbing a loose end of the clothesline, Battal quickly wrapped it around Celik's throat and drew it tight. Celik fought back fiercely, punching and flailing at the Mufti. But Battal was too big and powerful, and too bent on vengeance. Surging with pent-up rage, he ignored Celik's blows and yanked the line tighter.

The horror of being strangled was not lost on Celik.

Struggling to breathe, he saw a parade of his own garroted victims flash before his eyes as the life was slowly choked from his body. Failing in a last desperate attempt to break free, he stared at the Mufti with a combination of fear and defiance before his eyes rolled back and his body fell limp. Battal kept his death grip on Celik for another five minutes, less out of assurance than psychotic fury. Finally letting go, he stepped slowly from the dead man, staggering out of the storage room with trembling hands and a permanently disabled mind.

It was late the next morning when Celik's body was discovered by a Bosphorus fisherman. Surreptitiously dumped into the harbor, it had floated about the Golden Horn for most of the night before drifting ashore at Seraglio Point.

The expired body of Ozden Celik, the world's last Ottoman, was found just a few steps from the walls of Topkapi, in the shadow of the glory of his legendary ancestors.

85

Pitt and Giordino found Lazlo on the third floor of the Istanbul Hospital, situated in a pleasant but heavily guarded room overlooking the Bosphorus. The commando was lying in bed, reading a three-day-old copy of *Haaretz*, an Israeli daily newspaper, when the two men were allowed to enter.

"Don't tell me you are still front-page news back home?" Pitt asked as he entered and shook hands.

"It is good to see you, my friends," Lazlo replied, sheepishly putting the paper aside. "Yes, we are still big news in Israel. However, I am sad to report that I seem to be getting all of the credit. It was you who disabled the tanker," he said to Pitt. "And none of it would have been possible without the *Bullet*," he added to Giordino.

"I think it's safe to say it was a team effort," Pitt replied.

"Among other things, the three of us have improved my country's relationship with Turkey tenfold," Lazlo boasted.

"Not to mention helping keep Atatürk's vision of a secular Turkish government in play for a few more years," Pitt noted.

"I think somebody should put us in for a Nobel Prize," Giordino said with a smirk.

"I heard they found the body of Celik this morning," Lazlo said.

"Yes, he was apparently strangled, then pitched into the Golden Horn," Pitt said.

"Did you beat me to the task?"

Pitt smiled. "Not this time. A police detective told us they are pretty certain Mufti Battal is responsible. An undercover cop at Battal's mosque reported seeing a man matching Celik's description and dress in the building about the estimated time of his death."

"A pair of devils, in my book," Lazlo said.

An attractive nurse came into the room momentarily to check Lazlo's medication, then left under his watchful gaze.

"Anxious to get home, Lieutenant?" Giordino asked.

"Not particularly," Lazlo replied with a grin. "And by the way, it is now Commander Lazlo. I've received word of my promotion."

"Let me be the first to congratulate you," Giordino said, slipping him a bottle of whisky he had smuggled into the hospital. "Perhaps you can find someone around here to share it with," he added with a wink.

"You Americans are all right," Lazlo replied with a wide smile.

"How is the prognosis?" Pitt asked.

"I'm scheduled for surgery in Tel Aviv in another week, then will be subject to several weeks of therapy. But the recovery should be full, and I hope to report back to duty before the end of the year."

They were interrupted by the entrance of a man in a wheelchair, who rolled in with his leg in a cast.

"Abel, there you are," Lazlo greeted. "It's time you meet the men who helped save your life."

"Abel Hammet, master of the *Dayan*. Or ex-master, I should say," he said, greeting Pitt and Giordino warmly. "Lazlo here has told me everything you did. You really put yourself out on a limb, and my crew and I can't thank you enough."

"I'm sorry your tanker was still lost in the end," Pitt replied.

"The *Dayan* was a good ship," Hammet said wistfully. "But the good news is that we're getting a brand-new vessel. The Turkish government has committed to building us a replacement, apparently using the appropriated assets of one Ozden Celik to pay for it."

"Who says there's no justice in the world?" Giordino quipped.

As the men laughed, Pitt glanced at his watch.

"Well, the *Aegean Explorer* is due to shove off in about an hour," he said. "I'm afraid we're going to have to be on our way."

He shook hands with Hammet, then turned to Lazlo.

"Commander, I'd be glad to have you by my side any day," he said.

"It would be my honor," Lazlo replied.

As Pitt and Giordino moved toward the door, Lazlo called out to them.

"Where are you headed? Back to your shipwreck?"

"No," Pitt replied. "We're sailing to Cyprus."

"Cyprus? What's waiting for you there?"

Pitt gave the commander a cryptic grin.

"A divine revelation, I hope."

PART IV
Manifest Destiny

The Grotto

86

St. Julien Perlmutter had just settled into an oversize leather armchair when the phone rang. His favorite reading post was custom-built, as it had to be to accommodate his nearly four-hundred-pound frame. He glanced at a nearby grandfather clock, noting it was nearly midnight. Reaching past a tall glass of port parked on a side table, he answered the phone.

"Julien, how are you?" came a familiar voice over the line.

"Well, if it isn't the savior of Constantinople," Perlmutter replied in a booming voice. "I've read with glee about your exploits in the Golden Horn, Dirk. I hope you weren't injured in the affair?"

"No, I'm fine," Pitt replied. "And by the way, they call it Istanbul these days."

"Bilgewater. It was Constantinople for sixteen hundred years. Ridiculous to change it now."

Pitt had to laugh at his old friend, who spent most of his waking hours living in the past. "I hope I didn't catch you in bed?" he asked.

"No, not at all. I was just sitting down with a copy of Captain Cook's papers from his first voyage to the Pacific."

"One of these days, we'll have to go find what's left of the *Endeavor*," Pitt said.

"Aye, a noble mission that would be," Perlmutter replied. "So where are you, Dirk, and why the late call?"

"We just docked at Limassol, Cyprus, and I have a mystery I could use your help with."

The large bearded man's eyes twinkled at hearing the words. As one of the world's foremost marine historians, Perlmutter had a hunger for nautical enigmas that exceeded his appetite for food and drink. Having associated with Pitt for years, he knew that when his friend called he usually had something beguiling.

"Pray tell," Perlmutter said in his deep bassoon voice.

Pitt proceeded to tell him about the Ottoman wreck and its Roman-era artifacts, then he sprang the story of the Manifest and its list of contents.

"My word, that's an epic cargo," Perlmutter said. "A pity that little, if any of it, would survive after two millennia under the sea."

"Yes, the ossuary might be the best that could be hoped for."

"You would surely stir a hornet's nest with that," Perlmutter said.

"If any of it still exists, it deserves to be found," Pitt replied.

"Absolutely. Even without the cargo, an intact Roman galley would be a gem to discover. Do you have a starting point to conduct the search?"

"The purpose of my call," Pitt said. "I'm hoping that you might know of some unidentified ancient wrecks off the southern Cyprus coast. Any data on the historic trade routes around the island would probably be helpful, too."

Perlmutter thought for a moment. "I have a few

resources on the shelf that might be of assistance. Give me a couple of hours, and I'll see what I can do."

"Thanks, Julien."

"Say, Dirk," Perlmutter added, before hanging up. "Were you aware that Cyprus was known to produce the best wines in the Roman Empire?"

"You don't say."

"A glass of Commandaria, I've heard, tastes as it did two thousand years ago."

"I'll be sure and find you a bottle, Julien."

"You're a good man, Dirk. So long."

Hanging up the phone, Perlmutter took a long sip of his port wine, savoring its deep, sweet flavor. Then propelling his huge frame to his feet, he stepped to a ceiling-high shelf overflowing with nautical books and began humming to himself as he rifled through the titles.

It was less than two hours later when the satellite phone on the *Aegean Explorer* rang with a return call from Perlmutter.

"Dirk, I've found just a morsel so far, but it might be a start," the historian said.

"Every little bit helps," Pitt replied.

"It's a shipwreck, from the fourth century. It was discovered by sport divers back in the nineteen sixties."

"Roman?"

"I'm not sure. The archaeological report I have is quite dated, but it indicates that some Roman weaponry was among the artifacts recovered. As you know, Cyprus was never deemed of much military importance to the Romans but rather as a trading source for copper and grain. And, of course, wine. So the existence of weapons on this wreck might be of significance."

"Long shot or not, it sounds worth a look. Where is the wreck located?"

"She was found off of a town called Pissouri, which is near you on the southern coast. The wreck was located about a quarter mile off the public beach there. I found a later reference that the site was partially excavated in the nineties, however, and the artifacts put on display at the Limassol District Archaeological Museum."

"That's convenient," Pitt said. "Does the location hold up to the Roman trading routes?"

"Actually, the merchant ships of the day sailing from Judaea would have typically followed along the Levant coast en route to Constantinople. Same goes for the Roman galleys, which would generally hug the coastline to stay in calmer waters. But our knowledge of maritime practices in those days is limited."

"It may well be that they never intended to sail to Cyprus," Pitt replied. "Thanks, Julien, we'll look into the wreck."

"I'll keep nosing about for more. In the meantime, happy hunting."

As Pitt hung up the phone, his two children stepped onto the bridge with small travel bags slung over their shoulders.

"Jumping ship before we start our survey?" Pitt asked.

"You've got a starting point?" Summer asked.

"The good Mr. Perlmutter just helped me lay out a search grid."

"I talked Dirk into helping me attack the local archives,"

she replied. "I thought I'd see if we could find some local references to the Manifest, or perhaps a history of local piracy. You don't mind if we catch up with you in a day or two?"

"No, that sounds like a good idea. Where's your first stop?"

Summer gave her father a blank look. "To be honest, we haven't identified the local resources to visit. You wouldn't have any suggestions, would you?"

Pitt couldn't help but grin at the request while he glanced at a page of notes he had written while talking to Perlmutter.

"It just so happens," he said with a wink, "that I know exactly where you should go."

87

Summer and Dirk found the Limassol District Archaeological Museum in a modern building east of the city
center, not far from the town's scenic municipal garden.
A variety of pottery and artifacts from Cyprus's rich history, some dating to 2000 B.C., were displayed in simple
glass cases throughout the three wings of the building.
Summer admired a display of terra-cotta animal figures
from the Archaic Age while waiting for the museum's
curator.

"I am Giorgos Danellis. May I help you?" asked a
round-faced man with a Greek accent.

Summer introduced herself and her brother. "We are
interested in a fourth-century shipwreck that was discovered near Pissouri," she explained.

"Yes, the Pissouri wreck," Danellis replied with a nod.
"The display is in room three."

As he escorted them to the other room, he asked, "Are
you with the British Museum?"

"No, we work for the National Underwater and Marine
Agency," Dirk replied.

"Oh, sorry," the curator replied. "There was a fellow in
here a few days ago inquiring about the same exhibit. I
thought you might be related."

He stepped to a large glass case that was filled with
dozens of artifacts. Summer noted that most were ceramic

containers, along with some deteriorated wood fragments with rusty iron fittings.

"What can you tell us about the ship?" she asked.

"She dates to the first half of the fourth century," he said, pointing to a corroded silver coin on the lower display shelf. "This Roman denarius found on the wreck depicts Emperor Constantine with laurels, which indicates that the vessel was sunk around A.D. 330."

"Was she a Roman galley?" Dirk asked.

"There was some speculation to that end when she was first discovered, but most experts believe she was a merchant galley. Wood samples show she was built of Lebanese pine, which would tend to support the hypothesis." He pointed to an artist's rendition of a high-prowed galley with twin square sails that hung on the wall.

"The archaeologists believe she was a probably a merchant transporting grain or olive oil."

Dirk pointed to a sea-ravaged sword hilt that was tucked behind a clay pot.

"She had armament aboard?" he asked.

The curator nodded. "Allegedly, there was much more, but I'm afraid that sword remnant is all that we recovered. The archaeologists were forced to conduct a hurried excavation when it was discovered that the wreck site was being systematically plundered by thieves. I've heard stories that a great many weapons were removed from the site before the archaeologists arrived."

"How do you account for all those weapons on a merchant ship?" Summer asked.

The curator looked blank. "I don't really know. Perhaps

it was part of their cargo. Or perhaps a high-ranking official was traveling aboard."

"Or there's another possibility," Dirk said.

Danellis and Summer looked at him curiously.

"It seems to me," he said, "that this vessel may have been a pirate ship. It reminds me of the account I read in Caesarea of the captured Cypriot pirate vessel that was found with Roman arms aboard."

"Yes, that could well be the case," the curator replied. "Some of the crew's belongings were quite luxurious for the day," he added, pointing to a glass plate and stylized ceramic cup.

"Mr. Danellis, are there any other known shipwrecks from that era in Cypriot waters?" Summer asked.

"No. There's a suspected Bronze Age wreck on the north shore, but this would otherwise be the oldest wreck that I'm aware of. What exactly is your interest?"

"We're researching a Roman galley sailing on behalf of Constantine that may have been lost in Cypriot waters. It would have sailed at about the same time as the Pissouri shipwreck."

"I know nothing of that," he replied, shaking his head. "But you might want to make a visit to the monastery of Stavrovouni."

Summer gave him a skeptical look. "Why a monastery?"

"Well, aside from its beautiful location," Danellis replied, "the monastery played host to Constantine's mother, Helena, when she journeyed back from the Holy Land with the True Cross."

88

The *Aegean Explorer* crept close to the shoreline, then abruptly wheeled about and headed out to sea at its same plodding pace. A thin insulated cable stretched taut off its stern, disappearing below the surface. Fifty meters beyond, the cable tugged at a small, cigar-shaped towfish that glided through the water a few feet above the sea-floor. A pair of transducers on the towfish sent sound waves bouncing off the bottom, then recorded their timed rate of return. Processors on board the ship converted the sonar signals to a visual image, providing a simulated picture of the floor's contours.

Seated on the ship's bridge, Pitt studied a video monitor of the sonar images, watching an undulating, rock-strewn bottom scroll by. Standing nearby, Giordino took a break from staring over Pitt's shoulders and gazed over at the beachfront with a pair of binoculars.

"Enjoying the scenery?" Gunn asked.

"Could be better," Giordino replied. "Although it is enhanced by a pair of lovely young ladies seeking refuge from the sun in a sea cave."

The beach off Pissouri was a narrow strip of sand backed by high cliffs, atop which sat its namesake village. Though popular with the British servicemen stationed at the nearby base of Akrotiri, the beach was still one of the quieter ones along the southern coast.

"It looks like we'll soon be running out of beachfront real estate," Giordino noted as the ship slowly worked its way east while conducting the grid survey.

"Then that can only mean that we're getting close to the wreck," Pitt replied optimistically.

As if responding to his prophecy, the Pissouri wreck appeared on the screen a few minutes later. Giordino and Gunn crowded around as the image unfolded on the monitor. Far from appearing like an actual ship, the site was little more than an elongated mound, with small sections of the keel and frame exposed by the shifting sands. That even that much remained of the seventeen-hundred-year-old ship was a miracle in itself.

"It certainly presents the image of an old wreck," Gunn said.

"It's the only wreck we've found off Pissouri, so it must be Perlmutter's fourth-century ship," Giordino said. "I'm surprised it wasn't closer to shore, though," he added, noting that they were nearly a half mile from the beach.

"You have to remember that the Mediterranean was a bit shallower two thousand years ago," Gunn said.

"That would explain its position," he replied. "Are we going to dive it up?" he asked, turning to Pitt.

Pitt shook his head. "No need to. First, it's already been picked clean. And second, it's not our wreck."

"How can you be so sure?" Gunn asked.

"Summer called. She and Dirk saw the artifact exhibit at the Limassol Museum. The archaeologists who excavated her are certain it is not a Roman galley. Dirk believes it could be a secondary pirate vessel involved with the attack on the Romans. It might be worth a dive later on, but Summer indicated that it had been pretty well plundered before the archaeologists got to it."

"So we use this as a starting point?" Gunn asked.

"It's the best data point we've got," Pitt replied with a nod. "If the pirate ship came ashore here and wrecked, we can only hope that the Roman vessel is somewhere in the neighborhood."

Giordino took a seat near the monitor and tried to get comfortable.

"Well, let's keep searching, then," he remarked. "As the man said, Rome wasn't built in a day."

89

Summer drove east on the main coastal highway from Limassol, with Dirk relinquishing the driving duties since she had just come from England. A Crown Colony of Great Britain during the first half of the twentieth century, Cyprus still held visible reminders of its former British rule. English was spoken most everywhere, the currency in the southern Greek half of the country was denominated in pounds, and the road traffic traveled on the left-hand side.

Summer turned their rental car inland, following the well-paved highway toward Nicosia. The road began a gentle ascent as they approached the eastern extremes of the Trodoos Mountains. Traveling through mostly desolate hills, they turned off onto a narrow asphalt crossroad. The road climbed sharply, twisting its way up a small mountain. Perched dramatically atop the summit sat the monastery of Stavrovouni.

Summer parked the car in a small lot at the foot of the complex. Walking past an empty entry station, they approached a long wooden stairway to the summit. A beggar dressed in ragged clothes and a wide-brimmed hat sat nearby, his head hanging down in apparent slumber. The siblings tiptoed past, then climbed the stairs to the grounds of the monastery, which offered commanding views of the entire southeast portion of the island. Passing through an open courtyard, they approached a stern-faced monk in a woolen robe standing near the monastery entrance.

"Welcome to Stavrovouni," he said with reserve, then gazed at Summer. "Perhaps you are not aware, but we are adherents to the Athonite Orthodoxy here. I am afraid that we do not allow women into the monastery."

"My understanding is that you wouldn't be here if it wasn't for a woman," she replied tartly. "Does the name Helena ring a bell?"

"I'm very sorry."

Summer rolled her eyes at the monk, then turned to Dirk.

"I guess I'll stay here and look at the frescoes," she said, motioning toward the painted courtyard walls. "Enjoy your tour."

Dirk leaned over and whispered to his sister, "If I'm not back in an hour, then it means I decided to join up."

With his sister seething, he turned and followed the monk through an open wooden door.

"Can you tell me about Helena's role with the monastery and the history of the site?" Dirk asked.

"In ancient times, this mountaintop housed a Greek temple. It had been long abandoned and in a state of disrepair when Saint Helena arrived in Cyprus after her pilgrimage to Jerusalem. The good saint is said to have put an end to a thirty-year drought that had been baking the land. While on Cyprus, she had a dream in which she was told to construct a church in the name of the venerable cross. Stavrovouni, in case you didn't know, means 'Cross Mountain.' It was here she built the church, leaving behind the cross of the penitent thief she had brought from Jerusalem, along with a fragment of the True Cross."

The monk led Dirk into the small church, guiding him past a large wooden iconostasis to reach the altar. On the altar stood a large wooden cross, encased in silver. A tiny gold frame set within the cross protected a smaller wooden fragment.

"The church has suffered much destruction and vandalism over the centuries," the monk explained, "first by the Mamelukes and later by the Ottomans. I'm afraid little is left of Helena's legacy but for this sacred piece of the True Cross," he said, pointing to the gold-encased fragment.

"Are you aware of any other relics of Jesus that Helena may have left on Cyprus?" Dirk asked.

The monk rubbed his chin a moment. "No, none that I know of, but you should speak to Brother Andros. He's our resident historian here. Let's see if he is in his office."

The monk led Dirk down a corridor to their left, which housed a number of austere guest rooms. A pair of small offices occupied the end, where Dirk could see a thin man shaking hands with a monk and then turning his way.

As they passed, Dirk said, "Ridley Bannister?"

"Why, yes," Bannister replied, looking at Dirk with startled suspicion.

"My name is Dirk Pitt. I just read your last book about your excavations in the Holy Land. I recognized you from the dust jacket. I have to tell you, I've enjoyed reading about your discoveries."

"Why, thank you," Bannister replied, reaching out and shaking hands. A tentative look then crossed his brow.

"You said your last name is Pitt? You don't by chance have a relative named Summer?"

"Yes, she's my sister. She's waiting out front, as a matter of fact. Do you know her?"

"I believe we met at an archaeology conference some time ago," he stammered. "So what brings you to Stavrovouni?" he asked, quickly changing topics.

"Summer recently found evidence that Helena may have shipped more than just the True Cross from Jerusalem and that these relics may have been lost in Cyprus. We're hoping to find clues to the whereabouts of a Roman galley that sailed on her behalf."

The dim corridor light masked Bannister's sudden paleness. "A fascinating prospect," he said. "Do you have any inkling where the relics might be?"

"We're starting with a known shipwreck near a place called Pissouri. But as you know, two-thousand-year-old clues are hard to come by."

"Indeed. Well, I'm afraid I must be running along. It was a pleasure to meet you, Mr. Pitt, and good luck with your search."

"Thank you. And be sure to say hello to Summer on your way out."

"I will."

Bannister, of course, had no such intentions. Walking quickly down the corridor, he reentered the church and found a side exit on the opposite wall. Stepping into the sunlight, he crept cautiously toward the courtyard until spotting Summer studying a wall fresco. Waiting until she turned her back toward him, he quietly scooted across the grounds, reaching the upper stairway without being observed.

Jogging down the stairs, he nearly tripped on the beggar at the base before making his way to his car. He drove quickly down the winding road until reaching the highway, where he pulled to the side, parking behind a cluster of carob trees. There he sat and waited, watching the road for Dirk and Summer.

Seconds after he sped out of the monastery parking lot, another car started up. The driver wheeled alongside the base of the stairway, then stopped and waited as the mangy beggar rose to his feet and climbed into the passenger seat. Removing his hat, the beggar revealed a long scar on his right jaw.

"Quickly," Zakkar snapped at the driver. "Don't let him get out of our sight."

90

Summer was standing across the courtyard when Dirk stepped out of the monastery.

"How's things in the boys' club?" she asked with a touch of bitterness.

"Not the frat party you might think it is."

"Any luck?"

Dirk described what he had learned of the church's history and the display from the True Cross.

"I met with the resident historian, but he had little to add in the way of Helena's visit to Cyprus. The place has been ransacked so many times, there's no archival data left. The bottom line is, nobody has any knowledge of relics beyond the True Cross."

"Did he know anything about Helena's fleet?"

Dirk shook his head. "As far as anybody knows, Helena arrived and left Cyprus without incident."

"Then Plautius and his galley must have been attacked before she arrived."

She grabbed his arm and pulled him toward one of the courtyard walls.

"Come look at this," she said.

She led him to a trio of large frescoes painted on a linear section of shaded wall. The frescoes looked faded to the point of invisibility, at a quick glance. Dirk stepped closer and studied the first panel. It was a customary

Madonna and Child, featuring a haloed infant Jesus held in Mary's arms. Both figures' wide eyes and flat dimensions indicated it was a style of art from long ago. The next panel showed a crucifixion scene, Jesus on the cross, his head hung low in agony. Somewhat unusually for the genre, Dirk noted, the two beggar thieves were illustrated hanging from neighboring crosses.

He then stepped to the third panel, where Summer stood with a pleased expression on her face. It depicted a crowned woman in profile pointing toward the upper corner of the fresco. Her finger was pointing at a towering green mountain capped by a pair of crosses. The geological features of Stavrovouni were clearly visible in the hilltop rendering.

"Helena?" Dirk said.

"It has to be," Summer replied. "Now, look at the bottom."

Dirk peered closely at the lower portion of the fresco, observing a section of faded blue that represented the sea. The image of three ships on the water was barely visible beneath Helena's profile. Crude in representation, each ship was the same approximate size, and was powered by both sail and oars. With the proper perspective, Dirk could see that two of the ships appeared to be pursuing the third vessel. Studying the faded plaster, he pointed to the two chase craft.

"This one appears to be sinking by the stern," he said, "while the other one is turning out to sea."

"Look at the sail on the lead ship," Summer said.

Straining his eyes, Dirk could just see a faint symbol on the ship's sail. It appeared to be an "X" with a high-legged "P" written over its center.

"It's the Chi-Rho monogram that was used by Constantine," she explained. "It was the divine symbol that supposedly came to him in a dream before his victory at the Battle of Milvian Bridge. He used it on his battle standard and as an emblem of his rule."

"Then the picture is either Helena arriving in Cyprus with an escort . . ." he said.

"Or it is Plautius's galley fleeing two Cypriot pirate ships," she said, completing his thought.

A chip in the fresco obscured the path of the galley, but the continuation of a shoreline along the bottom indicated that it was headed toward land. Slightly above the horizon was another small image, of a nude woman emerging from the sea, a pair of dolphins at her side.

"The meaning of that is lost on me," Summer said as Dirk examined the image.

Just then, the dour monk walked by, having escorted a pair of French tourists through the church. Dirk hailed him and inquired about the frescoes.

"Yes, they are very old," the monk said. "The archaeologists believe they date to the Byzantine Age. Some have claimed that these walls were part of the original church, but nobody knows for sure."

"This last fresco," Summer asked, "is it an image of Helena?"

"Yes," the monk confirmed. "She's arrived by sea and envisions the church here on Stavrovouni."

"Do you know what this figure is?" she asked, pointing to the nude woman.

"That would be Aphrodite. You see, the monastery

549

here was built on the ruins of a temple to Aphrodite. The artist must have been paying homage to the site before Helena commissioned the church to be built here."

She thanked the monk, then watched him shuffle back to the monastery door.

"Well, we were close," she said. "Now we know there were two pirate ships, anyway."

"The image makes it appear that the Roman vessel was still afloat after battling the pirates. It was heading somewhere," Dirk muttered, staring at the image until his eyes turned blurry. He finally stepped away from the panel and joined Summer in heading toward the exit.

"I guess we got all we can from here," he said. "By the way, did you talk to Ridley Bannister?"

"Ridley who?" she asked as they descended the stairway to the parking lot.

"Ridley Bannister, the British archaeologist. He said he knew you."

Receiving a blank look, Dirk proceeded to describe his encounter in the monastery.

"I never saw him," she said. Then the wheels of suspicion began to turn in her head. "What does he look like?"

"Thin, medium build, sandy hair. I suppose women might find him handsome."

Summer suddenly froze on the steps. "Did you notice if he was wearing a ring?"

Dirk thought a moment. "Yes, I think so. On his right ring finger. I noticed it when we shook hands. It was solid gold with a funny design, like something out of the Middle Ages."

Summer's face turned flush with anger. "That's the guy

who stole the Manifest from Julie and me at gunpoint. He said his name was Baker."

"He's a well-known and respected archaeologist," Dirk said.

"Respected?" Summer hissed. "I bet he's here searching for the galley, too."

"One of the monks did mention he was working on a book about Helena."

Summer was fuming by the time they reached the car. The image of Bannister taking the Manifest in the basement of Kitchener's manor saturated her mind. She drove aggressively down the winding monastery road, her anger reflected in her driving. Entering the main highway, she never considered that the source of her wrath was in a car now following close behind.

Her temper waned as they reached the outskirts of Limassol. By the time they found the city's commercial docks, she actually felt encouraged.

"If Bannister is here, then the galley must exist," she said to Dirk.

"He certainly hasn't found it yet," he replied.

Summer nodded with satisfaction. Who knows, she thought, perhaps we're closer than we think.

91

"Shoving off already?" Summer asked.

She stood on the *Aegean Explorer*'s bridge, watching a pair of crewmen hoist in and stow the forward mooring line. It had been less than an hour since the ship had touched the dock at Limassol, and she and Dirk had climbed aboard.

Pitt stood near the helm, sipping a cup of coffee.

"We've got to get back around to the western side of the Akrotiri Peninsula in order to keep tabs on Rudi's AUV," he said.

"I thought you were surveying with the towed sonar fish?"

"We are. We actually completed our first grid off Pissouri and started a new survey grid to the west. But Rudi reconfigured the AUV for sidescan sonar duty, so we put her to work. She's currently running a large grid to the east of Pissouri. We'll keep pushing west with the *Explorer* and cover twice as much ground."

"Makes sense," she replied. "How much longer will the AUV stay under?"

"She'll be down another eighteen hours before surfacing. That will allow us a good run of our own before having to pick her up."

"Dad, I'm sorry we didn't come up with more promising research to go on."

"Your fresco seems to confirm the role of the Pissouri wreck as one of the pirate ships. If the galley exists, we've got a good chance of being in the ballpark."

The *Aegean Explorer* proceeded to steam south around the stubby Akrotiri Peninsula, then turned northwest toward Pissouri some twenty miles away. The research ship's sensors soon made contact with a pair of floating transducer buoys, which relayed data from the AUV as it glided over the seabed two hundred feet beneath the surface. While Gunn and Giordino reviewed the AUV's results, Pitt launched the towed sonar fish off the stern of the *Explorer*, sharing monitoring duties with Dirk and Summer.

It was nine the next morning when Summer stepped onto the bridge with a cup of hot coffee, ready to relieve her father in front of the screen.

"Anything new at the picture show?" she asked.

"A repeat is playing, I'm afraid," Pitt replied, standing and stretching. "The same rock and sand that's been rolling by all night. Outside of a small sunken fishing boat that Dirk picked up, it's been slim pickings."

"I just checked with Al in the survey shack," she said, slipping into Pitt's seat. "He said they've got similar results with the AUV."

"We're nearly at the end of this grid," Pitt said. "Shall we keep working west?"

Summer smiled at her father. "When it comes to finding a shipwreck, I know better than to question your instincts."

"Then west it is," he replied with a wink.

Captain Kenfield stepped over from the helm and spread out a local marine chart across the table.

"Where exactly would you like to configure the next grid?" he asked Pitt.

"We'll just extend the current grid, running as close to shore as we can get. Let's run another two miles west, to this point here," he said, pointing to a small coastal promontory on the map.

"Fair enough," Kenfield said. "I'll run the coordinates to Petra tou Romiou, as it says on the chart, or the Rock of Aphrodite."

Summer stiffened in her chair. "Did you say the Rock of Aphrodite?" she asked.

Kenfield nodded, then retrieved a dog-eared traveler's guide to Cyprus shelved behind the chart table.

"I was just reading about it last night. Petra tou Romiou, or Rock of Romios, takes its name from a Byzantine folk hero who allegedly tossed huge boulders into the sea to ward off pirates. The large rock formations are still visible in the surf. However, the site is also known from ancient times as the place where Aphrodite, the patron goddess of Cyprus, emerged from the sea in a wave of foam."

"Dad, that's it," Summer said, jumping from her seat. "The Aphrodite image was in the fresco. It didn't represent the temple at Stavrovouni, where the monastery stands. It's where the Roman galley was headed. Someone on shore, or perhaps the pirates themselves, saw the galley fleeing toward the rocks."

"It's roughly within sight of the Pissouri wreck site," Kenfield noted.

"I'll buy it," Pitt said, smiling at his daughter's enthusiasm. "The Rock of Aphrodite it is. Let's go see if the goddess will show us some love."

A short time later, they reached the end of the survey lane and pulled in the towfish. As the ship changed course to resume its search down the coast, a palpable optimism surged through the bridge. Caught up in the anticipation, no one noticed the small boat trailing a half mile behind, where Ridley Bannister followed the turquoise ship with a pair of binoculars glued to his eyes.

92

Six hours later, the goddess Aphrodite was showing the NUMA surveyors anything but love. The seabed around the Petra tou Romiou proved void of any man-made objects. Dirk had taken over the next survey shift, staring at an endless scroll of rocks and sand on the monitor, while Summer and Pitt loitered about, hoping for a strike. Giordino stepped onto the bridge, surprised to see that Summer's enthusiasm had waned to frustration.

"The AUV's due up in about forty-five minutes," he said to Pitt.

"We're only a few minutes away from finishing this lane," Dirk noted.

"All right, break off when we cross the end point, then we'll go pick up the big fish," Pitt said.

"Anything at all?" Giordino asked.

"If you have a fetish for rock gardens, you'd enjoy the seafloor here," Dirk said.

Giordino eased over to the helm and gazed out the forward window. Seeing they were near the shoreline, he picked up a pair of binoculars and scanned a pebble-strewn beach that ran west of the large rock formation.

"Any Greek goddesses lying about?" Summer asked with a hint of disdain.

"No, the gods have deserted the beach on this sunny afternoon. Even the shady sea caves are empty of spirits."

Pitt approached him with an inquiring look on his face. "Mind if I take a peek?"

As Pitt scanned the shoreline, Dirk announced that they had reached the end of the survey lane.

"Al, can you help secure the towfish?" he asked, turning off the sonar system.

"At your service," Giordino replied, and the two men headed for the stern.

Pitt kept his eyes glued to the shore, then turned to Kenfield.

"Captain, would you mind taking us in a little closer to shore, on a bearing of twenty degrees," he said.

"What's up, Dad?" Summer asked.

"Just exploring the possibility that King Al might have struck gold once more."

As the *Aegean Explorer* eased into shallow water, Pitt got a better look at the shoreline. From a low, pebbly beach around Petra tou Romiou, the terrain climbed dramatically to the east, rising in high chalky cliffs several hundred feet high. The Mediterranean's steady waves rolled into the base of the cliffs with a rumble, splashing foam high against the rocks at water's edge. Across the lower cliff face, scattered indentations were worn into the limestone where the sea had scoured away a hole, or sea cave, as Giordino had called them. It was the caves that had caught Pitt's attention, and he studied each one carefully. He finally focused on one in particular, a small black opening low above the water with tumbled rocks around its perimeter.

"Towfish is aboard," Dirk announced, stepping back onto the bridge with Giordino.

Pitt put down the binoculars. "Captain, what's the tidal stage right now?" he asked.

"We're just past high tide," Kenfield replied. "Tidal range is fairly minimal here, a couple of feet or so."

Pitt nodded with a slight smile, then turned to Gunn.

"Rudi, you've done some ocean modeling. How much of a change in sea level would you say the Mediterranean has witnessed in the last seventeen hundred years?"

Gunn scratched his head. "The sea level today is probably two to three meters higher than it was two thousand years ago. I can give you an accurate estimate if I check the NUMA database."

"That's not necessary," Pitt replied. He gazed at the sea cave once more. "I think she'd just about fit," he muttered.

"We really need to go retrieve the AUV now," Gunn pleaded.

"Okay, but before you go, you'll need to drop Summer and me in the Zodiac. Dirk, too, if you want to come."

"No thanks, Dad," Dirk replied. "I've had my share of goose chasing with Summer. I'll help with the AUV."

"But where are we going?" Summer asked.

"Why, to that cliff," Pitt said, pointing to the shore with a smile. "Where else are we going to find ourselves a Roman galley?"

93

As the *Aegean Explorer* slipped eastward to chase down the AUV, Pitt gunned the outboard on the new Zodiac and raced toward the shoreline. Summer sat on the bow, her long red hair blowing in the wind and a hopeful expression on her face, as they approached the sea cave. The low opening at water's edge reflected little light, telling Pitt that the cave did indeed penetrate well into the cliff.

Drawing near, Pitt could see that the entrance was wide enough for the Zodiac to slip through. Though the tide was now lower, the wave action made clearing the opening a treacherous proposition. Spotting an exposed grouping of flat rocks to the right, he nudged the Zodiac alongside and waited for a wave to carry it. Summer quickly jumped out and wrapped a line around a boulder to secure the craft.

"Looks like we're going to have to get wet," Pitt said, grabbing a flashlight and hopping out of the Zodiac.

Summer followed him as he crept along the rocks until being forced to wade into the water near the cave's entrance. A submerged layer of stones formed a crude ledge, which Pitt followed into the opening as a small wave rolled up to his neck. Flicking on the flashlight he held over his head, he could see the cave ran like a tunnel for at least twenty feet before expanding into the gloom beyond.

He stopped and waited as Summer navigated her way across the slippery rocks, grabbing his hand before almost falling under.

"Might be easier to swim," she gasped.

"I see a dry ledge just up ahead," Pitt replied, playing the light around.

Hugging the side wall, they worked their way forward, finding that the submerged ledge gradually rose until they stepped completely out of the water. Above their heads, the ceiling grew to enormous heights as the tunnel expanded into a large cavern. The water flowed through a curved channel in the shape of a large "U," indicating that it looped back toward the sea. Pitt could see that the water didn't appear stagnant but flowed with a mild current.

They followed the ledge a few yards farther as it led toward a large sandy rise. Pitt was surprised to see a soft, faint light bathing the interior cavern. Looking up, he could see where a few slim rays of sunlight slipped through a fissure in the cliff face.

Suddenly, Pitt felt Summer's hand clench his arm.

"Dad!" she cried.

He saw she was staring wide-eyed ahead. Turning to look, he expected to see a flying bat or perhaps a snake on the ground. Instead, he saw the hull of an aged ship.

The vessel sat upright on a sandy ledge, appearing little damaged under the dim light. Stepping closer, Pitt could see that it was built of an ancient design. An angled prow rose in a high arch that curled back over the open deck. Dozens of small round holes dotted the sides above the waterline, which Pitt recognized as perforations for oars.

There were no actual oars in sight, only a number of broken stubs that dangled from a few of the openings.

Approaching the dust-covered ship, they saw that its single mast had been shattered near the base, the thick pole now lying across the aft deck. Playing the flashlight beam across the high stern, Pitt could see the skeletal remains of a man draped over the wooden tiller.

"It's a galley," Pitt said with a grin. "An old one, by the looks of it. She probably snapped off her mast when she sailed through the cave entrance."

Summer remained in silent awe. Stepping to the bow, she finally found the words to call her father.

"Dad, look at this."

The galley's prow was a crumpled mass of timber at the waterline. Looking closer, they could see several bent copper spikes protruding in a horizontal band on either side.

"The only real damage to the hull," Summer noted. "They must have driven into the cliff face a few times before slipping into this grotto."

"It appears that she may have had a ram fitted here at one time," Pitt mused.

Using the spikes as a stepladder, he climbed up the bow, then pulled himself over the side. The sight on board nearly took his breath away. The entire deck was littered with skeletal remains clad in faded tunics or robes, a few with swords still clutched in their bony hands. A number of battle shields and spears were also scattered about, painting a grim picture of a bloody fight to the death.

"Any sign that it is Roman?" Summer asked from below.

"Of course it is."

Summer froze at the comment. It wasn't the cold tone in which the words were said but rather that they didn't come from Pitt.

She turned to see the figure of Ridley Bannister approach out of the darkness, his clothes wet from the chest down. In his hands, he carried a small video camera, which he turned on, bathing the cavern in a hazy blue light.

"Well, if it isn't the esteemed archaeologist Ridley 'Baker' Bannister," Summer sneered as he stepped closer. "Did you bring your gun this time?"

"Oh, no. That was Field Marshal Kitchener's revolver, actually. Quite empty of bullets it was, I'm chagrined to say." He held the video camera up for her to see. "It's nice to see you again, Miss Pitt. Now, if you'd be so kind as to step out of the way, I will proceed to document my discovery."

"Your discovery?" she said, her blood beginning to boil. "Why, you lying pig, you didn't find anything."

"It's as good as mine now. I suppose I should tell you that I'm on excellent terms with the Cyprus Director of Antiquities. I've already made arrangements for the exclusive film and book rights in the event of discovery, which you have kindly aided. I'll be sure to make a note of your generous contributions."

Bannister placed the camera to his eye and started filming the exterior of the galley.

"Is the Manifest cargo aboard, by the way?" he asked, scanning along the side of the vessel.

Focusing the camera lens on the damaged prow, he

didn't notice Summer rush at him until it was too late. Reaching out a long arm, Summer ripped the camera from his hands and tossed it into the rocks. A shattering sound ensued as the lens smashed, though the camera's bluish external light remained glowing.

Bannister stared at the damaged camera, then slowly became enraged. Grabbing the taller woman by her shirt lapels, he began shaking her in anger. A student of judo, Summer prepared to counter his grab with a takedown when a loud staccato burst through the cave. The gunfire was still echoing when Summer felt Bannister's fingertips slip free of her shirt. The archaeologist gave her a pained look, then slowly sagged to the ground. As he fell prone, Summer saw that his khaki pants had sprouted stains of blood in several spots.

Looking past him, Summer saw three men standing on the rise. Even in the low light, she could see that they appeared to be Arabs. The tallest of the three stood at the center, smoke rising from a compact Uzi machine pistol cradled in his arms. He slowly took a step forward, keeping the weapon aimed at Summer as his eyes scanned the galley.

"So," Zakkar said in halting English. "You have found the treasure."

94

Summer stood immobile as the three men moved closer. At her feet, Bannister clutched at his wounds, an uncomprehending look of shock etched in his face. Zakkar lowered his Uzi as he drew near, his attention focused on the galley.

"Gutzman will be pleased," he said in Arabic to his nearest associate, the bearded gunman from the Dome of the Rock attack named Salaam.

"What of these two?" Salaam asked, aiming a small penlight at Summer and Bannister.

"Kill them and throw their bodies into the ocean," Zakkar replied, rubbing a hand over the ancient ship's hull.

Having understood the conversation, Bannister tried pulling himself across the ground, grunting in pain as he clawed his way behind Summer. Salaam ignored him as he stepped close to Summer, then raised a pistol at her head.

"Run!"

Pitt's shout rang loudly from the deck of the galley, catching all of the Arabs by surprise. Summer watched the gunman in front of her glance toward the ship, his eyes instantly flaring in horror.

Whistling through the air at him was a *pilum*, the iron-tipped Roman javelin. Salaam had no chance to move before the razor-sharp spear struck him in the chest. The finely crafted weapon cut a path completely through the man's torso, its tip exiting his back below the kidney. The stunned man spit out a mouthful of blood, then dropped to the ground stone dead.

In the moment that Salaam was struck, Summer was already calculating her options. She instantly decided she could either lunge for the gunman's pistol, or run and dive into the water, or break for her father on the ship. The adrenaline was already surging through her veins, screaming for her brain to respond. But Summer let logic run its course before making a move. She quickly judged that the handgun would be no match for Zakkar's Uzi. And though her heart told her to run to her father, reason dictated that the water was much closer.

Suppressing her emotional urges, she took a powerful step to her right and then leaped. The sound of gunfire was already ripping through the air when her outstretched hands broke the water's surface and the rest of her body tumbled in after. The slope of the sandbar dropped away sharply, and she plunged into the depths without breaking her neck.

She instinctively swam down, following the slight current, which carried her away from the cave's entrance. She was a strong swimmer to begin with, and her pumping adrenaline drove her deeper, until her hand brushed the channel floor at a depth of fifteen feet. The water was pitch-black, so she tried to use the current to guide her forward, occasionally grazing against the walls of rock.

She swam hard for a dozen strokes, driving smoothly through the water. When her air began to expire, she eased toward the surface, confident that she had put sufficient distance between herself and the gunmen to catch a quick breath. With her lungs beginning to ache, she raised a fist over her head in the scuba diver's safe ascent pose and kicked toward the surface. She rose a dozen feet, and her upraised hand suddenly brushed against rock. An uneasy feeling crept over her as she groped along the hard surface. Slowly, she nosed her face up alongside her hand until her cheek was flush against the overhead rock, the water's current rippling against her face.

Her pounding heart skipped a beat as she realized the water channel had turned into a submerged tunnel, and there was no air to be had.

95

Zakkar's Uzi had opened fire the instant Summer dove into the grotto pool. His aim had been toward the galley, however, as he stitched a lead seam along the side rail a second after Pitt had ducked beneath it. Pitt quickly raced a few feet down the deck, scooping up a round wooden shield lying near his feet. Popping it up briefly, he flung the shield at Zakkar like a Frisbee, hoping to keep his attention away from Summer. Sidestepping the disk, Zakkar opened fire again, nearly catching Pitt at the rail with a short burst.

In his quick glance over the rail, Pitt had seen Summer dive for the channel and heard her splash in. The water remained quiet, and the gunmen weren't wasting shots into the channel, giving him confidence that his daughter had swum out of harm's way.

Bannister was proving equally adept at dodging bullets. In the confusion caused by Pitt's spear attack, he had dragged himself behind some low rocks, concealing himself, as he drifted in and out of consciousness from his wounds. The Arabs paid him little heed anyway. They were more concerned with avenging the death of their partner.

"Get aboard by the stern," Zakkar shouted at his accomplice, after checking on the impaled gunman. "I shall pursue from the front."

The Arab retrieved the dead man's penlight, then made his way to the galley's bow, keeping a cautious eye out for Pitt on the deck above.

Pitt had seen only the three armed men enter the cavern together and hoped there were no others. He had no idea who they were, but their readiness to kill was more than apparent. He knew it meant he would have to beat them to the punch.

Under the dim light, he surveyed the galley's main deck, spotting companionways at either end that descended to the rowing deck. Making his way to the aft companionway, he picked up a sword and another shield from the battle remnants lying about the deck. The shield felt unusually heavy, and he flipped it over to find three stubby arrows fastened to the back. They were throwing arrows, issued to Roman soldiers late in the empire. Each arrow was about a foot in length, with a heavy lead weight at its center and a bronze barbed tip at the end. Pitt tucked the shield under his arm, then climbed over the fallen mast that crossed the rear deck.

He could hear the sound of the two gunmen trying to board the ends of the ship as he moved aft toward the raised stern section. Stepping toward the centerline, he tripped over the skeletal remains of a Roman legionary and nearly fell through the open companionway to the lower deck. He cursed himself at the racket he made, but the accident gave him an idea.

Taking the sword, he jammed the tip into the deck plank so that it stood upright. He then hoisted the torso of the skeleton and wedged it atop the sword's hilt. He quickly wrapped it in a crumbling cloak that was lying beneath the bones, then spotted a broken lance nearby. He eased the spear through the skeleton's ribs, then concealed its base in the cloak while its business end protruded in a menacing manner. In the low light, the ancient warrior appeared almost alive.

Above him, Pitt heard a thud as the gunman climbing up the transom jumped onto the raised steering deck. Pitt quietly retreated to the fallen mast, climbing over the thick spar and hiding in its shadows. He silently unfastened the three throwing arrows from the shield, then fished through his pocket for a coin. Retrieving a quarter, he clenched it in his hand and waited.

The gunman moved cautiously, patiently scanning the main deck for movement before climbing down from the steering deck. He descended one of two ladders that were mounted on either side of the rowing-deck companionway. To Pitt's good fortune, the gunman climbed down the ladder closest to him.

Pitt held to the shadows until he heard the man's shoes hit the main deck. He then raised his hand and flicked his wrist, tossing the quarter high into the air. The coin landed right where Pitt aimed, near the base of the skeleton, tinkling loudly across the silent deck.

The startled gunman instantly turned toward the noise, spotting the cloaked figure holding a spear. He immediately pumped two shots from his automatic pistol into the skeleton, watching in amazement as it disintegrated into a small heap. His surprise was short-lived, for Pitt was already on his feet, flinging the first arrow from twenty feet away.

Finding the ancient weapon surprisingly well balanced,

Pitt was dead-on with his first throw, striking the man near the hip. The gunman grunted in pain from the penetration of the sharp projectile, wheeling around as the second arrow whizzed past his chest. Fumbling to remove the first arrow, he looked toward Pitt, only to see a third arrow flying in his direction. Too overwhelmed to shoot, he instinctively stepped to the side to avoid the incoming barb. Only there was no deck beneath his feet.

Falling where Pitt hadn't, he plunged down the open companionway with a gasp. The sickening crack of breaking bones echoed from the rowing deck a second later, followed by a morbid silence.

"Ali?" cried Zakkar from the bow.

But there would be no answer to his query.

96

For the second time in as many minutes, Summer faced a life-or-death choice. Should she turn back or keep going? She had no idea how far back the ceiling had become submerged. It could be five feet or fifty yards. But swimming against the current, light as it was, could make fifty yards seem like a mile. Following her instincts this time, she made a snap decision. She would keep going forward.

Kicking and stroking, she propelled herself through the tunnel, her arms and head occasionally bumping into the surrounding stone. Every other stroke, she would raise an arm above her, hoping to break the surface into a pocket of air. But every time her hand would drag against immersed stone. She felt her heart pounding harder, and fought a sudden reflex to exhale, as a creeping sense of panic began to set in. How long had she been underwater? she asked herself. A minute? Two minutes? It seemed like an eternity. But whatever the answer, she knew the more important question was how many more seconds could she hold out?

She tried kicking even harder, but it began to feel like she was swimming in slow motion as her brain labored for oxygen. Her arms and legs felt an odd burning sensation as the effects of hypoxia sapped her muscles. The black water seemed to turn even darker before her eyes, and she no longer felt the salt water stinging them. An internal voice yelled at her to remain strong, but she could feel herself slipping.

And then she saw it. A faint green glow appeared in the water ahead of her. Perhaps it was just a trick of the eyes or the first stages of blacking out, but she didn't care. Exhaling what little air was left in her chest, she summoned every last remaining reserve of energy and kicked hard toward the light.

Her limbs now burned with fire as her ears rung in a deafening tone. Her heart felt like it was going to beat out of her chest while her lungs ached to explode. But she ignored the pain, the doubts, and the urge to let go, and kept pulling herself through the water.

The green glow gradually expanded into a warm light, bright enough to show particles and sediment in the seawater. Just overhead, a silvery gleam caught her eye, appearing like a bowlful of mercury. With her energy failing fast, she kicked upward with a final, desperate surge of strength.

Summer emerged from the water like a show dolphin at Sea World, rising high into the air before tumbling back with a splash. Gasping and panting for air, she paddled to a nearby rock and clung to its barnacled surface while her oxygen-depleted body tried to restore order. She rested for nearly five minutes before regaining the strength to move. Then, in the distance, she heard muffled gunfire, and she remembered her father.

Taking her bearings, she found she was in a semisubmerged rock outcropping a hundred yards west of the cave. She quickly spotted the NUMA Zodiac, tied to the rocks beside two other small boats. Plunging back into the water, she circled around the rocks and began swimming toward the boats.

Her arms soon felt like lead weights, and several times the surf nearly flung her onto the shoreline rocks, but she managed to reach the boats without collapsing. The Zodiac didn't carry a radio, so she dragged herself onto the deck of the first of the two other boats, a small wooden trawler that Zakkar had appropriated. Inside its tiny, open wheelhouse, she found a marine band radio and immediately hailed the *Aegean Explorer*.

Dirk, Giordino, and Gunn were all on the bridge when Summer's frantic voice burst over the radio.

"Summer, this is *Explorer*. Go ahead," Gunn replied calmly.

"Rudi, we found the galley inside the cave. But three armed men showed up. I escaped, but Dad's still in there, and they're trying to kill him."

"Take it easy, Summer. We're on our way. Try to hide until we get there, and keep yourself out of danger."

Kenfield had already turned the *Explorer* around and was accelerating to top speed by the time Gunn hung up the transmitter. Dirk stepped forward and looked out the bridge window.

"We're six or seven miles away," he lamented to Gunn. "We'll never get there in time."

"He's right," Giordino said. "Stop the boat."

"What do you mean, stop the boat?" Gunn cried.

"Give us two minutes to launch the *Bullet*, and we'll get there in a flash."

Gunn considered the request a moment. Even to Gunn, Pitt was more than a boss, he was like a brother. If the tables were reversed, he knew exactly what Pitt would do.

"All right," he said with reservation. "Just don't get yourselves killed."

Dirk and Giordino immediately bolted for the door.

"Al, I'll meet you on deck," Dirk told him. "I need to grab something on the way."

"Just don't miss the bus," Giordino replied, then disappeared aft.

Dirk hustled down to the ship's lower deck, which housed the crew accommodations. Sprinting to his father's cabin, he burst in, stepping up to a small, built-in work desk. Above the desk was a shelf of books, and Dirk quickly scanned their titles. His eyes halted when he spotted a heavy, leather-bound edition of Herman Melville's *Moby-Dick*. Ripping the book off the shelf, he quickly flipped the cover open for a second.

"'To the great white beast, Ishmael,'" he muttered, then tucked the book under his arm and darted out of the cabin.

97

Pitt had nearly forgotten about Zakkar, who had finally clambered over the bow and now shouted for his partner. Met with silence, the Arab flicked on Salaam's penlight and aimed it at the aft end of the deck. The light's beam played upon the figure of Pitt, who stood with a shield in his hand and an upturned grin on his face.

But Pitt was already diving over the other side of the mast when Zakkar's Uzi barked, sending a burst over his head and into the raised steering deck. Pitt didn't wait for his accuracy to improve, quickly snaking across the deck and launching himself down the companionway as Zakkar chased after him.

The body of Ali lay barely visible in the small patch of light that reached the lower deck from above. Pitt could see that the Arab's head was tilted at an unnatural angle, his neck having snapped in the fall. Pitt quickly knelt alongside the body, searching the surrounding deck for the gun, but it wasn't there. Let loose during Ali's fall, it had bounced into one of the recessed rowing stations nearby. Pitt had left his flashlight on the upper deck while throwing the *pilum* and had no chance of locating the gun in the pitch-blackness.

As Zakkar charged aft overhead, Pitt moved forward, groping along a center walkway that divided the rowing stations on either side of the ship. He had left all his

Roman weapons above deck and now found himself defenseless in the unlit bay. His only hope was to get up the forward companionway as Zakkar descended in the stern.

But Zakkar knew he had his man on the run and didn't hesitate dropping down the aft ladder. Pitt could hear him descending and shuffled faster, spotting a faint ray of light ahead, which he knew was the open companionway.

His feet dropping to the lower deck, Zakkar spent only a second examining the dead figure of Ali before playing the small flashlight beam across the deck. He detected a movement at the far end, then locked the light on Pitt struggling to reach the forward ladder. He immediately aimed and fired a burst ahead of him.

Pitt dove for the deck as the bullets chewed into the wood around him. Several small crates were stacked near the base of the companionway, and he quickly crawled forward, ducking behind them for cover. Zakkar stepped closer and fired again, splintering one of the crates just inches from Pitt's head.

Unarmed, Pitt was in a hopeless situation. His only real chance was to somehow scale the ladder before Zakkar moved any closer. He again searched for a weapon, but only spotted another skeleton lying nearby. The long-expired body had belonged to another Roman legionary, as the bones were clad in an armored tunic and helmet. The dead soldier must have fallen through the companionway when he was killed in battle, Pitt surmised. Studying the armor for a moment, he suddenly reached over and plucked it off the dried bones.

By the fourth century, the Roman soldier had turned to

iron for much of his protective gear. Brutally heavy, it could withstand the sharpest spears and strongest swords. And perhaps, Pitt considered, it just might resist the slugs from a 9mm Uzi submachine pistol. Pitt slipped on the heavy circular helmet, which had an enlarged back piece that swooped outward to protect the neck. He then studied the armored breastplate. Known as a *cuirass*, it was an iron sheet molded in the shape of a man's chest, with matching back plate. Pitt could see it was obviously made for a man shorter than himself.

Wasting no time in trying to fit in the *cuirass*, he simply flung the twin plates onto his back, tying them around his throat with a leather strap. Crawling to the base of the companionway, he looked up at the deck overhead, took a deep breath, then sprang up the ladder as fast as his arms and legs could propel him.

Zakkar was still fifty feet away, running down the aisle with his penlight aimed at the ladder, when he saw Pitt spring up it. The experienced killer immediately stopped and raised his weapon. Holding the light beneath the barrel with his left hand, he took careful aim at Pitt and pulled the trigger.

The wood around Pitt exploded in a shower of splinters as the bullets sprayed into the ladder's supporting bulkhead. He felt three hard thumps on his back that knocked him forward like the blows of a sledgehammer, but he was able to keep moving. With his arms and legs pumping, he jumped onto the open deck as a second fusillade shredded the top of the ladder where his feet had just been.

Pitt made his way to the side rail, surprised to have

escaped the companionway unscathed. Still clad in his Roman armor, he prepared to jump over the side when he noticed another *pilum* on the deck, identical to the one he had flung at the first gunman. Deciding to take the offensive, he grabbed the spear and inched back toward the open companionway.

Zakkar had already approached the foot of the ladder and wisely flicked off the penlight. The galley was suddenly deathly silent as both men froze in their tracks. Zakkar then began slowly climbing the shredded ladder, moving quietly inch by inch. Unable to hold both the light and the gun as he climbed, he stuffed the light in his teeth, then held the Uzi up high.

Only his head had cleared the deck when he spotted Pitt moving a few feet away. The *pilum* left Pitt's hand quickly, rotating in a spiral as it shot toward the Arab. But the target was too small, and Zakkar easily ducked his head, leaving the *pilum* to harmlessly strike the ladder frame. Zakkar stuck the Uzi out and fired at Pitt without looking before rising up the ladder as his clip ran dry.

Pitt was already at the rail and threw himself over the side as the bullets flew by wildly. But the volley had thrown off his balance, and he landed awkwardly on the sand some fifteen feet below. A burst of pain flared through his right ankle as he rose and took a step, immediately hopping onto his other foot. With a twisted ankle, the water channel suddenly appeared miles away. But much closer was the body of Salaam. It lay just a few feet away, and Pitt knew he had been armed with a pistol.

Quickly hobbling over, Pitt bent over the dead man and searched around his hands.

"Looking for this?" came a sudden taunt from the galley.

Hesitantly peering over his shoulder, Pitt saw Zakkar looking at him with the dead gunman's pistol aimed squarely at his head.

98

Pitt didn't know why the Arab didn't immediately shoot him. Zakkar stood motionless for several seconds before Pitt noticed that he was looking past him. Pitt cautiously followed his gaze toward the channel, where an unusual disturbance appeared in the water.

A dull glow was visible beneath the surface, gradually growing brighter as a mass of bubbles agitated the waters above it. A glaring bank of xenon lights was the first thing to emerge from the depths, followed by an acrylic cockpit and then a long white hull. Pitt gave a grim smile toward the *Bullet* as it broke to the surface, then bobbed in the grotto channel.

Seated at the controls, Dirk and Giordino looked out of the cockpit in awe at the sight of the large cavern and the Roman galley parked at its center. Then they saw Pitt standing under the barrel of Zakkar's gun, both men bathed in the submersible's glaring lights. Looking up at the Arab, Dirk nearly choked in recognition.

"That's the terrorist from Jerusalem," he stammered to Giordino. "Keep the lights on him."

Before Giordino could respond, Dirk had bolted from his seat and opened the rear hatch. In an instant, he climbed to the side ballast tank, still clutching Herman Melville's book in his hand. The submersible was nearly ten feet from the bank as Giordino pivoted it to face the galley, but Dirk didn't wait for him to move closer. Taking a running leap, he jumped into the channel and swam to shore, holding the book over his head.

On the galley's deck, Zakkar surveyed the scene with agitation. He turned his pistol toward Pitt and fired a quick shot, watching him fall prone to the sand. Then he focused his attention on the submersible. Though he heard the splash of Dirk jumping into the water, he couldn't see him emerge on shore due to the *Bullet*'s blinding lights. Taking careful aim, he shot out one of them, then peppered the acrylic bubble with several shots before eliminating a second light. Then he noticed a tall figure emerge on shore with his arms stretched out in front of him.

Zakkar fired first, missing with a bullet that whizzed instead within a hair of Dirk's left ear. Dirk kept moving, marching directly toward the Arab without flinching. A surge of emotions ran through his body, from loving thoughts of Sophie to torrid flashes of anger and vengeance. But noticeably absent was any sense of fear.

Locking Zakkar in the sights of the Colt .45 he held in his outstretched hands, he calmly squeezed the trigger. Neither the roar nor the kick from the .45 slowed his pace, and he marched closer, squeezing the trigger with each step like some robotic soldier.

Dirk's first shot splintered the rail in front of Zakkar, and Zakkar flinched with his return volley, missing high. He didn't get another chance to fire. The next slug from Dirk's .45 tore into Zakkar's shoulder, nearly taking his arm off. He spun, then fell back against the rail, where he was hit again in the side.

Slumped over the rail as the life drained out of him, Zakkar wasn't allowed a slow death. Dirk marched closer, pumping five more shots into him, until leaving an ugly mass of red carnage streaming down the galley's hull. He stood staring at the dead terrorist as the cavern fell silent for a moment, then he turned at the sound of splashing water behind him.

Summer had helped guide the *Bullet* through the sea cave's entrance and came staggering up the submerged ledge. Reaching dry land, she ran up to Dirk, panting, "Where's Dad?"

Dirk nodded grimly toward the prone figure in the Roman helmet and armor lying near the first dead gunman. Giordino had since run the submersible to shore and hopped out, joining Dirk and Summer in rushing over to Pitt.

The head of NUMA stirred slowly, then looked up and gave his kids a weary smile.

"Dad, are you okay?" Summer asked.

"I'm fine," he assured. "Just got knocked a bit woozy. Help me to my feet."

As Dirk and Summer helped him up, Giordino surveyed the armor and grinned.

"Hail, Caesar," he said, thumping his chest with a closed fist.

"I should thank Caesar," Pitt replied, pulling off the helmet. He held it up, showing a crease near the temple where Zakkar had grazed it with a bullet.

"That'll ring your bell," Giordino said.

Pitt swung the *cuirass* off his back and examined it. Three neat, round bullet holes had pierced the breastplate, but they had just left indentations in the back plate. Only by doubling over the armor had Pitt's life been spared.

"There's something to be said for Roman engineering," he said.

Dropping the armor to the ground, he looked over at Dirk and the .45 still gripped in his hand.

"That Colt looks familiar."

Dirk reluctantly passed the weapon to his father. "You told me once how Loren had sent you a gun in Mongolia hidden in a cutout copy of *Moby-Dick*. I checked your cabin on a hunch and saw it on the shelf. Hope you don't mind."

Pitt shook his head, then gazed at the bloody muck that was left of Zakkar.

"You did quite a number on him," he said.

"That lowlife led the attacks at Caesarea and Jerusalem," Dirk replied coldly, leaving unsaid the fact that Zakkar was indirectly responsible for Sophie's death.

"It's pretty odd that he ended up here," Summer said.

"I suspect your British friend might know something about that," Pitt said, pointing toward Bannister.

The archaeologist had pulled himself upright against the rocks and stared at them with a dazed look.

"I'll go check on him," Giordino offered. "Why don't you guys find out what's aboard."

"Did you find the Manifest cargo?" Summer asked hopefully.

"I was a bit too preoccupied to find out," Pitt replied. "Come, somebody help a feeble old man aboard."

With Dirk and Summer's aid, Pitt hobbled up onto the galley, then climbed down the companionway to the dark galley deck. He limped over to the stack of crates that he had earlier used for cover.

"I suggest we start here," he said. Grabbing one of the smaller crates, he blew a layer of dust off of its side, then shined a flashlight at it. A faded red Chi-Rho symbol was visible on the wood.

"Summer, that's your Cross of Constantine," Dirk noted.

Summer grabbed the flashlight from her father's hand and studied the image, nodding quietly in excitement.

The crate showed damage along its side, where a burst from Zakkar's Uzi had riddled the edge. Pitt took the butt of his .45 and rapped it carefully against the damaged seam to open the crate. The narrow end piece easily popped off, causing the damaged front cover to fall away. A pair of well-worn leather sandals tumbled out of the open box, falling to the deck. Summer tracked the sandals with the flashlight's beam, noting a small slip of parchment strapped to one of the shoes. Shining the light closer, she illuminated a handwritten label penned in Latin:

Sandalii Christi

The translation was not lost on anyone. They were staring at the shoes of Jesus.

Epilogue
The Saviors

Hagia Sophia

99

The crowds had gathered outside the doors of Hagia Sophia in an immense line that stretched for more than six blocks. Pious Christians rubbed elbows with devout Muslims as pilgrims of both religions waited anxiously for the doors to open to the exhibit displayed inside. The venerated landmark building had been witness to count-less historical dramas in the fourteen hundred years it had dominated the skyline of Istanbul. Yet few events in its past had generated the kind of excitement that pulsed through the crowd clamoring for a chance to make their way inside.

Those in the crowd paid scant attention to the old green Delahaye convertible parked in front of the entrance. Had they looked closer, they might have noticed a seam of bullet holes stitched across the trunk, which the car's new owner had yet to repair.

Inside the building, a small group of VIPs stepped rev-erently across Coronation Square, admiring the dual exhibits beneath Hagia Sophia's towering main dome one hundred and seventy-seven feet above their heads. To their right, they found a display devoted to the life of Muhammad, containing the stolen battle pendant, a par-tial handwritten recitation of the Qur'an, and other artifacts gleaned from the personal collection of Ozden Celik. On the left side of the hall were the relics of Jesus, discovered on the galley in Cyprus. Dozens of armed guards began assembling around the display cases of both exhibits, preparing for the museum's formal opening to the public.

Giordino and Gunn were conversing with Loren and Pitt near a glass-encased ossuary when Dr. Ruppé joined them.

"It's magnificent!" Ruppé beamed. "I can't believe you pulled this off. A joint exhibit featuring relics from the lives of both Jesus and Muhammad. And in such a setting."

"With its historic legacy as both a church and a mosque, Hagia Sophia seemed like the perfect place to showcase the artifacts," Pitt said. "I guess you could say that the Mayor of Istanbul owed me one as well," he added with a grin.

"It certainly helped that the folks in Cyprus agreed to a tour of the Jesus artifacts while they construct a permanent exhibit for the relics and the galley," Gunn said.

"Don't forget the late Mr. Celik's contributions," Giordino said.

"Yes, the Muhammad relics all belong to the good people of Turkey now," Pitt noted.

"Another job well done," Ruppé said. "The public is going to be thrilled. It really is an inspired lesson in tolerance to combine the religious histories." He looked at Pitt with an arched brow. "You know, if I were a gambling man, I might think you were simply trying to hedge your bets in the afterlife."

"It never hurts to have insurance," he replied with a wink.

Across the square, Julie Goodyear stood enthralled before a small case containing several faded sheets of papyrus.

"Summer, can you believe this? It's an actual letter written by Jesus to Peter."

Summer smiled at the enthusiasm displayed on the historian's face.

"Yes, there's a translation below. He appears to be instructing Peter to make preparations for a large gathering. Some biblical archaeologists believe it could be a reference to the Sermon on the Mount."

After staring at the document for a short while, Julie turned to Summer and shook her head.

"It's just unbelievable. The fact that these artifacts were listed on a physical document that survived to this day is amazing enough. But then to have actually discovered all of the artifacts, and in excellent condition to boot, is nothing short of a miracle."

"With some hard work and a little luck thrown in," Summer replied with a smile. Spotting Loren and Pitt across the floor, she said, "Come on, I want you to meet my father."

As Summer led Julie across the floor, Julie made her stop for a moment at the very first item in the Jesus exhibit. Displayed in a thick, protective case was the original Manifest. Beneath it was a small tag that read "On Loan from Ridley Bannister."

"It's nice to see the original again, though frankly I'm surprised that Mr. Bannister agreed to loan it to the exhibit," Julie said.

"He nearly died in the grotto on Cyprus, and I dare say

he came out of the experience a changed man. It was actually his suggestion to include the Manifest in the exhibit, and he has already agreed to display it permanently, along with the other relics, in Cyprus. Of course, he has managed to produce a book and documentary film about the Manifest," she added with a smirk.

They stepped over to Pitt and the others, where Summer introduced her friend.

"It's a pleasure to meet the young lady responsible for all this historic treasure," Pitt said graciously.

"Please, my role was minuscule," Julie replied. "You and Summer were the ones that discovered the actual relics. Especially the most intriguing item," she added, pointing over Pitt's shoulder at the limestone ossuary.

"Yes, the ossuary of J," Pitt replied. "It created quite a stir, at first. But after careful analysis, the epigraphists deciphered the Aramaic inscription found on the front as reading 'Joseph,' not 'Jesus.' A number of experts postulate it's Joseph of Aramathea, but I guess we'll never know for sure."

"I would think it's likely. He was wealthy enough for an elaborate tomb and ossuary. Why else would Helena have included it in the collection? It's just a shame that the bones have vanished."

"That's a mystery I'll leave to you," Pitt said. "Speaking of which, Summer tells me that you've found a new clue regarding Lord Kitchener and the *Hampshire*."

"Yes, indeed. Summer may have told you how we found letters from a Bishop named Lowery who hounded Kitchener to turn over the Manifest shortly before the *Hampshire*'s sinking. Lowery was disabled in an automobile accident a short time later and ended up taking his own life in a bout of depression. I found a suicide note in his family's papers in which he admitted to his role in the *Hampshire* disaster. The ship was intentionally sunk out of fear that Kitchener was taking the Manifest to Russia for public release. At a time when the First World War was at a stalemate, the Church of England was apparently terrified of its contents, particularly in regard to the ossuary of J and its paradox to the Resurrection."

"I guess the Church is going to have a bit of explaining to do."

As they talked, Loren drifted over to a small painting displayed behind velvet ropes. Easily destined to be the most popular item of the exhibit, it was a contemporary portrait of Jesus on a wooden panel, painted by a Roman artist. Though lacking the skilled hand of a Rembrandt or a Rubens, the artist nevertheless had created a strikingly realistic portrait of a reflective man. Lean-faced, dark-haired, and bearded, the subject stared from the panel with a striking aura. It was the eyes, Loren decided. The olive-colored orbs nearly jumped off the panel, gleaming with a mixture of intensity and compassion.

Loren studied the painting for several minutes, then called Summer to her side.

"The only known contemporary image of Jesus," Summer said reverently as she approached. "Isn't it remarkable?"

"Yes, quite."

"Most of the Roman paintings that survived from that era are in the form of frescoes, so a freestanding portrait is quite rare. One of the experts believes it may have been created by the same artist who painted a well-known fresco in Palmyra, Syria. The artist likely painted frescoes in the homes of the wealthy of Judaea and supplemented his income with portraits. The historians seem to think he captured Jesus at the height of his ministry, shortly before he was arrested and crucified."

She followed Loren's gaze and studied the subject.

"He has a true Mediterranean look about him, doesn't he?" Summer said. "A real man of the sun and wind."

"Certainly nothing like the images created by the master medieval painters depicting Jesus as though he was born in Sweden," Loren said. "Does he remind you of someone?" she asked, entranced by the image.

Summer tilted her head while studying the painting, then smiled. "Now that you mention it, there is a resemblance."

"A resemblance to whom?" Pitt asked, stepping over to join them.

"He has wavy black hair, a lean face, and a tan complexion," Loren said. "The same features as you."

Pitt looked at the painting, then shook his head. "No, his eyes aren't quite as green. And judging by the background, he couldn't have stood more than five foot three and weighed much over a hundred pounds. On top of that, there's another big difference between us," he added with a slight grin.

"What's that?" Loren asked.

"He walked on water. I swim in it."

The afternoon heat had passed its zenith, and the sun was casting long shadows on the Jerusalem District Court Building when the final jury verdict was read. The television and print reporters were the first to exit the building, anxious to file their stories on the trial. The courthouse hounds and curiosity seekers who had filled the courtroom gallery filed out next, gossiping among themselves about the outcome. Last came the witnesses and attorneys, thankful that the long trial had finally reached its end. Noticeably absent, however, was the defendant. Oscar Gutzman would not stroll freely out the front door of the courthouse. Cuffed and under heavy guard, he was quietly escorted out the back door and into a waiting police van, which whisked him away to Shikma Prison to begin serving his sentence.

Dirk Jr. and Sam Levine lingered in the foyer, thanking the prosecuting attorneys for their good work, before stepping out into the fading sunlight. Both men wore the look of bitter justice on their faces, knowing that the verdict would never fully make up for the deaths of Sophie and her fellow antiquities agent.

"Fifteen years for aiding and abetting the death of agent Holder at Caesarea," Sam said. "We couldn't have done much better."

"It should ensure that he dies in prison," Dirk replied impassively.

"In his poor health, I'll be surprised if he survives the first year."

"Then you better get moving if you're going to try him on antiquities charges," Dirk said.

"Actually, we've already cut a plea deal with his attorneys. Although we had a solid case against him for trafficking in stolen antiquities, adding a few years to his sentence would have been an academic exercise."

"So what did you get out of him?"

"All charges were dropped in exchange for him cooperating in the ongoing investigation into the sources of the stolen artifacts in his collection. In addition," Sam said with a smile, "Gutzman has agreed to bequeath his entire collection to the State of Israel upon his death."

"That's a pretty good coup."

"We think so," Sam replied as they reached the bottom of the courthouse steps. "It will take a little of the sting out of our losses."

"Nice to know that something good will come out of all this," Dirk replied. He reached over and shook Levine's hand. "Keep up the good fight, Sam. Sophie would have wanted you to carry on."

"I will. Take care, Dirk."

As Sam headed toward the parking lot, Dirk heard someone call out his name. He turned to see Ridley Bannister, easing down the steps with the aid of a polished cane.

"Yes, Bannister," Dirk replied.

"If you've got a moment," the archaeologist said, hobbling up to Dirk. "I just wanted to tell you that, prior to the trial, I wasn't aware that you were involved with

Miss Elkin. She was a professional colleague of sorts, although we didn't always see eye to eye. Nevertheless, I just wanted to say that I always considered her a remarkable woman."

"I share your sentiment," Dirk said quietly. "Thank you, by the way, for participating in the trial. Your testimony was instrumental in putting Gutzman away."

"I knew that he bought stolen artifacts, but I never imagined he'd go so far as to hire trained terrorists to augment his collection. It's not difficult to get caught up in the allure of artifacts, and I carry my own sins in that regard. But you have to make right at the end of the day. You and your family showed me the way, in addition to saving my life. For that, I shall always be grateful."

"How much longer will you need that?" Dirk asked, pointing to the cane.

"Just another few weeks. The doctors in Cyprus did a splendid job of patching me up."

"It was good of you to agree to loan the Manifest to their new museum."

"It belongs with the other artifacts that NUMA bestowed," Bannister replied. "Perhaps it will make a few amends to your sister. Summer is quite a saucy young lady, by the way. Please tell her that I'd be honored to dine with her some time."

"I'll pass the word. What's next for you?"

"The Ark of the Covenant. I've uncovered a lead that suggests it may be hidden in a cave in Yemen. It looks promising. How about yourself?"

"I think I'm through working in the Mediterranean for a while," Dirk said quietly.

"Well, cheers to you wherever you end up next. And give my best to your father and Summer."

"Good luck, Bannister. I'll see you around."

Dirk watched as the archaeologist hobbled over to a taxi stand and hailed a cab. Dirk's own hotel was only a few blocks away, so he decided to proceed there on foot. Walking through the streets of west Jerusalem, he soon fell oblivious to the dense traffic and crowded sidewalks, his mind lost in an emotional fog.

He marched past the hotel and continued walking for another mile, entering the Old City through Herod's Gate. He stepped absently through the narrow streets, pulled to the east by an unseen compass.

Following a nun jaywalking across a side street, he looked up to find himself standing on the grounds of St. Anne's Church. He felt a calmness settle over him as he made his way around the back to the Pool of Bethesda.

The bench where he had shared lunch with Sophie was empty, and he took a seat under the shade of the sycamore trees. Lost in thought, he stared at the empty pools long after the sun had dipped beneath the horizon. He was still sitting in silent contemplation when the evening sky rustled up a cool breeze that carried the sweet scent of jasmine gently across the ancient grounds.

He just wanted a decent book to read ...

Not too much to ask, is it? It was in 1935 when Allen Lane, Managing
Director of Bodley Head Publishers, stood on a platform at Exeter railway
station looking for something good to read on his journey back to London.
His choice was limited to popular magazines and poor-quality paperbacks –
the same choice faced every day by the vast majority of readers, few of
whom could afford hardbacks. Lane's disappointment and subsequent anger
at the range of books generally available led him to found a company – and
change the world.

*'We believed in the existence in this country of a vast reading public for intelligent
books at a low price, and staked everything on it'*
Sir Allen Lane, 1902–1970, founder of Penguin Books

The quality paperback had arrived – and not just in bookshops. Lane was
adamant that his Penguins should appear in chain stores and tobacconists,
and should cost no more than a packet of cigarettes.

Reading habits (and cigarette prices) have changed since 1935, but
Penguin still believes in publishing the best books for everybody to
enjoy. We still believe that good design costs no more than bad design,
and we still believe that quality books published passionately and responsibly
make the world a better place.

So wherever you see the little bird – whether it's on a piece of
prize-winning literary fiction or a celebrity autobiography, political tour
de force or historical masterpiece, a serial-killer thriller, reference book,
world classic or a piece of pure escapism – you can bet that it represents the
very best that the genre has to offer.

Whatever you like to read – trust Penguin.